Born in the US, Ry Herman is now a permanent Scottish resident, and has been writing theatrical plays for most of his life. He's worked in a variety of roles, including submissions editor, theatre technician, and one job that could best be described as typing the number five all day long. He acts and directs, and performed at the Edinburgh Fringe Festival in 2019. He is bisexual and genderqueer. His hobbies include baking bread, playing tabletop roleplaying games, and reading as many books as humanly possible.

RY HERMAN

Love Bites

Jo Fletcher
BOOKS

For Beth
None of this would exist without you.

First published in Great Britain in 2020 by

Jo Fletcher Books
an imprint of
Quercus Editions Ltd
Carmelite House
50 Victoria Embankment
London EC4Y oDZ

An Hachette UK company

A CIP catalogue record for this book is available
from the British Library

PB ISBN 978-1-52940-630-6
EB ISBN 978-1-52940-629-0

This book is a work of fiction. Names, characters,
businesses, organizations, places and events are
either the product of the author's imagination
or used fictitiously. Any resemblance to
actual persons, living or dead, events or
locales is entirely coincidental.

10 9 8 7 6 5 4 3 2 1

Typeset by Jouve (UK), Milton Keynes

Printed and bound in Great Britain by Clays Ltd, Elcograf S.p.A.

THREE DAYS DEAD

Scottsdale, Arizona
26–29 August 1998

The first night Angela spends dead, it rains. An August monsoon pounding on the roof, hard and fast and mixed with hail. But it doesn't last very long. The sky is clear by the time she starts to stiffen. That begins around midnight with a subtle hardening of the small muscles in her eyelids, neck, and jaw. Before morning arrives, it's spread throughout her whole body, leaving her as rigid and inflexible as a loaf of stale bread.

She's lying on her right side, and her blood has pooled there, darkening one arm and one leg and the edge of her face and torso. It looks like a single giant bruise, as if someone slammed her body into a concrete wall just once, just on that side. The rest of her has been left a waxy, greyish white, except for her fingers and toes, which have turned blue.

After the sun rises, the city goes about its business as usual. Outside the walls of the house where Angela lies dead, birds sing before the weather gets too hot. Cars are stuck in rush hour traffic, drivers drum impatiently on their steering wheels, radios on, air conditioning blasting. The morning news programmes are still obsessively focused on Monica Lewinsky's grand jury testimony. For

1

those avoiding the news, the song of the day is 'The Boy is Mine', by Brandy and Monica, playing on so many stations it's hard to avoid. It wouldn't have been Angela's choice. Her favourite recent release was 'Venus', by Theatre of Tragedy: Norwegian gothic rock with Latin lyrics. But nobody is asking her. She couldn't answer if they did.

The temperature hits 107 degrees Fahrenheit that day. It's not quite that hot in the darkroom where Angela is lying, but it's nowhere near cool, either. By the end of the day, she's starting to smell.

The second night Angela spends dead, Tess comes into the room and watches her for two hours. Then she turns Angela onto her back. Angela's body is beginning to relax, the rigor mortis softening as she decomposes further.

A few hours after sundown, a woman walks her dog past the house. She's not exactly a neighbour – she lives around the corner – but she's seen Angela and Tess every now and then. She's never given them much thought. She doesn't do so now. Three other people also pass the house that night, but none of them pay any attention to it.

Morning comes, and another day goes by in an ordinary way. A greenish patch appears on Angela's lower right stomach as her intestinal bacteria eat through her gut. In the late afternoon, a palo verde beetle crawls across Angela's face, pausing on her cheek for unknowable reasons of its own. The temperature rises to a scorching 113 degrees.

The third night Angela spends dead is a Friday night, and more than six hundred thousand people across the United States go out to see Wesley Snipes kill vampires. *Blade* is still the number one movie a full week after its opening, although five hundred thousand people are watching *There's Something About Mary* instead. Angela never got around to seeing either film. The last movie she went to see was *Wild Things*, back in June. She didn't think it was all that great, but she'd been grateful for the air conditioning in the cineplex.

Late that evening, a pack of coyotes wander in and out of the neighbourhood's back yards, howling and yipping. A feral cat, alarmed by the noise, slips into a nearby ditch and scurries away. Overhead, a great horned owl flits from rooftop to rooftop, hunting for kangaroo rats.

Tess stays in the room the whole night this time, watching Angela's body whenever she isn't developing her photos. While Tess works, the greenish patch on Angela's stomach disappears. Her skin colour evens and fades to a snowy shade of white which is, to be honest, pretty much what it was before she died. She stops smelling of rotting flesh, and she doesn't start to bloat.

Tess notes these changes and leaves her pictures to dry. She grabs a utility knife from a drawer and presses the edge against Angela's neck.

She watches closely as the skin is dented by the blade, then springs back into place when she takes it away. The left side of Tess's mouth twitches into a half-smile.

The next morning, it rains again, hard and fast. But there's no hail this time. The weather cools down a little, only reaching 105 degrees at its hottest. Angela's advisor at the university sends her an e-mail, then another later in the day when she doesn't respond. No one else tries to get in touch.

Night falls.

Seventy-two hours after her death, Angela wakes up.

She's thirsty. Terribly, terribly thirsty. She tries to move her head. It feels like a stone, grinding against her neck.

Her gaze falls on a pair of shoes, then travels up. Tess is standing there, staring at her intently.

'What . . .' Angela is barely able to croak out the word. Her voice is a strangled rasp. She tries again. 'What did you do to me?'

'Well,' Tess says, 'I guess this means you won't be leaving me after all.'

3

PART ONE
The Bloodlust-Crazed Inhuman Trollop

CHAPTER ONE

Brookline, Massachusetts
6 November 1999

Angela puts on her makeup carefully. It's one of the most important parts of her preparations, and by far the most difficult.

First the lip liner – by feel. It requires a steady hand, so she likes to get it out of the way early. Slowly up and around, then the other way, down and across, setting the base, using precise movements that she hopes are shaping a perfect cupid's bow. She won't slip if she concentrates, but it's harder to concentrate when she's this hungry. That hunger, though, is the exact reason she needs everything to be perfect tonight.

Now the lipstick, almost as troublesome. She uses a brush and a liquid stain, applying it in even strokes. You'd think a tube would be easier to handle sight unseen, but she never got the hang of it.

Everything would be so much simpler if the mirror showed her reflection.

She could ask Shelly to take a look before she goes out, of course. But it's better if she gets everything right the first time. If she screws up anything major, there's a chance she could spend half the evening taking it off, putting it back on, asking Shelly again, taking it off again. That only happened once, shortly after she moved in, but she never wants it to happen a second time. Shelly had been giving her some extremely odd looks by the end of it.

The first few days in the house were the hardest, before she developed a routine. The absolute worst was the very first minute, hovering outside the open door, waiting for an invitation to come inside, wondering how long she'd have to stand there before she'd be physically capable of crossing the threshold. What a nightmare.

Eyeshadow next, which is a little easier as long as she brushes it on methodically. Angela starts small, and then blends it towards the edges. First a white primer up to the brows, then a coat of dark blue across the lids. Black in the crease. Smooth it out. Eyeliner can be tricky, but she's always had a knack for it. She just has to remember not to rush. Keep the motions deliberate. Look up, draw a line below. Shut the eye, draw another across her lashes. If she smudges it by accident, the dark eyeshadow will help conceal it. A dot of highlighter goes on the inner corner. Mascara is practically no trouble at all.

At least she doesn't need to bother with foundation. She doesn't think there's any way she could apply it evenly, not unless she enlisted someone else's help every single time. And there have to be limits to her housemates' patience. Not to mention their obliviousness. Fortunately, pale skin is in fashion where she plans on going. It's one of the main reasons she picked it; she blends in there, just the way she is. Or more accurately, just the way she is plus lipstick, eyeshadow, eyeliner, a painstakingly chosen outfit, and the right way of holding herself, not too eager but not too shy. But no foundation.

Rouge is still a good idea, though. Feel for the apples of the cheeks, a little bit worked into the middle of each. Now, ideally, she looks attractively alabaster and not quite so much like an upright corpse.

Angela puts her tools back in the makeup case and snaps it shut. Clothes come next. Out of the bathroom, across the hall to her bedroom. Why does she even bother keeping her makeup in the bathroom, if she can't use the mirror? Habit, probably. But it's a good habit. Anything that makes her seem normal is a good habit.

She opens her closet to look at her choices, and is greeted by a sweep of vinyl, lace, feathers, leather. She's not sure she owns any T-shirts or blue jeans anymore. It's certainly a far cry from her childhood bedroom, with its neat row of Catholic school uniforms in the closet and a crucifix prominently displayed on the wall. So much has changed since then.

Crucifixes make her uncomfortable now.

By far the greatest changes have come in the past year. Or rather, in the year, two months, and ten or so days since her death. The point of disconnect with what she used to be. She's reasonably certain she hasn't worn a plain bra or a pair of sneakers since it happened.

It occurs to her to wonder if she even can. Does she have a compulsion to wear goth fashion now? Could that be the source of the fictional stereotype, a grain of truth in the stories and myths?

No, that's ridiculous. She refuses to believe it. She wears these things to attract a particular kind of attention, and because she happens to like them. Why would this mysterious, theoretical instinct exist? Does it also force her to go to appropriate nightclubs? What would be the evolutionary basis for that – survival rates at the clubs on the savannah, deep in prehistoric times? Nonsense. There's no such thing as a lace instinct.

Maybe she should run an experiment, to be sure. Buy a bunch of different outfits: preppy, hippy, punk. See if she can step outside wearing one. She decides to add that to the list. Low down on the list, because it's a ludicrous idea. There are more important matters to test first. And she's definitely not going to mess around with her clothing choices tonight.

Angela picks a red-and-black corset top and a satin fishtail skirt.

Crimson gloves, tall heels. Enticing with a hint of elegance. She hopes. She wishes she could check.

Once she's finished dressing, she takes her hair out of its scrunchie, and it drops over her shoulders in straight blonde lines. She'd blend in better if she dyed it black, or maybe dark red, but she never has. So there, she maintains at least one piece of defiance against the cliché. As acts of individualism go, it scarcely counts at all, but it's something. Perhaps she's a terrible monster, but at least she's a terrible blonde monster.

She checks her handbag for her ID, phone, cash, and sleeping pills. She's running low on pills; she'll need to get her prescription refilled soon. A final look around the room, in case she's forgotten anything. She hasn't. There isn't much there to be forgotten.

With the closet door closed, hiding the wild indulgence of her clothing, the room is spare and spartan. The mattress, sitting directly on the bare tile floor, takes up the entirety of one wall, sheets and blankets in a tangle on top of it. Across from that, there's just enough room for her desk beneath the heavy drapes covering the single small window. Every now and then the code she's left running spits a number onto the computer monitor, each one a reminder of how much work she has left to do, work she has to put off tonight. A narrow bookshelf is squeezed into the last remaining wall space. Mostly reference books, plus a couple of tattered favourites from earlier days. *The Lion, the Witch and the Wardrobe*. A used-bookstore copy of *Annie On My Mind* that her parents, fortunately, never found.

The room's sole decoration is scattered across the ceiling. Glow-in-the-dark stars that light up dimly as she switches off the desk lamp. Familiar constellations – Draco, Andromeda, Orion raising his hand like an old friend. The star chart is completely accurate, the result of hours spent meticulously putting them in place with the help of a ruler and a stellar atlas. Angela gives them a faint smile as she leaves the room and shuts the door.

Up the stairs and out of the basement. Shelly is in the living room, perched on the settee, her hair unfussily pulled back into a ponytail, her nose buried in an unbound manuscript.

Good. Angela knows she could knock on Shelly's bedroom door if she needed to, but it's easier this way. The sound of pots clattering comes from the kitchen – Mike must be making a late dinner. She can smell the cooking steak from where she is. They don't bother to ask her to eat with them anymore, thank goodness. She's turned them down too many times, pleading work. Most of the time it's not even a lie.

The living room looks nothing like her bedroom; everything here reflects Shelly and Mike's taste. Sleek and modern, the settee black and chrome, the coffee table metal and glass. All of it out of place below a water-stained ceiling, in a room with dingy yellow-grey walls crusted with ancient wallpaper glue. A fixer-upper was the only place they could afford in Brookline, and a year and a half later they're still fixing it up. The furniture is aspirational, including the enormous dog crate in the corner for the enormous dog they don't own yet.

Shelly hasn't noticed her come in, so Angela deliberately steps on one of the creakier floorboards. Shelly looks up at the noise and quirks her eyebrows.

'Hey, Angela. Heading out for the night?'

'Yes,' she answers. 'How do I look?'

Shelly grins. A flash of broad bright teeth that make a striking contrast to her dark-brown complexion. She takes a thorough look at Angela's outfit, head to toe.

'I'm going to go with stunning. That sound good?'

'Flatterer.'

'You might want to put on a jacket, though.'

Angela shrugs. 'I'm just taking the tram over to Kenmore Square, I'm not going to be outside all that long.'

'Right, of course. But it's not a tram, it's a trolley, and you're taking the T. If you keep saying tram, everyone's going to know you're not from Boston.'

'Sorry. Old habit, hard to kill.' Angela smiles ruefully. 'At least I didn't call it the Metro, or SEPTA. So is my makeup all right?' She turns her face from side to side so Shelly can get a look from all angles. 'No smears?'

'You look great,' Shelly tells her. 'Seriously. Go have fun.'

'Thanks.'

Angela expects Shelly to go back to her book, but she doesn't. Instead, she keeps looking at Angela, her lips pursed, her expression thoughtful.

'Hey, I've been wondering. Would you like us to come with you some time?'

Oh, no. No, no, no. No. Angela makes an effort to keep her face neutral.

'You don't have to,' she says, maintaining an even tone. 'I know it's not your thing.'

'Eh, it couldn't hurt to try it.'

'Loud music, obnoxious drunks?' Angela gestures at herself, her clothes. 'Pretentious drama queens? You'd hate it.'

Shelly cocks her head, eyes narrowing. 'Do you not want us there?'

'Of course I do,' Angela says. Lying. 'I just don't want you to feel obligated to do something you don't like. Not because of me.'

Shelly glances at the manuscript to remember her place, then puts the pages down on the coffee table. Angela gets a queasy feeling in her stomach as Shelly turns to face her fully.

She clearly wants to talk.

'I'm only trying to . . . You've been living here for most of the year, and it feels like Mike and I never see you. I spent more time with you back when we were undergrads. We'd kind of like to hang out with you sometime, you know?'

'I can't – I have to finish my thesis. I'm sorry, but that takes up a lot of time.' Angela can hear how defensive she sounds as she says it. It must seem like a particularly lame excuse when she's on her way out the door.

'I know that.' Shelly holds out her hands in a placating gesture. 'I'm not trying to pressure you into spending time with us. I'm not even saying, don't do what you want when you take a night off – God knows you don't take that many. I just thought, next time you go out, we could go with you.'

Shelly's idea sounds reasonable. Extremely, frighteningly reasonable. Angela desperately tries to think of a polite way to turn it down.

'You could dress me,' Shelly suggests. 'That might be fun.'

'None of my stuff would fit you,' Angela says in a rush. 'I'm a stick, you have actual boobs. You'd have to buy new clothes to get in the club; that's absurd when you don't really want to go. Tell you what – next time I take a night off, I'll spend it here, with you guys.'

'You don't have to –'

'I want to. Seriously, it makes a lot more sense. And here's an idea: are you two still planning on painting the stairway soon?'

Shelly nods, slowly. 'Yeah, once we actually get around to buying paint for it.'

'That's perfect. Let me know when you pick a day, and I'll help out when I get up. We'll make it a house party, have a good time with it.'

'If you're genuinely sure you want to . . . All right, that sounds fun,' Shelly says, warming to the idea. 'We can put on some oldies. Buy snacks.'

'Snacks,' Angela echoes. 'Great.'

Feeling relieved, she forces a smile. It means she'll have to take an extra night off sometime to take care of business, but that's a small price to pay.

13

Then she notices Shelly is still studying her face.

'What? Is it my lipstick?'

'Are you all right?' Shelly asks. 'I mean, is everything OK?'

Angela's smile drops. 'I'm fine.'

'You haven't been looking so good lately—'

'I thought you said I was stunning.'

'Look, Angela, I don't mean to pry, but . . .' Shelly searches for words. 'I know whatever happened between you and Tess wasn't easy.'

'I'm fine.'

'You moved across the country. In the middle of grad school.'

'It's no big deal. I worked all that out with my advisor. I'm done with classes, I don't have to be there in person. I just need to finish my thesis.'

'That's not what I meant,' Shelly says, starting to sound a little frustrated. 'I'm trying to say, if you ever need someone to talk to, I'm here.'

'I know,' Angela replies in a quiet voice. 'And thank you. I appreciate it, I really do. But it isn't necessary.' She motions her chin towards the stack of paper on the coffee table. 'So, what are you reading? Is it any good?'

Shelly doesn't look happy that the subject has been changed. Angela wonders if she's going to force the issue.

In the end, though, all Shelly says is, 'Yeah, it's not bad. They're usually worth reading by the time they get to me. I have a minion who goes through the slush pile and weeds out the truly awful stuff before I ever see it.'

'That must be nice.'

'Oh, believe me, it is.'

From the next room, Mike calls out that dinner is ready. Shelly glances towards the kitchen door and heaves herself to her feet. 'Hope you have a good time tonight.'

'I'll try my best.'

'Good. You know, I think you might enjoy this book,' Shelly says over her shoulder as she heads into the kitchen. 'It's like *Buffy the Vampire Slayer* – all about monsters. Werewolves and vampires and witches and things. Very goth. Want to take a look sometime?'

'Sure, sounds great,' Angela replies weakly. 'Just my thing.' But Shelly has already turned away.

Angela flees out the front door.

CHAPTER TWO

Somerville, Massachusetts
6 November 1999

In her years as a slush pile reader, Chloë has encountered practically every kind of angel there is.

Sanctimonious angels are her least favourite. They have an annoying tendency to condemn her and everyone she knows to hell. Virtuous angels are a close second, though, because they're so dull. Wrathful angels are surprisingly relatable if you don't mind a few demons getting run through with flaming swords, and rebellious angels can go either way, compelling or repellant depending on how sulky they are. Wise angels are without question the best of the lot, but their appearances are few and far between.

If she never sees a sexy angel again, it'll be too soon. Conceited bastards.

Ever since the company she works for started publishing a line of 'inspirational literature', angels have popped up in at least a quarter of the submissions that get dumped in the in-box on her desk. Sometimes it seems like there's an angel for every possible purpose, and their personalities vary wildly depending on the taste and sanity of the author. Such is the glory and wonder of accepting unsolicited manuscripts. She's passed a few angel novels on to Shelly, the submissions editor for the imprints Chloë reviews, but most get sent back in their self-addressed stamped envelopes or tossed into the recycling.

But in spite of her experience with the species, she's having trouble getting a handle on the angel in the book she's currently reading. He doesn't seem to be doing much except hanging out in heaven and chatting with the occasional dead saint. He might be an entirely new type. A useless angel? A pointless angel? Maybe he's supposed to be avant-garde. Whatever he is, he isn't making a very good impression on her.

She can remember when paging through something like this would at least prompt her to work on her own writing. Right now, however, even the idea of it seems exhausting. Which isn't surprising, since she finds everything exhausting these days: writing and reading and walking out the front door. Getting out of bed each morning is a minor, pathetic victory.

Her thoughts are interrupted by her new housemate rapping on the doorframe between the living room and the kitchen. She jumps a little at the noise, startling the cat that had been dozing peacefully on her lap. And a startled Entropy is a destructive force of nature.

Ari doesn't manage to get all the way through asking, 'You got a minute?' before Entropy leaps away at such high speed that he transforms into a black-and-grey streak, using Chloë, painfully, as his springboard. He caroms off a wall before vanishing into her bedroom. In his wake, with the slow inevitability of an avalanche, the precariously balanced piles of odds and ends that Chloë assembled during her last futile attempt at cleaning topple over.

Ari and Chloë survey the resulting devastation.

In all honesty, it hasn't made much of a difference. Masses of books, old bills, dirty dishes, and unwashed socks are strewn over nearly every available surface in the house. And worse things, as well. Once Chloë found a half-eaten sandwich under a newspaper.

She couldn't remember making it, and was fairly sure there'd been no bread in the house for weeks.

The furniture isn't any better; it's been scavenged from whatever gets left on the sidewalk when the Tufts students move out – slanting bookshelves, chairs held together with duct tape, the sagging couch where Chloë sits. The building itself is as dilapidated as the landlords think they can get away with, peeling brown wallpaper on the inside and peeling brown paint on the outside.

'That,' Ari says as another pile collapses, 'is an extremely energetic cat.'

After allowing herself a small sigh, Chloë turns her attention to the figure in the kitchen doorway. 'Hi. I'm working, but I can break for a little while.'

'Great.'

As Ari walks into the room, she tosses the manuscript she'd been reading into the 'reject without passing on' area of the floor. Bye-bye, useless angel. The rejected submissions fan out from the couch in a sloppy arc. Chloë can judge how much she'd disliked a book by how far away it ends up; the more she hates it, the harder she throws it.

'So what's up?' she asks.

'Well,' Ari answers, 'I was hoping we could talk about a situation. In the house.'

'A situation?'

'Yeah.'

Chloë feels a sense of trepidation. She's been dreading the prospect of having a serious conversation with Ari since he moved in a few days ago.

She doesn't know him well. Financial desperation is the only reason she's taken on a subletter at all. The last rent increase made it impossible for Chloë to pretend that she could afford the place alone anymore, so she'd advertised the coffin-like 'half bedroom' on the far side of the kitchen as a sublet. Most likely, it's an illegal approach to the problem, but she figured someone out there had to be as desperate as she was. Although after a series of prospective tenants walked in, saw the state of the living room, and made hasty excuses to leave, she'd wondered if that was true.

Then Ari took one look around, said 'Great!', and signed the sublet agreement Chloë handed him without bothering to read it. She still isn't sure what his deal is. There's something odd about him she hasn't been able to put her finger on yet. Something odder than his being named Ariel, which might just mean that his parents were very Jewish. Or Shakespeare aficionados. Or big fans of *The Little Mermaid*. He looks a bit like a Renaissance painting of an angel himself, as it happens – he has the androgynous good looks, the long, wavy hair, and the large, soulful eyes.

If he has a job, it's not one that keeps predictable hours. Nonetheless, he'd prepaid two months' rent in cash, brought in a single suitcase worth of belongings, and then kept to himself for the most part. Trust-fund stoner is Chloë's first guess, although if he's smoking anything, he isn't doing it at home. He seems nice enough, but she's been waiting for the other shoe to drop.

He's going to pressure her to join his cult, she guesses. Or ask if he can deal drugs out of the kitchen. Or turn his bedroom into the world's smallest sex dungeon. Or, worst-case scenario, ask her to clean the place up.

She might as well get it over with. 'What situation did you want to talk about?'

'Your cat,' Ari tells her, 'keeps dropping on my head.'

'Oh,' Chloë says. 'Yeah, I'm sorry. He does that. Usually only with people he really likes, though.'

'It's amazing! Why – no, what I mean is, how? How does he do that?'

'He perches on the door lintels, waiting for someone to come through.'

'Amazing,' he repeats, peering at the narrow beam atop the doorway to the kitchen. 'They're only, like, half an inch wide.'

'He's very graceful.'

'Cats are such fantastic creatures, don't you think?' He continues to stare at the lintel, as if willing it to divulge its secrets.

'Has he scratched you?' Chloë asks.

'What? Oh, no. No, he kind of bounces off and falls after he hits. But that's why I'm concerned. I'm worried he might hurt himself.'

'Really? I'm pretty sure he'll be fine. Like I said, he's graceful.'

Ari doesn't look entirely convinced. 'Do you think there's any way to get him to stop?'

'Believe me, I've tried. But yelling, "No!" doesn't really do anything because, well, he's a cat. I thought about removing the lintels, but it's a rental and I don't think the landlord would like that.'

'No,' Ari acknowledges. 'Probably not.'

'Is this going to be a problem for you?' she asks, feeling nervous once again. She knows from personal experience how disconcerting it can be to suddenly find Entropy declaring war on your hair. If Ari decides to move out, she'll be right back where she started.

She waits while he thinks deeply.

'Nah, it's fine,' he says at last. 'If you say he'll always stick the landing, I'll trust you. Cats, just amazing.'

Chloë exhales with relief. 'Thanks for being willing to put up with it. I know animals leaping out of the sky isn't a standard household hazard.'

'Don't worry about it.' He airily waves a hand as he turns to head into the kitchen. 'I'll let you get on with your work.'

He's already halfway through the doorway when Chloë says, 'Hey, Ari?'

'Yeah?'

'I was wondering, what do you do? I mean, for a living?'

He turns back to her, a broad smile spreading across his face. 'I preach.'

'You what?'

Ari takes a step forward and winces as he treads on something hard or sharp lying concealed in the clutter. 'I preach. I'm a preacher.' He begins to pick his way more carefully across the detritus on the floor, moving towards the couch.

'Where do you preach?' she asks him.

'On the street.'

'Oh.'

'I've got a nice spot in the Public Garden. When they don't chase me away. I'll be heading out there later tonight, as a matter of fact.' He sits down next to her and clasps his hands across one knee.

'Tonight? But it's already dark.'

'I've been finding,' he says seriously, 'that preaching on the late side makes me less likely to get chased away. As long as I'm not too loud. Attracting some notice is important, but getting, let's call it, the wrong kind of notice has been an issue.'

Chloë isn't sure what to say. 'Does it pay well?'

'I don't really know. I haven't been doing it all that long.'

'And what do you preach?' she continues, despite the sinking feeling she's starting to feel in the pit of her stomach. 'I mean, what religion?'

'It's one I invented myself. I studied a lot of older religious doctrines first, but it's pretty much my spin on the whole thing.'

There it is, Chloë thinks, hearing a metaphorical shoe thud onto the floor.

Cult.

'Would you like to hear about it?' Ari asks eagerly, a zealous light coming into his eyes.

'I don't think right now is a great—'

'It's a very nice religion. It doesn't require any animal sacrifice at all.'

'That's . . . good?' she says.

'I figured you'd think so, because you're clearly an animal lover. There's no need to kill anything, bulls, goats, whatever. Definitely not cats. I have a whole little parable about why, if you want to hear it.'

'I really should get back to work,' Chloë tells him, patting the stack of manuscripts next to her a little too rapidly. 'So, you know, it sounds great, but, uh, you know.'

Ari's smile slips somewhat. 'Oh. Right, I totally understand.'

'It keeps piling up. The work.'

'Maybe some other time, then?'

He looks so put out that Chloë can't help but feel bad for him. 'Maybe. We'll see.'

'OK,' he says. 'Then I guess I'll leave you alone. Until you're not so busy.'

'Sure.'

Ari gets off the couch and makes his slow way back across the living room. Even taking as much care as he can, he manages to step on something that crunches under his foot. Throwing her an apologetic glance, he retreats into the kitchen, and soon after she hears the door to his bedroom shut.

Chloë massages her temples, trying to stave off an incipient headache, then runs her hands back through the tangled curls of her hair. When closing her eyes and holding still doesn't help, she roots through the couch cushions until she finds the Zoloft bottle. It's not a headache medication, but maybe it will help ease the muscle tension. Or something. Besides, it's time for her to take it.

Even if her housemate is an aspiring cult leader, Chloë tells herself, he seems harmless. She certainly hopes he is, anyway. Illegal landlords can't be choosers.

After she dry-swallows the antidepressant, she takes a new selection off the pile of unread submissions and flips it open. It's another religious text; the subject seems to be stalking her today. This one has a sanctimonious angel in it, and soon she's reading about all of the reasons she's going to suffer eternal torture in a lake of fire burning with sulphur.

It doesn't get any better from there.

CHAPTER THREE

The Parable Of The Monster And The Girl
Public Garden, Boston
6 November 1999

That's right, gather round, gather round. No need to be shy, come right up close. Welcome to the Public Garden. Preaching starts in two minutes, right here under the statue of the Good Samaritan. Which actually represents the first medical use of ether, did you know that? Yeah, that's why the Good Samaritan is drugging that guy. The more you know, huh?

Anyway, thanks to all, let's see, two of you – oh, wait, I didn't see the dog. Three. Thanks to all three of you for, like, giving me your ear on this cold November evening. It's so nice to be able to talk to you in person; it really helps keep the message from getting lost in transmission. I'm sorry it's so late, but the police here are starting to be really loose with their definition of a 'disruptive incident', so I'm trying to keep everything kind of low profile until all that blows over.

So, how about a parable? Everybody loves parables, right?

Cool, glad to hear it, that's great. Tonight's parable is called 'The Monster and the Girl'.

Once upon a time, there was a monster.

The monster was pretty miserable. So one day it got totally plastered on peppermint schnapps and watched Disney's *Beauty and the Beast* seventeen times in a row. It woke up the next morning with a nasty headache and a conviction that it could only be happy if it found true love with a beautiful girl.

Now, the monster realised that no girl would fall in love with a monster, so it disguised itself as a person, probably by putting on a hat or something. Thus camouflaged, it went out dancing at a nightclub. And at that nightclub – what's that you said, there? Yes, you're absolutely right! Guess you were paying attention to the title. At that nightclub, the monster saw a beautiful girl.

The beautiful girl was completely fooled by the monster's cunning disguise, and danced with it several times. Later that night they went home and had sex, which was only OK, because the monster was a little self-involved, but it had been a while for the beautiful girl and she was happy to be getting any at all.

The next morning, when they woke up, they discovered that they were in a relationship.

Things went pretty well for the first few weeks or months or years, but the monster slowly realised that it was still miserable. So it decided that there was something wrong with the girl, and started telling her so. The girl did her best to fix things, but the monster was never happy.

Eventually, the monster bit her. But by that time, the monster had pretty much convinced the girl that she deserved it, so she didn't leave. It's hard to keep perspective when someone's gaslighting you, and that monster made sure to tell the girl every day that all of their problems were her fault. Her head was tied up in knots. And the monster kept right on biting her.

But although the head games kept the girl under the monster's thumb for a good long time, one day, in the middle of a bite, the girl finally noticed that the monster was a monster. Maybe its hat fell off or something. Anyway, since she had seen both the Bela Lugosi version of *Dracula* and that terrible remake with Winona Ryder, she was terrified that the monster's bite would turn her into a monster as well.

She broke up with the monster shortly after that, still not knowing if she was fated to become one herself. The monster had a fit, because it knew that now it was doomed to stay miserable forever. The end.

Oh, except that they both were totally wrong about everything. The monster was simply an asshole and nothing was ever going to change that, and the girl really only needed a good night's sleep and a whole lot of therapy.

Just how it goes, I guess.

That was the actual ending, this time. All done.

Thank you, that's very kind, I appreciate it, thank you. Both of you have a nice night, now. And the dog. Can I pet the dog? No? That's cool.

Goodbye!

CHAPTER FOUR

Ascension, Boston
6 November 1999

The club sits off Kenmore Square, not far from the glowing neon Citgo sign that looms over the skyline, dominating the neighbourhood. It's across the turnpike from the better-known clubs on Lansdowne Street by Fenway Park. Close enough to them to be part of the nightlife scene, but far enough away to be its own little domain.

The building has three floors, and she slowly circulates through them. Two of them are solely for the music, dance floors spanning the entire space. Industrial metal blasts on the middle level. 'Butterfly Wings' fading out, Ministry's 'Bad Blood' taking its place. Trance and shoegaze are playing on the floor above.

Everything is painted black: walls and floors and ceilings, ductwork and piping. The lights are low except for a few coloured effects skittering around the rooms. If the place were empty, it'd be like walking into a void. But it's Saturday night, so it's crammed full of bodies and pulsing with sound.

Angela dances some when the mood strikes her, enough to blend in, but not too much. Her real goal is making sure she passes through the bottom-most floor, the bar, every twenty minutes or so. She wishes she could dance more. She used to dance more. She used to love going to these places so much. But these days, she has other things on her mind.

There are a few regulars she recognises from other nights, and occasionally she gets a nod from one of them. She nods back, but she doesn't really know any of them other than by sight. That's a deliberate choice. She splits her time among as many clubs as she can, and only goes out when she absolutely has to. It takes about two weeks before the hunger becomes uncomfortable; if she's careful, there's no particular place she needs to go to more than once every couple of months or so.

And she has been careful. But that means she's very, very hungry.

She struggles to stay focused as she slips through the gaps in the tightly packed crowd. The effect lights swirl and blink, throwing strange patterns over faces and bodies. All around her, people are dancing and drinking and talking, almost shouting as they try to make themselves heard over the music. Angela keeps to the edges. She's camouflaged like a leopard in the grass by the mass of stockings and corsets, boots and jackets, dresses and gloves.

Some of the clubgoers stand out more than others. Every now and then there's a splash of bright colour in amongst the black – pink or blue or gold. Sometimes there's a hat or a piece of jewellery that draws the eye. One bold young thing is wearing nothing but strips of tape. Not the kind of person that Angela is looking for. She isn't interested in anyone who's attracting too much attention.

The regulars are also off limits. Too dangerous, too much chance of being remembered. The same goes for the people who are obviously here as part of a group, or a couple. And she steers clear of the ones who spend all their time dancing by themselves. She learned early on that it's far too difficult to get a dedicated dancer off the floor.

On her third pass through the bar, she spots a likely candidate, sipping a drink and not talking to anyone nearby. After two more passes, her potential quarry is still in the same place. Perfect. Angela moves in, making a more thorough appraisal as she works her way closer.

The woman is perhaps in her early twenties, and has frizzy black hair, olive skin, and small, dark eyes. She's most of the way through a Jack and Coke, and it isn't her first. She's moving a little too slowly, taking care not to spill her drink with hands that are starting to get clumsy.

A labret juts out beneath her lower lip, and studded leather bands circle her neck and wrists. Her trousers and top are fairly plain, though, basic black. Clothes anyone might have on hand at home. If Angela had to guess, she'd say that the collar and wristbands are borrowed, and despite the labret, it's probably her first time here. And Angela is very good at guessing.

It takes some time before the next barstool over is clear. As soon as it is, Angela slides onto it and orders a gin and tonic. She waits no more than a couple of seconds before she turns towards the black-haired woman, raising her voice to be heard over the bar chatter.

'Hi.'

A glance, slightly wary. The look of someone who isn't sure why she's being addressed. 'Hi.'

'Are you here by yourself, too?' Angela asks, her tone friendly. Inviting. 'I hate coming to these places alone.'

A pause. A slight nod. 'Yeah.'

'People watching gets old fast, right?'

'I like the outfits.'

Angela listens carefully. Her seatmate isn't so drunk that she's struggling with her words, but drunk enough that she's articulating them deliberately, trying not to slur any. Angela smiles, cheerful and bright.

'I know what you mean,' she says. 'Did you see the girl who was only wearing, like, three pieces of electrical tape?'

The woman's eyes widen. 'Yeah.' She looks close to awestruck. 'Not something I'd ever wear outside, but damn.'

'Totally.'

Angela's drink arrives. She pushes a five across the bar to the bartender, and pretends to take a sip. Alcohol is a pleasure she doesn't indulge in anymore. Can't indulge in, although she very much wishes that she could, especially right now. But if dancing is something she does less than she wants to, drinking is off limits entirely. Swallowing more than a drop would make her gag.

As she sets the glass back down on the bar, she asks, 'So, what's your name?'

'Hazel.'

'Nice to meet you, Hazel. I'm Angela.' She glances towards Hazel's almost empty glass. 'What are you drinking?'

'Jack and Coke. You?'

'Gin and tonic. I like the way they glow.'

'Glow?' Hazel tilts her head, curious. Angela obligingly pushes her glass close to one of the blacklights playing across the bar. The two women watch as the liquid lights up, blue-white. 'Neat.'

'It's the quinine. Very fluorescent.' She leans towards Hazel, suddenly animated. 'You know what it's doing? It's absorbing the ultraviolet at three hundred fifty nanometres, and then emitting blue light at four hundred fifty. It has to come back out with less energy, so it's a longer wavelength.'

'Um, I'm going to go with, "pretty colour", if that's OK?'

'Sorry.' Angela feels like biting her tongue. Why is she letting herself get distracted tonight? She drags her attention back to the task at hand. 'Do you want one? My treat.' Hazel hesitates. 'You can buy the next round,' Angela assures her.

Hazel shrugs, acquiescing, and Angela orders another gin and tonic from the bartender.

'So, Hazel, what do you do?' Angela asks. 'When you aren't here, that is.'

'I'm an accountant.' Hazel grimaces, the words coming out short and clipped. 'Working towards my CPA licence.'

'You look like you're expecting me to run away screaming.'

'No, I'm expecting you to ask if it's as boring as it sounds.'

'Do people really do that?'

'They're usually too polite to say it out loud. But I can tell they want to,' Hazel says grumpily. 'And I actually have a job at a pretty interesting place.'

'Oh, yeah?' Angela raises her eyebrows in challenge. 'Do they let you keep the piercing in at work?'

'Well, no. But other than that. Honest.'

'All right,' Angela says. 'Then I won't ask if it's boring. Why don't you tell me what's interesting about it instead?'

Angela soon has Hazel chatting about her work. When the drink comes, Hazel doesn't notice Angela palming the tablets and crushing them with a quick, forceful squeeze. Or dropping the crumbled fragments into the glass as she slides it over.

She listens attentively while Hazel tells her about her job at a software company. Her group specialises in international tax law, which apparently is fiendishly complicated. Angela says the right words to keep her going, makes the right expressions to demonstrate interest, treads carefully on the deniable border between conversation and flirting. She's become skilled at that over the past year. A fact that disgusts her.

She wishes she could just make a pass at someone, a real one instead of this grotesque fraud. But that would be even worse than what she's doing now. Much, much worse. She's been on the other side of that, and knows exactly where it leads.

Angela can't start a relationship with anyone, no matter how much she wants one. It's too dangerous. Something like this, a horrific parody of a chance meeting in a club, is all she can allow herself to have.

Ever.

When the gin and tonic is halfway gone, Hazel starts forgetting what she's already said in the middle of a funny story about one of her co-workers.

By the time she finishes off the glass, she's been trying to explain something about German import policy for at least five minutes. Angela isn't entirely sure what the policy is, or why it's important, because Hazel is omitting half of the explanation without realising it.

Angela takes a deep breath to steel herself for what's coming next. And maybe to remind herself of a time when breathing was something she needed to do.

It's time.

'Hazel, are you feeling all right?' she asks, solicitous, nothing but concern in her voice. 'You don't look so good.'

'I think . . .' Hazel frowns, puzzled, her brows drawn down. She gestures weakly at her empty glass. 'I don't . . . I may have, have had too much . . .' She's swaying on the barstool.

'Are you going to be sick?' Hazel turns faintly greenish at the suggestion. 'Right, let's get you to the bathroom.'

'Yeah . . .' Hazel mumbles. 'That sounds . . . Yeah.'

Angela stands and slips an arm around Hazel's back, easing her off the stool. Hazel lets herself be led across the bar towards the women's bathroom, stumbling a little as she walks, leaning on Angela for support.

No one else notices anything is amiss. No one cares.

Angela can feel Hazel's pulse, the blood moving underneath the skin. And in an inevitable response, things start shifting and sliding just behind Angela's lips. Her mouth is full of saliva. She swallows it down. If Angela's heart still beat of its own volition, it would be racing. But it stays lifeless and silent.

She's left this far too long, and it's going to be difficult to stay in control. Stupid. But she hates this so, so much.

Pushing through the door, into the bathroom. Past a few other girls washing their hands or checking their makeup. She keeps Hazel between herself and the mirrors. It would get more than a little bit awkward if anyone noticed that only one of them has a reflection.

Angela muscles Hazel into an empty stall, shuts and latches the door. She sits Hazel down on the edge of the toilet seat. Reaches around and unbuckles the leather collar. Angela has an excuse prepared for this if she needs one – just letting Hazel get some air – but it doesn't matter at this point. Hazel's eyes are rolled back into her head, her lids halfway closed, and the only sounds she's making are incoherent murmurs. She's not aware enough of what's going on to protest.

Angela takes a long moment to look at what she's done.

'I'm so sorry,' she whispers.

And then, fangs fully extended, she bites Hazel in the neck.

CHAPTER FIVE

Somerville
6 November 1999

It's raining hard outside, water smearing across the window like a coating of Vaseline. Chloë usually loves rain, the calming white-noise sound of it. It isn't helping her mood tonight, though. Probably nothing could. Above her, the upstairs neighbours are doing something that makes repeated heavy thumping sounds. Chloë wonders what it could be. Basketball? Step dancing? Cattle rustling?

The blank document on the computer screen is taunting her at this point. She types a letter, and immediately erases it. After a moment, she tries again with a full word, hoping it will inspire her to continue on to a complete sentence. 'The' sits there, isolated and alone, for long minutes until she erases that, too.

The sky has already eased from grey to black, the early sunset of the Boston winter cutting the day short, and that one erased word is the most she's managed to write. It's the most she's accomplished, period.

Chloë can't blame the neighbours, not really. She can't even blame the cat now that she's managed to nudge him off the keyboard. Besides, it would be unfair to get irked at Entropy when he's been her only company for most of the day. Ari's been out for hours,

34

and she's been reluctant to talk to him since the animal sacrifice discussion, anyway. She hopes he isn't too wet, wherever he is.

She reaches over and scratches Entropy behind the ear, and he purrs contentedly, half-asleep. At least one of them is having a good day.

Gun, the thought enters her mind, unbidden. *You could shoot yourself in the head. It'd be quick and simple.*

Oh, hell.

'Where would I even get a gun?' she asks, talking aloud as if she's carrying on a perfectly reasonable conversation. 'You need a licence. And guns are messy. You can miss with a gun, end up brain damaged in the hospital, hooked up to a machine. Is that what you want?'

She knows they're called 'intrusive thoughts', although knowing what they're called never did her much good. It sometimes helps to think of them as trespassers, alien invaders, breaking into her head and occupying her mind. She'd been hoping they would end when her marriage did – remove the obvious cause and the effect should go away, shouldn't it? But the breakup happened more than two years ago, the divorce long since finalised, and here they are.

To be fair, it's been weeks since the last time this happened. The Zoloft has helped a lot. She still gets bad days, though.

She shouldn't have spent so much of the day in her bedroom. It can't be healthy, shutting herself in with nothing to look at but her cluttered desk and unmade bed. The walls are blank and ugly, interrupted only by the rain-smeared window; there isn't any art up anymore. All of it went with Alec when he moved out. The only traces left are a few lighter squares marking where the frames used to hang. She didn't even think he'd liked the pictures much.

In all honesty, he hadn't liked anything much by the end, not really. His disgust with the world and with her had grown worse every day; a mass of cold rage disguised as rationality, that was Alec.

She had emotions, while he had facts. Modern art is a con game – fact. TV remotes cause cancer – fact. If Chloë disagrees, it's because she's stupid – fact. Her parents played that game with her when she was a kid, too, and her Aunt Esther was the only one who'd ever called them on it. It's occurred to her that might be why she fell for the exact same brand of bullshit so easily with Alec.

She wishes she could afford to move someplace better, leave behind the bad memories that have accumulated like dead leaves. Even getting outside for a little while might help, but she knows she isn't going to do it tonight. It's too late and too wet.

Maybe she should make dinner, if she can scrounge up anything to make it with. The refrigerator is nearly empty, and she's afraid to touch the boxes and cans in the cabinets; some of them are years old. Cooking is too much of an effort, anyway. She's worthless.

Fuck. It's really bad today. She can't remember the last time it's been this bad. It couldn't possibly be getting worse, could it? Maybe it's time to get the dosage on her prescription upped again.

Entropy yawns, stretches, and begins industriously washing himself. Chloë watches him bathe. It's been a few days since she had a shower herself, and she's starting to feel grimy. It might be a good idea to take one before she heads in to work tomorrow.

She could slit her wrists in the bathtub, if she had a bathtub, which she doesn't. There's only a shower stall. Saved by her cheap-ass apartment. She can't start a car in the garage with the door closed, because she doesn't have a garage. Or a car, for that matter. And she can't stick her head in the oven – or rather, she could, but it's a crappy electric monster from the seventies so she'd probably just make her hair brittle.

Chloë lets out a harsh laugh, causing Entropy to interrupt his washing and turn towards her with a quizzical look.

Her mind is trying to kill her and she's worried about split ends.

She needs a distraction. Something else, anything else, to occupy her mind. There's always her job. Whether she gets anything else done or not, she'd better read some manuscripts tonight. She can only fall so far behind before Shelly starts asking if everything's OK. If she stopped reading them altogether . . . Chloë doesn't want to find out what would happen. She has to have some kind of income.

She forces herself out of her chair and wades through the mounds of clothing covering the bedroom floor, making her way into the living room, where the massive stack of unread works lies waiting. The topmost novel bears the unpromising title *Love Slave of the Night Creature*. Most likely not religion-themed, at least. Good. And how much can you tell from a title, anyway? It could be a comedy. Stupid title, silly characters, a wacky plot. She flips it open and her eyes fall on the Author's Note.

This book, it begins, *was written during a dark period of my life. I had convinced myself that no one loved me, and that I was in fact unlovable. I wrecked anything good before it had a chance to start, just to spare myself the trauma of destroying it later. This is dedicated to everyone who has suffered as I have suffered.*

OK. Not a comedy. She turns to the next page. Then stops short.

A number of phrases instantly leap out at her. In particular, 'naked, sweaty sextoy', 'bloodlust-crazed inhuman trollop', and a paragraph that ominously ends 'until the pineapple was fully inserted'.

Inserted into what? she wonders. She reads that section more closely. That turns out to be a mistake. She has serious doubts that what is being described is physically possible.

She abruptly decides that she doesn't need to read this one any further, and that trying to do so might cause her severe psycho-logical damage. Well, more psychological damage than she already has. She snaps the manuscript shut and flings it with some force. It flies across the room in a fluttery curve and lands with a faint, muf-fled thud on the far side of the rejection area.

At least it was distracting. Briefly.

She doesn't feel good about tossing it aside so soon, though. She can't help but think that she's let her profession down. Not so much that she's willing to pick it up again, but enough that she vows to delve further into the next few submissions. Unfortunately, the ones that follow aren't particularly good, either. None of them keep her mind from wandering, over and over, to uncomfortable places.

She's silently debating what to do next when the doorbell rings, scattering her thoughts.

It's been a while since she last heard it. No one has any reason to come by except for Ari, and he has a key. Her first guess is that he lost it, but when she walks over to the window, an elderly woman on the front walk gives her a wave. Chloë waves weakly back, dumbfounded.

Aunt Esther isn't quite the last person she would have expected to see, but it's still a surprise. Chloë's aunt – actually her great-aunt, or possibly not any kind of aunt at all but a cousin twice removed; Chloë has never been able to keep it straight – looks much the same as she always has. White hair, a wrinkled face, and a slight build that would seem frail if she weren't practically bouncing on her feet with energy.

Chloë goes to open the front door, letting in a gust of cold, wet air.

'Hello, dear,' Esther says brightly. 'I hope you don't mind, but there's some kind of snowstorm in Chicago so the plane I was on was forced to land in a tiny little airfield in Connecticut, and I wasn't about to wait around in a dreary old building for twelve hours, so I thought, who do I know nearby? And then I realised – Chloë! She's only a hundred and fifty miles away! So naturally, I hopped on a bus and the next thing you know here I am at your doorstep, which I hope isn't inconvenient, but is it all right if I spend the night?'

Esther's trouser suit is a lovely shade of violet, and appears to be freshly pressed. Rain drips off a matching umbrella. Chloë glances down at her own clothing, scruffy black slacks and a worn T-shirt of the same colour, leftovers from her days working in technical theatre. She wonders how she ended up feeling underdressed at her own front door. At least she doesn't lounge around wearing nothing but panties and a sweatshirt anymore. Having a housemate breaks you of that habit pretty quickly.

'Um, hi,' Chloë replies when she's able to gather her wits. 'You really should call ahead.'

'Oh, I didn't think I needed to stand on ceremony with you,' Esther answers.

'What if I hadn't been home? You'd have come all this way for nothing.'

It's been years since Chloë last saw Esther, although they've always tried to keep in touch. She used to babysit Chloë, and Chloë adored her. She still does, really, even if her aunt's eccentricities are sometimes less endearing to an adult.

'But you are home!' Esther points out. 'Everything worked out.'

'I suppose it did.' She steps aside to give Esther room to get through the door. 'Come on in.'

Well. It's certainly a distraction, anyway.

CHAPTER SIX

Ascension
6 November 1999

Angela drinks Hazel's blood in rapid gulps. It takes four quick swallows to take the edge off. Then she's able to slow down a little. Hazel shudders in her grip, and moans.

It's over quickly. Angela pulls back, then licks the streaks of blood dripping down Hazel's neck. It feels intrusively intimate, but it seems to help with the healing. Something in her saliva, Angela suspects.

And in fact, immediately after, the wounds stop bleeding. They're already closing up, two faint pinpricks above Hazel's collarbone. Soon they'll barely be visible at all.

The first thing she does is check Hazel's breathing. Steady, constant. Good. Then she checks her pulse. Still strong. Hazel doesn't seem to be having worse problems than anyone would, if they'd been drugged and dragged into a bathroom stall against their will.

Angela slams her head into the side of the stall. Once, twice, three times.

'Everything OK in there?' comes a concerned voice from somewhere beyond the door.

'It's fine. Sorry!' Angela calls back. She waits, listens. Whoever it was says nothing more.

There's a dent in the metal wall where Angela's forehead hit it. That was stupid.

Someday she's going to mess up even worse. She'll wait so long that she completely loses it and attacks someone in public. She'll accidentally hit a major artery and her victim will bleed to death in her arms while she desperately tries to lick the wound closed. She'll let herself get so hungry that she drinks too much, too fast. Or someone is going to have a bad drug reaction, and who knows what will happen then.

She's tried to be careful about the dangers, especially the one she worries about the most, the one that finally resulted in her own death. But even if she never preys on a single person more than once, never bites someone enough times to cause disaster in that particular way, at some point something is going to go wrong. Somehow, sometime.

She got a cell phone so she could call an ambulance, but what if it comes too late? And if it shows up in time, how on earth would she explain what had happened?

So far, she's never needed to make that call. So far.

There has to be a better way than this. Something she can do besides what she just did, or the other method. The one she was taught. But she hasn't come up with anything yet. No solution. Maybe she never will.

She certainly hasn't had much luck figuring out the rest of it. She has no idea why she doesn't cast a reflection. How is that possible? How does it even make sense?

Angela's beginning to feel dizzy – the secondhand drugs and alcohol are hitting her system. She leans against the wall, waiting for it to pass. She needs to be patient, anyway; she has to stay at least until Hazel is coherent enough to give an address, so Angela can bundle her into a taxicab and see her safely home.

Safe from any other predators out there, that is. It's a little late to say she's keeping Hazel safe.

Angela is suddenly glad she doesn't show up in mirrors.

She doesn't think she'd like what she would see.

PART TWO

It's Always Darkest Nowhere Near The Dawn

CHAPTER SEVEN

Tempe, Arizona
19 September 1996

Three years earlier. A different place, a different time, a different life.

'Don't move.'

Angela looks up, startled. She'd been so absorbed in what she was reading that she hadn't heard the other woman approach.

'Seriously, can you hold completely still for, like, half a second?'

Angela has no idea who is talking to her. The stranger's face is hidden behind a camera, so all Angela can see is a fall of hair too cherry red to be natural. A small woman in a ruffled black dress, a rectangular padded bag slung over one shoulder.

'This is going to need a long exposure time,' whoever it is explains. 'If you move, it'll blur out.'

'. . . all right,' Angela says.

'Great. Ready? Go.'

Angela tries to keep totally motionless. The camera clicks, then whirrs.

'Perfect,' the woman says. She lowers the camera, revealing a face with big honey-brown eyes and the delicate features of a china doll. Angela would put her in her late twenties or maybe early

thirties, if she had to guess. Short, almost to the point of being tiny –
Angela isn't tall herself, but she doubts the camera, woman reaches
five feet.

The woman holds out her hand. 'Tess.'

Angela takes it. 'Hi. I'm Angela.'

'Pleasure to meet you, Angela. So, what's your deal? You read outside at night a lot?'

Angela's eyes flick to the sheaf of papers she'd been studying,
then upward to the streetlight she'd been using as a lamp, the bulb
surrounded by a cloud of insects throwing themselves at it with sui-
cidal intensity. It's close enough to the park bench to make reading
possible, but it must look bizarre that she's doing it here.

She wants to explain that she couldn't stand being in her apartment for another minute after a whole day spent indoors. That the
park, grassy and quiet, had reminded her of home. It must use some
kind of irrigation system to have any grass at all in this climate,
which is probably a terrible waste of water. But Angela had been
grateful to find a patch of soft green interrupting the gritty brown
sand and dusty, spiky plants.

All this, however, seems like too much to tell someone she's just
met. 'I don't do it usually,' she says. 'What about you? Do you take
pictures of people at night a lot?'

'Hell, yeah,' Tess answers. 'Whenever I see a picture worth taking. You should see your hair under the streetlight. It's glowing.'

Angela touches her hair self-consciously. 'You're a photographer?
I mean, obviously you are . . . but, professionally?'

Tess nods, and sits down on the park bench next to Angela. Her
feet swing freely, not reaching the ground. 'Cigarette?' she asks,
offering one to Angela. Angela shakes her head no. Tess digs a
lighter out of her bag and lights it herself. Soon the scent of cloves
wafts through the air. 'That's what I do,' Tess continues. 'And that's
what brings me out at night. So what brought you out?'

Angela hesitates, then immediately berates herself for it. She should be able to carry on a conversation without retreating into shyness, for once, especially when someone is basically handing her one on a plate. Someone interesting, friendly, beautiful . . . 'Honestly, I'm out here now because I couldn't go out during the day,' she says.

'Oh? And why's that?'

'Just . . . too hot.'

Tess looks Angela over. 'Yeah. I can see that.'

Angela blinks at Tess, but the look she gets back is completely innocuous. 'I – I didn't want to put my foot out the door while the sun was up, you know?'

'Sure. I didn't get out until after sundown, either.'

Angela relaxes a little. The weather is a subject she can handle. And it should provide plenty to talk about, since the weather here is brutal. Her advisor has reassured her that it's a dry heat, but on the other hand, so's an oven. It's scorching even at night, but not quite as awful as daytime – close to bearable in denim shorts and a tank-top. The one perk is that she's not very sweaty; the air is so dry it wicks away sweat almost before it can form. Weather like this back on the east coast would have the backs of her thighs stuck to the bench, peeling off chips of sun-blasted paint whenever she stood up.

'Aren't you sweltering in that dress?' Angela asks Tess. It has full sleeves with lace around the cuffs, and layers of gathered fabric down to the ankles. 'I know I would be.'

Tess shrugs. 'I don't ever get too hot. What are you reading?'

'Oh, it's only an article,' Angela says, setting the pages aside. 'Homework, sort of.'

'You're in school?'

'Grad school. First year. I just started here.'

'Cool.' Tess blows smoke out of her nostrils, and doesn't say anything more.

In the lull that follows, there's no sound other than the faint hum of traffic over on the main road. Angela can just make out the lights of the cars, blinking in and out of sight as they pass behind the dark trees that line the distant street. No one else is sitting on any of the benches, or the wide, empty stretch of grass. She scratches distractedly at a mosquito bite on her leg, and tries to think of a way to keep the conversation going.

'Why didn't you use a flash?' she asks. 'For the photo?'

One side of Tess's mouth curls up in a kind of half-smile. 'I was trying to get the lamplight on your hair. If I'd used a flash, I would've picked up the flash instead.'

'Is that why you needed the long exposure? To get more light without—' Angela cuts herself off, wanting to take the question back as soon as she's asked it. No one is ever interested in nerd questions about optics.

Tess doesn't seem to mind, though. 'Yeah. Tricky shot. Even with a fast lens and high-speed film. Any movement would fuck it up.'

See, Angela tells herself. *No need to panic. You can talk to people.* 'That makes sense,' she says. 'But what about your hands?'

'What do you mean?' Tess asks.

'I was staying still, but you were holding the camera in your hands. Don't they, I don't know, shake? A tiny bit?'

'I have very steady hands,' Tess says. 'So. What do you do for fun, Angela the grad student?'

Angela shifts where she sits, very slightly, barely a motion at all. 'I don't know.'

'You don't know?' Tess asks, again showing her odd little half-smile.

'I only just – I haven't had time to meet a lot of people here yet.' It's the first excuse she can think of, and she's fairly sure Tess can see right through it. Her anxiety rises again. Angela reaches down to shuffle her papers, pretending to straighten them out, giving herself something to do with her hands. This isn't the first time she's worried that she might be boring, but the feeling is particularly strong tonight, when she's sitting next to someone who so obviously isn't. Someone bold enough to ask strangers for photographs. Someone with an artistic career. Someone who smokes and swears and wears elegant clothing and does all the other things that Angela has never allowed herself to do.

Because the truth is, she doesn't do anything much, and has never done anything much except shuffle to church or to school. Neither of which are of much use at the moment. She isn't going to church anymore, even if there's an annoying voice in her head calling her a heretic for it. And as far as school goes, the few friends she made as an undergrad, like Shelly, are thousands of miles away.

'Well, you've met someone here now,' Tess says. 'Want to go clubbing?'

'What?' Angela wonders for a moment if Tess somehow read her thoughts, until she realises it's a response to the last thing she said. 'Clubbing? You mean, tonight?'

Tess looks her up and down with a critical eye. 'Not tonight,' Tess concedes. 'You're definitely not dressed for it.'

'I'm not sure I can dress for it, if it means a dress like yours. I don't own anything like that.'

'In that case, shopping, then clubbing. Some other time. Tonight, how about I buy you a drink?'

'You really don't have to –'

'As a thank you, for letting me take your picture,' Tess says. 'Come on, one drink, how bad could it be? If I turn out to suck, you leave and never have to see me again.'

'Well. If you put it that way.' Angela is surprised to find she's smiling, too.

She's in a new city, isn't she? Maybe she can have a new life. It's time to try something different. Like following someone intriguing to a bar and seeing what happens.

'Great.' Tess stubs her cigarette out, then hops off the bench and stretches. 'Let's go.' Behind her, the stars that are bright enough to penetrate the glow of the city lights gleam like hundreds of distant cat's eyes, scattered across the wide southwestern sky. The swollen gibbous moon is huge on the horizon. 'Ever been to the Merc Bar?'

'No.'

'I'll take you there, then. Get you a gin and tonic,' Tess says as Angela joins her and they start to leave the park. 'There's a neat little trick you can do with them.'

'Oh? What's that?'

'You can make them light up.'

'Huh.' Angela cocks her head, considering. 'How does that work?'

'You know,' Tess says, 'I have no fucking idea.'

CHAPTER EIGHT

Somerville
15 November 1999

'Well, I'm off,' Ari says as he heads out the door. 'Thanks for the pancakes. They were amazing!'

'Anytime, dear,' Esther calls after him. 'Keep warm. And let me know if you save any lives.'

'Will do!'

Chloë manages not to roll her eyes. Approximately twenty minutes after first meeting Ari, Esther did a card reading for him and determined that he was going to save someone's life, in some unspecified way at some unspecified time. She's been bringing it up ever since as if it's certain to happen, which is exactly why Chloë has declined Esther's offers to tell her fortune as well. Ari, on the other hand, has been treating the whole thing with disconcerting seriousness.

She wonders how much of a crowd his preaching is going to attract after nine o'clock at night. The start of his work day, right after a healthy pancake breakfast. Well, it's not like Chloë sticks to reasonable working hours, either. She tries to return her attention to the manuscript she's reading.

She only gets a few words in before Esther interrupts her concentration. 'Mind if I make myself some coffee?'

'This late in the day? Won't it keep you up?' Chloë asks, throttling her growing frustration.

Esther is already walking into the kitchen. 'Not me. I like a cup in the morning and a cup before bed. First one makes the world seem fresh and new, and the last one, I swear, helps me to sleep. Do you want one?'

'No, thanks. I'd be shocked if there was more than one clean mug in the cupboard, anyway.'

'I could wash one out for you if you're busy. It's no trouble.'

'Really,' Chloë tells her, 'don't bother.'

Esther's 'overnight' stay has somehow stretched out to more than a week, and she hasn't given any indication that she plans to leave in the near future. The apartment is starting to feel awfully crowded with three people in it.

It helps that Esther spends a lot of time out of the house sightseeing – walking the Freedom Trail, visiting the parks of the Emerald Necklace, taking cruises out to the Harbor Islands. All the tourist expeditions no sensible person would want to do in the middle of November. Today she rented a car and drove up to Salem, returning with an armful of witchcraft-related knickknacks to add to the general clutter.

Whenever Esther is around, however, she keeps up a constant stream of chatter. Relentlessly cheerful chatter, which has grown more irritating with each passing day. However dearly Chloë loves her aunt, if this goes on much longer she's going to start screaming.

Chloë squirms in the overstuffed armchair. Formerly overstuffed, really; Entropy has taken to using it as a scratching post, so most of the stuffing is currently littering the floor. She prefers to read on the couch, but Esther has been using it as a bed, and the sheets and pillows mark it as her territory now.

Esther returns to the room, sipping her coffee with a sigh of contentment. 'You know, I think coffee's what's kept me alive all these years,' she says as she takes her place on the couch. 'Of course, back in the day, I never had one of those fancy electric coffee makers like you've got. They didn't exist. We had to boil the grounds in a linen bag. Tasted terrible, unless you heaped in the sugar.'

Chloë makes a noncommittal noise and flips a page in her book. She has a perfectly good excuse for not answering. The giant pile of manuscripts she needs to plough through is sitting right out in the open, not at all subtle. At some point, Esther has to take the hint.

At some point. Surely.

'Yep,' Esther continues, 'I remember when there were no coffee makers, no CD players, no computers . . . Heck, when I was a little girl, my house didn't have electricity at all. There wasn't even a radio. Can you imagine that?'

If Esther is bothered by the lack of response, she's showing no sign of it. It occurs to Chloë that her aunt might be doing this deliberately. Irritating her on purpose, trying to get a rise out of her, a reaction. But why would she do that?

Chloë has a sneaking suspicion she knows the answer, now that she thinks about it.

'That's because I'm old, you see,' Esther says. 'Unimaginably old. But I'm as alert and active as I ever was. Did I tell you I went rock climbing in Tibet last year? 'Cause that's the kind of gal I am.' She pauses to take a sip of her coffee.

Chloë stares at the words in front of her, although she isn't really reading them at this point. Now that Esther has brought up her 'unimaginable' age, Chloë knows what must be coming next.

She doesn't have to wait long.

'You know once, back in the day, when things got a little rough, Eleanor Roosevelt said to me—'

Chloë gives up on pretending to read altogether, and drops the manuscript to the floor.

'Why on earth,' she asks, 'are you still doing that?'

Esther is the picture of wounded innocence. 'Still doing what?'

On top of her other exasperating habits, Esther has claimed to be an ancient witch ever since Chloë was a small child. It was fun when she was too young to know better, and tolerable when she was a teenager because it annoyed her parents. But in the years since, the pretence has long worn out its welcome.

'You can't possibly expect me to believe you,' Chloë says. 'Eleanor Roosevelt? What, were the two of you chums?'

The older woman grins, shattering her innocent look. 'Well, we did have a . . . thing.'

'A thing? What kind of thing are you—' Chloë cuts herself off. 'No, never mind, I'm not going to ask. Because everything else aside, and there's a lot of everything else that I'm putting aside here, you have a normal, human lifespan. So whatever it was, it could not have happened, OK?'

'Eleanor lived until 1962,' Esther states with quiet dignity. 'And I wouldn't exactly have been a babe in arms by then myself, even if I did have a "normal, human lifespan". So in point of fact, it's entirely plausible.'

Chloë gets up off the armchair and stretches, working out the kinks in her back. She's been sitting still for too long, and is starting to feel it.

'All right, first, no one defends a real incident from their life by calling it "entirely plausible". You might as well say, "By the way, I'm making this all up." Second, don't think I can't tell what you're doing.'

'Oh? And what's that?' Esther asks.

'I appreciate that you're not just coming out and saying, "Hey, Chloë, get it together, your life is a sad wreckage of wasted time, dead hopes, and shattered dreams." But I'm hearing it.' There, it's out in the open. Maybe her aunt will finally stop poking at her. 'I mean, I think there's a comparison being made when you talk about how you're sky-diving at age ninety-nine or bungee jumping at a hundred and three in spite of your impoverished childhood. But I'm fine, OK?'

'Dead hopes and shattered dreams?' Esther raises her eyebrows and takes another calm sip of coffee. 'Have you been taking your medication?'

Chloë stops short. 'What do you mean? Why would you think I was taking medication?'

Esther reaches into the detritus cluttering the end table and plucks out a bottle of pills. 'Leaving this lying around is hardly hiding it, you know. Unless you like Zoloft for its great taste?' She rattles the bottle.

'All right,' Chloë grumbles. 'You caught me. But you don't need to worry, all right? I've got it under control.'

Esther looks around with a doubtful expression. She picks up a mass of papers and other debris from the floor, and lets it slide through her fingers back to the ground.

'Yes, I see,' she says, her tone dry. 'It looks like you have everything well in hand.'

'I have an extremely energetic cat. If I ever bothered to straighten anything up, he would knock it down again during the night.'

Esther doesn't look convinced by this argument. 'Is that also why you can't do your dishes? Or are you waiting for your extremely energetic cat to do them for you?'

Chloë wishes she'd kept quiet. She shifts her weight from one foot to the other, then back. A few days in her aunt's company and she's fidgeting like a child again. Typical.

'Who gives a damn if the place isn't clean, anyway? I don't care. Ari doesn't care. You're only here for a quick visit. It doesn't matter to anyone, so why should I bother?'

'Ah ha!' Esther cries. 'The truth is revealed at last!'

Chloë stares at Esther, whose expression resembles that of a cat who has eaten not just one canary, but a whole flock of them. 'What on earth are you talking about?'

'Loneliness. It's a terrible thing.'

'So is a complete non sequitur,' Chloë replies.

'You feel like you don't have anyone to keep the place clean for, so . . .' Esther makes an expansive gesture which takes in the mess on the floor, the apartment as a whole, and conceivably Chloë's entire life.

'I really don't see how you got that from what I said.'

'When was the last time you went on a date?' Esther asks.

Chloë takes an involuntary step back. She already misses the time when Esther was only badgering her to do a card reading.

'Are you kidding?' Chloë says. 'I am so not ready to date yet.'

'Why not?'

'It's too soon.'

'It's been two years, hasn't it?'

'Look, I'm not . . . I can't . . .' It's Chloë's turn to gesture wordlessly at the wreckage that surrounds them.

'Oh, sweetheart, you shouldn't let a bit of mess get in your way. I bet you're doing better than you think. I can see you're taking all the right steps – getting treatment, taking medication.' Esther peers at the Zoloft bottle. 'Two times a day.'

Chloë has no idea how to respond to that. So she doesn't. 'I, you know, I have work to do,' she declares. 'I need to read everything in the big pile there by Wednesday. I don't have time to dissect my love life, or lack of a love life, or whatever it is you're doing.' She grabs the manuscript she was reading from the floor and shoots a challenging look at Esther, who simply shrugs.

Chloë walks into her bedroom and shuts the door.

Ten seconds later, she opens it back up.

'Date who, anyway?' Chloë asks. 'It's not like anyone is lining up at the front door. What would my personal ad look like?

"Impoverished, divorced, insane writer seeks rebound relationship."
That's what everyone wants to take home to mother, right?'

'You're being a little bit hard on yourself, there.'

'The point is, my dating prospects are not what I would call
stunning.'

'All right, so don't date,' Esther says. 'But at least go out and have
fun sometime. When was the last time you did that?'

'I—' Chloë has to think hard about the question. She isn't immediately coming up with anything.

'That's what I thought. You need to get out of this house.'

'I go into the office once a week,' Chloë offers.

'Sounds thrilling.'

'Oh, wait! I went out for drinks with my officemate and some
friends of hers in September.'

'September was two months ago.'

'I still had fun,' Chloë counters, somewhat weakly.

'I suppose it's a start,' Esther says. 'So, was anyone there nice?'

'And here I thought we were past you trying to fix me up with no
one in particular.'

'Does that mean yes or no?'

'It means it doesn't matter!' Chloë shouts. 'Haven't you been listening? I'm a complete wreck. No wonder I'm not meeting anybody.
I can't even go outside!'

Chloë's eyes start to tear up.

Esther puts her coffee mug down and walks over to her. She gently rests her hand on Chloë's shoulder.

'You know,' she says, after a moment, 'sometimes, back during
the War, things got tough in Paris, too. But once, when the shelling
was so intense I could barely see, Gertrude Stein pulled me aside
and said, "Esther, maybe into every life a little rain must fall, but it's
always darkest just before the dawn and every cloud has a silver
lining, so let a smile be your umbrella and don't be afraid to stop

and smell the roses, because good things come to those who wait, a stitch in time saves nine, make love, not war, and loose lips sink ships!" '

Chloë snorts, trying not to laugh and failing.

'That was nice of her, don't you think?' Esther asks.

'Gertrude Stein said that.'

'Verbatim.'

'And which war was this?' Chloë asks her. 'Gertrude Stein was World War I, right? So, this is a conversation you had more than eighty years ago?'

'Gertrude Stein lived until 1946. She saw more than one war, dear.'

'All right, fine,' Chloë says. 'Let's just ignore the fact that none of that made sense, and that I'm pretty sure no one said "make love, not war" until the sixties, and that those weren't even good clichés.'

'Oh? What's wrong with them?'

'Everything. I mean, for instance, it isn't darkest just before the dawn. It's actually pretty bright. It's darkest when it's nowhere near the dawn. That's always bothered me.'

'I'm sure you're right.' Esther does not appear to be overly concerned by the details. 'Now get yourself out of the house before you start rotting.'

'You're going to keep pushing me until I do, aren't you?'

'Absolutely,' Esther tells her.

Chloë scrutinises Esther's face, and sees no sign whatsoever that her aunt will ever relent. To be honest, Chloë has to concede she has a point. It would be nice to get away from the stale air in her apartment, breathe something fresher for a change.

She's surprised to find that she feels up to it. At least for the moment, anyway. She isn't sure why, given that five minutes ago she was nearly crying. Unlikely as it may seem, her aunt's preposterous stories have derailed her incipient breakdown.

Not that she intends to admit it. 'Fine. You know what? You win.' Chloë grabs her coat off the lamp it's been flung over, and starts shrugging herself into it. 'I'm obviously not going to get any more work done tonight, anyway. You coming?'

Esther shakes her head, failing to conceal a satisfied smile. 'It's too late for my old bones. Go do young person things.'

'All right, then. Don't stay up for me. I'm off, heading out into the world to appease your tyrannical demands.' Chloë strides to the front door, and then stops, her dramatic exit interrupted as she spends the next few minutes looking for her handbag. Eventually, Esther finds it behind the armchair. 'Thank you,' Chloë says. 'Anyway, here I go. OK? Are you happy?'

'Have fun, dear,' Chloë hears Esther say as the door shuts behind her with a solid-sounding thud.

CHAPTER NINE

The Card Reading

I don't remember every card reading I've ever done. But I can recall with perfect clarity the one I gave Chloë when she was eight years old.

Her parents didn't approve of fortune telling. They claimed – loudly and often – to have rational ideas regarding childrearing and education. But they were out for the evening, and their plans for Chloë's upbringing didn't seem to be working very well anyway. The scribbled stories she'd shown me tended to focus on magic and monsters and brave Amazonian warriors rather than rationality.

I'd done my best to do things up right for the occasion, putting a fringed silk scarf across the table, lighting a couple of candles and turning off the lights. Chloë approved of the decorations, although she expressed disappointment at the lack of a crystal ball and damask wall hangings. Damask had featured a goodly amount in Chloë's writing, and I think she was hoping to find out what it looked like.

'This arrangement tells the past, present, and future,' I told her as I laid the cards down. 'Or it usually does. Tonight we're only doing the future.' At eight years old, she didn't have much of a past yet.

I can picture her to this day, shifting forward to watch the cards fall, moving to the edge of her chair with a little jump that made her mop of dark curls bounce, excitement in her bright-green eyes. But when I flipped the first card over to reveal Le Roi de Trèfle – the King of Clubs – she pouted.

'That's just a regular card,' she said. 'I thought you said these were old.'

It did look a great deal like a modern card. We still use the medieval French suits, after all. 'They are old,' I replied. 'Look closer.'

Chloë peered intently at the picture. 'Oh. It doesn't look the same rightside-up and upside-down. He has legs.'

It was an ornate drawing in the classic Paris pattern, the King's sceptre held high, fleurs-de-lis decorating his robes. I've never used a Tarot deck. The cards were from my piquet deck, which is what everyone used to use before Tarot became all the rage because some charlatan claimed it came from ancient Egypt. Which is ridiculous; playing cards didn't even reach Egypt until the Fatimid dynasty. I would know.

'This deck,' I said, 'was given to me by La Maupin herself, and she taught me how to use them, as well. You'd have liked her, dear. She was brave and dashing and clever, like the heroines in your stories.' And she could win the clothes right off your back, then use the same cards to gaze into your future later that night. While you still weren't wearing any clothes. I decided not to mention that part. 'In any case, Julie, that was her real name, was quite famous in her day. As an opera singer, as a swordswoman – this was back at the end of the seventeenth century–'

'You're making all this up,' Chloë accused.

'Not a bit of it. I've been alive a long, long time. I'm a witch, you see.'

Her eyes grew as wide as saucers. Then the questions came tumbling out. 'Are you really? Are you a good witch or a bad witch? Can you fly? Do you have a broomstick? Do you have a hat? Can you turn

people into toads? Will you turn someone into a toad if I ask you to?'
And on and on.

It took me some time to explain to her that good witches never
toadify anyone, not even Tiffany, whether she deserved it or not.
I only managed to get Chloë's attention back to the cards by prom-
ising to bring along a hat and broomstick next time.

'The King of Clubs,' I said, 'is Alexander the Great, fearsome and
mighty. That's why there's a lion at his feet.' It was a rather stylised
drawing, so if you didn't know it was a lion you might think it was
a dog. Or a handbag. 'All the face cards have names. There's also
Lancelot, and Julius Caesar, and Ragnelle –'

'Ragnelle?'

'She's another one from King Arthur's court. She married Sir
Gawain.'

'So what does the King of Clubs mean?' Chloë asked. 'About my
future?' When I told her it meant she would meet a tall, dark
stranger – which is the answer I gleaned from the card, no matter
how clichéd it might seem – she was displeased. 'Boys are gross.
I don't like that one.'

I flipped over the next card and found that the King of Clubs was
crossed by the Ten of Spades. 'Well, you're right,' I said. 'It's probably
not going to go well.' The Ten of Spades can be a rather savage card.
I elected not to burden an eight-year-old with the knowledge of precisely what that might entail.

'The next card,' she declared, 'should say I'm going to meet someone who is not tall, not dark, and not a boy. To make up for it.'

'It's difficult to predict what the cards are going to say.'

'*Show me*,' Chloë said.

I found my hand reaching to turn the next card over, placing it
face up on the table almost before I was aware that I was doing it.

I looked at Chloë sharply then, but the child was waiting expectantly for her divination. If anything unusual had happened, she

seemed oblivious to it. That was when I decided I might need to watch this one when she grew up.

The card was La Dame de Carreau, the Queen of Diamonds, a golden-crowned woman with a lily in her hand. 'Oh, look,' I said. 'It's Ragnelle. So you're right again. This one means a pale woman. And she won't be as tall as you, either.' That last part was a guess, but I didn't think it was a wrong one. I could already see in her bones that she was going to be a towering woman, like her mother. 'Now let's see what crosses her, shall we?' I turned over the card. 'The Seven of Hearts. Interesting. That can be a very strong affinity card, but it's never one of the smooth ones. You might have a pretty rocky time with her.'

Chloë was fidgeting in her chair, her interest rapidly waning. Her foot swung into the table leg, making the candle flames flicker and shake. I decided to hurry to the end of the reading. Childhood boredom does not mix well with open flame, and her parents were unlikely to be forgiving if an unauthorised fortune-telling session ended up burning the house to the ground.

The fifth card in the sequence was the Nine of Hearts. 'Ah, the Wish Card. Lucky you. That's one of the most auspicious cards in the deck.'

'Suspicious?'

'Auspicious. That means good. Your life is going to be full of magic, I think.'

That brought Chloë's attention fully back. 'Neat,' she said. 'I like magic.'

'I'm glad to hear it,' I said as I revealed the final card. The Nine of Spades.

'Is that auspicious?'

I hesitated before I replied. 'I'm afraid not,' I said slowly. 'The Nine of Spades tends to mean, well, dark things. Bad times.'

'How bad?'

'Sometimes very, very bad.'

Chloë frowned. 'So, what does it mean when the two Nines show up together like that?'

I couldn't answer. No matter how long I stared at the cards, the meaning wouldn't come clear.

CHAPTER TEN

ManRay, Cambridge, Massachusetts
15 November 1999

Angela circulates restlessly through the rooms. She doesn't like how thin the crowd is, or how small the club is. It isn't nearly as big as the one in Kenmore, and the lights aren't as dim. There aren't enough corners or edges. She feels too obvious, exposed.

This isn't one of her usual hunting nights, and it's throwing her off. But Shelly and Mike are painting the stairwell this coming weekend, and Angela wants to make absolutely certain she isn't hungry when it happens.

That means it's nearly a week earlier than she would ordinarily do this. She lacks the aching need she normally feels when she hunts. Without that driving her, she's finding it harder and harder to concentrate on what she's supposed to be doing. She keeps getting distracted by the music, by the lights, by the sound of people talking.

Nonetheless, she spots a likely prospect early on and starts angling in that direction. A woman in a miniskirt and lacy halter top, standing near the floor speakers with a glum expression on her face. But as Angela approaches, the woman is seized by a coughing fit that lasts half a minute before she finally recovers with a breathy gasp.

Angela backs off. She has no idea what would happen if she drank virus-infected blood, but it's one experiment she's never been tempted to try. *Go home and get better*, she thinks in miniskirt girl's direction. *Drink some cocoa.* Angela wonders why people go out clubbing when they're not feeling well. Do they want to get everyone else sick, too? She goes back to examining the crowd.

She's been here before, but never on a weeknight. The club is in Cambridge, at the far edge of her hunting grounds. It would be a fairly short drive across the river to get there, right over the Boston University Bridge, but that would mean finding a place to park. Quicker in the end to take the Green Line all the way downtown and then the Red Line north, the peculiar geography of the MBTA tracks telescoping the distance out by miles.

The drumbeat of the song that's playing pulls at her, loud and insistent. It's 'Adrenaline' – one of her favourites. She wants to lose herself on the dance floor. She walks away instead, further from the dancing, closer to the scattered clusters of people drinking and chatting.

So much is gone from her life. Cocktails. Sunbathing. The taste of pad thai. Everything about pad thai. She misses wrapping the noodles around a fork – she was always terrible with chopsticks. And carefully ordering it without peanuts, because she was allergic. Although judging by her runny nose whenever she's around anything with fur, she might still have all of her allergies. Shouldn't dander have stopped bothering her when she died? How unfair is that?

It doesn't matter. It doesn't matter that death didn't make her immune to the sniffles, and it doesn't matter that she isn't at the club to dance tonight. She's not there to have fun. If she didn't have a problem that has to be attended to, she wouldn't be there at all. She'd be at home, finishing her thesis so she can get her degree. That's the one thing that hasn't been taken from her yet, and she's not going to lose it if she can help it.

Besides, the fewer people she's exposed to, the better. It's safer all around if she spends most of her waking hours hunched in front of her computer. She starts to feel bad for thinking poorly of the sick girl. Angela's the one who should be staying home.

She's so lost in her own thoughts that she almost fails to notice the perfect target. Angela suddenly realises that the last four times she's made her circuit, she's seen the same woman in the exact same place, drinking alone.

Angela tries to take in as much as she can out of the corner of her eye. The woman is on the lanky side, at least a few inches taller than Angela, maybe more. Hard to tell with better precision when she's sitting down. Her hair is a mass of dark ringlets, and her skin is something like the warm colour of a good apricot. The reddish undertones mean her blood is close to the surface; she'll blush easily. She's wearing black clothes without any embellishments at all, unusually plain for this kind of place. Angela wonders if her potential victim meant to end up here when she went out this evening.

The woman looks up from her drink for a moment, and Angela sees that her eyes are a surprisingly bright, vivid green before she drops her gaze back down.

Whether she meant to end up here or not, she's here now. And she's clearly all by herself.

Angela stalks toward her prey.

CHAPTER ELEVEN

Excerpt From Angela's Experimental Log

TEST #33C
SUBJECT: How fast can I make my heart beat?
METHODOLOGY: Timed rate with stopwatch, five trials
RESULTS: Maximum heart rate 306.6 ± 1.3 beats per minute
COMMENTS: I really should have done more trials, but increasing my heart rate that much makes me dizzy. It's already a disconcerting sensation long before it gets to that point. Making my heart beat feels like clenching a fist inside my chest. It's useful, since it means I can fake having blood pressure in a doctor's office when I need to get a prescription refilled, but it's still strange. The fact that it doesn't beat at all when I'm not deliberately squeezing it, on the other hand, is something that stopped feeling unusual to me a while ago.

So what have I learned? Not much. The same could be said for most of these experiments. When I started doing them, I was hoping to discover more about what I was, what had happened to me, how it all worked. And I have found out a little. But it's frustrating. I can only run tests on myself, and there's no one to discuss them with. I will never publish my findings in *The Journal of Vampire Studies*, because it doesn't exist. No one knows any of this is real, and it'd be too dangerous to let anyone find out. So these are notes for an imaginary thesis. It will never see the light of day. Just like me.

I should be working on my actual thesis tonight, the one that will let me graduate. I need to take another look at the scatter plots and see if I can make sense of them. But frankly, if I have to stare at one more of those things today I'm going to go stark raving mad, so instead, here's an introduction to the Other Thesis that will never be written.

Vampire Physiology and Habits: A First-Hand Study of a Legendary Phenomenon

Vampires. No one believes in them, but everyone's an expert on the subject. After all, they're everywhere: in books, in films, on TV. So most people think they have a pretty good handle on what vampires are all about. But there's a lot of misinformation out there, and a lot of gaps in what 'everybody knows'.

Fictional representation cannot be assumed to be accurate. Let's take television, for example. Nearly every vampire you see on TV is the classic European Dracula type. Think about it – when was the last time you saw an Asian hopping vampire or an African mumiani on a show? It's like they don't even exist. Do they exist? I have no idea. But it bothers me that everyone assumes they don't.

The most basic facts are completely unknown. How many vampires are there in total? How would we find out? It's not like the Census Bureau has a 'vampire' category. And without one, there's no way to tell the difference between a town with vampires and a town where people just happen to bite each other a lot.

One benefit of not being able to publish this is that I don't have to take the jokes out. Academia, you are a humourless beast.

Anyway, all of this means that most people know far less about vampires than they think they do. And while I've only learned a tiny bit more so far, there are a few matters I can shed light on. So I'd like to start by dispelling some common vampire myths that I've found, from personal experience, are more falsehood than fact.

Myth number one: everyone a vampire bites either becomes a vampire or dies

I suspect this one does more damage to the reputation of vampires than anything else. And like many myths, it may have a basis in reality – I have reason to believe that if someone is exposed to enough vampire bites, then eventually one or both of these things will happen. But the key word here is 'eventually'.

Just do the math. Say you start with a single vampire, and this vampire only absolutely has to bite someone once a month – and bear in mind that's a conservative estimate already, although it's within the bounds of possibility, as I learned early on. Let's say that half of the victims become vampires, and half of them die. In that case, in two months you'd have two vampires, and in four months you'd have four, and everyone on Earth would become a vampire in less than three years:

$$2^{34} / 2 = 8{,}589{,}934{,}592$$

That's right, thirty-four months after the first bite, there would be more vampires than the entire current world population. Humans would be gone. There'd be nothing but packs of starving predators, with no one left to bite except each other.

In fact, turning people into vampires seems to be a long and difficult process. Which is why you're not surrounded by vampires right now.

Although it's possible you're surrounded by werewolves. I wouldn't know.

You might ask, what if far more than half of the victims die? That's a way the math could work. But then why aren't all the morgues full of bloodless cadavers with neck hickeys?

Death by biting has to be a relatively rare occurrence, or every vampire would create a substantial trail of very conspicuous corpses. That many vampire-related homicides would be impossible to ignore. You'd be reading about it in the news all the time.

There's only one logical conclusion – you can be bitten by a vampire at least once, and survive the experience.

I'm not saying biting people and drinking their blood isn't a problem. I'm not even saying it isn't evil. But it doesn't have to be murder. Not if you're very, very careful.

That's the truth. It has to be the truth. Because some nights, it's the only thing I have.

CHAPTER TWELVE

ManRay

15 November 1999

Chloë is not having a good time.

In the midst of so much shiny fabric and exposed skin, she's feeling distinctly drab. If she was worried about being underdressed beside Esther and her sharp trouser suits, that was nothing compared to this. She isn't sure how it's possible to feel underdressed next to people wearing lace lingerie and leather straps, but she does.

At least she's wearing black. It's undoubtedly the only reason she got in.

She had every intention of going somewhere fun when she got on the Red Line. She'd planned on going a long way, somewhere deep in the city, someplace she'd scarcely ever been. But she started having doubts when she realised she had no idea where someplace fun might be, close or distant or anywhere else. So she got off the T before it went too far, hopping out at Central Square in Cambridge only a few stops down. Easier to turn around and go home if it ended up being a disaster.

Central Square, though, is not a great spot for nightlife. Most of the neighbourhood is a hole in the ground, some massive construction project going on where there used to be shops and apartments. What little remains standing closes early.

Chloë wandered for a few blocks past empty space and darkened storefronts, trying to decide whether to go somewhere else or give up entirely, when she heard music coming from around a corner. Following the sound, she discovered what appeared to be the one lonely nightclub in the neighbourhood, and she'd felt almost compelled to go inside. She has them sometimes, these impulses, and over the years she's learned to pay attention to them. She ignored the one telling her not to marry Alec and look where that got her.

Before she'd even entered the club, she wondered if she'd made a mistake. The bouncer looked over her outfit with an expression of extreme scepticism before letting her through. As soon as she went in, she was sure of it.

She's been out of place and out of her league since she set foot inside. Half the crowd are dressed in spikes and boots and dancing like they want to punch someone in the face. The rest swirl around ethereally in outfits that look intended for a decadent sex party in a haunted mansion. Chloë doesn't have the faintest idea how to talk to any of them.

Given that she paid the cover charge, she figures she might as well make the best of it. So far, that's meant sitting at the bar nursing a fuzzy navel, and not doing much else. She isn't even bothering to ogle the scantily clad crowd. The music isn't bad, but tonight it's giving her a headache. At least it's not too loud where she is, far from any speakers.

When someone sits next to her and orders a drink, Chloë barely notices.

She used to like dancing. She used to go out to clubs in college. She's never been a social butterfly, but she had a life back then. Running lights for shows at the theatre in East Quad, drinking too much at the cast parties afterwards. Playing role-playing games once a week – *Ars Magica* and *Mage: The Ascension*. *Dungeons & Dragons* if the group was feeling old school. When she moved to Boston with Alec, she fell out of the habit of making friends, and never picked it back up.

Chloë tries to remember the last time she was somewhere like this. Well, not precisely like this – she's never run with a goth club crowd – but the same general idea. She thinks it was around 1995. Four years ago.

She decides to leave as soon as she's finished her drink. She swirls what little remains around in her glass. You're not supposed to drink alcohol while you're on Zoloft, anyway. Bad drug combination. She wonders if downing enough of both at the same time could kill her. It might be one way to do it.

She's taking her final swallow when a voice to her right says, 'Hi.'

Chloë turns, surprised, to find a woman sitting next to her wearing a short, glossy leather dress and fishnet stockings. The black dress contrasts with skin so pale as to be nearly luminous. Blonde hair frames her heart-shaped face. Her eyes are the colour of ashes.

'Hi?' Chloë says back, unable to keep the question out of her tone.

'Are you here by yourself, too?' the woman asks. 'I hate coming to these places alone.'

'I . . . Yes. Yeah. I was just, uh. I was thinking that.' Chloë is finding it hard to speak. Her mouth seems difficult to move.

'People watching gets old fast, right?'

Chloë shrugs, taking a second to pull herself together. 'I wouldn't know. I haven't been doing it.'

'Maybe you should. There's a girl around here wearing nothing but, like, two Band-Aids and a pair of striped tights.'

'Seriously?'

'Yep.'

'I hope she brought a coat,' Chloë says, 'or that's going to be a chilly trip home.'

74

The blonde woman laughs, bright and infectious. Chloë finds herself smiling back.

'So, what's your name?' the woman asks her.

'Chloë.'

'Nice to meet you, Chloë. I'm Angela.' She takes a sip of her drink and nods towards Chloë's empty glass. 'What are you drinking?'

'It was a fuzzy navel.'

'I like to get gin and tonics. I like the way they glow.'

'There are blacklights all over the place,' Chloë notes. 'They must flare up like the northern lights.'

'You want one?'

'Oh. Well. They're pretty and all, but I can't stand the way they taste.'

'Why don't I get you another fuzzy navel, then?' Angela offers.

Chloë hesitates. 'I really shouldn't.'

'You can buy the next round.'

Chloë decides to throw caution to the wind. 'Sure, why not?' She's already had one. Another won't do too much damage, right? She feels more in control of her tongue now, anyway.

She watches Angela as she orders the drink, chatting easily with the dauntingly tattooed bartender until he turns to grab the schnapps. Chloë can't help but notice how beautiful she is. She wonders why Angela sought her out. Most likely, the answer is the obvious one – she was lonely and bored, just like Chloë.

'Do you usually come here with other people?' Chloë asks.

Angela shakes her head. 'Not these days. I haven't lived in Boston long enough to make a lot of friends. What about you?'

'I usually don't come here at all. Most nights I stay at home. Me and my cat.' *And also my weird evangelist subletter and my elderly relative who won't leave*, Chloë thinks. But that's more information than a random stranger is likely to care about.

'What's your cat's name?' Angela asks.

'Entropy.'

'Oh, fantastic name. I like that. I think cats are great, but I'm horribly allergic to them.' Angela sounds almost apologetic. 'I get itchy eyes, runny nose, the works.'

'Sounds awful.'

'Eh. There are worse problems.' Chloë's drink arrives, and Angela pushes it over to her, gripping it across the top like a gearshift. 'So, Chloë, what do you do? When you aren't here, that is.'

'Well . . .' There are a few possible responses to that. Chloë falls back on her standard answer, even if it's less true than it used to be. 'I write a bit.'

'Really? Wow. That's so cool. I wish I was artistic.'

Angela sounds honestly impressed, which takes Chloë aback. 'I wouldn't – I mean, it's, uh, writing is just something I like to do. And lately I haven't been . . . I'm not making a living at it, you know?'

'But that's kind of the point, isn't it?' Angela asks. 'If you wanted to be making money, you'd be, I don't know, selling life insurance or something, right? Writing is the kind of thing you have to be really passionate about.'

'That's a little strong, don't you think?'

'Is it?'

Angela looks directly at Chloë as she asks, and Chloë feels her stomach flutter nervously. She isn't sure why.

'All right,' Chloë says. 'Yes. I guess I am passionate about it.'

'I thought you might be.' Angela is still studying Chloë's face. 'You've got the eyes.'

'Eyes?'

'You have very intense eyes.'

'You're, uh, you're going to make me blush here.'

'Ooh,' Angela says, smiling. 'Tempting.'

And now Chloë finds herself completely speechless. Angela couldn't possibly be flirting with her. Could she?

After a few moments that feel like a very long time, Angela tears her gaze from Chloë's. 'So. How do you survive if writing doesn't pay?'

This seems like safer territory. Chloë calms herself down. She's probably misinterpreting things, anyway. It's never a good idea to trust your judgement on alcohol. She leans her elbow on the bar and rests her cheek on her hand.

'Mostly,' she says, 'I read bad books.'

'You read – what?'

'I'm a slush pile reader at a publishing company. I get all the unsolicited submissions. Our nation's first line of defence against appalling literature.'

There's a strange expression on Angela's face. 'Really? There can't be a lot of people who have that job, can there?'

'I wouldn't say a lot. A few, I guess. It's a pretty literary town, there are a bunch of publishers based here.'

'Which one do you work for?'

'Compass Rose.'

Angela's eyes suddenly widen. 'Wait. Are you Shelly's minion?'

'Well, I work with Shelly Butler, yeah. Do you know— Hey!'

Chloë isn't sure exactly what happens, but her fuzzy navel glass shatters on the floor. The ground between them is soaked with alcohol, a spreading puddle saturated with ice and broken glass, like a tiny glaciated sea in shades of muddy orange.

'I'm so sorry!' Angela's apology is almost shouted, loud and rushed. 'Did any of it get on you? I swear I'm never that clumsy – I must be drunker than I thought. Are you OK?'

'I'm fine, don't worry about it,' Chloë reassures her. 'It's no big deal, you paid for it, anyway. It's fine.'

They slide off their barstools and move away from the wreckage so the bartender can sweep up the glass. The pool is still widening; Chloë hadn't started on the drink before it got knocked over, although that might be for the best in any case. Her shoes stick to the floor after they hit the edge of the spill, making a sound like Velcro every time she lifts them.

The bartender shoots them an unappreciative glare, his scowl made more menacing by the metal piercings dotting his face. He keeps it pointed at them until they move farther off. Angela leaves her nearly untouched gin and tonic behind on the bar. The few chairs scattered across the room are fully occupied, so by an unspoken mutual agreement they back away until they hit a pair of dusty pool tables further in the room. Chloë wonders how many goths play pool. Not many, going by the dust. Certainly none tonight.

Apparently judging that they're out of glaring range, Angela leans against one of the tables, resting a hand on the green felt. 'I feel terrible about that.'

'He probably has to deal with that all the time. Alcohol, glass, it happens.'

'I guess.'

'I bet he's already forgotten about it.' Chloë risks a look over her shoulder at the bartender and finds his expression unchanged. She turns back to Angela, clearing her throat. 'Or not. Um, so how do you know Shelly, anyway?'

'I met her when we were both undergrads at Haverford. She was a couple of years ahead of me, but we kept in touch after she graduated. I'm her housemate now, though, actually.'

'Really? Small world.' Chloë has a sudden realisation. 'You must be the mysterious woman in Shelly's basement!'

Angela tilts her head, her eyebrows drawing together. 'She talks about me? And she said I'm mysterious?'

'No – I mean, yes, she has mentioned you, a little. But she never called you mysterious. That's just how I thought of you.'

'Oh, did you?'

'Only because she said you were always down there working, and never came out, which obviously isn't true, since you're here, and, and, uh . . .' Chloë looks for a graceful way to finish, and eventually gives up. 'Does Shelly really call me her minion?'

'Well. Yes.' Angela smiles contritely. 'Does that bother you?'

Chloë shrugs. 'Nah. She's not technically my boss, so I probably should be insulted, but as far as the job description goes it's pretty accurate, honestly.'

'You're the one who passes the good books on to her, right?' Angela asks.

'Yeah, which is a pity. It means she never has to suffer through the really, really bad ones.'

'Like what?'

'Like the Irish potato famine children's book,' Chloë says immediately. 'Among other things, it explains to kids why it's better to get married at age fourteen, so that there will always be, and I quote, "No bastards in Ireland!" '

Angela looks simultaneously delighted and appalled. 'What does that have to do with the potato famine?'

'I have no idea. It also came with crayon illustrations of people dying of starvation, though.'

'You're kidding.'

'Not at all. The title was *I'm So Hungry I Could Die*.'

'Wow.' Now Angela appears to be the one at a loss for words. 'Just . . . wow.'

'It was kind of remarkable. It holds a special place in my heart.'

Angela laughs again. Chloë decides she rather likes making Angela laugh. When she stops, the look she turns on Chloë is speculative.

'You know, I don't think he likes me resting my ass on the pool table, either,' Angela says, inclining her head towards the bar. 'Or at least he's still staring. Do you mind if we go somewhere else? Other than the bar, that is? I don't really want to go back there.'

'Sure.'

Angela weaves her way deeper into the club, with Chloë following close behind, until they reach a small padded bench at the edge of one of the dance floors, out of sight of the bar and hopefully out of mind. Angela perches on the armrest and motions Chloë towards the seat. Chloë settles into it. A song Chloë doesn't know pulses over them from the speakers. Close by, a woman in a velvet dress spins in graceful circles, her eyes closed. A slim man in a tight mesh shirt glides past her. Off to the right, someone is coughing.

'So, I feel like I've been going on about me,' Chloë says after a brief pause, louder now to make herself heard over the music, her mouth close to Angela's ear. 'What about you? What do you do for a living?'

A look of surprise flashes across Angela's face, as if she hadn't expected to be asked. 'I'm a grad student.'

'Oh? What are you studying?'

'Astrophysics.'

Chloë blinks. 'Wow. My turn to say wow. I wouldn't have guessed that.'

'Why not?' Angela asks, frowning slightly. 'Do I come across as dumb?'

'No!' Chloë says quickly. 'No, not at all. It's more that you . . .' Chloë gestures at the dress and fishnets.

Angela's expression softens. 'I don't look the part?'

'You don't fit the stereotype.'

'Oh, come on,' Angela purrs, leaning close to Chloë. 'You don't think I'm the type that likes to stay up all night?'

Chloë swallows. 'You make a valid point.' *Angela is just a very friendly person*, she tells herself. *This doesn't necessarily mean . . . anything. At all.* 'Anyway, I'm, I'm impressed,' Chloë manages to choke out. 'I'm pretty certain astrophysics isn't the easy option.'

'I wish it was. Then maybe I'd be finished with my thesis.'

'What's it on?'

'I'm trying to figure out how to take a picture of a planet in another stellar system,' Angela tells her. Chloë concentrates on the words, trying not to lose any of them to the background noise. 'We know they're out there, because they make their stars wobble when they orbit, but no one has seen one yet. Which means there's a lot we don't know about them. How hot they are. What the weather's like. If there's anybody living there.'

'I'm guessing it's not easy to find out?'

'Imagine you're trying to snap a photo of a firefly. But the firefly is next to a lighthouse. And you're here, and the lighthouse is in San Francisco. So, yeah.'

'This is what you're passionate about, isn't it?' Chloë asks. 'I mean, astrophysics.'

'Yes,' Angela says. 'Yes, it is.' She gazes at Chloë contemplatively. 'You must be at least a little bit of a science fan yourself, if you named your cat Entropy.'

'It seemed to fit. He's a living force of destruction and disorder. I could tell you stories.'

'Please do.'

'I once came home to find one of my dresser drawers was open and all of my socks and underwear were gone. He'd hidden them around the house. That was back in January, and I'm still finding them in weird places every once in a while.'

Angela raises her eyebrows. 'How does a cat even open a dresser drawer? I mean, mechanically, how does he pull one out?'

'I have no idea,' Chloë admits. 'Never caught him at it. I ended up child-proofing them. It's worked so far.'

'You're an intriguing person.' Angela is giving her that speculative look again.

'Well, I have an intriguing cat, I guess.'

'Do you want to dance?' Angela asks.

'I – What?'

Chloë feels as if the floor has suddenly dropped away from the room.

'I want to go back out on the dance floor,' Angela says. 'Would you like to join me?'

She holds out her hand. Chloë looks at it.

'Come on.' Angela's hand is still extended. 'Come on.'

Chloë takes it and lets herself be led into the press of dancers. The room seems very warm. Angela's touch is cool. When they get to the middle of the floor, Chloë is achingly aware of how close Angela's body is to hers.

Whatever song is playing is heavy on the bass and drums, and most of the lyrics seem to be about sadomasochism.

But Chloë isn't really paying attention to the music.

PART THREE

The Monster And The Girl

CHAPTER THIRTEEN

Scottsdale, Arizona
5 October 1996

Just after midnight, Angela splashes water on her face and tries not to have a panic attack.

'It's a mortal sin, you know,' the angel in the bathroom mirror tells her. 'It'll kill your soul. And when was the last time you went to confession, anyway?'

'Shut up,' she hisses at him. 'Shut up, shut up, shut up!'

She only met Tess two weeks ago, though it feels like it's been years. Two weeks of drinking, dancing, doing things she's never done. Wearing clothes she's never worn. Clothes that Tess picks out for her – black and shiny, slinky and smooth. Sexy. Clothes from a shop she never would have walked into without Tess taking her by the hand.

And now she's in Tess's house.

They'd come here after a night out clubbing, calling it quits early, Angela already tired and more than a little bit drunk. It's an old house by Scottsdale standards, dating from the 1950s, all dark wood floors and panelling instead of tile and plaster. A wrought-iron fence, and more wrought iron over all the windows. Tess took her through rooms that looked mostly unused, dusty furniture and bare shelves, a kitchen with an empty cupboard. No pictures or decorations on any of the walls, not even Tess's own photos.

But then they reached the darkroom at the centre of the house. There, everything was clean and functional. Tubs, tools, chemicals, things Angela didn't know the name or purpose of. A slot processor, Tess told her. An enlarger. Negative carriers. A drum scanner. Angela understands enough about telescopes to grasp the basics of lenses and images, but this is another world altogether, almost alchemical in its mystery. And it's here, in one corner, that she sees the filing cabinets that contain Tess's work in neat albums and folders, hundreds of photos and thousands upon thousands of negatives.

The darkroom probably used to be an oversized walk-in closet before Tess transformed it into what it is now. It's clearly become the heart of the place, the space where Tess works and plans and even sleeps. Her bed is in there, a metal-framed cot as practical and utilitarian as the rest of the room.

That's where Tess is right now. Sitting on the bed. Waiting for Angela to return.

Angela is certain she hasn't misread the signals. She's sure of it. Unless she isn't. What if she's wrong?

'Plus, there's Romans chapter one, verse twenty-six to think about,' the angel says. 'Also Colossians chapter three, verse five. Galatians chapter five, verse nineteen. Oh, and First Corinthians chapter six, verse nine. But honestly, mostly Romans one twenty-six.'

For this cause God gave them up unto vile affections, Angela recites in her head automatically. *For even their women did change the natural use into that which is against nature.*

She knows all of those verses by heart, not just the one from Romans. All of the warnings against fornication, uncleanness, lasciviousness. Inordinate affection and evil concupiscence. Against everything she wants to do.

Of course she knows them by heart. It's not like he can tell her anything that isn't in her head already.

'Jesus didn't say any of that. That's all Paul,' Angela replies. 'And if you're going to throw Bible verses at me, how about the Book of Samuel? Jonathan and David strip naked and kiss. Because they love each other. Not really tricky to figure out what that was all about.'

I'm arguing with a figment of my imagination, she tells herself. *I really, really need to get a grip.*

She knows it's years of indoctrination doing the talking. All the dire pronouncements that were heaped on her at church, at Catholic school, and at home. It's hardly the first time she's had this kind of internal conversation. She knows exactly where it comes from and exactly how it's likely to go. That doesn't make it any easier to ignore.

This isn't even the first time she's been admonished by a bathroom mirror. That goes back to tenth grade, after her furtive kiss in the girls' room with Irene Gallagher. Their noses had bumped and they'd fumbled at each other's clothes without achieving much and the kiss still smashed through her body like a brick hitting a window. A very nice brick that made her think yes, this, oh my God, this.

And when Irene had gone, there was the angel in his iridescent robes, looking the way she'd always pictured him when she mouthed the prayer, her favourite one as a child. *Angel of God, my guardian dear, to whom His love commits me here* . . . Except now he was glaring at her with stern eyes while she tried to figure out what it all meant. Judging her while she tried to fit together the girl who'd just kissed Irene with the girl she'd been brought up to be, the one who was going to get married in a church wedding and start having kids right away. His stare was unforgiving. She'd wondered if she was already damned.

The kiss with Irene never led to anything more. Angela had been too scared and too confused. She never told anyone about it. She's never been out. Not to any of her friends, definitely not to her parents or her sisters. She didn't even join the Gay–Straight Alliance at Haverford.

'Maybe you should go home,' the angel says.

She takes a deep breath. If she's ever going to stop being a coward, then she'd better start now. It's well past time for her to cast aside the judging face in the mirror, the nagging voice in her mind.

'"Then Jonathan and David made a covenant, because he loved him as his own soul,"' Angela reels off from memory, aloud this time. '"And Jonathan stripped himself of the robe that was upon him, and gave it to David, and his garments, even to his sword, and to his bow, and to his girdle." Want to hear any more?'

'I know the rest of it.'

She continues anyway. '"And they kissed one another, and wept one with another, until David exceeded." You know what "exceeded" means there, in the original? I looked it up.'

'The word in Hebrew,' the angel answers, 'is *higdil*. "Became large."'

'Yeah.'

'Which can mean lots of different things.'

'Sure it can.'

'And you're skipping a lot.'

'What am I skipping?' she asks. 'The part where David says, "I have found grace in thine eyes"? The constant talk about their spirits being intertwined? What?'

'This is all kind of beside the point.' The angel looks exasperated.

'You know something? You're right. This is pointless, and stupid, and meaningless. You're not real. I'm talking to myself.'

'I know,' he says. 'I wish we could meet in person. We might have a better conversation if you could really hear me.'

'What's that supposed to mean?' she asks. He doesn't answer. 'Never mind, I don't care. I'm done with this. Goodbye.'

She closes her eyes and wills him to disappear.

When she opens them, he's still there.

'Screw it,' she says, and leaves.

Down the short hallway and through the living room. She makes her way over a thick, dark-red rug that fails to keep the floorboards from creaking. Past a pair of spindly chairs and an ageing camel-back sofa. None of the furniture here would look out of place in an antique shop. Except for the darkroom, of course, but even that has the air of a mad scientist's lab from an old movie. A bubbling retort and a Tesla coil would fit in nicely.

Angela puts her hand on the doorknob and pauses. 'I will find grace in thine eyes,' she murmurs in a near whisper, 'if I'm very, very lucky.'

She pulls open the door to the windowless interior.

Tess is still sitting on the bed where Angela left her, lit only by the red glow of the safelight. Except now she's slumped over, her face pressed against her hands. She hasn't changed out of her club clothes, a high-necked dress dripping with falls of lace.

'Tess?' Angela steps into the room. 'Are you OK?'

Tess looks up, and the sight of her fine-boned face makes Angela feel almost giddy. But Tess's black eyeliner is running the tiniest bit, and her eyes are wet. They might be tinged with red, or that could just be the safelight.

'You were in there a long time,' Tess says.

'Sorry. I was . . . It took me a while, that's all.'

'I thought maybe you'd left.'

Angela sits on the bed next to Tess. Near her, but not too near. Not near enough to touch. 'Why would I do that?' she asks.

Tess doesn't answer, doesn't move.

'I'm right here,' Angela tells her.

'Listen.' Tess shifts a little closer to Angela, a short jerk sideways like a tight spring uncoiling. 'I feel like we've grown really close in the last couple of weeks.'

Angela's heart is pounding so hard she's sure Tess must be able to hear it. She feels lightheaded, almost dizzy, like she might topple over. She puts a hand on the bed frame to steady herself. 'I feel the same way.'

'I've never met anyone like you.'

'That can't possibly be true.' Heat rises in Angela's cheeks. She can't remember the last time she was so aware of her own body. Every reaction, every twitch. She's equally aware of Tess, seated beside her, indenting the mattress, creating a gentle slope Angela could slip down if she let herself, closing the last few inches between them.

'I mean it.' Tess's voice is low and intense. 'I don't . . .' She makes an odd little noise, almost a laugh. 'I'm used to hanging out with idiots, Angela. People who think they're artists, you know? All of them like, "Oh, no, Mercury's in retrograde, I need my homeopathy or my biorhythms are going to be out of alignment." You're not like that. Not at all.'

'OK, well, that definitely isn't me,' Angela admits. 'And I've never met anyone like you before, either.'

Tess leans back. 'Bullshit.'

'It's totally true!'

'Copycat,' Tess says, straight-faced. 'I can't believe you copied me.'

'I did not! I—'

'Imitation is flattery, you know. You keep it up, I'm going to start to think you're hitting on me.'

Angela stops short in the middle of another protest, unable to find her breath. Her hand clutches the bed frame more tightly.

Unspoken words gather between them.

There's a body next to hers, indenting the mattress.

'Angela,' Tess says eventually, 'if you're, if we . . . There's stuff you don't know about me. Stuff that would scare the shit out of you.'

Angela shakes her head. 'I don't believe that.'

'I'm serious. You'd run away screaming. Hell, you probably *should* run away screaming. I'm not good for people.'

'I wouldn't run away, if you told me whatever it was. I'd stay right in this room.'

'It's not just one thing. It's a whole big mess of them.'

'I don't care.'

It's only been two weeks, but Angela already feels like she knows Tess as well as she's ever known anyone. She can't imagine a confession that would send her away. Not now.

Tess looks Angela over as if assessing her answers, weighing and judging. Her mouth is a thin, serious line.

'Do you promise?' she asks.

'What?'

Tess puts her hand on Angela's. Tess's touch is icy, so much colder than the warm night air that Angela wonders if she's ill.

'If I tell you about me,' Tess says, 'do you promise that you won't run away?'

'All right.' Angela's eyes are fixed on Tess's. 'I promise.'

'You're sure?' Tess's voice is sharp.

Whatever Tess has done, it won't change who she is. Won't make her a different person from the one Angela wants more and more with each passing day. 'Yes. I'm sure.'

Tess nods. 'Keep that in mind, then. Because it's going to get real hard to remember in a minute.' She turns her head away.

'Tess, no matter what it is, it won't make any difference to how I—'

Tess turns her head back. Her mouth is open, and there are fangs in it.

Angela's eyes widen, but she manages not to flinch. If her heart was pounding before, it's battering at her rib cage now, racing in her chest like a drumroll on timpani.

I promised, she tells herself. *I promised*. It's the only coherent thought she can manage.

'So, the first thing,' Tess says, 'is that I need to ask you for a big, big favour.'

CHAPTER FOURTEEN

Red Line to Quincy Center
17 November 1999

Chloë is feeling cheerful as the train launches itself out of the tunnel and into the light. It's an unusually bright, clear morning for Boston in November – still cold, but the Charles River sparkles in the sunlight as the Red Line crosses the Salt and Pepper Bridge. The snow has held off so far this year, and the Esplanade remains a dull grassy green along the banks, a few joggers on the path braving the morning chill.

It's Wednesday, so Chloë is making her weekly pilgrimage to work. She generally spends most of the commute with her nose buried in a manuscript, but she always makes sure to poke her head up for the crossing. It's the prettiest part of the trip, both now and at night on the way back, when the dark cityscape is illuminated by the weather beacon at the top of the Hancock Tower and the Citgo sign over Kenmore Square.

When the train goes back underground, she returns to her reading. There's a long way to go yet. When she started at Compass Rose, the publishing company's office was in Chinatown, but last year they moved all the way out to Quincy, south of the city proper, thanks to Boston's rapidly rising rents.

Chloë managed to read a good chunk of the submissions in time for the trip, pushing through them in a fourteen-hour marathon session yesterday in spite of distractions. She's still behind, but then, she's always behind. Since Compass Rose accepts unsolicited manuscripts, they receive uncountable numbers of them, even just for the imprints that Chloë and Shelly handle. Writing a book and having it published is a common dream. Chloë herself is no exception.

The remaining half hour of her commute is spent leafing through one last collection of short stories. Chloë finally wedges it into her bag as the train pulls out from Wollaston, one stop away from her station.

She draws her coat closer against the cutting wind when she disembarks from the T at Quincy Center. From there, it's only a couple of blocks to the building, then a trip up an ageing elevator to the sixth floor. She nods at Mike as she passes him in the outer room, and he waves back without looking up from his computer. He's already deeply involved in whatever inscrutable tasks he performs to keep the website running and deal with any book orders that come through it. She'll talk to him later, unless it's one of his game days when he leaves early. She's never been entirely clear on what kind of game it is. He's tall, so possibly it's basketball. But maybe it's *EverQuest* or *Ultima Online*. It could be unicycle jousting, for all she knows. She should ask sometime.

The small office Chloë shares with Shelly is a few doors down; long and narrow, a subdivision of a larger room, the resulting space barely five feet wide and almost unnavigable. In addition to their desks, it's crammed full of boxes of office supplies, as well as filing cabinets containing years' worth of records, forms, and contracts. It likely violates several fire codes. Chloë feels right at home here.

Shelly is already there, wearing a bright-orange dress that would have made Chloë look sallow. Earth tones and muted plaids are more her speed. But somehow, the colour works for Shelly, setting off her dark eyes and bringing out deep russet tones in her hair.

As Chloë thumps down her sack, Shelly scoots her chair back so she can see around the shelving sandwiched between their desks.

'Hi, you.'

'Hey.' Chloë slides into her own mismatched chair and starts sorting books. 'How was your week?'

'Fabulous. I managed to drag Mike out of the house for once. We took a day trip over to Sturbridge and saw all the Ye Olde Village stuff. I learned how to cooper a firkin.' She glances at Chloë's bag. 'Anything good this time around?'

'Not really,' Chloë says. 'Mostly a lot of glurge. What's a firkin?'

'It's a little barrel. So, you only got treacly crap? Nothing inspiring in the inspirational lit?'

'Why do we even publish those?'

Shelly shrugs. 'They sell. And some of them are good. Uplifting.'

'Yeah, well, you only have to read the uplifting ones. I get to read the ones that tell me I'm a tool of Satan.'

'Chloë, the Tool of Satan,' Shelly chants rhythmically. 'That has a nice ring to it. Like "Hamlet, the Prince of Denmark".'

Chloë makes a snorting noise. 'Interesting comparison. Does that mean I'm tragic and doomed? And Oedipal?'

'Fine. Like "Rudolph, the Red-Nosed Reindeer". You'll save Christmas.'

'Much better.'

Shelly returns to her work, and Chloë fires up the ancient PowerBook on her desk. Once it finally boots, she begins updating the status of the entries. *Love Slave of the Night Creature* definitely gets a checkmark in the column labelled 'Rejected'. She makes a note to remind herself what kind of rejection letter to send.

'I ran into your housemate a couple of days ago,' Chloë says casually. 'Angela.'

'Yeah,' Shelly replies, still engrossed in her work. 'She said.'

'Oh, really? Did she, uh, did she say anything else about it?'

95

There's a slight squeak of wheels as Shelly moves her chair back once again. She looks at Chloë curiously. 'Why?'

A long pause follows before Chloë responds.

'Is she seeing anybody?'

Shelly blinks, then bursts out laughing.

'Thank you,' Chloë says, 'for making that awkward moment so very, very comfortable. Really, thanks.'

'No, I'm sorry.' Shelly is still laughing, struggling a bit to catch her breath. 'It's just, now I know what I should have told her last night.'

'Told her?'

'She asked if you liked girls.'

Chloë's body stops functioning for a fraction of a second. *So that's what it means for your heart to skip a beat*, she thinks with odd detachment.

'Are you OK?' Shelly asks. 'I didn't mean to give you a seizure, there.'

Chloë makes an attempt at speaking. 'What . . . what did you tell her?'

'I said I didn't know.' Shelly examines Chloë. 'You used to be married, though, didn't you?'

'Bisexuality is very fashionable these days.'

'Really?' Shelly asks. 'I mean, you are?'

'Yeah. At least, I think so.'

'You think so? What does that mean?'

'I haven't actually . . .' Chloë gestures vaguely. 'I've never done anything with a woman. I think I've always been attracted to women, but men have been a lot easier to find, I guess. So it never happened.'

'I suppose that makes sense. But, so, what if something did happen?'

'With a woman? I'm pretty sure I'd be able to run with it, yeah.' Chloë thinks back to the nightclub. And smiles. Yes, she definitely thinks she could run with it . . .

'Huh,' Shelly says. 'What exactly did you two do Monday night?' Chloë blushes deeply. 'Oh my God, you look like a tomato. Chloë likes An-ge-la!' she sings with a wicked grin.

'Cut it out!' Chloë throws a wadded-up rejection letter at Shelly, missing her completely. Shelly snickers, but when Chloë makes pleading puppy-dog eyes at her, she mimes zipping her lips closed.

Chloë considers whether her love life to date would have been different if she'd ever acted on one of her girl-crushes. Most likely not. Flipping the genders around probably wouldn't have made her any less of a psycho magnet.

'What's she like?' Chloë asks. 'Angela, I mean.'

'Yeah, I kind of figured out who you meant.' Shelly thinks for a minute. 'She has a really cute ass.'

'I'd noticed that, thanks.'

'I know, right? I swear, you could bounce quarters off that thing.'

'Seriously, though,' Chloë says.

'Seriously?' Shelly leans back in her chair as she considers the question. 'She's very sweet. But I think she's lonely. She spends almost all her time working. She's usually up all night plugging away at her thesis. We live in the same house, and I hardly ever see her.'

'So she probably doesn't have a lot of free time.'

'That's one way to look at it. Another would be that she desperately needs to get out more, so maybe it'd be good for her to be swept off her feet by some genius novelist.'

'You can't call me a genius novelist,' Chloë protests, 'when you've never read anything I've written.'

'And whose fault is that?'

Chloë shifts uncomfortably. 'I don't think I've got anything in good enough shape yet.'

'Give me whatever is closest. I bet it'll be good. You're an award-winning writer.'

'That was years ago, and it was a minor award for a short story,' Chloë says. 'It's not like it was a Pulitzer or something.'

'Still.'

'I'll submit something to you sometime, OK? Just not right now.'

'Promise?'

'Promise.'

Chloë quickly turns her attention back to the grim work of crushing people's dreams. Rejection letters are her least favourite part of the job, but they have to be written. Or partially written, anyway; she uses a template for the bulk of the text, but likes to add a relevant sentence or two to let the author know that someone genuinely read what they submitted.

Not that adding a personal touch to the letters matters much, judging by the reactions of a certain vocal fraction. Her second least favourite part of the job is fielding threatening phone calls from rejected authors.

She only gets one call like that this morning, thankfully. But it's obvious what kind of conversation it's going to be the second she picks up the telephone and hears a voice shaking with poorly suppressed rage. She forces herself to be polite to the man accusing her of idiocy, prejudice, and malevolence. Or accusing her pen name, actually. She doesn't sign the letters with her real name. It helps to make it feel more impersonal.

'When I was a little girl I thought, maybe I'll get a job in publishing,' she grouses once he hangs up. 'Surround myself with books and stories. Literature, belles lettres, the life of the mind.'

'Don't complain to me,' Shelly says, invisible behind the shelving. 'You have to do that one whole day a week. I get four times as many of those.'

Chloë grunts, and starts trying to figure out how to shove more submissions into a file drawer already packed tight. She's attempted a few strange geometric configurations without much success when she notices that Shelly is standing nearby, staring at her with a calculating look.

'Um, is something the matter?' Chloë asks.

'Do you want me to tell her you're interested?'

'What? No!' Chloë twists around to face Shelly and somehow manages to bang her elbow against the open file drawer.

'I'm just offering to help out.'

'Well, thanks. I guess. But please, please don't.'

'Why not?'

'First, because we're not in seventh grade. Second, because she probably won't care. It wasn't anything. We danced one time, and then made vague promises to call each other. She was being friendly.'

'Right. That's why she asked me if you might be pounceable. Friendliness.'

'Maybe she was just curious. I was practically drooling. I'd have wondered, too.'

Shelly's eyebrows draw together. 'Why are you trying so hard to convince yourself that she's not interested?'

Because I'm completely insane, and she should probably avoid me at all costs, Chloë doesn't say aloud.

Instead, she says, 'I don't know.'

'Well. I won't tell her if you don't want me to. It's your call.'

'Thanks.'

Shelly watches her for a moment, but doesn't press any further. Soon, she withdraws back to her desk.

Chloë grabs a random submission from the pile of as-yet-unread manuscripts that have been dumped on her desk over the course of the week. She rips open the Manila envelope, slides out the cover letter, and starts tapping a new entry into the computer.

But her thoughts won't stop drifting back to Angela's hair, and lips, and laugh.

CHAPTER FIFTEEN

Brookline
17 November 1999

The first thing Angela does when she wakes up is check her code.

It's her highest priority, coming even before her next self-test. Tonight, she's planning on a session with a mirror and a flashlight – will the light bend around her body before it hits the glass, or go straight through it? Is it some kind of refraction effect that's making her invisible to reflective surfaces? Probably not, but it's worth checking out. There's always a chance she'll learn something new.

The code comes first, though. The data for her real work always has to come first. She started it running on her Linux box in the early hours before dawn, and it's been steadily humming away, crunching the numbers as she slept. If she got it right this time, she can at long last move on to the next step.

When the screensaver vanishes, all it reveals is a string of error messages plastered across the monitor.

Crap.

Angela gets out of her chair and paces around the small confines of her room. She knows she has great data, maybe something significant enough to be published in one of the really prestigious journals like *Nature* or *Science*. She just has to beat it into submission.

The images she's working on are from the Hubble Space Telescope. Getting research time on the HST had been a hard-fought battle all by itself. For every one proposal that's accepted by the committee, seven others are turned down. Hers was accepted. She would really like to prove that she deserved it.

But she needs to fix her code before she can write a paper – any paper at all, much less one that might be accepted by a big-name journal. And of course, her thesis depends on the paper. And her career depends on her thesis.

'No pressure, though, right?' she mutters aloud.

One of the images she took shows a disk of debris around a star, a cloud of dust tens of billions of miles across. Within that disk, she thinks she sees a gap. If there's a gap, that could mean there's a planet in there somewhere, sweeping up the dust as it orbits. But first she has to prove the gap is real, which means creating a program that will take the image and spit out a surface brightness profile, a precise mathematical map of light and darkness.

It shouldn't be taking her this long. It's supposed to be a minor part of the overall task, one small piece of the bigger picture. She's been stuck on it for days, nonetheless. Every time she's tried to run it, it's come up with gibberish. She needs to go through every line of code with a fine-toothed comb, track down the point where everything went wrong – or, more likely, find one of many ways that everything went wrong; so far, after each problem she's fixed, a different one has popped up, hydra-like, to take its place.

She's on the verge of starting when she glances at the date and time in the corner of her computer screen, and realises what day it is. She stops, her fingers hovering over the keys.

Angela hadn't been planning to go out tonight, no matter how spectacular it's supposed to be. Still . . . it's not something that happens every night of the year, right? And no one in the astronomy world would begrudge her taking some time off for it. It's practically a national holiday for star-gazers.

It also might be a chance to see those bright-green eyes again.

Angela puts her computer to sleep and fishes the napkin with Chloë's number on it out of her handbag; she made sure to get it that night at the club, before they parted ways. She could give Chloë a call, find out if she'd be interested in this kind of thing. She might be.

Before Angela reaches for her phone, though, she hesitates.

This is exactly what she's spent the past year telling herself she should never, ever do.

She knows what will happen if she gets involved with someone. Where it will lead. Secrets shared, then teeth and blood. Then worse. So much worse. No matter how it starts, it will end in disaster.

Her eyes flick to the blank computer screen. One press of a button and she could get back to work. Another night alone with her code.

Is that going to be it for her? Crouched in a basement, peering at her data, only coming out when she needs to feed? That's been her life since moving to Boston – does it have to be the sum total of her existence, for all time?

Maybe she can have more, if she's careful. Just a little bit more than she has now without catastrophe happening. It's not like a phone call is a lifelong commitment. Chloë might not even say yes. And if she does, who knows how far it will go? One date, a few days, a few weeks?

She's making excuses for herself already, because she's lonely and pathetic. Because that night at the club is something she desperately wants to recapture.

Laughing at Chloë's jokes. Trying to make her blush. Looking into her green, green eyes. Flirting, talking, connecting with someone without planning to drink her blood the entire time.

Angela wonders, not for the first time, what it would be like to kiss Chloë.

It doesn't have to be more than that, she tells herself. *Nothing more than what any two normal people might do together.*

I don't have to do what Tess did. I don't have to be like Tess.

Before she has a chance to change her mind, she picks up her phone and dials.

CHAPTER SIXTEEN

Somerville
17 November 1999

The telephone is ringing, and Ari isn't sure what to do about it.

He's alone in the house for once. To be honest, he's been enjoying the solitude. Things have felt awkward here lately; as much as he loves talking to people, sometimes he worries that he doesn't quite have the hang of it yet. He knows Chloë has been unsettled in his presence ever since they discussed his vocation. And her aunt is nice, a wonderful woman, really, but man, she will talk your ear off given half a chance.

The sun slipped behind the horizon a few minutes ago, and the gradually darkening twilight held the promise of a peaceful evening. He'd grabbed an apple to munch on from a bag Esther brought home the other day, and started browsing his housemate's bookshelves in search of a nice mystery novel when the telephone began to ring. And ring.

He tries to decide whether or not to pick it up. It probably isn't for him. It isn't his phone; he doesn't even know the number. But he's the only one around, and what if it's an emergency? There doesn't seem to be an answering machine – should he take a message? If he writes a message down, where could he leave it? It's not like another piece of paper is going to stand out from the general mess.

The phone continues to ring. It doesn't seem about to stop anytime soon.

Maybe he can help whoever's calling, somehow. It's his job to help people, after all. For all he knows, taking this phone call could be his entire purpose for being there, the reason he felt drawn to this apartment in the first place. Right, problem solved, question answered – he has a clear duty. And if he needs to take a message, he'll find a way, no matter how difficult the task might be.

He picks it up.

'Hello?' says a woman's voice on the other end of the line.

'Hi there!' he exclaims. 'How may I be of service to you?'

There's a pause.

'I think I may have the wrong number,' she eventually says. 'I was trying to get hold of someone else. Sorry to bother you. I'm going to give it another go and see if I can manage to dial the right—'

'Wait, don't hang up!' He figures there's no reason he shouldn't take a shot in the dark before she goes. It never hurts to check. 'There's something I'd like to ask you.'

'Um, all right, I guess.'

'Are you by any chance,' he says, 'in need of succour?'

'. . . I'm sorry, what?'

'Or comfort, or guidance? I'm just saying, if you called the wrong number, maybe there was a reason for it, you know? A reason you reached me instead. A wise woman once told me there are no coincidences.' The wise woman was Esther, and she'd said it last night, but it seems applicable. 'So you should know that it's my mission to give help to the helpless, hope to the hopeless, and redemption to the, uh, to the redemptionless. No, that's not quite right, is it?'

'Are you being serious? Who is this?'

'Unredeemed!' he shouts in triumph. 'That's a much better word than redemptionless. No, wait, on second thoughts, it doesn't work, either.' Ari tucks the phone between his shoulder and his ear and starts groping through the haphazardly piled books on the shelves; he's sure he spotted a dictionary in there somewhere. 'Unredeemed sounds more like an unused coupon than a person, don't you think?'

'Who am I talking to?' The woman's voice has become very cold.

Ari stops, one hand on a battered copy of *The Hero and the Crown*.

'Sorry, I should have said. I'm an angel. That's why I might be able to help you out. I've come down to Earth so I can spread my gospel of personal salvation through radical self-actualisation and self-acceptance.' A long silence answers him. 'An angel is like a . . . heavenly emissary?'

'Shut up.' If her voice was cold before, it's furious now. 'I am not speaking to you. I am never speaking to you ever again.'

'Have we met?' Her voice does sound familiar, now that he thinks about it.

'I know what you're trying to do, and it's not going to work. You can't stop me from doing anything. Because I don't have to listen to you anymore. Do you understand me?'

'Why don't you calm down and tell me what the problem is?' Ari's becoming anxious. Somehow, he's blown it again.

'Do you understand me?' the woman repeats.

He gives up on the dictionary search and takes the phone back in hand. It was giving him a crick in his neck, anyway. 'Um, hey, just so I know – who are you?'

There is only a click in reply. She's hung up on him.

He's still staring at the phone, wondering what just happened, when Chloë comes in through the front door. She blinks for a few seconds at Ari, who's standing with the telephone in one hand and an apple in the other, a guilty expression plastered across his face.

'It's all right, you can make calls if you need to,' she says. 'But let me know if they're long distance. Or . . . you weren't calling a 900 number or something, were you?'

'No!'

'It's just, if you're going to be running up a whole lot of charges –'

'I was only picking it up. Someone – It rang.' He hurriedly tries to explain himself. 'Esther wasn't here, and you don't have an answering machine, and . . . and it was probably a wrong number, anyway.' He jams the phone back down onto its base.

'Oh. Well, OK. Don't worry about it, no big deal.' Chloë drops her bag on the ground and tosses her keys on a table.

So she isn't upset with him, at least not over this. Good, that's a relief. And in that case, he decides, he might as well press his luck further.

'Hey,' he says, as she unbuttons her coat and drapes it over a lamp. 'Listen. I feel like we got off on the wrong foot.'

'What do you mean?'

'You seem tense whenever I'm around.'

She regards him warily. 'Well, I have been kind of worried you're going to start preaching at me or something, yeah. Should I be?'

'Hey, if that's the issue, I can be off duty when we're at home from now on.' He holds up a hand in what he hopes is a reassuring gesture. 'No preaching, no problem. Anything else?'

'I guess that's it. Unless . . . Is there anything about your religion that might catch me by surprise? Any strange practices? Chanting? Exorcisms? Ritual suicide?'

'Well,' says Ari, looking around at his surroundings, 'not in the apartment.'

'I guess that's fair.'

'No offence, but it's kind of messy here. You need some space to perform an exor –'

'I said we're good!' she says hastily. 'Really. No need to explain.'

Ari beams at her. 'I'm so glad we had this talk. I don't want my vocation to be a problem for you.'

'Sure. Me too.' She nods and heads towards her room, but comes to a halt in front of the door, her hand hovering over the knob. 'You know, actually, now that we're on the subject . . .' Chloë trails off.

'Yes?'

She turns back around and takes a couple of hesitant steps in his direction. 'You're sort of like a rabbi, or a pastor, right?'

'Not exactly.'

'But you give advice sometimes? I mean, is helping people out one of the things you do?'

'Absolutely!' he tells her. 'Are you unredeemed?'

'What?'

'Never mind, it's not important. What's the problem?'

Chloë moves further into the room and sits heavily in the armchair. 'Well. If someone was a bit messed up . . .' She pauses. 'Or, let's say, very, very messed up. Is it fair to inflict yourself on someone new? While you're still crazy?'

Ari sits across from her on the couch and thoughtfully strokes his chin. He looks at her with a penetrating gaze.

'Crazy's a strong word, isn't it?'

'I think once you've been institutionalised, you have a right to call yourself crazy,' she says.

'Good point. In that case, I suppose it depends.'

'Depends on what?'

'On what kind of crazy you are.'

'I guess that makes sense,' Chloë says cautiously. 'So what would the bad kind of crazy be?'

Ari furrows his brow as he tries to think of an example. 'Well, like, in this new relationship – are you going to pull a *Fatal Attraction* and kill a rabbit or something?'

She stares at him. 'Excuse me?'

'That would definitely be the bad kind, wouldn't you agree? And for the record, animal sacrifice is never the answer.'

'You know what? Never mind.' Chloë stands up. 'Thanks for trying, but I think I'll handle this one on my own.'

'Are you sure?'

'Absolutely. Don't worry about it.' She starts sidling towards the kitchen. 'Listen, I should make myself some dinner, so if you don't mind . . .'

Once again, not his most successful intervention. Oh, well. Some days are like that. He always tries to take it philosophically. He's only been doing this in person for a couple of weeks, so he probably needs more practice. Unless Chloë isn't someone who stands to benefit from his sort of help. Not everybody is. The most he can do is provide assistance where he can and hope for the best.

He should try to get a better prophecy out of Esther sometime. Someone around here is going to find him useful, that much is clear, but figuring out who it might be is proving more elusive. It'd be nice to know some specifics.

He gets started on finishing his apple as Chloë scurries off. Just after she disappears into the kitchen, though, the phone rings again.

Chloë pops her head back through the doorway, looking startled. She glances at Ari, but he shakes his head. It isn't going to be for him this time, either; he'd have thought that much was obvious. After a moment, she returns to pick it up.

'Hello? Oh, hi!' she says. 'No, of course I don't mind. What's up?'

She motions for Ari to go away so she can talk in private. He tries to mime back that he can't go to his room until he's finished the apple, because there isn't a trashcan there where he can throw the core away. Going by her puzzled expression, he's not entirely sure it gets across. He chews faster.

'Tonight?' she asks, returning her attention to the telephone.

'Yeah, I'm pretty sure I'm free. Why?' She listens briefly. 'Sure, yes, I'd love to. Oh, that's fine, I don't mind staying up. I'm at 10 Warwick Street, the downstairs apartment. But, um' – she glances quickly at Ari, then at the piles of junk surrounding her on the floor – 'just honk and I'll come out. OK, great. I'll see you then.'

She hangs up, and grins goofily at the phone.

Far too late to do any good, Ari at last manages to swallow. 'Going out tonight?'

'Yeah. Yeah, I guess I am. Well . . .' she adds after a short pause. 'Technically, I'm going out really, really early tomorrow morning.'

CHAPTER SEVENTEEN

Appalachian Foothills, Western Massachusetts
18 November 1999

Chloë can't help but notice that Angela isn't dressed for hiking at night. In fact, Angela isn't dressed for hiking at all. But Chloë is the one who's stumbling as she makes her way along the rough path up the slope. She clutches at a sapling with her free hand to keep from falling over as she trips again, and barely manages not to drop her flashlight.

Angela, in contrast, is so sure-footed she might as well be walking down a brightly lit hallway. Even with both hands occupied, one with her own flashlight and the other with a rolled-up sleeping bag. Even though she's dressed in a black silk cheongsam over white thigh-high stockings.

Chloë had needed to ask what kind of dress it was.

'Are you all right?' Angela asks as Chloë recovers her footing.

'Yeah, I'm fine. Thanks.'

'We're almost there.'

'How far is almost?' Chloë tries to keep her tone light. The stubbed toe isn't helping.

'It's really close, honest.'

Chloë's opted for jeans, a flannel shirt, and a heavy coat. Admittedly the nicest jeans and flannel shirt she could find. Angela wears the dress well, though, Chloë has to admit. And at least she's in big black boots and not something insane like high heels. It all looks natural on her, like she was born wearing it.

Chloë finds herself wondering whether or not Angela has any piercings, and where.

'We've got maybe another quarter-mile or so to go,' Angela says. 'You'll know when we get there.'

It's late. It was close to midnight when Angela arrived in an ageing Corolla to pick Chloë up. They drove for quite a while before starting the hike – although a good chunk of their travel time was spent getting out of town, in spite of the light late-night traffic. The Big Dig, Boston's massive, endless, eternally over-budget roadworks project, has turned a city already known for its incoherent street layout into a tangled minotaur's maze.

When they escaped the city limits, Angela headed west, towards the low mountains of inland Massachusetts. The trees at the side of the road stood bare, stark and black. For most of the trip they were practically the only car on the road, and the dark loneliness of the highway made the world seem empty.

An inconspicuous exit finally led them to a series of twisting back roads, all steep and angled sharply uphill. On one that looked much like the others, Angela manoeuvred the car into a nearly invisible passing place, and from there they'd started walking up the trail.

'Thanks for inviting me along, by the way,' Chloë says.

'Well, it's supposed to be a once-in-a-century kind of thing. Not to be missed.'

'So is that what it takes to drag you away from your thesis?'

Angela brushes a stray strand of blonde hair out of her face, sending her flashlight beam skittering through the treetops. 'Everyone plays hooky sometimes.'

Chloë finds that comforting to hear, if only because it means there are cracks in Angela's perfection. She's been feeling a little intimidated, walking behind someone who manages to look flawlessly put together while hiking in the dark. It's reassuring to learn that Angela's only human after all.

'So,' Chloë says, 'how is a meteor storm different from a regular old meteor shower, anyway?'

'Lots more meteors.'

'I probably could have guessed that without asking, huh?'

Angela smiles. 'Most meteor showers aren't all that impressive. In a normal year for the Leonids, you'd maybe see one meteor every couple of minutes or so. Tonight, it could be twenty times that, something like six hundred an hour at the peak. If it's a really good night, it might get to thousands of meteors an hour. Like fireworks.'

'Sounds more interesting than dinner and a movie.' Whatever else she may feel about trekking through the underbrush, Chloë certainly isn't bored.

'I'm glad you think so.'

'I mean,' Chloë says hesitantly, 'not to presume that this, uh, that this is a . . .'

'Is a what?'

All Angela had said on the phone was, 'I was wondering if maybe you wanted to come?' Chloë hadn't asked if that meant what she hoped it did. It occurs to her that she probably should have.

Now is better than never, she supposes, even if she isn't doing a very good a job of it. 'I was trying to figure out if this was, if we were on . . .'

'A date?' asks Angela.

'Yeah. That. I mean, I thought it might be, but I didn't want to assume, if it wasn't—'

'Well, I hope it's a date. Because, you know, I brought breath mints and everything.'

'Oh,' Chloë says, a little confused. Her eyes widen when she picks up on the hint.

Angela glances at her sidelong, seeming suddenly shy. 'But, I mean, if you thought it wasn't–'

'No! I mean, I did. Was. Hoping it was. A date.'

'OK,' Angela says. 'I mean, good. Great.'

The conversation lapses into a somewhat charged silence.

'We're here,' Angela says a short while later, as they emerge from the woods.

The clearing is bordered on three sides by ancient oaks, growing so close together that their branches intertwine. The grass is filmed with frost, which glitters in the light of the moon, dipping low on the horizon as it sets. The final side of the clearing is a sheer drop into a valley.

Chloë walks to the edge and looks down the cliff. It's a nearly vertical rock wall punctuated by patches of greenery. Far below, she can just make out the dark gleam of a stream.

Then she looks up.

'Is it me,' she asks, 'or are there, like, five hundred times as many stars up there as there usually are?'

'That's why we came all the way out here,' Angela says, coming up behind her. 'There's no light pollution.'

The snow is late in coming for the season, leaving the night still and clear. They spend some time just taking in the view.

'I found this place not too long after I moved to Boston from Phoenix,' Angela continues after a while. 'One night I started driving west, I don't even know why. I needed to get away from everything, I guess. Anyway, now it's my favourite place to look at the sky. Sometimes the science can get a little, I don't know, abstract. No one looks through a telescope anymore, you run computer scripts while the equipment looks at everything instead. You could spend your whole life studying this without ever seeing it. I like to come here to remind myself what it's all for.'

'Do you get out here a lot?'

Angela shakes her head. 'Not as much as I'd like. A few times right after I found it, but hardly at all lately. I haven't had the time.'

A streak of light flashes across the sky.

'Hey, there goes one,' says Angela. She moves almost imperceptibly closer to Chloë, her arm brushing the sleeve of Chloë's coat.

Chloë debates with herself internally until she reaches an uncomfortable conclusion, then takes a breath.

'Listen . . . you should know I'm divorced. It's not like it's a big deal or anything, but I figured it was first date kind of information, you know?'

'OK,' Angela says.

'I didn't want weeks to pass or whatever and then, surprise! Not that, I mean, just in case.'

'Is it all right if I ask about it?'

'Um.' Chloë hadn't considered the possibility of conversation beyond letting Angela know. 'Yeah, I guess so. Sure.'

She doesn't have anything to hide. Not about the divorce, anyway.

'I'm just curious,' Angela says. 'If it's not something you want to talk about . . .'

'It's fine. Really, it is.' Chloë picks her words with care. 'It was a pretty miserable marriage. We were both too young to have any idea what we were doing, and he was, he was a very angry person. Things got bad, after a while.'

'I'm sorry.'

'Hey, it, it's all in the past. I'm pretty much – I mean, one way or another, all bleeding stops eventually, right?'

Angela grins. 'I like the way you put it.'

'Thank you.'

Angela looks at the ground, thinking, then lifts her gaze back up, her expression turning serious. 'My last long-term relationship was with someone who wasn't very happy,' she says. 'She started blaming me for that at some point.'

Chloë is surprised to hear Angela say something that sounds so achingly familiar. 'Yeah. I know how things can get turned around like that.'

'I kind of thought you might.'

'You get blamed until you start to believe it yourself.'

'Exactly that.'

'This is going to sound odd,' Chloë says, 'but in a way this is nice. Not that you went through that, but that you know what it's like.'

'Yes. I know what you mean.'

Angela slips her hand into Chloë's. It's picked up the chill of the night, and feels cool and smooth. They smile shyly at each other.

'I used to think I took on all the blame for what happened because I'm a lapsed Catholic,' Angela says. 'We get all of the guilt and none of the benefits.'

'Huh. Sounds a lot like non-religious Jews, so I'm with you there.'

'Oh, yeah? Were you always that way, or did you used to believe in it?'

'The first one, I guess. My family was laid back about the whole thing. We never went to synagogue, and I got ham sandwiches in my lunchbox for school. How about you?'

Angela looks rueful. 'I was really serious about it when I was younger. My family was . . . not laid back. It made coming out of the closet kind of difficult.'

'I can imagine.'

'I'm an atheist now, though.' She pauses, then mutters, 'So I don't have to have any more close, personal conversations with my guardian angel about my sex life.'

Chloë laughs. 'What, really? I mean, are you serious?'

'Totally. But don't worry, I know what it sounds like.' Angela's face takes on a rather sheepish expression. 'Believe me, that little phase of my life is well and truly over with.'

Angela sounds like she's beginning to regret bringing it up in the first place, so Chloë decides to do her a favour and change the subject. 'Well, anyway. Here's hoping we both have better luck with romance from here on out.'

Angela gives Chloë a grateful look. 'I like to think I've learned from the experience. I've actually made a little promise to myself – I am never dating anyone with serious mental health issues ever again.'

'Oh,' Chloë says in a small voice. She takes a step back, and Angela's hand falls from hers.

'Is everything all right?' Angela asks, looking puzzled. 'Did I say something wrong?'

'No, no. Not at all.'

I could jump off the cliff, Chloë finds herself thinking without wanting to. *Five steps, a leap, and I'm gone.*

She tries as hard as she can to squash the intruding thought into oblivion.

'Because it's not like I have much right to talk,' Angela says. 'I should come with a warning label that reads, "Don't get too close".'

Over the edge and all the way to the bottom, Chloë thinks. *Smash like a watermelon when I hit. What am I doing out on a date? I'm insane. At some point, she's going to notice.*

Stop it, stop it, stop it.

'You know,' Chloë says quickly, 'maybe we should switch to a cheerier topic.'

'Oh, of course. I'm sorry. I didn't mean for everything to get so depressing.'

'No, don't be. I'm the one who started with the heavy stuff. It's just not what I wanted to talk about for the whole . . .'

'Sure. We should get ready, anyway. I don't think it's going to stay quiet up there for much longer.'

Chloë strives to get her mind under control as Angela unrolls the sleeping bag on the ground. Casts around for something else to talk about, anything.

'When's the storm supposed to start?'

'It's already started,' Angela says. 'But the visibility changes throughout the night, and I think there are pockets of different density. We've probably been passing through one of the sparser ones for a while.'

This is good. She can focus on this. 'Passing through?'

'The Earth is passing through the meteors. Right now the whole planet is colliding with a stream of leftover comet debris. A big field of flying bits of ice and rock.'

'Which then become falling, burning bits of rock?'

'You got it.' Angela unzips the bag. 'I brought this along because the ground gets a lot colder than the air. Standing up isn't too bad, but you should use this unless you want to literally freeze your ass off when you sit down.'

'Right.'

Chloë's mostly managed to calm herself. She huffs out a breath that frosts in the night air, and manoeuvres her legs into the bag. When she's settled, she turns her attention back to the sky; she's noticed a few more lines of brightness arcing across it.

As she begins to warm up, though, she glances over at Angela's arms, bare below the short sleeves of her dress. 'Say, aren't you cold?' Chloë asks. The thought has been nagging at the back of her mind all night. 'I'm in a heavy coat and I'm freezing and you're, um, not.'

'Don't worry about me. I don't ever get too cold.'

'You don't?'

'No. So, the best place to watch is going to be right over there.'

Angela indicates a section of the sky. 'You want your eyes facing that way, and the top of your head pointing towards Leo.'

'Because these are the Leonids?' Chloë guesses.

'Exactly. So over there is where they're going to have the highest transverse velocity.'

'I'm going to assume that's a good thing.'

'The best,' Angela promises.

Chloë turns and squints at the arc of horizon that her head is supposed to angle toward. She doesn't see anything that looks even vaguely like a pattern in the scattered mass of stars.

'I have no idea what Leo is supposed to look like,' she confesses. 'And I really have no idea how they got "lion" out of any of that.'

'Leo's not visible tonight, anyway. It's in the direction you're look-ing, but it's right below the part you can observe. It might pop its head up next month, maybe.'

'See, I had no idea. I only know the myths.'

'I'm the opposite,' Angela says. 'I can find the constellations, and I know their names and what they mean, but I've got no idea what most of the myths are. So I can tell you that Andromeda is over next to Pisces, but I mainly have an idea of who that is because she was in *Clash of the Titans*.'

'Really?' Chloë brings her gaze back to Angela. 'I thought they'd teach astronomers that kind of stuff.'

Angela shakes her head. 'I got Stellar Evolution and Statistical Mechanics. No myths. What's Leo's story?'

'He was the Nemean Lion.' Chloë chews her lower lip thought-fully as she tries to remember more. 'Let me think . . . His thing was that his hide couldn't be pierced by any weapon made by man. But then Hercules came along and fought him with his bare hands. So that was the end of the Nemean Lion. Oh, and Hercules figured that an impenetrable hide would be pretty handy as armour, but he couldn't get it off the lion because, well, impenetrable. Until he thought of using the lion's own claw as a knife. Anyway, that's why Hercules is wearing a lion skin in all those pictures.'

'Poor lion,' Angela says.

'Yeah, no one ever thinks about it from the lion's point of view. At least he got a constellation out of it, I guess.'

A quick string of bright flashes catches Angela's attention. 'Oh, hey, look, there they go!'

Chloë leans back to watch. Within a few minutes, dozens of shooting stars have traced thin paths of light through the dark night, gleaming streaks that vanish the moment after they appear.

'They're gone so quickly,' she says. 'Blink, and you miss one.'

To her surprise, Angela slides down to lie on the outside of the sleeping bag. She presses her body into Chloë's, nestling against her. Chloë shifts her arm to hold Angela. The silk of the dress feels smooth and slippery beneath her hand.

'Why did you ask me out?' Chloë asks her quietly.

'What?'

'I was just wondering.'

'Well, when we got to talking at the club, I thought you were the most interesting person I'd met in a long time. And I found myself thinking, "I wonder if she'd be interesting to kiss, as well." So I decided that maybe I should try that, too.'

Angela turns to look directly at Chloë, their faces close, her eyes posing a quiet question. Chloë leans in and kisses her.

Angela's lips are cool and soft and dry. They open as the kiss continues.

After a long moment, the two of them draw apart, only by a few inches, still keeping close. Chloë feels short of breath. She leans in again and kisses Angela on the neck, right beneath her ear. Angela closes her eyes and makes a faint murmuring sound.

'Definitely,' Angela says, 'interesting.'

Angela cuddles up against Chloë once more, and they go back to looking at the sky. It takes a while for Chloë's breathing to return to normal.

The meteors are coming so rapidly that sometimes several appear at once, criss-crossing each other, making brief, shining spiderwebs and filigrees overhead. As they watch, one explodes like a roman candle.

'Whoa. What was that?' Chloë asks.

'It was a bolide. They break into fragments when they hit the atmosphere.'

Angela hasn't even finished speaking when what looks like a burning flame shoots across the sky, nearly as bright as a lightning flash. Chloë blinks as afterimages float across her eyes in its wake.

'And that,' says Angela, 'was a fireball.'

'Are there going to be more of those?'

'I hope so.' Angela rests her head against Chloë's shoulder. 'It's so beautiful up there. How do you even describe it? The words people like to use, jewels on black velvet, candles floating in the sea, nothing quite works. Do you know what I mean?'

'Yeah, I think I do.'

'Maybe eyes. Bright, glowing eyes. That's almost right. Maybe something up there is looking back at us.'

'I think it's too big to be one thing. That's the whole universe up there.'

'The whole universe. Yes, that's exactly what it is.' Angela snuggles in closer. 'You know, I decided I wanted to be an astronomer during a meteor shower. A different one, the Perseids. I was visiting Nantucket for the summer, and I went out for a night swim. There's a patch of sea out there that glows when you move in it – it has bioluminescent algae – and it's amazing at night. So I was floating on my back there, and up in the sky were the meteors, and past them the stars and the Milky Way, as clear as I've ever seen them. Jupiter was out that night, too. And I got this incredible sense of place. Me, floating on Earth, spinning through the meteor stream, and the galaxy, and the universe. Right there watching it all.'

Angela lifts her head and looks out into the meteor storm.

Chloë, however, turns to look at Angela, watching her watch the sky.

PART FOUR

Love Slave Of The Night Creature

CHAPTER EIGHTEEN

Scottsdale, Arizona
5 October 1996

Angela stretches in the narrow bed, languid and relaxed. There's a pinprick of pain in her neck where Tess bit her, but it's overwhelmed by the more pleasant ache between her legs. A nice reminder of what they've been doing, all through the long night.

My Lord and Saviour Jesus Christ can fuck right off, she thinks, feeling bold. Then she instantly tries to take it back. At least she didn't say it out loud. Although that probably doesn't matter to someone who knows her innermost thoughts.

Myths and make-believe, she reassures herself. *Fairy tales. Fiction.*

She's still wrestling with blasphemy when she's blinded by the camera flash.

'Don't move,' Tess says. 'Stay just the way you are.' Another flash.

Angela tries to blink away the spots in her vision. Past them, she gets a blurry and confusing impression of a naked Tess, the camera held to her face. Pink nipples on pointed breasts. Further down, a triangle of light brown hair, her natural colour.

Flash.

'What . . .' Angela, bewildered, gathers the sheet to cover herself. 'What are you doing?'

'Immortalising the moment.' Tess lowers the camera, looks Angela over. 'I asked you not to move, though.'

'Tess, I'm not wearing anything!'

'I noticed.' The half-smile plays over Tess's lips. 'You've been like that for hours. Don't tell me you're getting shy now.'

'You weren't taking any pictures when we were in the middle of it!'

Tess sits on the bed, the springs creaking under her. She takes hold of Angela's hand. 'Don't worry about it. They're only for me, angel. So I can always remember right now, exactly the way it is.'

Angela still feels uneasy, but can't quite pinpoint why. Tess has already seen everything, after all.

'So these aren't going to show up in a magazine sometime? Or anything like that?'

Tess laughs. 'Of course not. This is personal stuff.' She lets go of Angela's hand and raises the camera to her face again. 'Can I take a couple of you like this? I kind of like you shy.'

'Well . . . OK.' Angela forces herself to relax again, feeling guilty for overreacting. A few pictures. Personal pictures. No big deal.

Flash. Flash. Flash.

Tess puts the camera aside and lies on her stomach next to Angela, her chin in her hands. 'So. I had a great time. We should do this again.'

'I . . . Yeah. Me, too.'

'"Yeah"? Just, "Yeah"?' Tess pokes her sheet-covered belly with a finger. 'Come on, you can do better than that. Be a little descriptive. How does it feel to be freshly fucked?'

'Well, I think I'm going to hell for it,' Angela says, smiling. 'But other than that, it was fantastic.'

She feels Tess stiffen next to her. Sees her eyes narrow, her mouth turn down into a frown. 'What's that supposed to mean?'

'It was just a joke.'

Tess hurls herself off the bed, and starts picking her clothes up off the floor. 'Just a joke?' She steps into her panties, shrugs herself into her bra. 'It was just a joke? You think you're going to hell because you slept with me, and I'm supposed to think that's hilarious? Ha fucking ha.'

Angela sits up, struggling to keep the sheet around her, feeling more exposed than ever. 'I didn't mean it like that.'

'How exactly did you mean it? It was, I don't know what it was. It was . . . racist? Speciesist? Undeadist? It was undeadist, Angela.'

'What? No!' Angela is standing up now, moving closer to Tess, who's shimmying back into her club dress. Tess yanks it down over her head and glares at Angela, waves of anger radiating from her. Angela nearly reaches out to touch her, but thinks better of it.

'You can't say that kind of shit to people,' Tess spits out.

'It wasn't because of what you are! That's not what I meant!'

'Well, what, then? Huh? What?'

'I meant because you're a girl!'

Tess stops, pauses, stares at Angela suspiciously. 'Are you serious?'

'Yeah, I mean, the Bible has a lot to say about, you know, that we're both girls, and that we're not married – not that we can be, not legally, married that is, and definitely not in the Catholic Church – but it doesn't, I'm pretty sure it doesn't have anything to say about the other thing.' Angela is aware on some level that she's babbling, but can't stop. 'The, the teeth and the rest of it, I don't think that ever comes up, not as far as I know.'

Tess is calmer, looking Angela over in appraisal. 'Because we're girls. That is, like, seven different kinds of fucked up. Gotta say, I'm not thrilled that you threw a homophobic comment at me, either, you know?'

'Oh my God.' Angela feels almost nauseous. 'I'm so sorry. I didn't mean . . . I wasn't thinking.'

'Don't worry about it.' The half-smile is back. Tess reaches over to the counter where she left her pack of cigarettes and shakes one out. Angela is relieved to see that she looks amused. 'Just don't say that kind of shit to me again, all right?' Tess says as she lights up.

'I won't. I'm really, really sorry. If there's anything, anything at all I can do to make up for it—'

'How about you come here?'

Angela walks forward and Tess gathers her into a one-armed hug. Angela falls into it gratefully. She rests her chin on Tess's shoulder.

They stay like that, holding each other, as the minutes pass. Tess takes a drag on her cigarette every few seconds, blowing out scented smoke that slowly clouds the small room.

'Hey,' Tess says, finally pulling away, leaving a hand on Angela's waist. 'It's only an hour or so until dawn, which means bedtime for me. You should head on home.'

'Oh. All right.'

Angela starts gathering up her clothes, shoving aside her disappointment at being kicked out of the house. She's embarrassed to find that her things have been flung around the room with messy abandon. Her panties are entangled with the photo enlarger, and her stockings somehow ended up under the bed.

She'd been looking forward to sleeping next to Tess, lying in her arms. Although it's not like she'd ever been promised that. She should feel lucky, she tells herself. The night nearly had a much worse end.

'You still look like your favourite puppy died,' Tess says as she watches Angela dress. 'Seriously, chill out.'

'I'm sorr—'

'Listen,' Tess cuts her off, 'you've probably figured this one out by now, but I've got a bit of a temper. You're going to have to get used to that.'

'Used to that?' Angela pauses in the middle of pulling up a stocking. 'So, um, does that mean I'm invited back?'

Tess chuckles, deep in her throat. 'What, you thought I was breaking up with you? This was nothing. Don't worry about it.'

'Breaking up with me?' Angela stares at Tess, her stocking forgotten, half-unrolled on her leg. 'Are we a couple now?'

Tess tilts her head, smiles. 'Aren't we?'

Angela smiles back tentatively, trying out the idea in her mind. 'I guess we are.'

CHAPTER NINETEEN

Brookline
21 November 1999

'You're not seriously planning to wear that, are you?' Shelly asks Angela.

'What's wrong with it?'

'It's embroidered. I'm pretty sure you're not allowed to paint wearing anything that's embroidered.'

'There may be a law about it,' Chloë says.

'Then I'm an outlaw,' Angela tells them. 'A fashion outlaw.'

Shelly and Mike have set out paint cans, brushes and rollers, paint trays, everything that might be needed. They've picked blue for the walls, white for the banister posts, and brown for the rail. Or to be more precise, Horizon Haze, China Cup, and Log Cabin. A sea of plastic covers the carpet, which was only laid down a few months ago and is relatively pristine. Shelly's admitted that the carpet probably should have come after the painting instead of before, although she only conceded it after extended protestations that she had a plan and it made perfect sense.

Angela bounds the rest of the way up the stairs and joins the other three on the landing, the tarp making crinkling noises beneath her bare feet. The silk dressing gown she's wearing is chain-stitched all

130

over with vivid images of mythical creatures – dragons, griffins, gargoyles, demons. Truth be told, Angela checked her closet pretty thoroughly for anything appropriate, and this was the best she could come up with. A final confirmation that she doesn't have any jeans or tank-tops or sneakers left at all. But there are solid, rational explanations for that, she reminds herself. Most of her old clothes were thrown away at Tess's insistence.

Although a tiny voice in the back of her mind keeps pointing out that she is, in fact, dressed in something utterly absurd. She really should add a casual outfit or two to her wardrobe.

'Anyway,' Angela says, 'this is old and ratty and I sleep in it. It's perfectly fine to paint in.'

'Well, I'm not going to object to you hanging around in your pyjamas,' Chloë says.

'But embroidery!' Shelly protests.

'You know, I brought in an extra pair of hands to help out.' Angela bumps her hip against Chloë affectionately. 'You should be thanking me instead of complaining.'

'That's another thing. Chloë is my minion, not yours. I should be the one forcing her to volunteer for unpaid work at my house.' Shelly turns to Mike. 'Angela is stealing my minion.'

Mike gazes serenely at her, his eyes mild behind his thick glasses. He straightens up from his relaxed slouch against the banister, looming over them as he unfolds to his full height. Mike is tall and gangly, taller even than Chloë. Since his dark hair is thinning prematurely on top, his height and high forehead make it look as if his head is trying to grow through the fringe that remains and escape. His head is the only place he lacks hair, though; the rest of his body is so thickly furred that at first glance, he could be mistaken for wearing a sweater instead of a short-sleeved shirt. Shelly once confessed to Angela that she likes to pet him.

'What is Angela offering your minion to sway her?' he asks.

'Angela makes out with the minion,' Angela replies herself, before Shelly has a chance to answer.

'Then I think,' Mike says, 'that Angela wins this round.'

'The minion agrees,' Chloë puts in.

'All right, fine.' Shelly throws up her arms in surrender. 'Shall we get this wall painted?'

Obligingly, Angela picks up a paintbrush and dips it in the can. She starts on the area by the landing, and Chloë moves to work next to her. Soon they're all slapping blue paint over the hideous shade of taupe currently disgracing the wall.

Having Chloë so close makes Angela notice how hungry she is. It's been long enough that Angela is acutely aware of the warmth of Chloë's body, the blood circulating beneath her skin.

But the hunger isn't painful, not yet. It's been a couple of weeks, and she'll need to go out hunting soon, but she's not starving. Her body hasn't even dropped below 85 degrees; she checked with a thermometer when she got up. Still well above room temperature. Angela can keep it together. At least for now. She's sure she can.

'Seriously, though,' Chloë says quietly to Angela, 'if you want me to lend you my button-down, I've got a T-shirt on under it.'

Angela knows it would be sensible to take her up on the offer, but she shakes her head. 'It's no big deal. And I'd look pretty silly wearing a button-down over a dressing gown.'

'I was figuring you'd take the dressing gown off.'

Angela dabs at the wall and turns to Shelly. 'Chloë is asking me to wear nothing but her shirt and a pair of panties.'

'We were never that obnoxiously cute, right?' Shelly asks Mike.

'Never,' he says solemnly as he works on the moulding near the ceiling.

'Sure you weren't,' Angela says. 'And no one, absolutely no one I know ever called me long distance, sobbing, "Oh, woe is me, there's this guy at work and he will never, ever notice me!"' She claps the back of her hand to her forehead and heaves an exaggerated sigh.

'You did that?' Mike glances down at Shelly with a lopsided grin. 'I had no idea.'

'If I did, it was only because someone was so completely oblivious that I had to –'

'Throw yourself at me in a supply closet like a wanton hussy?'

'Really?' asks Chloë, delighted.

'Well, yes, I did,' Shelly admits. 'But it totally wasn't like the way he made it sound.'

Angela makes a dubious-sounding snort. 'So you chastely threw yourself at Mike in a supply closet?'

'Look, I just happened to already be in the supply closet, OK? Mike came in looking for some pens or something –'

'It was Post-It Notes,' he clarifies. 'Green Post-It Notes. I remember because I never did end up getting them, and I actually really needed some.'

'Anyway,' Shelly continues, 'I had been lusting after him since the day he showed up at the office. This was back when the website was being launched, a little while before Chloë got hired, and he was dealing with weird internet emergencies every minute. So I couldn't figure out if he was totally uninterested, or just too busy to notice all of these obvious signals I'd been throwing off.'

Angela paints her section of the wall in smooth, even strokes as she listens to the story. It strikes her that she's having a good time. Somewhere along the line, this has transformed from a social obligation she couldn't avoid to exactly what it was supposed to be – an evening spent with friends. It might even be a double date, if house painting counts as a date. It's been a long time since she's done something like that. Since she's done anything resembling that. She lets the chatter wash over her like a warm bath.

Maybe, she thinks, *I'm ready to rejoin the human race after all.*

'I didn't have the slightest notion how she felt back then,' Mike is saying. 'I thought she was just chatty.'

'Shelly chats with me all the time,' Chloë notes. 'Has she been hitting on me all along without my ever knowing it?'

'Shut up,' Shelly answers evenly. 'So, we were alone in the closet, and something snapped in my head. I decided I was going to find out one way or the other, whatever it took.'

Mike nods in corroboration. 'And that's what she did. I was very surprised.'

'Because that's when she threw him on the floor and had her way with him, right there in the closet,' Angela says as she redips her brush.

'I did not! I asked him out! We kissed one time!'

'First, she gazed in awe at his throbbing, vein-laden meat pipe—'

'That's a reasonable description of it,' Mike agrees.

'Please do not mention any part of this conversation to anyone else at work,' Shelly says to Chloë. 'I'm begging you.'

'And then mounted him then and there,' Angela says. 'I swear this is the truth. Don't believe her if she tries to tell you it's not.' She finishes her section of the wall with a satisfied flourish.

'You be quiet, or I'll paint you Horizon Haze.' Shelly waves her brush threateningly.

'Feel free to give it a try.' Angela grins. 'If you think you can take me.'

Chloë hovers her own brush inches away from Angela. 'Oh, really?'

'Do it,' Angela tells her. 'I dare you.'

Chloë darts her hand forward. Angela leans to the side, fast as a whip, and the brush misses her.

'Oh, it's on,' Angela says, her eyes glinting. Chloë goes in for another attack, but Angela grabs her wrist. There's a quick tussle, which ends with Chloë tumbling backwards onto the landing with

Angela sprawled triumphantly across her, dangling a paintbrush over Chloë's face.

'Um.' Chloë blinks at the paintbrush suddenly hovering above her. 'Angela is apparently bizarrely strong.'

Shelly rolls her eyes. 'You two need to get a room.'

'What a nice coincidence,' Angela says. 'I've got one just downstairs.'

CHAPTER TWENTY

Brookline
21 November 1999

As soon as the painting is finished, Angela and Chloë slip away to Angela's bedroom, giggling and holding hands.

Angela draws Chloë through the door and shuts it behind them. Chloë only has time for a quick impression of the room – a whirring computer, a closet stuffed full of impractical clothes, a mattress on the floor – before Angela is pressed against her, kissing Chloë hungrily. Chloë runs her hands down Angela's back and kisses her back with equal intensity.

She feels the blonde woman clutch at the edges of her shirt, and thinks again about the surprising strength of those arms. She wonders if her clothes are about to be torn off of her. She wouldn't mind at all if they were. Or if Angela threw her on the mattress.

Then abruptly, Angela steps back, her grey eyes wide, her expression nervous.

'Is something wrong?' Chloë puts her arms down, caught up short. She looks Angela over, concerned, trying to figure out why she's pulled away.

'No.' Angela turns her face aside. Her voice is quiet. 'No, nothing's wrong. It's just that – if you could, if you'd be willing to take the lead here . . .'

Chloë is surprised by the sudden display of shyness. Surprised, and a little taken aback. Angela has been the one pushing things forward since the evening they met, tonight included. There'd been a part of Chloë, she begins to realise, that had been counting on the other woman's experience.

You're being ridiculous, Chloë tells herself. *How difficult can this possibly be? It's not like you've never had sex before. It's still sex, just with different bits.*

Of course, it's been a long time since she's done this with anyone at all. But you never forget how, right? Like riding a bicycle. And it shouldn't be more difficult with another woman, should it? Since you already know where everything is, and how it works?

Chloë nods, trying not to let any of this show on her face. 'Sure,' she says. 'I can do that.'

Angela gives her a thankful look. Not saying anything. Waiting.

OK, I need to get a grip, Chloë thinks. *Start with what you'd like yourself. Figure it out from there.* Well, maybe not the clothes-ripping and mattress-throwing. Angela's clothing looks expensive, however much she tried to claim it wasn't anything special.

Chloë wordlessly takes Angela by the hand and leads her to the bed. Angela lets herself be led.

Once they're seated, she kisses Angela again, at first more hesitantly than she did at the door, but growing impassioned as she feels Angela kissing her back. She goes a step further, kissing Angela on her forehead, her cheek, her neck. Emboldened, she undoes the tie holding the dressing gown shut. She slides it off of Angela's shoulders and licks her along the collarbone. Angela shuts her eyes and shivers with pleasure.

Chloë smiles at the response, her earlier worry overtaken by the desire heating her like a furnace. She reaches behind Angela's back and unclasps her bra, taking it off to reveal small, perfect breasts.

She slowly works her way down Angela's body, stroking and kissing her pale skin, lingering for a while at the breasts, teasing the nipples until they redden. She moves back up, her mouth seeking Angela's once again, but is stopped by a gentle hand.

'Keep going. Further down,' Angela breathes. 'Please.'

If anything, Chloë is reassured to get direction. A pathway in the wilderness. She trails a series of light kisses across Angela's stomach. When she reaches the belly button, her lips hit a smooth nubbin of metal. Angela does have piercings after all.

Chloë runs her finger down the crease where Angela's thigh meets her groin. The other woman's breath quickens. Chloë slips her hand under Angela's panties and lets it rest there, and Angela wriggles at the touch, unable to hold still.

A quick move of her hands to grasp at the sides of the panties, and then Chloë pulls them off, Angela arching her hips to help Chloë along. She pauses, feeling as if she's about to enter territory both unknown and strangely familiar. Then she nuzzles her lips against the newly exposed blonde thatch of hair as Angela moans and parts her legs.

Chloë shifts to the side so she can run the flat of her middle finger across the opening, finding that it's already slick and wet, watching Angela's face as she does, every sharp breath she sees feeling like a jolt to her own body. She stays on the outside for a while, stroking gently as Angela squirms and makes soft noises beneath her.

When the moment feels right, she slips her finger inside. Angela gasps and clutches Chloë close. Chloë starts moving her fingers, in and out, brushing her thumb gently across Angela's clit.

'Slower,' Angela urges her. 'A little bit . . . Ah. There. Just like that.'

Chloë is happy to comply.

Gradually, Angela starts panting, then thrashing. Chloë listens to the sounds Angela is making, learning her body, slowly increasing the pressure.

Angela cries out, her whole body tensing as Chloë brings her to a shuddering climax. Chloë feels as though she is on the verge of orgasm herself simply from seeing it, from feeling Angela's inner muscles clench around her fingers. She keeps them there as the contractions slowly subside.

Angela is beautiful when she comes.

'You're not even undressed yet,' Angela says when she catches her breath. 'That's not fair.' She gazes at Chloë with a languid smile.

'I can fix that.' Chloë strips off her overshirt and T-shirt, then reaches behind her back to unclasp her own bra. After she slips it off, Angela pulls her in close and runs her fingernails down Chloë's back. Chloë leans into her, feeling their bodies crush against each other.

'You're still wearing jeans,' Angela points out.

Chloë reaches down to unbutton them, then stops. As much as she wants to feel Angela's hands on her, her mouth on her, she wants to make Angela come again even more.

And, after all, she's been asked to take the lead.

'They don't come off yet,' she says. 'It's still your turn.'

'Very, very unfair,' Angela responds, without any resentment at all.

Chloë moves her head between Angela's legs and starts licking her with long, slow movements.

Angela is already nearly there. Chloë begins changing the pace. Rapid flicks, then back to long strokes, then small circles. Angela makes incoherent sounds of pleasure. Chloë plunges her tongue inside, and Angela makes a noise that's almost a scream. Then she makes the same sound again, and again, as Chloë drives her tongue deep and pulls it out slowly, moving it up to the spot that makes Angela tremble uncontrollably, and then back down, back in, over and over as Angela presses herself against Chloë's mouth. She grabs Chloë's hair with her hands and writhes, stuttering out a fragmented shout as she climaxes a second time.

'OK,' Angela pants a short while later. 'Now it's definitely your turn.'

This time, Chloë makes no protest. She unbuttons her jeans and pushes them down and off.

'Lie down,' Angela whispers.

Chloë lies back on the mattress. Angela sits upright and brushes her fingers delicately across Chloë's body. She caresses the sides of Chloë's breasts, and runs her hands down her torso. Chloë reaches up to touch Angela's hips, but Angela shakes her head and pushes her hands back down.

'Your turn means you don't do any of the work,' Angela chides her.

Chloë endeavours to lie still, with some difficulty, while Angela takes her time exploring her body.

The moment before Chloë would have begun pleading for it, Angela slides her hand under the waistband of Chloë's panties, her gaze locked on Chloë's eyes. Angela's fingers, long and dexterous, start repaying the favour performed by Chloë's earlier.

Chloë is already poised on the brink, so aroused she's finding it difficult to breathe. She can no longer tell how much time is passing. Every touch of Angela's fingers seems to shoot straight up her spine, electric currents of sensation. Angela keeps watching her face intently as Chloë begins to buck her hips and grasp the bedsheet with her hands. She feels that growing warmth again, starting between her legs but soon spreading everywhere, fast, like a wildfire.

Chloë spasms, coming hard, Angela's eyes still on hers. She feels the orgasm in her whole body, rocketing from her pelvis to her breasts, to her fingers, down her legs to her toes. It doesn't stop. She has no idea how long it lasts.

When Chloë's body finally relaxes, Angela lies down beside her.

'You still aren't completely naked, you know,' she says.

'Well,' Chloë replies, 'maybe I should do something about that.'

Angela grins. 'There's plenty of time. After all, we're only just getting started.'

CHAPTER TWENTY-ONE

Somerville
21 November 1999

They've pushed aside the dirty dishes cluttering the kitchen table to clear enough space for the game. It's cramped, but it's better than trying to play in the living room; at least the curling brown linoleum of the kitchen floor is tidy, relatively speaking. Ari doesn't have to worry about knocking over a pile of something or other every time he shifts his chair.

He looks over his hand and decides to go with the Ace of Clubs. He slides it out and places it down between them, face up.

'So that's one point to me, right?' he asks. 'For leading the trick.'

'Exactly,' Esther says. 'Now, let me see – I have point of five, a quint and a quart, and a quatorze of Kings, plus the repique, of course, which gives me . . . ninety-eight points.'

'The score is ninety-eight to one?'

'Yes.'

'Before the first trick is over.'

She looks up from her hand. 'Well, you really should have taken all five cards during the exchange.'

'We don't play piquet where I come from,' Ari says defensively. Endless choir practice is practically the only form of entertainment back home. Getting away from that for a while is, frankly, one of the major perks of being here. Hymns of praise can become pretty boring after enough repetition.

Esther chuckles. 'I didn't think you'd had much opportunity to gamble. But that's why we're playing for pennies tonight, dear. I'm sure you'll pick it up quickly.'

After a few tricks in which the difference between their scores only grows, Ari feels far less certain of this.

It's a nice way to spend the evening, nonetheless. Some card games, some conversation, and of course, since Esther is one of the players, quite a lot of coffee. It's certainly a pleasant break from the trials of street preaching. Which isn't to say he doesn't like what he does, but it can be frustrating. A lot of the time, he isn't sure whether or not his message is getting through. The whole point of doing it in person is to make certain his words are heard clearly, but he can still never be 100 per cent confident that anyone is truly understanding what he's trying to say.

He's on a break tonight, though, and there's no need to take his work home with him. It's time for simpler pleasures, like losing at cards. And getting to know his housemate's aunt better.

During a rare pause while Esther decides which card is the best one to defeat him with, Ari casually asks, 'So, do you mind if I get some snacks?'

'Go right ahead, dear,' Esther says, concentrating on her hand.

'Is there anything I should avoid? Non-kosher, non-halal?'

She glances up, an amused glint in her eyes. 'I'm not hungry, thank you.'

Ari nods to her and puts down his hand. So much for that. The old woman remains a mystery to him. He's tried making subtle enquiries about her religious leanings before. Testing the waters to see if she might be interested in his brand of theology. So far, she's been skilfully evasive. There's a chance she's Jewish like her niece, of course. But if he had to guess, he'd peg her as some kind of pagan based on all the witchy stuff she brought back from her Salem trip.

He starts rooting through the cabinets, looking for something to nibble on. There isn't a lot to choose from, and even less that looks anything but ancient. Those apples that briefly made an appearance in the fridge are long gone. What on earth does Chloë eat? She can't be getting take-out all the time, like he does; she never goes outside. Well, she used to never go outside. That's changed recently.

He goes back to the table with a box of Wheat Thins which has a sell-by date that's at least in the current calendar year. 'Chloë's out pretty late tonight,' he says as he sits down. 'Again.'

'Mm,' the old woman replies, possibly in agreement.

'Doesn't seem usual for her.'

'Maybe she has a new hobby. I'm glad that she's getting out of the apartment. She was beginning to grow mould in here.'

Ari raises his eyebrows. 'Are there any nocturnal hobbies?'

'Of course. Drive-in movies. Star-gazing. Bass fishing.'

'Bass fishing?'

'Bass bite more at night.' Esther chooses a card and slaps it down with an air of finality. And, of course, wins yet another trick.

So much for gossip. Ari has a lingering suspicion that Esther knows more than she's saying, but if there's any juicy information to be had, Ari isn't able to read it in her impassive face. No wonder she's such a good card shark.

The other things she can do with the cards, however, can't be explained by an expert poker face. Although he supposes he should call it a piquet face, if he's trying to be accurate.

'I haven't saved anybody's life yet,' he suddenly says.

'It can take time for a prediction to fully mature.'

'Could I maybe get a second reading sometime? To clarify how it'll happen?'

'I don't see why not,' Esther says. 'I take it your religion isn't one of the ones that condemns fortune-telling.'

Ari shrugs. 'I don't like most of the rules that condemn people. Only keep the good stuff, that's my motto.'

'Fair enough. How about now, then? I've already got the cards in my hand. What would you like to know?'

Ari purses his lips thoughtfully. He didn't expect to get a reading right away, so he doesn't have any specific question ready. 'Hm, let's see. How about, when will I be of help to someone around here?'

'Let's see what they have to say.'

When she performed a divination for him the first time, nothing out of the ordinary occurred. She'd looked over the cards for a while, as if reading a book, and told him what they meant.

This time is markedly different. Her eyes roll back until only the whites are showing, and her hair stirs in a sudden draft. The overhead light flickers with a faint buzzing sound. Ari notices the distinct, sharp smell of electricity, like the scent of the air before a thunderstorm.

'*Once December's ides have flown,*' Esther chants,

'*Take a journey to the West.*
Find the girl who waits alone,
High upon the mountain's crest.
In the images of night,
Seek her place in heaven's dome.
Test her wrath and watch her flight,
And at its nadir, send her home.'

She blinks, and her eyes go back to normal. The light pops back to full brightness. 'You got a rhyming one this time. Congratulations. They're somewhat rare, although I'm afraid they're also somewhat annoying.'

'What does it mean?'

'I have no idea.'

So his future continues to be murky. But, he reflects, it could have been worse. At least he's got a more solid idea of the timing. No doubt he can figure out the rest.

And this one feels more like a proper prophecy. That's undoubtedly better. He'd already been heartened by the first prediction; it's good to know that his current mission of wandering the Earth, providing counsel to those in need, is going to bear fruit sometime. He trusts the instinct that brought him to this place, but a heavenly emissary should come equipped with a suitably portentous prophecy. It just seems appropriate.

Esther tosses down the Queen of Diamonds, and promptly takes the card he puts out in response. Then, with almost alarming speed, she proceeds to win the rest of the tricks.

'So,' she says, 'at the end of the first deal, that's three points for you, and a hundred and nineteen points for me.'

Ari gives a low whistle. 'If that happens every time, how much am I going to owe you by the end?'

Esther raises her eyes to the ceiling as she does a quick calculation. 'Well, after six deals, that would be eighteen for you, and . . . seven hundred fourteen for me. Add them together, plus the extra hundred, all in pennies would come to, hm. Eight dollars and thirty-two cents.'

Well. That isn't so bad. On the other hand, though . . . 'What do you normally play for, dollars?'

Esther grins. 'A dollar a point is a bit small-time, actually. Your deal this time around.'

Ari takes the deck and starts shuffling it. 'So what should I know about being the dealer?'

'Having the deal makes it harder to win.' Esther looks apologetic. 'Quite a lot harder, really.'

Ari reaches for his coffee mug. It seems likely to be a long night.

CHAPTER TWENTY-TWO

The Boxing Match

Here's a story that I swear is true. Or at least, close enough to be entirely plausible. Marlene Dietrich kissed me once.

She punched me in the face once, too. I treasure both memories.

All of this happened before she was famous, you understand. She'd already been in a few small films when I met her, but she was introduced to me as Marlene from Schöneberg, not the Legendary Marlene Dietrich.

Der blaue Engel was the movie that made her a star. *The Blue Angel*, with Marlene as Lola Lola, the transcendent temptress. She seduced the whole world with that role. After that, she moved to Hollywood and our paths never crossed again.

The first time I ever saw her, she was slamming her fists into a punching bag. I can still replay the scene in my mind like one of her films. Dreamy blue eyes, arched brows, long legs, and arm muscles like steel cables. I was instantly smitten. Who wouldn't be? Her boxing coach was standing right beside her, screaming in her ear. Punch faster! Hit harder! Move your hips! It's a wonder she didn't throw a punch at him instead of the bag.

Sabri Mahir, that was his name. A Turkish tyrant who taught by shouting, cursing, and rambling on interminably about his dream of perfecting the human body. Although he might have been pretending to be Turkish, we were never sure. He owned the Studio für Boxen und Leibeszucht, which was the only place open to women then. And I will say this about him – unpleasant as he was, the training he gave was real, for men and women alike. I suspect he didn't see people as individuals so much as walking collections of muscles.

Which meant if you took what you could from it, it would make you stronger. Marlene took what she could. She had a hunger for it. Watch her movies. The first time you see her, she'll look as cool as an autumn dusk. But the second time, you'll see that hunger lying just beneath her skin. I don't think she'd have been what she was without it.

Marlene and I only sparred together once, and that was how I learned that she had a straight left like a steam engine piston. I was flat on the floor in under twenty seconds.

She took me out for a drink afterwards to make up for it.

We went to a place on Bülowstrasse, past an imposing, humourless doorman and through to an overheated back room. It was all done up with paper lanterns, palm trees, and swathes of silk. Beads and veils draped everywhere you looked. There was a trio playing tango music in a corner. They sounded fairly good after the third glass of wine.

I'm sure we discussed all sorts of topics that evening, but I don't remember most of it. I was quite drunk from very early on, and also thoroughly distracted by the fact that I was sitting next to my crush. She had a presence that drove away thoughts of anything but her.

Not to mention that the night she knocked me down is the same night she kissed me, which looms a good deal larger in my mind than the rest of it. She tasted of lipstick and cognac and cigarettes. She knew I was carrying a bit of a torch for her, I'm certain, because she'd taken me to a place where you could get away with that kind of thing. There were quite a few of them around Berlin then, if you knew where to look. It never went any further than that one kiss, though.

One other thing I do remember is asking her why she was taking boxing lessons. I was curious. There weren't a lot of women doing it then, obviously. I loved the physical power of it, myself, that pure feeling of strength and motion. But I wanted to know what was driving her. What was fuelling that hunger.

'I want to learn how to fight,' she told me, 'because I want to be prepared for anything, Esther. The world is full of predators, and no matter how we struggle to foresee our fates, no one can ever know exactly what the future holds.'

Mostly, though, I remember the kiss.

And the straight left.

CHAPTER TWENTY-THREE

Brookline
21 November 1999

Angela is the one who finally says, 'OK. I think . . . I'm done.'

'Are you sure?' asks Chloë.

'Pretty sure. Any more and I'm going to dissolve or something.'

Angela relaxes into the blissful haze of afterglow. The two of them lie close together, Chloë tracing abstract patterns on Angela's skin with her finger.

Angela closes her eyes. If she were able to purr like a cat, she would. She's enjoying the snuggling almost as much as the sex itself. It's been so long since she's touched anybody, except to bite them.

She runs her tongue over her teeth, and is reassured to find that nothing is out of the ordinary anymore. She kept it together. Not one nip, in spite of arousal layered on top of hunger, an almost over-whelming combination.

She can do this.

The fangs came out a couple of times during the course of things, but she'd managed to keep Chloë from noticing. There had been a few dangerous moments near the beginning when a probing tongue would have discovered everything, but she got past them. Just a momentary problem. Nothing that spoiled their time together.

There's a small, rebellious part of her that comes close to wishing Chloë had noticed after all. That everything had been exposed. Maybe it's not such a small part of her; there have been times when she's practically dared Chloë to guess that something's up. Going to the mountaintop without a coat on. Showing off her strength on the stairs. But if the truth had come out this evening, it surely would have brought things to a screeching halt. She might have missed out on this perfect night.

She wonders if she should tell Chloë now, right this minute. But as she feels the warmth of Chloë's body, naked beside her, she can't bring herself to do it. Everything's going so well. She doesn't want to risk wrecking it.

Maybe she'll never have to. It's not like they've pledged to be together forever. Things might end before she has to say anything irrevocable, before she does anything unforgivable. Who knows what's going to happen? It might simply never come up.

And if it does, if she has to finally say something, there'll be a better time for it. The right time. She'll wait for that.

'So, how was it? For you?' Chloë asks, breaking her out of her reverie.

Angela opens her eyes and smiles. 'How do you think it was?'

'I'm guessing good?'

'You're guessing right.'

'I was just . . . I was asking because . . .' Chloë clears her throat. 'That was my first time with another girl.'

Angela turns on her side, lifting her head up to look at Chloë. 'You're kidding.'

'Nope.'

'I never would have guessed. You figured out what to do pretty damn quick, then.'

'Well, you were very, um, responsive.' Chloë's face reddens. It's as adorable as Angela thought it might be.

'I was very loud, you mean,' Angela says. 'It's a good thing we're in the basement, or I'd never hear the end of it from Shelly.' She sinks back down onto the pillow.

'So, are there any perks that come with losing my girl virginity?' Chloë asks, smiling. 'Will I get a certificate?'

'Absolutely,' Angela tells her, grinning back. 'And your invitation to the secret lesbian New Year's party should come in the mail.'

Chloë stretches her long frame out on the mattress. 'Oh, good. Is it going to be a big one this year?'

'Are you kidding? 2000 AD. Everyone everywhere is going to go nuts.'

'Yeah. We'll be living in the future.'

'What do you think it'll be like?' Angela asks. 'Dawn of a new era of peace and understanding?'

'No, I think the Y2K bug will cause the end of the world. At midnight on the night, everything will just, like, catch on fire.'

Angela laughs. 'Lights out for civilisation. It had a nice run.'

'At least that Prince song would finally stop playing on the radio 24/7.'

'You're right,' Angela agrees. 'Even the apocalypse has a silver lining.'

Chloë starts to cuddle up close to Angela once more, but Angela holds up a finger, asking for a moment first. She reaches over and clicks off the lamp. The two of them are instantly plunged into near total darkness, the only light coming from the glow-in-the-dark stars overhead. No longer able to see, they twine together, seeking each other by touch.

Angela doesn't think that lying next to Chloë is going to bring out her fangs again tonight, not when she feels so calm, but there's no reason to take unnecessary risks. If she can't be seen, she can't give anything away.

'It's like a cave in your room,' Chloë says in an almost hushed tone. 'Other than the ceiling, I mean. How do you get it so dark in the middle of a city? Where I live there's always a streetlight or something outside.'

'Tinfoil on the window. And drapes over that. I told you, I work nights. Have to keep the light out if I want to be able to sleep during the day.'

She feels Chloë shift in her arms, rolling on to her back to gaze up. 'Are those actual constellations? That's Orion, isn't it?'

'Yes.'

'He's the only one I can always recognise.'

'Do you know what his story was?' Angela asks.

'Some of it. He was a mighty hunter,' Chloë says. 'I remember he was stung to death by Scorpio because he was planning to kill every animal on Earth. Or else he was killed by Artemis for being an obnoxious jerk, it depends on who's telling the story. What else do you have up there?'

'Up and to the right of Orion is Taurus, the bull.' Angela starts to point, then realises it's of no use in the darkness. She tries to guide Chloë with her voice instead. 'There's a big bright star above Orion's left arm. See it?' She feels Chloë nod. 'That's Aldebaran. You can think of that as the bull's right eye, if you want. Aldebaran means "the follower" because it trails after the Pleiades – that's the line of stars off to its side.'

'Go on.'

'The stars across Orion's waist are Mintaka, Alnilam, and Alnitak – the belt, the string of pearls, and the girdle. His left shoulder is Bellatrix, the warrior woman. Across from her is Betelgeuse, which means armpit.'

'Armpit?'

'Yes.'

'There's a star named armpit?'

'Well, it's his armpit.'

152

Chloë laughs and pounces on top of her. Angela giggles uncontrollably as Chloë tickles her. She tickles back and they roll around on the bed until Chloë runs out of breath.

'So,' Angela says when they stop. She's on top of Chloë now, comfortably splayed across the taller woman's lean form. She makes her heart beat while she's there, in case Chloë can feel it. 'I haven't asked yet. How did you like your first time with a girl?'

'Very much. Very, very much.'

'Good. Because I'm starting to seriously consider calling you up and asking you out sometime.'

Chloë folds her arms around Angela. 'I'd have to check to see if my incredibly busy schedule is clear. I need to be at work at least once a week, you know.'

'You poor thing. Do you think maybe you could fit me in somewhere?'

'I think that could be arranged.'

'Mm,' says Angela. 'I'm glad.' She slides off of Chloë, leaving an arm and a leg draped across her lover, keeping close. 'Tell me something about you. Anything that I don't know.'

She feels Chloë tense ever so slightly. 'There's not a lot to tell.'

Did she tread too close to uncomfortable territory? Angela wonders if the reaction has anything to do with what Shelly told her a couple of days ago. The aftermath of Chloë's divorce. Maybe best to ease it back a little. 'It doesn't need to be a big revelation or anything,' she says gently. 'You said you had stories about your cat. Why don't you tell me a couple of those?'

'Ah.' The tautness in Chloë's muscles uncoils. 'He's a strange little beast. Nimble as all hell. I've seen him run straight up a plaster wall. And he likes to drop on people's heads.' She pauses, thinking. 'The day I drove him home from the animal shelter, my car caught on fire. That's when I decided on his name. It's also why I don't have a car anymore – I couldn't afford to get a new one after that.'

'Wait, but that can't be because of something he did, can it? I mean, this isn't an arsonist cat or anything, right?'

'No, but things do tend to break around him,' Chloë says. 'It's a general trend. I once read somewhere that all cats are little Buddhists. They attempt to reduce your attachment to material possessions by destroying them.'

Angela laughs. She's laughing a lot tonight. She likes it. 'I'm looking forward to meeting your marvellous cat.'

'But you're allergic.'

'I can put up with a few sniffles to meet a creature out of legend.'

'Well, you should wait until I clean the place. Clear away all the dander and . . . It could use some cleaning. A little.'

'All right. Now tell me more. I like your stories.' Angela checks her teeth with her tongue once again. Nothing sharp pricks it, so she kisses Chloë gently on the mouth. 'I like you.'

'I like you, too.'

Chloë kisses her back, and Angela almost manages to lose herself in the moment and forget about everything else.

CHAPTER TWENTY-FOUR

Brookline
22 November 1999

Chloë's lips are raw by the time she slips out of bed, a little while before dawn. Her mouth is no longer used to doing so much kissing in a single night. She's not about to start complaining about the sting, though.

She switches the light on and starts getting dressed. Angela watches as Chloë steps back into her panties, slips on her bra. The blonde girl is still naked, half-covered by the sheet. Her body could be carved out of marble except for her enigmatic grey eyes, following Chloë's movements.

'Give me a call tonight, maybe?' Angela asks.

'I will,' Chloë promises. 'You sure you don't want to get a bite to eat or something?'

Angela shakes her head. 'I'd love to, but seriously, I'm about to collapse. For some reason,' she adds teasingly, 'I'm kind of worn out.'

Chloë grins as she pulls on her jeans. Angela does look like tiredness is rapidly overtaking her. When she blinks, it takes a few moments for her eyes to open again. For her own part, Chloë feels the odd, buzzing energy that comes when you've gone past exhaustion and come out the other side. Probably a good thing, since it's not a short trip back home.

'See you again sometime soon, then?'

'Yes.' Angela sinks deeper into the mattress. 'Soon.'

They haven't discussed what they are to each other. Dating, it certainly seems like. Lovers, obviously. Girlfriends? Chloë hopes so, but she doesn't ask. Not now, not yet. If they are, there'll be time to say it.

But right now, her flannel overshirt is buttoned all the way up and her shoes are tied, so she's run out of excuses to linger.

'Well . . . Goodnight. Or good morning, I mean. Sweet dreams.'

Angela tilts her head to blow her a final kiss, and then lies back down on the pillow as Chloë backs out of the room, her eyes on Angela until she gently shuts the door. She creeps silently up the stairs, readying herself for the cold trip home.

She doesn't expect to find Shelly and Mike awake and in the living room. They look up at the same time to see Chloë as she reaches the head of the stairs.

Oh, right, she realises a bit too late. *Monday. Some people have to go to work on Monday.* She should have noticed the light was on.

They're having an early breakfast, last night's cold pizza for Shelly, sausages for Mike. The couple sits close together on the settee, plates and soda bottles and pizza boxes spread out across the glass-and-metal coffee table. Shelly is wearing bright pink pyjamas and Mike is in nothing but a pair of shorts. With his legs and chest visible, Mike looks even hairier than usual.

The three of them blink at each other. Shelly pauses mid-motion, a slice halfway to her mouth.

'You spent the night,' she says.

'Um. Yes.'

'Did you . . . want something to eat?' Shelly asks. 'There's plenty left.'

Chloë thinks about begging off, but she is, honestly, pretty hungry. Not to mention that scuttling out the door seems even more awkward than staying.

'Sure. Thanks.'

Mike wordlessly offers her a piece of pizza, and Chloë accepts it gratefully. She takes a seat in a leather-upholstered chair across the table from them, and tries to think of ways to act nonchalant.

'So how far did you get?' Shelly asks. 'We've got money riding on it.'

Chloë nearly chokes on the bite she's just taken. 'What?'

'Mike thought you wouldn't get past kissing after only a couple of dates, but I said you'd at least get to second base.'

Chloë feels herself blushing. Yet again.

'Shel, you're embarrassing Chloë,' Mike warns her.

Shelly ignores him as she watches Chloë's face get redder and redder. 'Oh my God. You totally did it with her!'

'Are we back in high school?' Mike asks the ceiling.

'Hush, you, that's an improvement. Last week my commentary was from the seventh grade.'

Mike chomps a piece of sausage off his fork and tries to look uninvolved. Shelly whacks him lightly on the shoulder and turns back to Chloë.

'So?' she asks. 'You went all the way?'

'Well.' A shy smile lights on Chloë's lips. 'Yes. We . . . Yes.'

Shelly literally claps her hands together with excitement. 'Oh, that's fantastic! I'm so happy for you!'

'You know, you seem weirdly thrilled about all this, considering you weren't there,' Mike says to her.

'Are you kidding? This is amazing. It's like finding out your sister had sex with your, uh . . .'

'Hot cousin?' Mike suggests.

Chloë raises her hand. 'Can we not accuse me of incest, please?'

'With your best friend,' Shelly finally finishes. She hits Mike on the shoulder again. 'Sicko. Angela's still down there, I'm guessing? No longer among the conscious?'

'Yeah,' Chloë says between mouthfuls of pizza. 'She needed to go to bed, and I need to get home and feed the cat. And then go to bed.'

Shelly tilts her head, looking oddly serious, and watches Chloë eat for a few moments. Then she nods. 'That's a pretty normal schedule for Angela. You're never really going to see her during daylight hours.' Suddenly, the grin leaps back onto her face. 'Wait, if you're going home to bed now, does that mean she kept you up all night long?'

'Well, yes, but it wasn't all . . . There was talking, too.'

'Sure, yes, talking,' Shelly says dismissively. 'So. How was she in bed?'

Mike puts his face in his hands. 'Shelly. Come on.'

'Hey, Chloë has blackmail material on me after last night's conversation. It's only fair that I get something to hold over her head, too. Speaking of which, you're being awfully prim this morning, Mr Meat Pipe.'

'A gentleman may be free to discuss his own meat pipe,' Mike states in dignified tones, 'but that doesn't mean he will talk about a lady's, um . . .'

'Let's not look too hard for a metaphor,' Chloë says, 'since I'm not going to be describing it, no matter what Shelly asks me.'

Shelly tosses the crust of her breakfast into the empty box. 'Well. You look like you're in a good mood, so that answers my question anyway.'

Chloë sighs happily. 'Yeah. If I were a bell I'd be ringing, if I were a banner I'd wave, all that goofy stuff.' She pours herself half a glass of soda instead.

'Huh.' Shelly peers at her assessingly. 'You seem pretty smitten.'

'Well, it's early on still. But she's smart, and she's gorgeous, and she's other things I am not going to talk about so don't ask anymore, but yeah. Why wouldn't I be?'

'Good,' Shelly says. 'Maybe I can stop worrying about you now. And Angela, for that matter.'

'Worrying?'

'Yes, worrying. Ever since you told me about your divorce and, well, I mean, you know.' Shelly glances sidelong at Mike.

'You can say I've been diagnosed with depression in front of Mike,' Chloë says. 'It's all right.' Mike inclines his head in acknowledgement.

'OK. Yeah, that. I didn't think I should make a big deal out of it or anything, but . . .' Shelly shrugs. 'I'm glad you're getting laid.'

Chloë puts her empty glass down on the dog crate next to her chair. 'I doubt that's the recommended therapy. But thank you. I think. And on that hideously embarrassing note, I should go keep my cat from perishing of hunger.'

She stands and stretches, unable to suppress a yawn. Now that she has food in her stomach, the long night is starting to catch up with her. The other two get up to escort her to the door.

'I'm guessing we might be seeing more of you around here?' Mike asks.

'I hope so.'

'Great,' Shelly says. 'Come out of the basement and say hi when you do. If you ever come up for air.'

'I sincerely apologise for Shelly being Shelly,' Mike says.

'Oh, come on,' Shelly says to him, her voice growing fainter in Chloë's ears as she heads down the walk. 'Be fair. That one was barely innuendo at all.'

The sun is only a scant inch over the horizon as she starts making her way to the nearest Green Line stop. Brookline is still sleepy, not yet hurrying along in the caffeinated press of rush hour. The trees cast long shadows across wrought-iron fences and Victorian buildings, and dry brown leaves crunch under her feet.

She knows that sex isn't the cure-all Shelly believes it to be, but the fact that this budding romance exists has got to be a good sign, wherever it ends up going from here. Her life might be coming back together, more than two years after she finally freed herself from the mess that wrecked it. She wonders how long it will be before she's able to go off the meds. Two more years? Never? Soon enough that she won't ever have to bring it up with Angela?

As she crosses Beacon Street to the centre platform, her thoughts turn, unbidden, to Alec. Tall and tanned and seething with rage. That's the only way she can remember him these days. Screaming at the car when the engine light went on, snarling at a waitress who brought him a cappuccino instead of a macchiato. Finding a way for every single one of their friends to offend him, until he ran out of friends to get mad at. Was it so much worse at the end because she was the only person left, the sole target for all that anger? The two of them trapped together, him yelling at her, how useless she was, how pathetic. Worthless.

Other memories surface. The gritty, unpleasant taste of activated charcoal in the hospital. Weeks under observation in an institution after that.

Chloë shakes her head to clear it as the trolley pulls up. He's gone. She's allowed to have friends again. People are coming back into her life, one by one. Shelly, Mike, Esther, even Ari. And Angela.

Images of Angela flash through her mind as she drops into her seat. Angela smiling. Angela naked. Angela draped over her in the dark. Angela coming, gasping at her touch, muscles clenched, mouth open, eyes closed.

The doors fold shut and the trolley starts moving with a jolt. Memories of the night before keep Chloë warm and awake as the sun crawls higher into the morning sky, and she starts the long journey home.

PART FIVE

I'm So Hungry I Could Die

CHAPTER TWENTY-FIVE

The Underworld, Phoenix, Arizona
31 October 1996

Angela is dancing to Concrete Blonde, her hands held high, her skirt swishing around her knees. She loves this outfit. Tess found it for her last week, and it makes her feel slender and elegant instead of awkward. She spins around another time, just to make the skirt twirl again.

It's Halloween night, and the whole gothic community of Phoenix has come out to play, masked in their finest monster makeup. Zombies and demons and bleeding ballerinas. Angela's face is painted like a skull. Everyone is beautiful. And one person is more beautiful than anyone else.

She sees Tess dancing close by out of the corner of her eye, decked out as a vampire, red-lined cape and all, her own private joke. She's streaked two lines of stage blood down her chin. When they were getting dressed, she'd said that this is the one time of year she can go out with her fangs on full display, exposed to the world, and think nothing of it.

I'm at a club with my girlfriend, Angela thinks, savouring the idea. She feels like she can do anything, anything at all. It's as if she's become an entirely different person. Tess has even been talking

163

about taking her to get a piercing. Not something she would have done before, not something that would ever have occurred to her.

And half an hour ago, in the club bathroom, she said a final goodbye to her old self, to the part that had kept her away from all of this for so very long.

'I'm done with you,' she'd told the face in the mirror. 'You've got no more hold on me.'

'And yet, here I am,' the angel said in return. 'How are you? Are you doing all right?'

'I'm fine. Great, actually. No thanks to you.' She'd peered at him more closely then. 'Why do you look different?' She couldn't determine what had changed about his face – was his expression softer than she was used to? His iridescent robes were gone as well, replaced by a spotless white suit and tie. Elegant enough to befit a celestial entity, but not nearly as ostentatious. Definitely not what she'd come to expect.

'Perhaps,' he said, 'you're starting to see me better.'

'You know what? I don't really care what you look like. Goodbye.'

She'd stuck her tongue out at him, and walked away. Leaving him behind for good. Seeing him was the only sour note in the evening, and she's determined not to let it get to her.

Her thoughts return to the present when Tess moves closer and cups a hand against her cheek, careless of the white makeup plastered there. Something in Angela's chest melts like warm butter at the touch.

She can't keep herself from glancing furtively around, though, checking to see if anyone's watching.

No one is. No one cares. People come here with girlfriends, boyfriends, sometimes both at once. This isn't somewhere she needs to be self-conscious. She relaxes, and draws Tess into a close embrace.

She could get used to this.

She could get used to everything, her whole new life here. Even the weather is beautiful at long last, warm enough for short sleeves without being oppressively hot anymore. The approach of winter is finally making her appreciate Phoenix. At this time of year in Pennsylvania, she'd have been switching over from a fall jacket to a winter coat, steeling herself against the bite of the frigid air every time she went outside. She doesn't miss the cold.

If the scenery on the drive over to the club wasn't much, strip mall after endless sprawling strip mall, outside the city limits the Sonoran desert has a surprisingly lush beauty of its own, one that Angela is becoming more entranced by with each day that passes. An arid, peculiar landscape of saguaro and palo verde, cholla and ocotillo, brittlebush and prickly pear. Living here has its charms.

'You know, Halloween always makes me feel romantic,' Tess says in her ear. 'Do you want a Halloween gift? Would that be weird? Like, I don't know, a telescope. Do you need a telescope?'

Angela smiles. The telescopes that she uses cost millions of dollars to build, sometimes billions; you can't pick one up in a store. Still, it's nice that Tess is trying to be thoughtful. 'You don't have to get me anything.'

'But I want to.'

'How about candy, then? That's more traditional for Halloween, isn't it?'

Tess screws her face up into a look of mock distaste. 'Human chow. Yuck. But all right, candy it is.' She lifts Angela off the ground and whirls her around. 'I'll get you a hundred pounds of candy. Whatever kind you want.'

'Maybe not a hundred pounds,' Angela says breathlessly. 'How about one pound?'

'Really nice candy, then,' Tess counters. 'Truffles and shit like that.'

'Sounds wonderful.'

'Good. Glad that's settled.' Tess gives Angela a gentle squeeze and puts her back down. 'I love you.'

Angela can feel her heartbeat thump against her chest where Tess is pressed against her. She shuts her eyes and lets Tess move her to the music.

She's young and in love and dancing.

Everything is beautiful.

CHAPTER TWENTY-SIX

South End, Boston
11 December 1999

Angela is so ravenous it's hard to think about anything else. There's a fine red mist over her vision that makes everyone she sees look like a walking juice box.

'I'm not sure this is really my thing,' Chloë says nervously.

Angela plasters a smile onto her face. 'Please let me buy you one present? It can be something no one will ever see but me.'

Over the past few weeks, Angela's life has settled into an easy rhythm. She spends the first part of almost all her evenings with Chloë, and then after they separate she plugs away at her thesis until dawn. Early on, she introduced the television-lacking Chloë to *Buffy the Vampire Slayer* – a show Angela loves despite its many inaccuracies – and they've been watching it with Shelly and Mike every Tuesday night. Chloë, in turn, lent Angela her copy of *The Silent Tower* by Barbara Hambly. In the rare hours Angela can snatch to read it, she's become engrossed by the adventures of Joanna and Antryg. And also by Chloë's own short fiction, loose double-spaced pages handed over with obvious nervousness. There was no need for Chloë to worry. Angela loved her droll stories about unconventional heroines and enigmatic cats.

The astronomy work is going more slowly than it did when Angela dedicated nearly every waking moment to it, but not as slowly as she would have thought. Whenever she does settle down to chip away at it, she has more energy and focus than she used to. She's happy. She can't remember the last time she was so happy. But there is one big problem. Dividing her nights between Chloë and work hasn't left her any time to feed.

Except that's a lie, of course. One that's becoming increasingly hard to tell herself. She could have hunted on any of the scattered nights she wasn't with Chloë. Or even a night when she was – all she had to do was wait until Chloë headed home. The clubs are open late enough. It wouldn't have killed her to step away from her thesis and hold off on reading the next chapter of *The Silent Tower*. It never seems to happen, though. She hasn't set foot inside a club since the night she met Chloë.

The truth is, she hasn't wanted to hunt. It's been over a month at this point, though. She needs to do something about it soon.

But not now. Not tonight. She can keep it together just a little while longer, just a few days more. It can wait. She's only putting it off until she figures out what to do.

'A present?' Chloë asks, glancing around. 'What did you have in mind?'

Tonight they've gone to the Fetish Fleamarket at Angela's urging. It only happens twice a year. When she went last summer, she found a better selection of the things she likes to wear than she can get at the shops in town – even though all the stalls were low on stock right before closing, the only time she could show up.

Unsurprisingly, they made it to this one near the end of business hours as well. The customers are beginning to thin, draining away little by little until the packed crowd drops to a few sparse clumps. Oddly enough, it's being held at the Boston Center for the Arts, nestled among the brownstones of the South End. The whole of the

Fleamarket has been packed into the Cyclorama, an enormous circular room beneath a copper skylight dome, built back in the nineteenth century to house a single giant painting of the Battle of Gettysburg.

A maze of booths sprawls across the space. Some are selling corsets and high-buttoned shoes that would have looked familiar to the Victorians who designed the place. Others are offering items they never would have dreamed of. Although, Angela considers, possibly they would have if they'd heard of latex and silicone rubber; she's heard the nineteenth century could get pretty kinky.

As far as Angela can tell, Chloë's mostly been enjoying browsing through the racks of bondage gear and sex toys. She hasn't blinked at the equipment catering to more obscure tastes. But she does seem unnerved by the idea of being given a gift. Angela sees Chloë's gaze flick from a booth proudly advertising genuine medical supplies to another that sells bridles, riding crops, and insertable pony tails.

'I was thinking lingerie,' Angela reassures her. 'You're not about to get a surprise crash course in BDSM.'

'Oh. OK, sure.' Chloë sounds relieved. 'I don't promise I'm going to look good in fancy lingerie, though.'

'I promise you will to me. In it, out of it, whichever.'

Angela is rewarded by an immediate reddening of Chloë's cheeks. She still likes making Chloë blush.

But she hadn't anticipated that the rush of blood to Chloë's face would make her fangs spring out like a pair of switchblades. She clamps her lips tightly together and desperately tries to convince them to retract.

Chloë doesn't help matters by stepping in closer.

'In that case, buy me whatever you want,' Chloë whispers to her huskily. 'Would you like a private showing later tonight?'

Angela turns away from Chloë and pretends to study the display of violet wands.

'Probably not tonight,' she mumbles into the shelving. 'I have to get some work done.'

'Are you sure?' Chloë runs her hand suggestively down Angela's arm. Still not helping.

'Seriously. Want to. But I can't. Has to be a present for later. We'll unwrap it together sometime. Soon.'

'All right.' Chloë sounds a bit put out. 'I know I shouldn't keep you from your work. Maybe tomorrow?'

'Maybe tomorrow.'

Angela can't blame Chloë for being disappointed. It's been almost a week since the last time they were in bed together. But it was hard enough not to get bitey the first few times, and it's getting more and more difficult the longer she goes without feeding. The way she feels right now, she doesn't trust herself at all. She hopes that by tomorrow she'll have her urges under control.

I must be sending insane mixed signals, Angela thinks. *Hi, let me buy you sexy underwear. Now don't let me see you in it. Even though I really, really want to see you in it. What am I doing?*

'I'll go look for something,' Angela says. 'You stay here. I don't want to spoil the surprise.' Angela flees to another booth before Chloë can protest.

She takes a good long time looking through the lingerie. She shakes her head when the woman in the booth asks if she needs help. Without saying a word, she moves further away and acts as if she's preoccupied with the garter belts. She doesn't want to talk to anyone with a heartbeat.

She waits until she calms down enough to get her teeth back to normal.

No more sharp fangs distorting her smile.

Everything is fine.

In the end, she picks out a lacy dark red set that will contrast nicely with Chloë's eyes. Red and green. It'll be like Christmas.

When she asks, she finds out they can't giftwrap it for her, but they do put it in a fancy bag.

On her way back to Chloë, Angela catches a glimpse of a head of hair the same dark red as the lingerie, weaving its way to the exit. She stops, stunned, but when she tries to get a better look, whoever it was is gone, vanished out the door.

It can't have meant anything, anyway. Lots of people have dyed hair, especially here. Tess is in Arizona.

Tess used to buy Angela's clothes.

This isn't the same thing at all, she protests to herself. It's only briefs and a bra. Nothing more, nothing less. Giving someone a gift doesn't have to mean anything sinister.

Upon her return, she finds Chloë with a salesman about to demonstrate the proper use of a violet wand. Chloë's already obligingly rolled up her sleeve.

'There you are,' she says as Angela walks up. 'I was beginning to wonder what had happened to you.'

'Sorry. There were a lot of choices, and I wanted to find something special.' She looks from Chloë to the salesman and back again. 'Are you sure about this?'

'I'm being brave and daring. And it's on the lowest setting. He says it'll give me kind of a tingling sensation.'

'That's right!' The salesman plugs one of the devices in and motions to Chloë to lift her arm. 'It's all set. Now, do you have a pacemaker or any kind of heart disease, or do you think you might be pregnant?'

Chloë freezes, her arm halfway up. 'Do I think I might be what?'

'I'm required to ask those questions, that's all,' he says reassuringly. 'It's perfectly safe.'

'Really?'

'I've never seen anyone get seriously hurt by one of these,' Angela tells her. 'As long as he keeps it away from your eyes and your chest, you should be fine.'

'And any metal or jewellery,' the salesman adds. 'Oh, and if you're wearing alcohol-based hair gel, it could ignite.'

Chloë blinks as she considers the information. 'I see. Um, no pacemaker, no heart disease, no hair gel, and pregnancy would be a medical miracle.' She smiles at Angela, who stifles a giggle. 'Anything else?'

'Epilepsy or other seizure disorders?'

'No. Are you selling a lot of these?'

'They're very popular. OK, here goes.'

He turns on the wand and holds it close to Chloë's arm.

'Ow!' she yells immediately, pulling her arm back close to her body. She cradles it as she glares at the salesman.

He looks disapproving. 'You're supposed to feel a tingle.'

'That was not a tingle!'

Angela slips her own arm into the one Chloë doesn't have protectively clenched to her chest. And, she's pleased to note, her teeth don't do anything they're not supposed to do. No more problems now, even when the two of them are touching. Good.

'Come on, my brave and daring girl. I think I should rescue you from the tingling now. Here's your present, by the way.' Angela passes her the bag.

'Thank you. That was nothing like a tingle.'

Angela pulls her away from the salesman. He takes a step towards them, looking fully prepared to argue that it was, in fact, a tingle, even if it takes the whole night to convince them.

Chloë half turns and growls, 'Back off,' over her shoulder. It's in a tone of voice that Angela has never heard from her before, sharp but somehow distant, like a shout heard from a long way off. It almost makes Angela want to move away herself. The salesman retreats immediately, backing into his display case and nearly dropping the violet wand.

'OK, tigress,' Angela says to her, grinning at the unexpected display of fierceness. 'Now it's really time to go.'

The two women make their way back out to the street, arm in arm. It's started to rain, a light drizzle that doesn't soak them so much as gradually get them damp. It's just enough moisture to make misty halos appear around all the street lamps, and wet the sidewalks until they turn from light grey to dark grey. The lights from shop windows cast bright streaks across the street.

Chloë shifts her present under her coat to keep it dry, holding it awkwardly through the cloth. 'Hey,' she says. 'I know you have to work tonight, but did you want to grab a quick bite somewhere?'

And out pop the fangs again. Is Chloë trying to make things this difficult?

Angela forces them back in through sheer willpower. 'I really shouldn't.'

'Are you sure? Addis Red Sea isn't far from here. It's a favourite of mine. Do you like Ethiopian food?'

'I haven't ever tried it.' She never had the chance, and now she never will. 'But you know me. Never hungry right after I wake up.' She laughs. She wonders if Chloë can hear how fake it sounds. 'I have to wait hours or it makes me nauseous.'

'You must have the slowest metabolism in the world. Do you ever eat?'

'I'm fine. Remember, for me, all I'm doing is skipping breakfast.'

'Someday I'll get used to your weird schedule. My mystery woman, who walks only by night.'

'I'm supposed to be the mystery woman?' Angela says quickly. 'I've never seen the inside of your apartment. I picked you up in front of it one time, and that's it.'

'That's not a mystery. That's because you have allergies.'

'And when do I get to read what you're working on now? Your older stuff was great, but I'd love to see more.'

'I don't have anything that's ready for someone else to look at yet,' Chloë says uneasily.

'See? You're the cryptic enigma here.'

They wander up Tremont Street for a few blocks, heading towards Boston Common, passing dimly lit wine bars and cafés offering thin-crust pizzas with escarole and Gruyère. The old row houses, in red brick and limestone and granite, extend down all the side streets. Prized real estate these days, pretty and proud and well maintained. The neighbourhood's been a gay and lesbian enclave since the 1940s, and over the intervening decades it's changed from a collection of crumbling tenements to an upscale arts district. It's one of the wealthier parts of the city now, a rival to the old money of Beacon Hill across the Common to the north. Changing times, Angela reflects.

'It was all right that I bought you those, wasn't it?' she asks suddenly, gesturing at the bag beneath Chloë's coat. 'I didn't pressure you into it or anything, did I?'

'What? No, not at all. I was just afraid you were going to buy me something like one of those electric cattle prods back there.'

'OK. Good.'

'Why would you think that?'

Angela kicks at a piece of litter on the sidewalk. The wind picks up the crumpled cardboard box and carries it into the gutter. It slowly becomes waterlogged in the thin stream running there, and collapses in on itself. 'It's stupid. Tess – my ex – used to pick out all my clothing for me.'

'Are you saying she told you what to wear?'

'Pretty much,' Angela says. 'I mean, it was complicated, because I liked the clothes. She had good taste. But, yeah. Everything had to be her choice.'

'She sounds horrible.'

'She was, most of the time. But every now and then she was amazing. I guess I was dumb enough to believe that every now and then made up for the rest of it.'

'It's not about being dumb,' Chloë says. 'At least, I hope not. It's not like I can point any fingers.'

'What was your ex like?'

'Alec?' Chloë thinks carefully before she answers. 'He was the kind of person who didn't like anybody or anything. You ever meet someone like that? I thought I was special because he acted like I was the only person he could stand to be around.' She shrugs. 'That didn't last. He spent a lot of time screaming at me in the last year or so. He'd keep a lid on it for a while, but sooner or later something would set him off. And then he'd explode.'

'I'm sorry. That must have been awful.'

'I stayed with him way longer than I should have. Then there was one fight where he started yelling, "I don't love you!" and I felt something snap between us. Physically snap, like that was the last thread holding us together and he'd broken it. The next day I told him, "*You're moving out.*" I didn't actually think he would, I thought he'd make me leave instead, but he went. Out the door, then and there. He came back once to pick up his stuff, and the only time I saw him after that was when we finalised the divorce. I think he's in Connecticut now.'

'Do you hate him?' Angela asks.

'Some. It feels weird to say that. It's hard to admit that you hate someone, you know? But he kind of wrecked me, for a while. It's hard to forgive that.'

They've wandered out of the South End and all the way through the Theatre District, walking beneath the flashing marquees advertising plays and musicals, passing by the fringes of Chinatown on the other side of the street. It isn't long before they reach Boston

Common, getting close to the Park Street T stop. On a midwinter evening, the park in the middle of town is nearly empty of people. The streetlamps glow like will-o'-the-wisps beneath the trees, turning the damp grass silvery.

'I'm not sure I hate Tess for what she did to me,' Angela says slowly. 'There are things I think she did to other people that I can hate her for, and I do. But I feel like I was too, I don't know, too complicit in what happened to me to blame her for everything. I was there, making decisions. Letting things happen, because it was easier than saying no.'

'Do you mind if I hate your ex for hurting you, even if you don't?' Chloë asks. 'Because I really, really want to.'

Angela smiles. 'Please be my guest.'

The two of them halt at the head of the stairs down to Park Street. It'll be the end of their night together once they reach the bottom. Angela will go west on the Green Line, and Chloë will travel north on the Red. One heading home to work and one to sleep.

'Should I drop by your place again tomorrow? Usual time?' Chloë asks.

'Actually, why don't I come over to yours this time? I really would like to see it.'

'What about the cat?'

'I'm pretty certain I can survive the sniffles for a night.'

Chloë seems reluctant. 'It's sort of a mess.'

'I'm not going to break up with you because you've got some dirty laundry on the floor. Come on, how about it?'

'Well . . . OK,' Chloë says. 'Why don't we catch a movie or something, then go back to my place after?'

'Sounds great.'

They hug at the top of the stairs, holding each other close. A knot of disembarking passengers starts pouring out of the station, swerving around the two women embracing. A gust of heated air from the open doors follows in the wake of the crowd.

Angela stands on tiptoe so she can rest her chin on Chloë's shoulder and feel her breath, warm against her ear. The coils of Chloë's curly hair, wet from the rain, brush against her cheek. Angela is grateful for the winter chill tonight; it should disguise how cold her body is. Everyone's skin feels cold after they've been outside in Boston in December.

If she doesn't think about it, the hunger is a dull roar in the background. She can ignore the crowd of people, the blood pulsing through the arteries of every last one of them. It's nothing she can't handle. She can hold Chloë with no risk that she'll turn her head and bite.

Angela is sure she can keep it together for another night. Just one more night, and then she'll figure something out.

CHAPTER TWENTY-SEVEN

Somerville
11 December 1999

Chloë has worked herself into a decent-sized panic by the time she bursts in through the front door. She makes a quick survey of the living room.

'Oh, God.'

From over in the kitchen, Ari and Esther look up from that weird card game they like to play. The one that uses the prophecy cards.

'Is something the matter, dear?' Esther asks.

'Yes. I need to clean. I need to clean right now. This place is not habitable for humans.'

'It's a good thing that it's only been a year or two since the last time this place got straightened up,' Esther comments, 'or you could have had a really tough job ahead of you.'

Chloë is not amused. 'You know, given that you're staying here rent free, I do not find the whole sitting and mocking thing you're doing very endearing.'

'Oh, I'll help out.' Esther levers herself to her feet. 'I was just waiting for you to ask. Show no patience with the elderly and infirm, why don't you?'

Ari is likewise putting down his cards and getting up. 'I can pitch in, too, if you want.'

'Oh. Well, thank you both. That would be great.'

Chloë doesn't know where to start. Everything is jumbled together, on the tables, on the floor, on the chairs. Manuscripts are scattered like leaves. Cat toys have been batted under every piece of furniture. There are piles of compact discs. Empty boxes. Pens. Shoes. She starts to despair when she realises used tissues need their own category.

If Angela sees this, she's going to notice that something's wrong. Very, very wrong.

She picks a blender up off a chair. How long has she had a blender? And why was it sitting in a chair? Was it comfortable there? She shoves it behind the couch.

Ari and Esther are milling about the living room, picking over the various piles. She decides to leave them to it and heads into the kitchen. She can start on the dishes. The two of them might have a better idea of how to organise the clutter than she does, although she doesn't have high hopes of it. And there's a good chance that if they dig deep enough, they're going to come across some of the underwear Entropy hid around the house. She knows she never found all of it. Well, it's far too late to be embarrassed about that now.

The dirty dishes in the sink have risen to truly lofty heights. She isn't certain that she has any dish soap. Washing the dishes is a lost cause. She opens the cabinet beneath the sink and starts shovelling plates into it.

Suddenly and disconcertingly, a collection of broken handbags is thrust in her face. Her field of vision is filled with snapped straps, broken zippers, burst seams.

'Where do these go?' Ari asks.

'Throw them away, I guess. No, wait, don't!' Some of them are bulging with unknown contents. Makeup? Money? Candy? She has no idea. 'Just put them somewhere neat for now. I need to sort through them.'

He lays them down gently and presumably neatly next to the broken sewing machine on the kitchen table, and then he wanders back out to the living room. One set of objects successfully moved from somewhere to somewhere else. She isn't sure if that counts as progress.

She returns to the task of getting her dishes out of sight.

'Is that really the best idea?' Esther is leaning against the door-frame between the two rooms, watching Chloë work.

'It's saving me a lot of time.' Chloë starts laying a row of filth-encrusted glasses next to the oven cleaner.

'Hm. So, what's the occasion? Expecting company?'

'As it happens, yes. Someone's coming over tomorrow night. And would it be all right to ask if you and Ari could maybe find some-place else to be for a while?'

Esther arches an eyebrow. 'Is this a special someone?'

'Yes, actually.'

Esther's face lights up. Her grin immediately jiggles all of the deep wrinkles on her face into place. Smile lines, every last one.

'I knew you needed to get out more.'

'Don't give yourself too much credit,' Chloë says. 'All you did was force me out of the apartment. I had to do the rest of the work myself.'

'So how long has this been going on?'

'We've been going out for a few weeks.'

'Have you, now?' Esther says. 'Then why haven't I met this special someone yet?'

Because, Chloë thinks, *Angela is a normal, sane person and I am des-perately trying to keep a wall between her and my deranged life so she doesn't run screaming. Because a sane person might have second thoughts if they knew about my fortune-telling live-in aunt who likes to imply she had a fling with Eleanor Roosevelt. And my exorcism-performing cult-leader housemate. Or if they knew about the mess. Or about me.*

She glances down at the bowl she's attempting to slide between the drain trap and a stack of plates. 'I'm acting like a crazy person, aren't I?'

'It's not an ideal approach to the problem,' Esther agrees.

With a sigh, Chloë starts putting the dishes back in the sink.

She realises Esther is still waiting for an answer to her question. 'I wanted to be sure that it was going somewhere before I brought her round.'

It's close enough to the truth. Esther seems to accept it, at any rate. 'I take it things are going somewhere, then?'

'Um. Maybe? We haven't talked about it that much. Not seriously.'

'Why not?'

Chloë rolls her eyes. 'Because it's only been a few weeks. And now you're just prying.'

'Yes,' Esther says with no guilt at all. 'I am. Consider it my revenge for being kept ignorant.'

'I am not obligated to tell you all the details of my love life.' Chloë marches past Esther, back into the living room. The dishes will have to wait until she gets some soap.

'I'd guessed some of it, anyway, to be honest,' Esther says as she passes. 'You come home glowing.'

'She makes me feel pretty glowy.' The living room looks much the same as it did before – no surprise there. Ari is sitting in a corner, picking objects up, peering at them intently, and then putting them back down in what Chloë can only suppose is a more organised way. 'Anyway,' she continues, 'tonight she asked why we never come to my place, and I couldn't think of any sane-sounding reason not to. Because "it might be dangerous to living organisms" is not a sane-sounding reason. So, the cleaning, it must happen.'

Ari pauses, then slowly lowers the feathered cat toy he'd been studying. 'Did you, I just noticed, I wasn't eavesdropping, but I mean, you're standing right over there so I couldn't help hearing, did you say "she"?'

'Er, yes. She. Her. Her name's Angela.' Chloë has a sudden, horrified thought. 'Your religion doesn't forbid that kind of thing, does it?'

He tilts his head slightly, thinking about it. 'Frankly, I haven't put anything about it in my religion yet, one way or another.' He shrugs. 'It's not the type of thing I've really been concerned about. I was surprised, that's all.'

'Oh. Good.' Or at least not bad, which is better than nothing. 'Yours is one of the few, then.'

'Honestly, for a lot of them, it depends on how you look at it,' Ari says. 'Like, there's some stuff about it in the New Testament, but it's not part of the Gospels. It's all in Paul's epistles. The guy wrote a lot of letters and put his own spin on things after the fact. It's interpretation, and interpretation can change.'

'Huh.' Chloë mulls that over for a moment. 'Well, I'm glad you're so flexible about it.'

Ari nods, and goes back to his sorting.

'Anyway, we'll make ourselves scarce when Angela comes over,' Esther says. 'Don't worry about that.'

'Sure,' Ari agrees. 'How late do you want us to stay out?'

'You don't have to be gone the whole night or anything, I just wanted a little time without—Um, what the hell are these?'

Beneath the armchair, Chloë has found what looks like a graveyard for shredded cotton balls. There are mounds of them, piled into drifts and tiny hills. She lifts one up, and sees that a string is dangling from it limply. It couldn't be . . .

'Entropy attacked the savage tampons,' Esther says. 'He got a whole big box of them open. Most of them are under there, but I've been finding them all over the place.'

Chloë buries her face in her hands. 'It's not that I can't have any nice things. I can't have any things at all!'

Esther picks one up and flicks the string, which swishes like the tail of a strange animal. 'They do sort of look like mice, don't they? The little dear was going by natural instinct.'

'I refuse to believe that cats are evolutionarily programmed to attack feminine hygiene products.' Chloë says. 'My cat is weird. And what am I supposed to do about Entropy, anyway? Angela's allergic. I'll have to shut him in the bathroom for the night.' As soon as she says it, she realises the problem with that idea. 'That won't work, damn it. What if she has to go to the bathroom?'

'How about the bedroom?' Ari suggests.

'I kind of don't want my bedroom off limits, either,' Chloë says drily.

Esther pats Chloë on the shoulder. 'I'm sure you'll think of something.'

Chloë begins stuffing eviscerated tampons into a plastic bag. 'I just want everything to be perfect for her.'

'Of course you do.'

She looks for a place to hide the plastic tampon bag, but can't find any out-of-sight areas that aren't full to bursting. So far, their efforts have hardly made any difference to the size of the mess. There's plenty of space on the couch, though, so she throws the bag onto it and follows that up by moving more piles there from the floor.

Esther interrupts with a gentle hand on Chloë's arm. 'I can sleep on the floor if I have to, but I think you might want to leave her somewhere to sit down.'

Chloë pauses. 'You're right. I don't think I'm thinking straight. Maybe I'm getting a little overwrought here.'

'At least it's nice to see you excited about something for a change.'

Ari suddenly looks up. 'You know what? It's actually kind of amazing.'

'Er, what is?' Chloë asks.

'Two women, falling in love. I mean, now that I'm really contemplating the spiritual significance of the concept. It makes you reflect on the vast, magnificent panoply of human existence, doesn't it?'

'I . . . guess so?'

His smile is beaming. 'Your love is a beautiful thing.'

'Oh, well, that's . . .' Chloë is at a complete loss as to how to respond to that. 'Thanks?'

'Life on Earth is such a rich tapestry. Love, in all its many forms and phases –'

Esther quickly intercedes. 'Ari, why don't you spend a little time straightening your own room? In case Angela wants a full house tour.'

'Oh, yeah. Sure. I'll go do that.' He rises and strides out of the room, passing through the kitchen to his bedroom, where he promptly begins rearranging his few possessions into a tidier configuration.

'He means well,' Esther says sotto voce, sounding apologetic.

Chloë starts the process of moving everything off the couch cushions and back onto the floor. 'Oh, he's all right. Sure, he sometimes makes a comment from outer space, but I've lived with worse.'

'I'm sure you have. Now' – Esther goes on in a more normal tone, clapping her hands together with a single brisk slap – 'shall we get the rest of it squared away?'

'Is there any point?' Chloë sits down heavily in the small clearing she's made on the couch. 'Look at this place. We've barely started. It's never going to get fixed in one day. Angela is going to come here and expire from cat dander and toxic mould, and she'll never want to see me again, and I'll grow old and die alone, unloved, unmourned, and hiding my dirty dishes.'

'Now you genuinely are being overwrought. Getting something done is better than getting nothing done.'

'I suppose you're right.' Chloë heaves herself off the couch. 'I should probably start by keeping Entropy out of here before he decides to undo everything we manage to accomplish.'

Esther straightens a pile of books as Chloë heads over to shut the bedroom door. Entropy shoots out just before it closes and streaks across the room, scattering small objects in his wake.

'Yeah,' Chloë says heavily. 'Exactly like that.'

She stalks off after her cat, trying to think of the best way to imprison him before he makes her task even more hopeless than it already is.

CHAPTER TWENTY-EIGHT

The Treaty Of Westphalia

I wanted to take a moment to say that I understand how things can end up getting a bit messy sometimes.

I remember a period in my life that seemed like nothing but turmoil and chaos, when I was a younger woman, back during the Thirty Years War. Absolutely everything was going wrong, especially right after the Defenestration of Prague.

But once during those dark years, when Queen Christina of Sweden and I were lying naked in bed together after a night of passionate lovemaking, she turned to me and said, 'Esther, although millions have already perished in this senseless struggle, I believe that the Treaty of Westphalia will be signed and the warring powers of Europe brought to peace, because in the end, love will always triumph over even the worst adversity.'

And of course, she said it in that adorable Swedish accent.

CHAPTER TWENTY-NINE

Harvard Yard, Cambridge
12 December 1999

The sky is clouded over, not a single star to be seen, and a bitter wind is whipping across Harvard Yard. The university is quiet as Angela walks through, the buildings empty and the grassy quads deserted. The only sounds she can hear are the leafless trees creaking in the stiff breeze and the plasticky rustle of her dress as she walks. The hunger is a dull roar in the back of her mind. It's getting palpably worse with each passing day. She woke up tonight feeling like a rabid animal.

She drove into Cambridge instead of taking the T, even though it meant she had to park on a back street halfway to Porter Square and walk half a mile down. Now she's wasting more time taking a roundabout route through the university grounds. But driving and detouring let her avoid being trapped in a packed subway car, kept her away from any crowded streets. It's easier to stay in control when there aren't any people around.

She tries to turn her attention to something else. Anything else. She focuses on the red-brick buildings. Harvard. It's a place with a lot of meaning for her, even though she never went to school there. Over a century ago, women were working in astronomy here, toiling over thousands of photographic plates, classifying the spectra of the stars. Williamina Fleming, Annie Jump Cannon, Henrietta Swan Leavitt, Antonia Maury. And later on, Cecilia Payne, who used their data to figure out what all those stars are made of. The elemental ingredients of the universe.

They were treated like crap, of course. Underpaid, unappreciated. Other people taking credit for their work. But still. It means something that they were here. Maybe she'll apply for a job at the Center for Astrophysics when she graduates; it'd be nice to be able to stay in Boston. She can try to make her own small contribution to history. If they're hiring then. If she graduates.

If she doesn't die of hunger first.

Her need slams into her like a physical blow as soon as she walks out through the gates. A car horn blares from somewhere in the stopped traffic on the street a moment after she steps through, the dark quad behind her giving way to bright lights and noise. The university may be silent, but Harvard Square is bustling.

The neighbourhood is a hive of activity, the sidewalks packed with people making their way to the bookstores and boutiques, restaurants and bars. Businesses catering to the young, the well-off, and the over-educated. A meeting point for throngs of Christmas shoppers, as well as the swarm of students taking a break from studying for exams.

On a normal night, she likes it here. She is, after all, young and over-educated, and the fact that she never needs to buy groceries might push her into well-off, even on a grad student's stipend. She doesn't stand out here. Any subculture that has ever had its moment has its fashions on display somewhere in the square; she can wear a full-length vinyl dress and not attract a second glance. It doesn't rate a look in a neighbourhood where living statues are competing for the best location.

This isn't a normal night, though. She keeps her head down so she can't see anyone's neck, her eyes on her feet as she makes her way down Mass Ave. She's about to turn onto Brattle Street when she hears someone behind her calling her name.

'Angela? Angela, is that you?'

The voice sounds familiar, but she can't quite place it until she turns to look. She sees someone approaching her with rapid steps, dodging past the people in her way. Frizzy black hair, olive skin, dark eyes.

Hazel.

A vivid memory of the taste of Hazel's blood rushes into her mind. Hot and warm and wet in her mouth.

Angela bites down on her tongue. Hard. The pain replaces everything else, drives away the hunger. For the moment.

Hazel skids to a halt in front of her. She has an eyebrow piercing now, still healing, a barbell with crystal beads. Leather pants and a sharp red jacket. Angela doesn't think the clothes are borrowed anymore.

'It is you.' Hazel is smiling broadly. 'Hi.'

'Hi, Hazel.' Her tongue is still aching, making her lisp the name a little. But it's better than attacking someone in public. Better than attacking someone anywhere at all, she quickly corrects herself.

She can get through this. It's only someone who wants to say hello. A brief conversation and then she'll make her excuses.

People are pressing around them on the busy corner, jostling the two women as they pass. Angela steps out of the way, drawing Hazel between the pillars fronting the bookstore entrance nearby.

Hazel takes the opportunity to step up close to Angela. 'I'm so glad I ran into you.'

'It's nice to see you, too. How've you been? How's work?'

'What? Oh, it's fine.' Hazel waves a hand through the air as if brushing the topic aside. 'But listen. I feel rotten that I never got a chance to thank you.'

'To thank me for what?' Angela tilts her head, perplexed. She's not sure where this is going, and definitely wants it to end soon.

'For seeing me home, of course. After the club.'

'Oh.' Angela feels sick to her stomach. 'Don't . . . It was nothing. You don't need to –'

'It wasn't nothing,' Hazel cuts her off. 'Not a lot of people would have done that.'

'Really, it wasn't a big deal.'

Hazel shakes her head. 'I can't believe I got that drunk. You must think I'm horrible.'

'What? No, I don't. Not at all.'

'Say . . .' Hazel bites her lower lip shyly. 'Are you busy tonight? Would you like to – I was just thinking – maybe go get a drink or something? I promise I won't pass out on you this time.'

Hazel's lips are painted bright red. Arterial red. Angela could drink her blood right here, behind the pillar. No one would notice, or if they did, it'd look like one goth girl kissing another, nothing unusual in Harvard Square. Except for the screaming. No. No, no, no. She'll need to go somewhere else with Hazel, get her drunk, for real this time, she didn't bring any sleeping pills with her.

'Hey, do you have fangs now?'

'What?' They've come out without her realising. She blinks, unable to think of anything to say.

'You do!' Hazel says. 'That's awesome. I've been getting a lot more into the scene, myself.' She gestures at her clothes. 'But I haven't had the guts to go that far. Are they permanent or temporary?'

'Oh. They're, they're temporary.'

Hazel nods. Smiles again. 'So, how about that drink?' She rests her hand lightly on Angela's arm.

Angela jerks away. 'I don't know if that's such a good idea.'

'Oh.' Hazel's smile starts to fade. Her voice is uncertain. 'I thought that we, you know, before I . . . I thought we had a nice time talking, and –'

'I'm on my way to meet my girlfriend!' Angela blurts out.

'You . . . ? Oh!' Hazel takes half a step back, looking mortified. 'Is that something you told me about the first time we met? Because I'm really sorry if it was. Some of that night is a blur.'

'No,' Angela says. 'No, it's new. I met her about a week after that.'

'Oh. Just my luck. Bad timing, huh?'

'Bad timing,' Angela echoes.

The conversation ends shortly after that, much to Angela's relief. Hazel presses her phone number on Angela, pretending that 'in case you break up with your girlfriend' isn't the subtext, and Angela dutifully records it in her cell phone, pretending that she might use it sometime. Then there's nothing left to say but a pair of awkward goodbyes.

Once Hazel is out of sight, Angela ducks into the first café she sees and heads straight into the bathroom. She sits on the floor of a stall, her head on her knees. She isn't sure how long she stays there.

When she finally lifts her head and checks the time on her phone, she has only a few minutes to get to the movie theatre. She isn't late for her rendezvous with Chloë yet, but if she stays in the bathroom much longer, she will be. Even though she's still feeling shaky, she gets up and goes to meet her date. The girl she hasn't bitten.

Hasn't bitten yet, a voice in the back of her mind insists on adding.

She hurries over to the Brattle Theatre. Brattle Hall is an odd building for a cinema, looking more like a large house that wandered into a business district by mistake, got lost, and decided to stay. Angela goes down the stairs to the ticket window and sees no sign of Chloë, inside or out, so she buys tickets for both of them. The cashier has a long, swan-like neck. If Angela looks closely, she can see the artery pulsing underneath the ear.

She grabs the tickets and ducks into the lobby as quickly as she can. She keeps herself as far as possible from the man selling concessions, moving to the far wall to make a determined study of the flyers and posters there. At least the room is empty aside from the two of them. The movie is about to start; everyone else must already be inside.

Her gaze drifts over ads for events and shows. Tonight marks the end of Horror Movie Week at the Brattle. Tomorrow, Muppet Week starts. There's a production of *Pippin* going on somewhere near the Museum District. She makes a mental note to tell Chloë. It's the sort of thing she'd like.

All of the holiday stuff is coming up soon. Some of it's already started. The Christmas Revels on the Harvard Campus – for some reason they're set during the Italian Renaissance this time around. The Boston Pops Holiday Concert. First Night downtown. That'll be huge this year. She and Chloë should at least go out to see the fireworks. She smiles to herself. Lesbian New Year's.

At first, she doesn't consciously recognise her own picture; there's just a vague feeling that something isn't quite right. It's only when she looks at the flyer a second time that she realises what she's seeing.

She pulls the flyer out of the rack and stares at it. There she is, lying on a bed, relaxed, her eyes half-lidded. Blood dripping down her neck. Tess was never fussy about cleaning up after herself. The photo's been cropped for the flyer, showing her from the collarbones up. The full one, she remembers, is a nude.

She reads the words on the flyer in haphazard fragments, barely able to take them in. Art Opening. Photography Exhibition. The name of a gallery in the Back Bay. Three photographers. Tess's name.

Her thoughts are a jumble. Should she call a lawyer about the photo? She knows she won't. Is Tess coming to town? Will Angela run into her on the street? Was that really her at the Fetish Fleamarket after all?

Is this the kind of thing that's going to happen from now on – every piece of her past that she wants to forget is going to call out her name and pull her aside for a chat?

I'm in hell, she decides. *Somehow, tonight, I woke up in hell.*

Chloë rushes in through the door, out of breath.

'Sorry I'm late. The T got stuck at Porter for, like, twenty minutes.'

Angela shoves the flyer into her handbag. 'It's fine. I got the tickets.'

'Has it started?'

'They're probably not past the previews yet.'

Chloë proffers her arm, and Angela hesitates for only an instant before she takes it. She's relieved to find that it doesn't make the hunger any worse. Too many other things on her mind, she guesses.

She leans against Chloë as their eyes adjust to the darkened theatre. On the screen, Kermit the Frog is talking to Michael Caine. An ad for next week's shows. They haven't missed anything. They hurry to a pair of seats at the back.

As soon as they sit down, Angela rests her head on Chloë's shoulder. She feels better with Chloë around. Calmer. If it can just be this way for the rest of the night, maybe everything will be all right.

At least I have this, she thinks to herself.

I still have this.

CHAPTER THIRTY

The Parable Of The Lady In The Tower
Public Garden
12 December 1999

You guys are lost? How can you be lost? You're in the middle of the Public Garden. The Common is right over there, and if you walk that way you'll hit the end of Newbury Street.

The Public Garden. It's like a . . . garden. That's open to the public. Are you tourists?

You're all pretty drunk, aren't you?

Well, as long as you're here, do you want to hear a parable? Parable, it's like a story. Great, that's great, gather round. This parable is called, 'The Lady in the Tower'.

Once upon a time, there was a tall tower with no doors and only one window—

I'm sorry, what? Why would that be illegal? No, I don't know anything about fire codes. What, are you a fire safety inspector or something? Oh, you are.

Well, maybe it was built by, like, evil contractors. Relentless fiends who would build anything for the right price. Yes, I'm sure it would have been torn right the hell down if you'd ever taken a look at it. But let's say you never got a chance to do that, OK?

Look, why don't we back up a little.

Once upon a time, there was a lady who hired a bunch of unscrupulous contractors to build a tall tower with no doors and only one window, on a lonely island where no fire inspector would ever see it.

When it was finished, she dwelt in a room at the very top of the tower, looking at the world through a magic mirror and never daring to show her face at the window. She lived in isolation because she knew the world was full of monsters—

I don't know how she got food up there.

No, she didn't let down her hair, that's a different story. Besides, don't you think it would be really painful to have someone climbing up your hair? Not to mention the amount of conditioner you'd go through every week. I'm guessing she let down a basket on a rope or something. That work for you? Good. Moving on, then.

One day, a traveller came to her island, the first to visit there in many years. Oh, come on, this person obviously came on a boat, all right? Can I keep going, please? The traveller called up to the tower, asking to see the lady's face, for tales of her beauty had spread throughout the land.

The lady saw the bold adventurer through her magic mirror. While she was greatly attracted to the daring stranger, she was also cautious. For in this land, monsters took the form of people, and there was no way to tell the one from the other until they were close enough to bite. But she had grown tired of living alone, seeing only shadows of the world.

So she went at last to her window and invited her visitor up, in spite of the danger—

No, I don't think the traveller came up in the basket. I guess there was also a ladder? I mean, she had to get into the tower in the first place, somehow. Yeah, that's true, if there was a ladder she didn't need the basket. Maybe there wasn't a basket. I know I said there was a basket. Forget the basket.

The stranger placed the ladder against the tower and started to climb.

Are we back to that again? Seriously? Maybe she had the food delivered. On boats. Sure, yes, her magic mirror had internet access. Oh, you're right, I did say the traveller was the first person to go there in years. But this isn't really—

HELPFUL ANIMALS. All right? Birds. Her friends the birds brought her food every day.

The traveller told the lady that she was the fairest maiden in all the land. She was very flattered, and also very lonely. And yes, sure, also very horny. I mean, she'd been up in that tower for a long time. So she drew her guest in close for a kiss, knowing that if she'd let in a monster by mistake, then this would be the moment—

I don't know what kind of birds. No, I don't know how many, either. Larks. Call it larks. A hundred of them, bringing berries. Yes, only berries, sure. Is it really important what she did for protein?

No, she didn't eat the larks.

. . . you know what? Forget it. You guys want to go get a pizza? Awesome. Let's go.

I don't know how this story ends, anyway.

CHAPTER THIRTY-ONE

Somerville
12 December 1999

'I'm never letting you pick a movie ever again,' Chloë says as she walks through the front door. She looks up to check the lintel as soon as she's inside. Entropy managed to evade capture both last night and this morning, and an attack from above is probably not the best way to introduce someone to her apartment.

From behind her, Angela says, 'I cannot tell you how sorry I am. I had no idea it was going to be that bad.'

'Oh, I'm not being serious,' Chloë replies. 'I mean, it was the worst movie ever, yeah, but I'm not going to blame you for that. I was surprised you didn't take me to *Sleepy Hollow*, though. I'd have pegged you for a Tim Burton fan.'

'I don't really watch a lot of films. I should've let you choose.'

'It's fine. I could have said no.'

'What kind of thing do you like to see, usually?'

'Whatever catches my interest, I guess.' After confirming that the lintel is clear, Chloë does a quick scan to make sure there are no bottles of antidepressants in view. None are out in the open as far as she can tell. 'I thought *Mansfield Park* was good. I'm a sucker for textual interrogation and romantic endings.'

So far, it hasn't been their most successful date. The movie they'd gone to see at Angela's request had been monumentally awful. The plot had been something incomprehensible about a vampire sorceress who abducts a mute girl for reasons that were never made entirely clear. It had mostly been an excuse to show scantily clad women making out for ninety minutes.

On top of that, both of them have been tense all night. Chloë's been almost panicky, and Angela has seemed nervous, too. Fidgety, distracted. Distant. And weirdly insistent on getting away from crowds. They'd come straight back here after the movie.

Chloë's made a couple of ventures towards asking her what's the matter, but Angela's brushed them aside. It's not the first night that's happened recently, either. Chloë has an uneasy suspicion that something is going wrong between them, and she doesn't know what it is. Hopefully, Angela will tell her when she's ready. But if not, then Chloë suspects that at some point she's going to have to force the issue.

She doesn't want to. Confrontations with Alec never went well, and she remains wary of them. *But Angela*, she reminds herself, *isn't Alec.* Bringing up a problem doesn't mean it will blow up in her face. Chloë has the right to ask what's going on. Even if the very idea of doing so makes her guts twist with anxiety.

Chloë takes a final look around the room. The Zoloft may be out of sight, but the place is still a mess. Of course it's still a mess. It's better than it was last night, but straightening everything up in a single day was an impossible task. In spite of all the effort, it looks like an explosion at a yard sale. Chloë thinks she's managed to get the worst of it out of sight. No used tissues or shredded tampons, anyway.

'So, is it all right if I come in?' Angela asks.

She's still lingering outside the door.

'Oh, yes! No cat about to pounce, he's hiding somewhere. I'm guessing he's mad at me for trying to take him prisoner. Come on in.' Chloë ushers Angela through the door. 'Welcome to my humble abode. It's, uh, it's a little cluttered right now.'

'Trust me,' Angela says as she enters, 'I'm sure I've seen . . .' She trails off as she looks around. 'OK, wow, I haven't actually seen worse.'

'Oh, God.' Chloë can feel her panic rising. 'I don't, I mean, I didn't, I really didn't want you to –'

'Hey.' Angela turns to face her. 'Don't worry about it. It was just a joke. I didn't mean to upset you. It's OK.'

'It's not OK!' Chloë breaks into a sweat, damp and clammy on her skin. No wonder everything has been going wrong. She couldn't get her act together with twenty-four hours' notice. 'I should have done more. The least I could have done was make the place clean for you.'

Angela lays a hand on her shoulder, then quickly takes it away again. 'Chloë. Everything's all right. I'm not about to run off into the night.'

Chloë nods, and tries to pull herself together. She wouldn't mind turning around and heading straight back outside herself. She takes off her coat instead. Angela, as usual, hasn't bothered to wear one.

'Well.' Chloë takes a deep breath, and regrets it. The place doesn't smell all that fresh, either. 'Let me know if you start feeling wheezy or anything, all right? We don't have to stay here if it's a problem.'

'I dosed myself up on, like, mega-antihistamines earlier tonight. I'm pretty sure even your paranormal hyperkitty won't be able to break through.' Angela gives her a reassuring smile. A tense one, maybe, but reassuring, nonetheless.

'OK.' Chloë feels some of her panic drain away. Angela's smile has that effect on her.

It helps that Angela is looking particularly beautiful tonight. *There are*, Chloë thinks, *some good reasons to bring Angela home.* Her black vinyl dress flows down her body like dark water, shining wherever it catches the light. It makes her skin look almost translucently white, and gives her grey eyes a gleam of silver. Hypnotic eyes, easy to get lost in.

Which may be why Chloë is so startled when she hears Esther's voice calling out from the kitchen.

'Oh, are you two back already? Hello!'

Angela's head whips around towards the sound, her smile vanishing. 'I thought you said there wasn't going to be anyone else here tonight?'

'There wasn't supposed to be,' Chloë grumbles. She turns to shout through the kitchen doorway. 'Hi, and yes, we are! You haven't left yet?'

Esther bustles into the living room. 'I'll be on my way soon. Sorry to interrupt your date, I must have lost track of time.'

Esther is already dressed to go out, wearing a stylish forest-green jacket, but Chloë is nearly certain that 'lost track of time' could be phrased more accurately as 'waited around long enough to check out the new girlfriend'.

'Is Ari here, too?' she asks her aunt.

'No, he went out to preach about an hour ago. He shouldn't be back until late.'

'Preach?' Angela asks Chloë quietly, her eyebrows raised.

'Yeah, it's his thing. I'll explain later.'

Esther is now standing directly in front of them. Angela takes half a step back. Possibly she doesn't like being examined, which the older woman is doing pretty blatantly. If Esther is planning on leaving immediately, she isn't showing any sign of it yet.

'Angela, this is my aunt,' Chloë says with a certain degree of resignation. 'Well, great-aunt. Esther. Aunt Esther, this is Angela.'

'Pleased to meet you,' Angela says politely.

'Likewise, I'm sure,' Esther replies. 'Chloë has told me almost nothing about you whatsoever.'

Angela hesitates, then grins. 'You know, I could say exactly the same thing.'

Esther nods firmly, as if she expected nothing else. 'And what do you do, Angela?'

'I'm a grad student. You?'

'I'm a witch.'

Chloë winces a little, but Angela doesn't even blink. 'A good witch or a bad witch?'

Esther makes a tsking noise. 'Chloë hasn't even told you that much?'

'Well . . .' Angela looks sideways at Chloë. 'We both seem to like some mystery in the relationship.'

'I see,' Esther says slyly. 'So you won't be wanting to see any of Chloë's embarrassing baby pictures, then.'

'Are you kidding? I want to see all of them!'

'Not to interrupt this fascinating discussion about me,' Chloë says, 'but why on earth do you have embarrassing baby pictures of me? Do you just carry some around with you wherever you go?'

'If you don't want me to know where you keep your albums,' Esther tells her, 'don't ask me to help you clean.'

She sidles over to a pile which mostly consists of CD cases and starts digging under them. A few clatter to the carpet with soft thuds. Chloë sighs. Well, Entropy would have got around to it at some point, anyway.

'If you show her the one where I'm wearing an upside-down soup bowl as a hat . . .' Chloë says as Esther triumphantly pulls a photo album out from the bottom of the heap, 'I'm going in the other room.'

'That sounds cute,' Angela says.

'The soup was still in it.'

'That sounds cuter.'

'Well, then.' Esther settles on the couch and blows some dust off the album cover. Its spine creaks stiffly in protest as she opens it. 'Shall we see how much we can make Chloë blush?'

Angela freezes. Her smile remains fixed on her face, but it drops away from her eyes.

'Maybe . . . on second thoughts, maybe we should take a rain check on that. Since you were about to go out, and I don't, um, I'd rather not mortify Chloë too badly tonight.'

Esther shrugs amiably and sets the album back aside. 'Some other time, then. You're right, I should be on my way. Chloë, would you help me find my car key? I put it down in the kitchen somewhere and it's disappeared.'

Chloë obligingly follows Esther into the kitchen. She's about to point out that the key is sitting in the middle of the table when Esther grabs her arm and pulls her further from the doorway.

'Oh my goodness, she's gorgeous!' Esther whispers.

'Um. I agree?'

'And she seems charming as well, at least from what little I've seen. I'd say you have excellent taste in women.'

'Well, thank you,' Chloë says. 'I think. Although I'm going to be honest, it sounds kind of creepy when you put it like that. Is this what you dragged me in here to talk about?'

'No.' Esther glances at the doorway, then back to Chloë. 'Is Angela feeling entirely all right tonight?'

'I . . . don't know. She has seemed a little bit off. Why?'

'I'm not sure. She's very pale.'

'Oh. That isn't – I mean, that's normal for her. I don't think she sees a lot of sunlight. She works on a night schedule.'

'Does she now?' Esther says, her brow wrinkling.

Chloë frowns. 'Are you trying to hint at something? Because if you are, I am totally not getting it.'

'No, not really.' Esther shakes her head. 'No doubt it's nothing out

202

of the ordinary, like you said. I'm an old woman and sometimes get odd notions. Pay me no mind.'

She picks up the car key and walks out of the room, leaving a perplexed Chloë to follow along after her.

In the living room, Angela is examining the books on Chloë's shelves. She straightens when the other two come back in.

'It was lovely to meet you, dear,' Esther says as she heads to the front door. 'Perhaps you'll be here when I get back?'

'Probably not,' Angela says. 'I have to work later tonight. But another time, for sure. You owe me a soup hat.'

Esther chuckles, then steps out into the night, shutting the door behind her with a click. There's a silence after she leaves. Chloë wonders if anyone else is going to burst in, Ari ringing the doorbell or Entropy racing through, but no one does.

'So,' Chloë says, turning back to Angela. 'Where were we, before we were interrupted?'

'Well, let's see. We walked through the door, you took off your coat—'

'And then I fell into a blind panic over your seeing my place for the first time. Right.'

Angela steps closer to Chloë. 'You don't have to. I'm not that scary, am I?'

'I know. I'm jittery tonight, that's all.' Chloë shrugs nervously and decides to move to a different topic. 'So. Can I get you something to drink?'

Angela shakes her head. 'No, thanks. I'm not that much of a drinker. Oh, except when I'm out clubbing,' she adds hastily.

'Well, I didn't, I mean, if you wanted juice, or something . . .'

Looking back, Chloë realises that except for that first gin and tonic, which Angela barely touched, she's never seen her drinking. Surely that's something she should have known, after a whole month? Sometimes, she can be really oblivious.

'No, nothing,' Angela says. 'Don't worry about it. I'm good.'

They stand awkwardly for a moment, not quite looking at each other. Chloë places a tentative hand on Angela's arm. 'In that case – Wow, you're cold. Are you OK?'

'I'm fine.' Angela's voice is tight. 'It's from being outside without a coat.'

'Maybe I should get you warmed up?' Chloë asks. Angela doesn't answer. Chloë tries again. 'Because now that I've got you alone in my place at last, I should probably take advantage of you. If, if you'd like that.'

She tugs gently on Angela's arm, angling her towards the couch. After a brief hesitation, Angela lets herself be led. They sit, Angela's dress making a soft rustling sound as the vinyl brushes against the upholstery.

Chloë's glad she stripped the sheets off this morning. She can live without the reminder that she's about to do this on her great-aunt's bed.

She leans in and softly kisses Angela on the lips. They're almost icy, like her arm was. 'There.' She kisses her again, and this time, Angela kisses her back. 'This is a much better use of our time, don't you think?'

Chloë feels Angela's body relax into hers. The tension she's sensed throughout the night dissolves as they caress. Chloë holds her close, and then pulls back to look at her. That pale and perfect face, framed by blonde hair like gold embroidery thread. So beautiful.

'Definitely a better use of the time,' Angela says as she runs her fingers through Chloë's curls. 'I very much agree.'

'That's what I was hoping you'd say. Oh, and just so you know, I'm wearing the underwear you bought me.' Chloë leans in for another kiss.

'Good. I'm looking forward to it.'

It's a long kiss. Chloë doesn't mind the chill; she's sure they'll warm up soon. She wraps her arms around Angela, feeling the contours of her body beneath the smooth, slightly sticky material of her dress. Angela trails her fingertips delicately down Chloë's leg.

'Feeling a little less jittery now?' Angela asks when they finally break apart. 'Not so worried about your apartment? Not so nervous about me coming in?' She bends her head and presses her lips against Chloë's neck, her tongue darting out for a quick lick.

'Much less jittery,' Chloë murmurs. 'I guess I just needed a reminder that you don't bite.'

Angela goes completely still. Then, without another word, she gently disengages herself from Chloë's arms and withdraws to the other side of the couch, her face turned away.

Chloë sits there, stunned.

This is all backwards, she suddenly thinks. *I should be the one with the problem here. Aren't antidepressants supposed to kill your sex drive?* She slumps against the back of the couch, struggling not to feel rejected. She almost wishes that the Zoloft did have that effect on her, so she wouldn't have to deal with her gnawing frustration. At the moment, having no desire at all sounds like it might be the better option.

Like the brush-offs she's been getting whenever she asks if Angela's unhappy, this isn't the first time something like this has happened lately. Although this is the first time Angela put a stop to it right in the middle of foreplay. Chloë had hoped things were turning around when she got the sexy underwear as a present last night. Apparently not.

It's time, she decides, to ask the questions she's been afraid of asking. No matter how much the thought makes her heart race.

She has to find out what's wrong.

CHAPTER THIRTY-TWO

Somerville

12 December 1999

Angela is keeping her face averted, so she can't see Chloë's expression. It hardly matters. She can practically feel the disappointment radiating from the other side of the couch.

Get back in, she silently commands her fangs. *Go away. Please, go away.*

They don't. The two spikes stay relentlessly present. Sharp and insistent, impossible to ignore. Thirst starts clawing its way up her throat like a trapped animal. The need is so strong she can barely think about anything else.

She hears soft sounds of movement from behind her as Chloë straightens her clothing. Getting herself back together. Giving up.

'Angela. What's going on with you?' Chloë asks.

'Nothing!' Angela says, not turning around. 'Nothing's wrong. Everything's good.' She expects her voice to come out as a dry croak. To her surprise, she sounds perfectly normal.

'Is it?' Chloë's reply is hesitant. 'Because sometimes I feel like you're giving me mixed messages.'

Angela wants to scream. But she says, very softly, 'I don't mean to.'

She truly doesn't. She wants more than anything to tear off Chloë's clothes. Kiss her all over.

Bite her neck.

'Do you want to talk about it?' Chloë asks. 'Is it something I'm doing?'

'No! Look, it's not you. I've been having a rough few days. I . . .' Angela battles with her instincts, trying to get them under control.

She could turn around right now. Show Chloë her fangs. Worst-case scenario is that Chloë would run out of the room screaming.

No. That's not the worst-case scenario at all. The worst-case scenario is that Chloë would stay. Be understanding. Kind. Talk it over, think about it. And then offer her a drink again. A different kind of drink.

'I need to ask you for a big, big favour,' Tess said.

Angela keeps her mouth firmly shut as she turns to face her girlfriend. Rather than say anything, she reaches into her handbag and pulls out a piece of paper, which she hands to a puzzled-looking Chloë.

Frowning, Chloë unfolds it. 'Is that – that's a picture of you, isn't it?' She scans the flyer more closely. 'Wait . . . the photographer, is that *the* Tess? Your ex?'

Angela nods, her lips pressed together into a tight line. Swallowing on a dry throat. Nothing there to swallow.

Chloë looks up from the paper, wide-eyed. 'Do you think she put this out on purpose? So you'd see it?'

Angela pulls back, blinking. It hadn't occurred to her that it could be some kind of deliberate revenge. Or even Tess's fucked-up way of trying to get in touch. Angela sure as hell isn't dropping by the gallery to find out.

'Why didn't you tell me?' Chloë goes on. 'I mean, I can understand how upsetting this has got to be, but I wish you'd let me know.'

It doesn't matter what Tess had in mind. Angela turns her face away again before she speaks. 'It was hard to talk about.' Especially when she only found out about it this afternoon. *Liar*, she berates herself. *Filthy liar.* She doesn't know why she feels so vile about this one in particular. What's one more lie on top of all the others? 'It's still hard to talk about.'

'Well, I'm glad you finally said something.' Chloë sounds noticeably less tense. 'You can always do that with me, OK?'

'I'm sorry I kept quiet about it.' Which would be the truth, if they were discussing what the problem really was. 'That wasn't fair.'

She wonders if Chloë is going to press any further. Wonders if everything will come rushing out of her mouth if Chloë asks her about Tess. About anything.

'Hey, it's all right,' Chloë reassures her. 'I'm not mad at you.'

Chloë doesn't ask anything else when Angela doesn't respond. She lets it lie there, no questions after all. Crisis averted.

Maybe, Angela thinks, *I haven't completely destroyed this.* Maybe some part of the evening can be salvaged. She could cry with relief. And disappointment.

She can't keep facing away from Chloë whenever she wants to talk, though. It's beginning to look ridiculous. She twists back around, putting her elbow on the back of the couch, her hand just below her nose, covering her mouth. Like resting her chin on her hand, only higher.

It has to look just as absurd as having her head turned the other way, if not more so. Chloë is certain to notice. She has to say something, make some comment. Doesn't she?

Angela looks up to find Chloë taking a deep breath, trying on a shy smile. 'You know, I was worried you were upset with me, but since you're not, I've been wanting to . . . We've never really talked about where we're going. The two of us, long term.'

'Are we a couple now?'

Tess tilted her head, smiled. 'Aren't we?'

'I guess we are.'

Angela doesn't make a sound. *Ask me why my hand is in front of my mouth*, she thinks, trying to prompt the question by sheer force of will. *Come on. You have to have realised it's not normal. It's obvious. I'm acting bizarre.*

'I think you're incredible, you know that, right?' Chloë says.

'You shouldn't,' Angela responds, breaking her silence. 'I'm, I'm not all that.'

'Yes, you are.'

'Don't.' She shifts uncomfortably. 'I mean, I've got lousy taste in movies, right?'

There's a slight hesitation before Chloë says, 'OK, I'll admit that much is true.'

Her gaze drops down to Angela's hand, and her brow creases in confusion. *Good*, Angela thinks. *Ask me about it. Ask me why my body is ice cold. Ask me why I just blatantly changed the subject, even though I'm pretty sure it hurt your feelings. Maybe badly. Please, I'm begging you, ask.*

Chloë doesn't. She stands up instead. The upholstery creaks as she rises from the couch. 'We probably should have guessed from the poster,' she says with a nonchalance that sounds forced.

It takes Angela a moment to realise Chloë is talking about the film. 'The poster?'

'Yeah, it was a lesbian vampire movie. It's a cliché, like soap opera amnesia, or angel glurge. Never a good sign.'

Chloë is gazing out the window, watching the wind blow through the leafless tree outside. Angela drops her hand away from her mouth.

Look at me. Turn and look at me when I talk.

'I don't know what that word means,' Angela says. 'Glurge.'

'Oh, glurge means a sentimental little inspirational story about the triumph of the human spirit. Like an angel popping up from nowhere to bring someone out of despair through the power of fortune cookie wisdom. That kind of thing. I read hundreds of them every year.'

Chloë is pacing now, back and forth in the limited space allowed by the clutter. She still isn't looking at Angela, who starts to feel an unreasonable rage building.

'What does that have to do with lesbian vampires?'

'They're a different kind of cliché. Although I guess you could write glurge about lesbian vampires. But they're usually about sex fear.'

Turn and look at me. 'Sex fear?'

Her mouth is wide open on both words. Sex. Fear. Gleaming white fangs obvious for anyone to see. If anyone were paying attention.

'Monsters are people's fears made manifest, right?' Chloë answers. 'The vampire myths everyone knows best started with the Victorians, so they're all about terrifying sex. Sexual domination, sexual perversion. And when it's a woman, you get the vampire as a lesbian sexual predator. The horrible vampire women out to seduce and destroy poor, innocent girls.'

There's a long pause while Angela takes that in.

'I see,' she says icily. 'Well, thanks for clearing that up.'

Chloë stops pacing and glances over. 'Is everything all right? I know I keep asking that, but–'

Angela gets up from the couch, and starts making her way towards the door. 'Maybe I should go.'

Chloë chases after her. 'No, wait, don't go. What did I say?'

Angela is already fiddling with the lock. 'Look, let's call it a night.'

'I was lecturing you. I do that sometimes. I'm sorry.' Chloë lays her hand on Angela's arm.

Angela goes still. She can feel the pulse in Chloë's palm. A double-beat rhythm, one-two, one-two, one-two. 'Will you please, please back off?'

Chloë holds on more tightly. 'No! Look, would you for once just tell me what's wrong?'

Angela turns and grabs Chloë's arms, moving faster than a

human can. She spins Chloë around and thrusts her against the wall. It's easy. So easy. It doesn't matter that Chloë is bigger than she is. It's no more difficult than picking up a soda bottle and twisting off the top.

She keeps a firm grip on both of Chloë's wrists, pinioning her arms against her sides. Chloë is too stunned to say anything, or maybe she simply hasn't had time.

With a darting movement, Angela presses her mouth against Chloë's neck.

And bites.

CHAPTER THIRTY-THREE

Somerville
12 December 1999

At first, Chloë doesn't know what to make of what's happening.

When Angela pushes her against the wall, she wonders if it's foreplay. When Angela's mouth lands on her neck, she decides it must be. Her body is relaxing into the kiss when she suddenly feels a sharp, intense pain.

Chloë screams.

She tries to pull away, but Angela's grip is as solid as a pair of handcuffs. Her arms don't budge when Chloë strains against them. Chloë can feel Angela sucking on her neck. Swallowing. Swallowing more.

The pain has subsided to a dull ache, but she's starting to feel dizzy. Black fuzz gathers at the edges of her vision, and the room blurs away. Everything is moving in slow motion. She can't tell how much time has passed. A few seconds? A minute? More?

This doesn't make sense. None of this makes any sense.

Another useless push against Angela. She isn't sure Angela even notices.

It's hard to keep her eyes from shutting. Every time she blinks, it becomes a fight to force them back open. Sometime soon, her eyelids are going to go down and not come up again.

'Angela,' Chloë manages to say, her voice barely above a whisper. 'Angela. *Stop.*'

Angela stills for a bare instant, then jumps back. Her eyes are wide as she stares at Chloë. Her lips are wet.

Chloë's neck throbs where the cool air hits it. She's so lightheaded that she nearly topples over when Angela lets her go. She braces herself against the wall for support.

'What,' Chloë begins. Stops. Tries again. 'What was that?'

Almost instantly, somehow, Angela is all the way across the room, crumpled against the far wall. As far away from Chloë as she can get.

'I'm sorry, I'm sorry, I'm sorry, I'm sorry . . .' Angela is practically chanting the words, only those words, over and over. She's covered her eyes with her hands. Chloë wonders why she isn't explaining what she did, why she did it. There has to be some kind of explanation.

When Chloë lifts her fingers to the stinging spot on her neck, they come away bloody.

'You bit me.' She should be yelling, screaming it, but it comes out a blank statement of fact. Dull surprise is the strongest emotion she can muster.

Angela looks up at her. Her eyes are as wet as her lips. 'I'm so, so sorry.'

Chloë is at a complete loss, utterly unable to process whatever's going on. 'Why did you bite me?'

Angela makes a sound that's something like a choking laugh. 'Haven't you put it together yet?'

'Angela, what the hell just happened?'

'I'm up all night long!' Angela's voice rises. She's nearly shouting. 'I don't need a coat in December because I never feel the cold! And,

and' – she makes a sweeping gesture indicating her black vinyl clothing – 'and who dresses like this? All the time? Then I took you to that movie, and you still didn't get it, and—'

'Didn't get what? I don't understand what you're talking about!'

'Me,' Angela says. 'Vampire.'

Chloë shakes her head, trying to clear it. 'What?'

'I'm a vampire. As in, evil, vile thing. Complete with neck biting, and no sunlight, and living on blood.'

'That's . . . that's not possible.'

This can't be happening. Chloë's mind lurches after anything that would make the world rational again. An answer that would force everything to make sense. Maybe one of them has gone insane. Or both of them have.

But even as Chloë tries to dismiss the idea, a nagging part of her points out that what Angela is saying would account for an awful lot. The more Chloë thinks about it, the more pieces belatedly fall into place. She's never seen Angela eat food. Not once, in a whole month. Angela works only at night, and she sleeps during the day. All day long. Every single day.

Chloë abruptly recalls the moment earlier in the evening when Angela hovered outside the front door, waiting for Chloë to ask her to come inside. You have to give them permission, she remembers. That's one of the rules she's seen come up in books. You have to invite vampires in, or they can't cross the threshold.

And Chloë had invited her right in.

'I can't, I don't . . . Why did you . . .' Chloë tries to think of something coherent to say. Her thoughts have begun to jumble, overlapping one another like dozens of voices all talking at once. 'You're a vampire?' she finally asks, stupidly.

'I'm so sorry,' Angela says once more, rising to her feet.

Chloë can only watch, open-mouthed, as Angela runs out through the front door.

PART SIX

Bloodless Cadavers With Neck Hickeys

CHAPTER THIRTY-FOUR

Scottsdale, Arizona
3 September 1997

The corner of the living room is one of the few places in the house she's managed to carve out as her own.

The darkroom is Tess's entirely. Angela sleeps in that room almost every day, but if she and all her possessions vanished tomorrow it would look the same. Any trace of Angela near Tess's precious equipment is treated as an alien invader and summarily removed. And while she may have more reasons to use the bathroom than Tess does, everything in it marks it as Tess's property. Tess's towels, Tess's hair dye, Tess's choices in soap and shampoo and toothpaste. Angela's only contribution is a toothbrush.

The kitchen is hers, though. The messy rituals of cooking, eating, and washing up are things Tess has no interest in. They've never had a meal together. Well, Angela is there when Tess feeds, of course. But Tess doesn't like to watch Angela eat.

And, without question, the desk in the living room is hers. Shoved into a corner, but absolutely hers. Papers carefully ordered on the surface in neat piles, unmatched mugs with traces of tea lingering at the bottom, the hum of her computer and the whirr of her box fan. A little intrusion of the modern day staring down the antique furniture scattered across the rest of the room.

It could hardly be anyone else's. God knows she spends enough time sitting here.

Angela squints at the screen as she pages back to the beginning of the document, bracing herself for another round of edits. The Time Allocation Committee will look for any excuse to reject a proposal so they can winnow down the stack. It has to be perfect. She starts proofreading her writing from the top.

According to theoretical models, planets can sculpt complex structure in their natal discs during the process of formation, which should be observable at the debris disc stage. Features such as gaps and spirals could be considered signposts of recently completed planet formation. However, complex structures might form with no planets present, so considerable care in data analysis and modelling is necessary to attempt to elucidate the origins of imaged structure in any given disc . . .

She frowns at the wording and makes some minor changes. It's the fifth time she's been through it today. Or maybe the sixth? Her eyes are tired and the letters are blurring together.

She's debating with herself whether 'determine' might be a better word to use than 'elucidate' when someone grabs the back of her chair and spins her around.

'What—' It's all she has time to say before Tess's hand hits her face.

The force of the blow knocks her out of the chair and sends her sprawling to the floor. The fan topples over and starts making a stuttering noise.

Above her, Tess is waving some kind of paper in the air. Her face is contorted in rage. She's screaming something, words that Angela has to sort out from the ringing in her ears.

'Did you think I wouldn't *notice*?'

Angela doesn't answer, doesn't even get up from the carpet, all her attention taken by the pain blooming in her jaw. She tries to open her mouth. It hurts, but she doesn't think it's broken.

That means Tess wasn't using her full strength. She doesn't ever use her full strength on Angela. Never has, and never will. It's important to remember that. If she had, it would have shattered the jawbone like glass. Angela has seen Tess put her fist straight through a cinderblock wall.

Tess doesn't hit her that often. Only when she's very, very angry. And Angela can always calm her down. She will, as soon as she can think straight.

'I said, did you think I'd never notice?' Tess asks again.

'Notice?' Angela croaks from the floor. The carpet fibres scratch against her skin. She still doesn't get up. Safer that way. Tess wouldn't kick her when she's down. 'I don't, what did I do, I don't know . . .'

Tess drops whatever she's been waving around in front of Angela. Not a piece of paper. A photo. Dark streaks are blotted across the image, obscuring whatever it used to be a picture of.

Oh, crap.

Light will only spoil a photo if it hasn't been fixed. Tess must have been planning to play with this one, dodge it or burn it or something. Angela hadn't known that Tess had left one out, left it unfinished. Hadn't known she'd get caught.

Tess crouches down, brings her face close to Angela's. 'How many times,' she asks, too quietly, 'have you opened the door when I'm asleep?'

'Almost never! Only, only a couple of times.'

'Fuck.' Tess stands back up and stalks away from Angela, across the living room. 'Fuck, fuck, FUCK!' She kicks at one of the spindly wooden chairs. Its leg snaps in two and it topples to the ground. The fan, the chair, Angela. Soon the whole room is going to be broken on the floor. 'That could kill me, Angela. I could die.'

She's right. She's absolutely right. Tears streak down Angela's cheeks. 'I'm sorry! It was just open a crack, I was so careful, I promise. The sun didn't come anywhere near you!'

'You're sorry.' Tess gives her an incredulous look. 'You almost murdered me in my sleep, but you're sorry.'

'Yes! I'm sorry!' Angela is outright sobbing now, tears pouring out, snot clogging her nose. She draws herself into a sitting position and tries to explain. 'Last night, I was – I had to go to the bathroom. I had to. I tried to hold it, I tried, but it hurt so much.'

'You had to go to the bathroom.' Tess's voice is flat. 'You've been risking my life so you can pee.'

'It hurt!'

'Then pee in a goddamn bucket!' Tess is across the room again in a blur of movement, screaming in Angela's face. 'Pee in the goddamn corner! Pee anywhere you want except outside the fucking DOOR!'

Angela has never been sure exactly what will happen if Tess is exposed to sunlight. Tess almost never answers questions. Whenever Angela asks about what she is, what she can do, Tess grouses that she isn't a test subject and doesn't do party tricks. It's maddening to Angela, a constant itch she hasn't been allowed to scratch. But she's learned to stop asking.

It's been clear since the beginning, though, that sunlight hitting her girlfriend would mean something very, very bad. Angela should have known better.

'Maybe . . . maybe it would be easier if I didn't sleep in there,' she says, barely loud enough to be heard.

Tess stops short, her mouth snapping shut, cutting off the rest of her diatribe. She opens it again, just wide enough to growl out a single word. 'What?'

'Safer for you.' Angela sniffles, wishing there was a tissue within reach. 'If I slept out here on the couch instead. I mean, I already do that when I've got classes, or –'

'No. Absolutely not.'

'But it'd be less dangerous. For you.'

'It wouldn't be dangerous if you didn't act like a moron!' Tess snaps at her. 'What the hell were you thinking?'

'I wasn't thinking. It was stupid.'

'Goddamn right it was stupid.' Tess's tone is calmer. 'Look, I want you in there because you're my girlfriend. I want to sleep in the same bed with you. You're already leaving me by myself half the time as it is. You get your own room, all of a sudden we're nothing but housemates. And then one of these days you'll tell me you want to get your own place.'

'That won't happen.'

'It will. Once you start drifting apart like that, you keep on drifting. You'll move out of the room, then out of the house, then one day I'll get a call and you'll tell me you're seeing someone else.' Tess frowns, suddenly suspicious. 'That's not what this is about, is it? You want your own bed so you can fuck other people?'

'No!' Angela gives Tess a pleading look. 'Don't start that again. Please.'

'That better not be what this is about.' But after leaving that to hang in the air, Tess lets it drop. 'Hey, I love you. You're my angel. I want you next to me when I'm asleep. Is that so hard to understand?'

Angela hesitates. There's a lot she'd like to say. Ever since she moved in, she's been struggling. Sometimes she gets scarcely any sleep at all. More than sometimes. Usually. Constantly shifting between a daytime schedule when she has classes and a night-time schedule when she doesn't leaves her exhausted and disoriented. Even when the school is on a break, the smell of chemicals in the darkroom keeps her up and makes her feel sick.

And lying next to Tess's still, unbreathing body all day long doesn't feel like snuggling with a girlfriend. It feels like trying to fall asleep next to a corpse. It's worse when Tess hasn't fed for a while and her flesh is cold to the touch, like some half-defrosted hunk of meat in the bed.

But Angela doesn't think this is the right time to bring any of that up. Tess could have died. Angela could have killed her. Putting up with a little discomfort seems like a small price to pay in comparison.

'OK,' Angela says. 'You're right. We're girlfriends. We should sleep in the same bed together, whenever we can. And I, I'll bring in a bucket. Something.'

Tess doesn't reply for an agonisingly long time, but then says, 'All right.'

She offers her hand to Angela. Angela takes it and finds herself being pulled to her feet, then drawn into an embrace. Angela sags with relief against Tess, letting the smaller woman bear the whole of her weight. The knot in her stomach unclenches.

She has to remember the good times whenever things get like this. That's what keeps her going. Late nights drinking and dancing. Caressing her girlfriend's naked curves during foreplay, during sex, in the afterglow, still a wonder to her after almost a year. Tess buying her extravagant gifts on a whim – jewellery, clothes, candy, exotic flowers. Feeling the fangs behind Tess's closed lips when they kiss in public, a secret only the two of them share.

As long as she can keep Tess happy, everything will be all right. She starts planning how she's going to explain the bruises on her face to her classmates and professors the next time she has to go in.

Tess pulls back from the embrace, flashes a bright smile up towards Angela.

'Let's go out. Go to a club, cheer ourselves up. We haven't done that for weeks.'

'Oh.' Angela can't help but glance towards her computer, the screensaver drawing abstract patterns across the monitor. 'I really can't. Not tonight.' She attempts her own smile back at Tess. 'I've got to keep working on this stupid Hubble proposal.'

'Just for a few hours. Come on, you need a break, anyway.'

'Tess.' A pleading note enters Angela's voice. 'It's due in two days.'

'Yeah, but that's not tonight, or even tomorrow night. Don't work yourself to death. It's not good for you.'

'I have to. Look, as soon as it's submitted, I'm all yours.'

Tess is no longer smiling. She takes a half-step towards Angela's computer. 'You know, sometimes I think you love that thing more than you love me.'

Angela moves between Tess and the computer, panic setting back in. So much effort sitting in that hard drive. 'Don't be ridiculous. It's work, that's all.'

She knows she's being paranoid. Tess wouldn't do that to her. Nevertheless, some part of her mind is trying to figure out how long she can hold Tess away from the computer if she has to. Even thinking it feels like a betrayal.

The answer, of course, is not very long. Tess can toss her aside like a ragdoll if she feels like it.

Tess looks from Angela to the computer. Her fingers slowly uncurl. 'I miss you,' she says grumpily. 'You've been spending all your time messing around with that thing.'

Angela lets herself exhale.

'I know, I'm sorry. And you know what? You're right. I can get away for a few hours. Let's go out.'

'You sure?'

'Yeah, I shouldn't neglect you. Especially after . . . I shouldn't neglect you. Come here.' Angela holds out her arms and, after a moment, Tess lets herself be held.

Angela decides to e-mail a copy of the HST proposal to herself as soon as she can steal some time tonight. It's common sense. You should always have a backup. She'll send it as an attachment while Tess is changing for the club.

'I love you so much,' Tess whispers in her ear.

Angela can spare a little time to go out, if it'll keep her girlfriend happy. Nothing's going to get done on a night when Tess is feeling resentful, anyway. In the long run, coaxing her into a better mood now means Angela will have more time to work later.

Lost in her own thoughts, she hardly notices the sharp sting in her neck when Tess latches on and starts to feed.

CHAPTER THIRTY-FIVE

Davis Square, Somerville
15 December 1999

Esther's feet crunch on a thin layer of snow as she walks away from Davis Square, groceries in hand. A small flurry finally arrived last night, the first of the year. And a sign of more in the days to come, if she's reading the weather right. She hopes she is; there's nothing quite like a white solstice to relieve the gloom of long winter nights. The sun is out for the moment, but a bank of dark clouds blowing in from the east promises another snowfall sooner rather than later.

The light dusting that's already fallen has given everything a bit of sparkle in the late afternoon light. It's still new enough to be pretty. Fresh and clean, the white yards and rooftops like blank sheets of paper, waiting to be written on.

She nearly slips when she steps on a frozen puddle, but manages to catch herself before she falls, clutching the plastic grocery bags to her chest. Wouldn't do to drop them, break all the eggs in the carton. Or break her hip, for that matter. You might only be as old as you feel, but ageing bones are still ageing bones.

Esther turns onto the side street where Chloë lives, passing by the laundry service on the corner. Immediately after comes Chloë's building, a squat structure covered in peeling brown paint. Even the snow can't do much to cheer it up. She lets herself into the apartment with the spare key.

Neither Chloë nor Ari are there to greet her, but past the kitchen, music is quietly slipping out from under the door to Ari's room. It's the *City of Angels* soundtrack again; right now it's on 'What You Don't Know About Women'. He plays that CD quite often. There's something a tad self-indulgent about the choice, in Esther's opinion, but who is she to sit in judgement?

Chloë, no doubt, remains barricaded inside her own bedroom, at least judging by the firmly shut door. She's barely poked her head out for days. Esther raps gently on the barrier.

'Chloë? Would you like some dinner? I bought groceries.'

There's no reply. Small surprise there. After Chloë's tearful, semi-coherent description of what happened on Sunday night, she hasn't said much of anything. An understandable reaction, all things considered, but Esther can't help but wonder how long it's going to last.

She considers asking Ari for advice again, but truth to tell, his suggestions haven't been all that useful. His particular brand of religious mysticism is too off-putting to Chloë to get through to her. Ah, well. If it isn't Chloë he's here to help, he must be around for some other reason. The cards, after all, have indicated that he's going to be of crucial aid to someone. Esther is firmly of the belief that everyone and everything fulfil some role in a greater plan. Even if, in the current situation, Ari's place in the plan seems rather obscure.

Esther heads to the kitchen and starts putting the groceries away. There's plenty of space on the shelves for them now that she's cleared some things out. She's done what she can to continue cleaning in bits and pieces, whatever she thinks might help. It's not as if Chloë ever asked her to stop. She doesn't think anything she's thrown away will be missed. Some of the 'food' she got rid of had to have predated Chloë's divorce.

She's almost done when the telephone rings. She pauses with a bag of chilli peppers halfway in the crisper. There's a chance, she supposes, that Chloë might come out to answer it.

After a few rings, it becomes clear that isn't going to happen. And she knows Ari won't willingly get it either; he's peculiar about the phone for some reason. Esther shuts the refrigerator door and goes to pick it up herself.

'Hello?'

'Um, hi,' says the voice on the other end. 'This is Shelly? I work with Chloë. Is she home, by any chance?'

'She's home, yes,' Esther answers. 'But she hasn't come out of her room in quite some time. I can see if she'll emerge to talk, if you like, but I doubt it.'

'Oh. Well, yes. I'd appreciate that.'

Esther pulls the phone away from her head and yells at the bedroom door. 'CHLOË! PHONE CALL FOR YOU!'

Once again, there's no reply. She stares at the door for a while, hoping it will open. When it doesn't, she brings the phone back to her ear.

'No good?' Shelly asks.

'I'm afraid not. Sorry.'

'She didn't make it into work today, or come over to watch *Buffy* last night, so I wanted to check on her.'

Ah, yes, that's right. It's Wednesday. Chloë should have put some time in at her barely-a-job. 'Is she in trouble?'

'No, no, I covered for her,' Shelly reassures her. 'I figured she was probably having a bad time because of . . . I thought she might not be doing too well.'

At least Chloë hasn't managed to get herself fired, on top of everything else. Esther already has her work cut out for her without that getting thrown into the mix.

'I know she's alive, at least,' she says to Shelly, 'because I can

227

hear something moving around in there from time to time, and I know it's not the cat, because the cat makes a good deal more noise than that.'

'Oh.'

'She seems fairly determined to wallow for a while.'

'Yeah, I thought she might be back to doing that. I don't know exactly what's going on, but I think a few days ago she had some kind of fight with her, uh . . .' Shelly hesitates.

'Girlfriend,' Esther supplies. 'I know.'

'Oh. Good. Angela seemed pretty upset.' Shelly sighs. 'She won't talk to me about it, either.'

'Mm,' Esther says noncommittally.

'Say, do you mind if I ask, are you Chloë's mother?'

Esther laughs. 'No. Her aunt. I'm staying with her while I'm in town. There was a bit of business I needed to take care of here.'

'Ah. Well, I'm glad she has you there to look after her. Let her know that I called, OK?'

'I will,' Esther promises.

After she hangs up, Esther grabs the rag and spray bottle she's left on an end table. She's managed to clear off a few surfaces, but they're in need of a good scrub. She only has time for a few quick wipes when the door to Chloë's room creaks open.

Chloë stands in the doorway and gazes blearily out. She's wearing the same pyjamas Esther spotted her in yesterday, and the day before. Her eyes are red-rimmed and bloodshot, and her hair, always easily tangled, looks like an untrimmed hedge. An incongruously cheerful Hello Kitty Band-Aid has been slapped over the two neat puncture marks on her neck.

Frankly, Chloë looks like death warmed over. Maybe worse than that. Death briefly microwaved.

'Well, well, well,' Esther says. 'She walks, like unto the living.'

'Who was on the phone?' Even Chloë's voice sounds slightly rusty.

'Shelly. You missed work.'

'Oh, hell. I completely forgot.'

'It's fine, apparently. She's worried about you, though.'

'Shelly . . .' A frown line appears between Chloë's eyebrows. 'Do you think I should warn Shelly? And Mike? About what Angela is? She's been living in their basement for months.'

'If she's been there for months without a problem, I doubt they're in much danger.'

'Maybe. Do you think so? I've got no idea what kind of behaviour is normal for . . . you know. Them.' Chloë stumbles over to the armchair and collapses into it.

Esther puts the cleaning supplies down and takes a few steps towards Chloë. She tries not to get too close; she knows she has an uncomfortable tendency to hover over anyone in distress. It generally doesn't help.

'You don't know?' she asks. 'I thought you'd been observing one of "them" pretty closely for some time now.'

Chloë ignores that. 'I can't imagine how I'd break the news, anyway. "Hey, Shelly, your housemate is a supernatural creature. You must believe me, your co-worker with mental health issues." That should work perfectly. Did anyone else call?'

'Not that I'm aware of.' Esther waits a short while, but Chloë doesn't seem inclined to say anything more. Eventually, she ends the lull herself. 'I'm worried about you, too, actually.'

'Huh. Maybe you should be,' Chloë says. 'Do I look like I'm getting any paler to you?'

'No.'

'All right. How about my teeth? Could you check my teeth? Any fangs?'

Chloë tries to bare all of her teeth in a grimace and thrusts her face towards Esther.

Esther gives them a brief inspection. Nothing seems amiss.

'They're fine. Chloë, that's not what I'm worried about. You've hardly come out of your room for three days.'

Chloë draws away and sinks back into the armchair. 'So?' she asks sullenly.

'Well, recent studies have proven that if you don't eat anything at all, you die.'

'That would solve a lot of problems, now, wouldn't it?'

Esther stares at her. 'What is the matter with you?'

'What's the matter with me?' Chloë sits up. 'What do you think is the matter with me? What's been the matter with me for the last two years? Why do I sit in this place rotting for weeks at a time, not writing a single damn word, not able to think, not able to do anything except read other people's shitty writing and bitch about how worthless I am?'

Chloë pushes herself up and wanders over to the window.

Esther wishes she had come to visit a good deal sooner. Years ago. Before Chloë's divorce. Before her marriage, ideally.

She'd always meant to give Chloë some guidance. Ever since she first spotted her potential, back when Chloë was a child. But somehow the years slipped by without Esther noticing. They do that rather often, these days. Time keeps getting away from her. She'd been involved in other matters, gone off travelling, had things to do.

She'd been belatedly prompted to intercede when she'd learned about Chloë's trip to the hospital. Pills. It happened quite a while ago, but Esther only found out last month. Third hand, from a cousin she happened to meet in an airport. A cousin who only knew about it because Chloë's parents had complained about having to pay for the ambulance. Sometimes, it's hard to have faith that everything is proceeding according to a plan.

As if reading Esther's mind, Chloë suddenly says, 'Mom and Dad would not approve of the way my life is going. They'd definitely object to the existence of certain things.'

Esther snorts. 'Your parents have a remarkable ability to disapprove of whatever doesn't fit their preconceptions.'

Chloë glances over at her. 'What about you? You seem pretty accepting of the stuff your crazy niece blurted out hysterically a few nights ago.'

'Everything else aside, the two little round holes in your neck were fairly convincing. I don't doubt the evidence of my own eyes. I hope you won't, either.'

'No. It all makes a bizarre kind of sense to me.' Chloë drums her fingers against the windowsill. 'So you believe me. I wonder if anyone else would. My parents would pack me off to the mental hospital if I tried to talk to them about it, wouldn't they? Not that I'd blame them this time.'

'I'd blame them.'

'I know.' Chloë looks out at the darkening sky and scratches at the Band-Aid on her neck. 'Have you noticed that things seem to get worse and worse every year these days?'

Esther isn't at all sure where that comment came from. 'What do you mean?'

'I don't know. Sometimes it feels like the party's ended and everyone's hung over. Maybe the crazies are right. Maybe the world really is going to end in a couple of weeks because 2000 is a big round number. It'll all be a big smoking crater when the clock runs out.'

'I don't think so.' Esther shakes her head. 'No. Things are the same as they always were, good and bad.'

'Well. That's depressing.'

Chloë picks her Zoloft bottle up from where she's hidden it and takes it into the kitchen. Esther follows a few paces behind and watches as Chloë fills a water glass. The CD playing in Ari's room has moved on to 'With Every Breath I Take'. Esther wishes it weren't something quite so maudlin, although it probably doesn't matter much; Chloë doesn't seem to be paying it any attention.

'Did you skip three days' worth of your meds?' Esther asks.

Chloë shrugs. 'I guess so.'

Esther taps her foot on the linoleum and fixes Chloë with her most disapproving expression. 'Relapse is such an ugly word.'

'You know, you can't relapse into mental illness unless at some point you stopped being mentally ill.'

'Only a few days ago, you were feeling downright perky,' Esther points out. ' "Glowy", I think was the word you used.'

'Well, it didn't take much to change that.' Chloë swallows her pill and chugs a few gulps of water.

'No, you're right,' Esther says. 'Most people take it in perfect stride when they find out their girlfriend is one of the living dead.'

Chloë makes a frustrated noise, nearly choking on a swallow as she puts her glass down. She coughs a few times to clear her throat. 'You can't have it both ways. You can tell me hiding in my room and skipping my meds is bad, or you can tell me it's normal, but you cannot do both.'

'Why not?' Esther asks.

'I don't know,' Chloë says. 'Look, this isn't fair. I can't do this. I don't have enough energy to figure out why you're wrong right now.' She glances past Esther towards the telephone in the other room. 'I just wish . . .' she starts, trailing off.

'What?'

'Nothing. It doesn't matter. I'm sorry I'm such a mess.' She brushes past Esther and trudges back towards her bedroom. 'And I thought I was doing so well, you know?'

'But you were.'

Chloë's laugh is a harsh, sharp bark. 'Are you kidding? Look at me! I've completely fallen apart. I've been wearing the same underwear for three days. I'm not up to dating anyone. What was I thinking?'

'That's amazing,' Esther says. 'I can't believe how fast you've somehow made this out to be your fault.'

'It is my own damn fault. I should know by now that I shouldn't ever try to depend on other people to make me happy.'

'Because they'll hurt you?'

'Because it's stupid. It's too much to ask.'

Esther steps up next to Chloë. 'Can't two people ever be happy to be with each other because they're in love?'

'The last time I thought that, someone bit me.'

'Do you think,' Esther says, 'it would help if we did a card reading?'

Chloë blinks, surprised by the sudden change in subject. 'What? No. I'm not eight years old. Where did that come from? I thought we got past this in November.'

'It could clarify matters for you.'

'No. Come on, it's nonsense. Make-believe isn't going to be useful right now.'

'That's a bold stance coming from someone with a vampire girlfriend.'

Chloë's eyebrows crease at that, but before she can reply, the telephone rings.

Chloë jerks back in surprise, and stares at it as if she doesn't completely understand what it's doing. On the fifth ring, Esther once again picks it up herself.

'Hello?' says the voice on the other end. 'Chloë, is that you? Please don't hang up.'

Esther recognises it. Angela.

She turns to Chloë. 'It's her.'

'It is? What, what does she want?'

Esther hands her the phone. 'Why don't you ask her?'

Chloë quickly covers the mouthpiece with her hand. 'Because what if,' she hisses to Esther, 'she wants to drag me back to her lair and make me her mind-controlled slave?'

'Through the telephone?'

Chloë thinks about that. 'OK, you have a point.'

'And didn't you say her "lair" is the basement of Shelly's house?'

'She could have another one somewhere,' Chloë says, without sounding particularly convinced.

'Are you going to talk to her or just clutch the telephone?'

'Fine!' Chloë takes a deep breath and brings the phone to her ear. 'Angela!' she says brightly. 'Hi! Um, what's up?'

Chloë listens as Angela says something Esther can't quite hear. Chloë remains mute. After a pause, Angela says something else.

'What?' Chloë says. 'No, it isn't . . . I mean, sure, it can be in a public place if you want, but I wasn't, I didn't think . . .' She trails off, then starts again. 'How about the Diesel Café? In Davis Square?' She takes a quick glance at the clock. 'Would maybe an hour from now work for you? Great. So . . . I'll see you there, I guess.'

Chloë hangs up the phone and turns to Esther.

'Well,' Chloë says, 'if I'm going to be supernaturally enslaved by my girlfriend, I think I want to take a shower first.'

'That might be wise, yes. It's been a few days.'

Chloë takes a step towards the bathroom, but stops when her hand touches the doorknob. 'Was agreeing to meet her tonight a really, really bad idea?'

'I don't honestly know,' Esther tells her. She wishes she could say something more useful. If Chloë had agreed to a fresh card reading, perhaps she'd be able to. But she doubts there's time now, not with Chloë needing to get herself ready. Ah, well. It's no use worrying over might-have-beens.

It's a good sign that Angela suggested meeting in public, however. Shows consideration. That gives Esther some hope about how things might turn out. Even if she only has a reading nearly two decades old to go by, she remembers it hinting at a rocky path to a worthwhile destination.

Although, of course, it offered no guarantees that the destination would ever be reached. The cards can be cryptic that way at the best of times.

Chloë gives her armpit a sniff and wrinkles her face. 'Wow. Yeah. Definitely time to pull myself together.' She heads into the bathroom, shutting the door behind her.

Whether things go well or badly tonight, Esther decides, if nothing else she's relieved it's getting Chloë to clean up and go outside.

CHAPTER THIRTY-SIX

Excerpt From Angela's Experimental Log

TEST #48A

SUBJECT: How quick is my reaction time?

METHODOLOGY: Ruler drop test, three trials and then I gave up

RESULTS: Inconclusive, less than 1/16 inch

COMMENTS: This was a complete waste of time. It was supposed to be a simple test where I held a ruler between my thumb and forefinger, let it go, recaught it, and then looked at how far it had dropped. The problem is, it didn't drop far enough to have a measurable result. So there's not really a lot I can say about this one.

Why am I still doing these? What's the point?

Screw it. Screw all of it. I should write about the things I've actually learned. So here's the next vampire myth in the Imaginary Thesis.

Myth number two: vampires live only on blood

As far as I know, admittedly using a very low population sample, all vampires drink blood, and need to do so to survive. But from personal experience, I can attest that there are vampires who pick a particular chosen victim and feed not just on their blood, but on other things as well.

That kind starts out by telling you that they love you.

And when they do, things can be really great, at first, anyway. Maybe they've got a few problems, but you're pretty sure you can deal with it, because they love you, right?

But after a while, things start to go wrong. They get kind of cold, or they get angry for no reason. But you figure, hey, all relationships have their troubles, don't they? So you try to talk it out, make everything happy again.

But it doesn't work. They get mad at you for bringing it up at all. So, after a while, you learn never to bring up anything bad. Just smile and stay happy and maybe things won't get any better, but at least they won't get any worse.

But they do get worse. You don't know why. Everything's going wrong, and somehow it's your fault. You're not doing it right. You're not loving enough. If you loved them enough, everything would be fine, but it's not, so you need to love them more and more, but it never seems to be enough, and you think, what's wrong with me? It isn't her fault, she told me what I'm not supposed to do, but I keep fucking up.

And then one day, when she slaps you, nothing unusual, not even a hard slap, but you start screaming and screaming and kicking and biting and that was it, it was over, and it was all my fault, because if I had loved her enough, everything would have been all right, but I couldn't, I didn't have it in me, I couldn't love her enough, because I'm bad, I'm a bad, mean person and I can't really love anybody, I can't . . .

I'm sorry.

CHAPTER THIRTY-SEVEN

Diesel Café, Davis Square
15 December 1999

Chloë feels a cold wind against her back as she stands in line. Some-body must have opened the door again. The flurries that finally arrived last night have turned into a fully fledged blizzard, starting almost the moment she stepped out of her apartment to come here. It was a chilly walk over, and a blast of snow and freezing air blows into the café every time someone enters or leaves.

She glances to her right. Angela is still sitting at the table, gazing out the front windows at the steadily building snowdrifts outside. The line moves again, and Chloë shuffles forward to order a latte.

After she picks up her coffee, she goes back to the table and slides in across from Angela.

'Hi again.' Chloë gestures at her mug. 'Are you sure you didn't want me to get you one?'

'No. I mean, I don't—'

Chloë realises her mistake. 'Oh, I guess you, uh, can't. Is that true? Do I have that right?'

'Yeah.' Angela grins and affects an exaggerated Bela Lugosi accent. 'I never dreenk . . . *coffee*.' Chloë does not smile. Angela's grin fades. Her eyes search Chloë's face. 'There's snow in your hair.'

Chloë brushes a hand through her curls. It comes away wet, the snowflakes melting at her touch. 'Yeah, with my hair, it stays there unless I towel it off.'

'I like it. It looks like sugar frosting.'

Chloë feels the blood drain away from her face. So she's a dessert now. Does she always remind Angela of food? Does everyone?

Angela catches the change in Chloë's expression, and looks appalled. 'I didn't mean, I wasn't—' Angela stops, and bites her lower lip. She starts on a different tack. 'So, how have you been?'

'I've been all right.'

'All right?'

'Well, let's say I was kind of thrown by what happened.'

Angela drops her eyes and plucks at her fishnets. 'I know.'

'I didn't think I was going to get attacked. By you.' Angela shrinks further down into her chair. 'I don't need that kind of thing in my life again,' Chloë says. 'Ever. I'm done with it.'

'I know,' Angela says again.

'It's not OK. It's not at all OK. I can't even put into words . . . I can't believe you did that.'

Angela stares at her shoes and says nothing.

Another bundled-up customer comes in from outside, bringing a freezing gust and a light dusting of snow in with them. Chloë shivers, but Angela doesn't seem to notice. Well, of course she doesn't.

Chloë takes a sip of her latte, then another. Two seconds later, she can't remember what it tasted like. She puts the mug down on the table with a clink, and heaves a sigh. 'Look, why are we here?'

'I asked you to come here because I wanted to apologise.' Angela looks up at Chloë, her eyes wet. 'I'm so sorry about what happened. I didn't mean to hurt you.'

'Well,' Chloë admits hesitantly, 'I don't think it ended up being a severe wound, if that's what you're worried about. I didn't actually faint from blood loss or anything.'

'It looked like you came pretty close to it. And that's not the only thing I meant. I'm sorry I hurt you in any way. At all.'

Chloë studies Angela's face during the silence that follows. She has a lot of questions, and isn't entirely sure how much she wants to know the answers.

She decides to ask anyway. 'So. Do you, I mean, have you ever . . . There's the whole, you know, um, vampires are supposed to kill people . . .'

Angela blanches, her skin turning even paler than its normal lily-white sheen. 'Oh! I, I haven't. Killed anyone. I try to be very careful, and I haven't killed anyone. Ever.'

Chloë feels somewhat ashamed of having asked. 'I was pretty sure – I, you know, I thought so, but I thought I'd better check.'

'Of course.'

'And will I, I mean, am I going to turn into a vampire?' Chloë absently fingers the Band-Aid on her neck.

'No. You'd be one by now, if it was going to happen, and it would have started right away. You'd know. It's not like it's a subtle event.' There's another long pause while Angela seems to be trying to put together what she wants to say. 'I'm pretty sure it can't happen after only one bite.'

Chloë does not feel particularly reassured. 'So, how many does it take? Is it three, or something? More than that?'

'It takes a long time,' Angela says, looking sombre. 'At least it did for me. I don't think there's a set number. Just, enough bites, and then one day, if you die from it . . . Maybe that's something that can happen by accident, or maybe that's how things always go if it's been going on for a long enough time. Or maybe it happens when somebody is trying to kill you, I don't know for sure. But then you come back, and there you are.'

Chloë wonders what going through that must have been like. But seeing how unhappy Angela looks just thinking about it, she decides not to ask. Maybe not every single one of her questions needs an answer. She quickly moves on to something else. 'So, how many of the other myths are true? You know, garlic, crosses?'

'Oh,' Angela says. 'They're, well . . .'

She belatedly looks around to see if anyone is likely to overhear. Chloë checks the room out as well. The place is packed in spite of the weather, but the couples seated at the tables next to theirs look far too preoccupied with their own conversations to be listening to anyone else's. If anything, the low current of background noise in the crowded room is helping to keep things private. Discussions taking place only a few feet away have dissolved into an anonymous murmur by the time they reach the table.

'I'm sorry,' Angela says quietly. 'I've never talked about this kind of thing, not outside of my own head, or in stuff I only write down when I'm alone. For some reason it feels a little embarrassing. Like it's a rash, or something.'

Chloë watches her, not saying a word.

'But if anyone deserves to know, it's you,' Angela continues. 'So . . . right. Garlic and crosses make me pretty uncomfortable. I have no idea why – it doesn't make any sense to me, and believe me, I have been making a serious study of my, I guess you'd call it my condition. My reaction to them could be psychosomatic, I've never been sure. Crossing running water feels weird, but if I'm in the subway and it goes over the Charles I don't collapse or anything. Was there anything else you wanted to know?'

'I've also been wondering, how old are you? I mean, really?'

'Ah.' Angela's face takes on a misty, faraway look, and she gazes off into the unseeable distance. 'I'll say only this. In the year that I was born, Europe was nothing more than a squabbling collection of tiny countries, its eventual union not yet imagined. Gerald Rudolph

Ford had just become president of this land, and cell phones and compact discs were but distant dreams in the minds of visionaries and madmen . . .'

'Stop it,' Chloë says. 'This isn't funny.'

Angela is instantly sober again. 'I'm sorry. You're right, it's not. Anyway, yeah, I'm twenty-five. I haven't been this way all that long. I think I might not age and die naturally, but I'm not completely certain about that. Tess dropped some hints about it, but she really didn't tell me much.'

'Tess – she was the one who . . . ?'

'Yes,' Angela says curtly. 'Anyway, I know at least some of the myths about vampires aren't true, at least not for me. I'm definitely not immune to every kind of illness. And I don't think I can fly or turn into a bat or anything like that. I spent a while trying to, in the first few months, and I pretty much just felt like an idiot.'

'But there are some myths that are accurate, aren't there?' Chloë asks. 'You need an invitation to go inside a building, right?'

'You noticed, huh?' Angela's lips tighten a little. It isn't really a smile. 'Yes, that one's real. Only if someone lives there, though. Getting in here wasn't a problem. Oh, and I don't have a reflection.'

'You don't?'

Angela tilts her head towards the café's front windows. When Chloë turns, she sees herself reflected in the glass, but no sign of Angela. As far as the windowpane is concerned, Chloë is sitting alone.

Chloë looks back and forth between the window and the woman seated across from her. 'Doesn't anyone ever notice that?'

'People don't notice a lot of things.'

'How is it even possible?'

'I don't know yet,' Angela tells her. 'I haven't been able to work it out, at least not so far. Especially since it happens to my clothes when I'm wearing them, too, which is weird. Or, that is, even weirder. There's one myth that says we don't have reflections because we don't have souls.'

'I don't believe that,' Chloë says immediately. 'Not for one second.'

'Thanks.' Angela's smile is real this time, if a bit wan. 'So, does that pretty much cover what you wanted to know?'

'Well . . .' There is one more thing Chloë's been curious about. She's been staring at Angela's mouth for the whole conversation, and she still can't figure it out. 'How come I never noticed your, uh . . .'

'My what?'

'Your fangs. I mean, it's obvious you have them – I've got puncture wounds in my neck.' Chloë taps a finger on her Band-Aid. 'But I can't understand why I don't see them when you talk.'

'Oh. You don't see them because they're retractable.'

'Excuse me?'

'Like a pit viper,' Angela adds helpfully.

'Like a what?'

'Or some other snakes, rattlesnakes and puff adders – there are a bunch of them. Their fangs fold up into the roof of their mouth when they're not in use.' Angela's tone becomes more animated as she starts to warm to the topic. 'I read up on it when I was trying to find out about myself. It was one of the only things I ever learned that made complete sense. And they're fascinating creatures. Their teeth have a hollow centre where the venom goes, like a hypodermic needle.'

'Venom?' Chloë ask, a little nervously.

Angela stops short. 'I don't think there's venom in mine. I've never noticed anything like that. Although there may be some kind of clotting agent in my saliva, to help the wounds close. And . . .' She leans forward. Her eyes narrow as she searches Chloë's face. Chloë isn't sure what she's looking for. 'I've wondered if it might create some sort of bond. Have you noticed anything different in how you feel about me? I mean, I know you must feel . . . I meant weird and inexplicably different.'

'I don't think so,' Chloë says. Her emotions are a churning mess, but she isn't having any she doesn't recognise as her own. 'I might have had some kind of reaction, though,' she adds as an after-thought. 'It itches. Not a lot, but some.'

'So you're allergic to me? That's great.' Angela drops back, pulling away from the edge of her chair. She makes a noise that isn't quite a laugh. 'Anyway, it turns out that vampires have the same kind of fangs as vipers, or at least I do. They come out when I'm hungry, or when I'm excited, or both. I try not to get too hungry and too excited at the same time.'

'Oh.' Chloë suddenly makes a connection. 'Oh!'

'Yeah,' Angela says, looking down at her shoes again. 'When I haven't fed for a while and I get, when I'm aroused, that's one of the times I feel particularly bitey. I worry about getting carried away. In the heat of the moment.'

'I guess that explains some things, at least. How long can you go without, I don't know what to call it . . . without feeding before it's a problem?'

'I seem to be all right if I do it around once every two weeks.'

'Two weeks.' Chloë stirs her coffee, mostly to have something to do with her hands. 'So how many people have you bitten since we started going out?'

'None. Or, that is, only you.'

'None?'

Angela shrugs. 'I didn't feel like it. It's not exactly something I like doing.'

'So when you bit me it had been . . .'

'About a month. A little more.'

'You were starving yourself?'

Angela looks at her sharply. 'Are you trying to make excuses for me? Don't.'

'I'm not,' Chloë says. 'I'm trying to understand.'

'Do you know what I was doing, that first night at the club?' Angela asks, her voice so quiet that it almost doesn't reach Chloë across the table. 'I was drugging your drink. I only stopped because I figured out who you were. That's what I do, Chloë. I drug girls, I drag them into the bathroom, and I drink their blood.'

'Oh.' It's all Chloë can manage to say.

'I'm a predator,' Angela continues, 'just like you said. The horrible vampire woman, out to destroy innocent girls. And I've been lying to you by omission since the night we met.'

Chloë feels dizzy, even a little nauseous. 'You drug girls.'

'With sleeping pills.' Angela's words are stark, almost affectless. 'I'm a monster. Don't start to believe anything else.'

Chloë rises to her feet, pushing her chair back, standing up unsteadily. The floor feels like it's pitching and rolling beneath her. 'Listen, I'll be right back. I'm sorry. I have to –' She waves her hand vaguely towards the back of the café. 'I'll be right back,' she repeats.

Angela says nothing as Chloë flees from the table.

Chloë pushes her way through to the other side of the crowded café, squeezing past the bodies jammed between the counter and the condiments table. Beyond that, customers are spilling out of the booths onto extra chairs borrowed from other tables. There seems to be no end to them, an interminable mass of people talking, sprawling in their seats, blocking her way. When she makes it to the bathroom, she sees to her relief that it's unoccupied. She ducks inside and slams the door shut.

The bathroom is quite nice as they go, black tile and red-painted walls, reasonably clean except for a floor muddy from wet shoes. It's quiet there. She twists the deadbolt and spends a few moments just breathing, holding still as her nausea slowly subsides.

She almost misses it when it's gone. As soon as she doesn't feel sick to her stomach, she has time to think. To remember Angela's confession. *I'm a predator.* How many girls been taken into a bathroom like this one, to meet sharp teeth and blood? It almost happened to her. Did happen to her, after a long delay. She flinches with remembered pain.

But, the thought comes to her mind insistently, she didn't die. Angela doesn't kill anyone. Not if she's telling the truth, anyway. And Chloë doesn't think she's lying. She has no reason to believe that other than instinct, but she does. Even with everything else Angela told her, and even though it was all said much, much too late. Maybe she believes it because her memory of the bite goes past the pain, to Angela huddled against the wall, covering her eyes. To Angela running out the door.

So, Chloë doesn't think Angela is a murderer. Damning with faint praise. But surely it counts for something, under the circumstances?

Chloë goes to the sink and splashes some water on her face. It has a chilly bite to it. She lets it run, hoping that it will get warmer.

She looks in the mirror while she waits. Tries to imagine what it would be like to see nothing there. Tries to ask herself what she'd do in Angela's shoes. Or rather, Angela's big black shiny boots. Probably very practical for the snow. Her mind is all over the place. She attempts to force it into some semblance of order, not very successfully.

The water is almost too hot now, so she quickly dabs a little more on her face and shuts it off. A faint trace of steam rises from the sink. She pulls a paper towel out of the dispenser and dries herself off.

Are the things Angela has done inexcusable?

Maybe. But maybe not. It seems like the answer should be yes, that there should be no question, but Chloë finds that she isn't as ready to accept that as she might be, as she normally would be. Angela's situation isn't a normal one. It isn't anything like normal.

Or is Chloë making excuses for someone again, the way she did for years with Alec?

She needs to know more. She needs to know why. Because she's not even close to convinced she'd have managed things any better than Angela has. It's not like she's been perfect herself. Not at all. Although she's not sure how much it matters now, there's plenty she hasn't said that she should have. Needed to. Didn't.

There's a conversation she should have had with Angela a month ago, but she'd avoided it. Kept to the topics that seemed safe instead. Kept quiet, stayed evasive, and hoped it would go away.

She unlocks the door and steps back into the crowd and the noise. She can't hide in a bathroom forever. There are things she has to get out in the open.

CHAPTER THIRTY-EIGHT

Diesel Café, Davis Square
15 December 1999

Angela drums her fingers on the table, lost in her own thoughts. She doesn't notice Chloë approaching until she's a couple of tables away; she'd given up on trying to spot her five minutes ago. Angela watches while Chloë manoeuvres herself through the small spaces between the last few chairs.

'I was worried you'd run away out the back door,' Angela says. She's not quite joking.

The knot in Angela's stomach hasn't gone away with Chloë's return. Especially since Chloë isn't pulling out her chair, isn't sitting back down. And the expression on her face could only be called grim.

'No,' Chloë says. 'I . . . I don't think this place even has a back door.'

'Oh.'

Chloë keeps standing. Angela raises her eyebrows in an unspoken question. At this point, she'd rather Chloë get it over with.

'Listen,' Chloë finally says, 'I think you should know that, I mean, I want to tell you, that, uh . . . I think about suicide sometimes.'

'What?'

That was not on any list of things she thought Chloë might say.

'Not as much as I used to,' Chloë continues, 'but I'm not as stable, not as sane as I think you maybe thought I was. I'm on antidepressants. They don't always work.'

'Oh.' Angela takes that in. 'Are you saying – did I make it worse?'

'No!' Chloë shakes her head. 'No. I'm trying to say that there are important things I should have told you, and I didn't, OK?' Chloë sits back down at the table at last. She looks out the window, her eyes fixed on the swirling snowflakes. 'So, I'm telling you now. I don't want to leave my room, or even move, for days and days sometimes. I lose interest in doing anything or going anywhere, or even eating. I wanted you to know you weren't the only one lying by omission.'

Angela is still scrambling to catch up. 'Wait, you can't possibly believe that's the same as what I've done.'

'I'm not making comparisons. But it matters, OK? You told me you didn't want to date anyone with mental health problems, and I didn't tell you I had mental health problems.'

'I sort of knew. Shelly said something about it.'

Chloë's head whips back around to face Angela. 'She did what?'

'Not like that!' Angela adds quickly. She wants to bite her tongue. Making trouble between Chloë and Shelly is the last thing she wants to do. 'She was just talking about you in general – she wasn't being mean.'

'What did she say?'

'Not much. She didn't make a big deal out of it or anything.'

Angela can tell she's doing a terrible job of explaining things, but she can't seem to find the right words. It was the night after that first date on the mountaintop. She'd been gossiping about it with Shelly, giddy with the thrill of kissing Chloë even a full day later. Shelly was teasing her, then all of a sudden grew serious, telling her how much she respected Chloë, mentioning Chloë getting treatment, dealing with the difficulties of her past.

'Maybe Shelly should have made a big deal about it,' Chloë says. 'If you'd been with someone else, someone who wasn't so wrapped up in their own problems, they might have noticed yours.'

'Look, it doesn't matter to me. To us. If there is still an us.' Angela has somehow stumbled into saying what she's been wanting to say all night, at what might be the worst possible time. But now that it's out, there doesn't seem to be anything she can do but push forward. 'Which I guess means I'd better ask, is there? Still an us?'

Somewhere to her left there's a loud burst of chatter as a small knot of friends walk out into the night, laughing about something she can't make out. Chloë puts her hands around her coffee mug as the door swings shut behind them. Angela wonders if there's any heat left in it. She wishes she could put her own hands over Chloë's to warm them; it's only a few days after a bite so she might even be able to. But she isn't sure it would be welcome. It might even be grotesque, since she'd be using Chloë's own, stolen blood to do it.

'I don't know,' Chloë says. 'About us. You frightened me. When you exploded like that. I know I was being kind of obtuse—'

'No,' says Angela. 'Don't ever blame yourself. Ever.'

'It brought back some bad memories.'

Angela nods slowly. 'And you don't want to make the same mistake twice.'

'Would I be?'

Well. There it is. Neatly wrapped up in a three-word question.

In a small voice, Angela says, 'Maybe you would.'

Chloë stares into her coffee mug.

'You know, I've missed you,' Angela says softly. 'Even just over the last few days. I miss talking to you. I miss your green eyes, and your curly hair, and . . . I think you're the best thing that's happened to me in a long time.' She feels a tear race down her cheek. 'And I've screwed it up. I hate being undead.'

Angela sees Chloë slowly reach across the table, lay a hand on her shoulder. 'Hey, it's all right,' she says. 'Don't, you shouldn't—'

'No, it's not all right. How is any of what I've done forgivable?'

'If it was a matter of survival . . .'

Angela shrugs off Chloë's hand. 'So what? How can I ask you to accept that? To be complicit in it?'

Chloë slumps back in her chair.

'Why do you do it that way?' she asks. 'With the drinks, and the bathrooms, and the rest of it?'

'Because it's the best I could come up with,' Angela answers glumly. 'I've tried other things. Animals, blood bags. None of it works. It's like living on nothing but Diet Coke – you start to starve. I need to drink fresh, human blood, in secret, every couple of weeks. It doesn't leave me with a lot of options.'

'Why . . . You said you drug girls. Why only women?'

Angela runs her finger along the metal rim edging the table, focusing her eyes on it instead of Chloë's face. 'Because,' she says, 'it's a lot trickier if you need to go into a bathroom with a guy.'

'Oh. I thought maybe—' Chloë cuts herself off, shakes her head. 'Never mind.'

Neither of them says anything. The silence between them makes all the other sounds seem louder. Clinking spoons, muffled half-sentences, names called out as orders come up.

'What if . . .' Chloë takes a deep breath. 'Have you ever tried to find a volunteer?'

'No,' Angela says flatly.

'But—'

'I'm not going to do that.'

'You can't possibly want—' Chloë's voice has risen almost to the point of yelling. Angela looks at her in mute appeal, and she drops back down to a near-whisper. 'You can't possibly want to go on drugging people.'

'Of course I don't,' Angela hisses back. 'But volunteering? That's how I ended up this way. And I might've been lucky to survive it at all; I don't know if everyone does. You think I'm going to do that to somebody else? No. It'd be worse than what I'm doing now. Much, much worse. Believe me, I know. You can't help me with this.'

Both of them are quiet again for a long time after that.

'Maybe it's for the best, anyway, if we don't . . .' Chloë says at last. 'I mean, maybe we're not good for each other.'

And that's that, Angela thinks. Quick and easy as a thread being cut. And it's obviously the right decision. If Angela were in Chloë's position, she'd make the same choice.

She should have made that choice. Weeks ago, long before it ever got to this point. She should have been brave enough to end things herself. Or strong-willed enough not to start anything in the first place.

For that matter, she should have ended things with Tess when she had the chance, years ago. But she didn't, and now she has to live with the consequences of that. With what she's become.

What if she'd been even more out of control that night? What would have been the outcome if Chloë didn't get through to her when she said, *'Stop'*? How long would she have kept going? What if she'd hurt Chloë badly?

What if she'd killed her?

Something like that could still happen. She has a predator's instincts. Maybe it's only been luck that the worst hasn't occurred. Maybe it's inevitable. Even if she never crosses the lines she's set for herself, never bites the same victim again and again until they're either a monster or a corpse.

She needs to face up to what she is.

'You're right,' Angela says. 'You're absolutely right. I don't think it would be safe for you.'

Chloë frowns. 'I didn't mean . . . This isn't just because of you. I'm not so wonderful.'

'Don't,' Angela says, standing up. 'Just don't.'

She turns and heads towards the exit at a reckless pace, excusing herself as she brushes past other customers. She knocks aside a man with a glass of lemonade, and a large dollop of his drink splashes onto the floor. He looks at the expression on her face and decides not to make an issue of it, turning aside to let her pass.

'I'm sorry,' Chloë calls after her.

Running, running, she's always running away. She takes a final look back as she wrenches open the door. Chloë is watching her, clutching her nearly untouched coffee. In the crowded café, Chloë looks forlorn and alone.

Angela turns and scurries out of the building, into the falling snow.

PART SEVEN

You're Surrounded By Werewolves

CHAPTER THIRTY-NINE

Scottsdale, Arizona
26 August 1998

'Who the hell are they?'

Angela can't keep the snarl out of her voice as she dumps the thick pile of photos in front of Tess. They slide across the small table, some of them capsizing over the edge and dropping to the floor.

Tess continues to stare through her loupe for a few seconds, transfixed by whatever image she's singled out to put on the light box. Her dark-red hair is pulled back in a braid to keep it out of the way, making her features look sharp and angular in the stark white light coming from the bulb below.

When she looks up and swings around on her stool to face Angela, her eyes are distant. They always are in the first moments after she stops working. Her gaze slowly comes into focus as she looks down at the scattered photos.

'Where did you find these?' Tess frowns. 'Have you been snooping?'

Angela laughs. It comes out high and thin. 'No, I've been cleaning. Cleaning your house, and guess what I found shoved behind a bookcase.'

'And?'

'That's all you've got to say? "And?"'

'I don't know why you think this is supposed to be a big deal.'
Tess's tone is calm, patient. An adult trying to reason with a toddler.
'So I'm not a virgin. So fucking what? Did you think you were my
first?'

Angela doesn't feel like being reasonable. She's angry and miserable and much, much too hot. Even though there's an air conditioner
churning away in the kitchen now, the darkroom is an oven. Temperature affects how photos develop, and Tess likes it on the warm
side. But this year has been hotter than usual, making it unpleasant
in there at night, and torturous during the day. August is always the
worst. The monsoon rains don't cool the place down enough to matter; they mostly make it more humid. It's raining tonight, hard and
savage and mixed with hail in spite of the heat. Angela can hear it
clattering on the roof like a horde of rats trying to scratch their way
through. The weather makes no sense. Two years in this climate
and she still can't figure out why anyone would build a city here.

Sweat is already soaking the ridiculously impractical waist-
cinched dress Tess is having her wear today. Her whole body is damp
and itchy, sweat on the back of her neck, sweat in the creases
between her thighs and her groin. Her fingers have left smears of
moisture across the photos where she touched them.

Tess, as always, looks like she doesn't notice the heat. Doesn't
care. She's dressed all in black wool, infuriatingly indifferent to the
murderous weather. The air conditioner is one of the few concessions she's ever bothered to make about the house, and that didn't
happen until Angela literally fainted back in June. Half from the
heat, half from exhaustion.

Even then, the heat was the only part of it Tess was willing to
acknowledge; she still stubbornly refuses to let Angela sleep in
another room. She won't take any steps to protect herself, either.

They had one of their worst fights when Angela asked about putting up blackout curtains so she could leave the darkroom without putting Tess in danger. Angela eventually gave up, pleaded insomnia to a doctor at the university health centre and got herself a prescription for sleeping pills. Tess may keep her trapped in there during the day, with the chemical stench and the stifling heat, but at least she can sleep through it now.

A second air conditioner in the living room might make the whole house bearable, but she knows asking would only lead to another argument. And Angela never, ever wins arguments with Tess.

She's starting one anyway.

'Don't try to pretend it's normal to have a folder full of naked pictures of your exes –'

'I'm a photographer, idiot.'

'– hidden in your house!' Angela rolls over Tess's interruption. She's not going to let herself get sidetracked. Not this time. 'Something you never once mentioned to your girlfriend!'

'Maybe it's because I knew you'd freak out about it.'

'Dozens of them!'

'Not everyone was raised by religious crazies, Angela. Some of us slept around.'

'Stop trying to change the subject!'

'The only "subject" is you having a hissy fit over nothing.'

Angela stops, takes a deep breath. As usual, this isn't getting her anywhere. Tess will always twist away, turn it around, throw it back at her. She needs to focus, ask the questions that really matter.

'How far back do these photos go, anyway?'

Tess only snorts. She shakes a cigarette out of a pack and lights it. The scent of cloves starts to mingle with the acrid odours of developer and fixer.

Angela grinds her teeth. Tess never answers questions about her age.

The photos haven't been much help, despite Angela poring over them for hours after she found them. They're all in the grainy black-and-white style Tess prefers. Men and women, most of them probably in their late teens or early twenties. Some with a trickle of blood oozing down their neck.

No clothes to help determine the decade. Angela tried to judge based on hairstyle, but didn't have much luck. A few look like they have eighties hair, but that doesn't mean much – the eighties weren't that long ago. Did she spot styles from the seventies or sixties? Or were they just retro? Or was she just wrong?

They're closing in on their second anniversary, and Angela doesn't know whether Tess was born in 1969 or 1869. She doesn't know whether or not it's possible for Tess to have been born in 1869.

Ask questions that matter.

'Are any of them still around? The people in the photos?'

Tess stares at her. 'What the hell is that supposed to mean?'

'Can I talk to one of them?'

'I'm not going to put my girlfriend in touch with my exes,' Tess says flatly. She takes a long drag and blows the smoke out through her nose. 'That's weird. Seriously, I don't know what's got into you lately, but I don't like it.'

What's got into me is that I'm going to leave you, Angela thinks. But she doesn't say it out loud.

She started to consider it in earnest the last time Tess hit her, weeks ago now. She doesn't remember what the fight was about. All she remembers is the thought that sprang into her head, of dragging Tess's body out of the darkroom and into the sunlight. Seeing what would happen.

She's worried she might kill Tess if she stays with her much longer.

If the thought of leaving didn't send her into a panic, she'd be gone by now. She doesn't know why it frightens her so much. She has plenty of reasons for going. She's spent weeks wondering if a vampire's bite creates some kind of bond with its victim, an addiction that keeps her fluttering around Tess like a moth.

Maybe she's simply still in love with Tess. She might be. She wants to be, in spite of everything. Falling out of love feels like giving up. But lately, being with Tess has been like pouring herself into a well with no bottom.

'You haven't actually answered any of my questions,' Angela points out. 'Again.'

Tess heaves a sigh. Angela hates when she does that. It's entirely theatrical, since she doesn't need to breathe.

'Your questions are stupid. Stop acting like a crazy person.' Tess presses her hands against the sides of her head, the cigarette dangling between two of her fingers. After a few moments, she abruptly grinds it into an ashtray. 'Angel. I cannot deal with this right now.'

No answers. More secrets. Tess's whole life is based on secrets. She's dropped hints about what a careless word might do. Angela used to wonder about torch-bearing mobs, amateur vampire hunters, vivisectionists, angry rival vampires. More recently, she's wondered if the consequences would be far more prosaic. A psychiatric ward. Jail. Either would still be a death sentence for Tess – locked in a room with a window. For someone so strong, Tess is strangely vulnerable.

It occurs to Angela that Tess might spend her life terrified. If she is, it's a revelation that's come too late for Angela to care.

Tess slides off her stool and steps closer.

'You know, I'd feel more talkative if I weren't so distracted.' She starts toying with the laces on Angela's dress.

'Are you serious?' Angela pulls away from her. 'Now?'

Tess pouts. 'It's been weeks.'

'It hasn't been weeks.'

'It totally has – you're never up for it these days. Come on, I can't resist you. You look so damn luscious.'

Angela rolls her eyes. 'You cannot possibly think that's going to work.'

'Please?'

'Christ, don't whine.'

'Pretty please?'

There's no talking to Tess when she gets like this. It's just going to continue until Angela gives in. And it has been a while. She hasn't exactly been offering herself eagerly lately.

'All right. Fine, whatever.' Angela undoes her top buttons and yanks the dress down off her shoulder. 'Go ahead. But as soon as you're done, we're getting back to what we were talking about.'

Tess wraps her arms around Angela. Her fangs are already extended.

Angela winces at the first shock of pain. It gets easier after that, a dull ache and the unpleasant sensation of Tess sucking away. She settles in to wait.

After a while, the first wave of dizziness hits. She's going to need to lie down after this. Juice and a cookie before she does; that usually keeps it from getting too bad.

This is the last time, Angela thinks. *One way or another, I am never letting her do this to me again.*

The dizziness is getting worse. The room starts spinning. Spots of brightness and darkness flash across her vision. That isn't normal. And it can't be a good thing. Something's wrong.

'Tess? Are you about done?'

Her head is throbbing, fuzzy pulses of pain. She doesn't remember it ever feeling like this before. Is Tess taking longer than usual? Angela isn't sure. She suddenly wonders if any of the people in those photographs are alive. What exactly would Tess do to protect her secrets?

'Stop it.' Angela wants to shout, but it comes out a murmur. 'Stop it, stop it . . .'

Tess is still drinking. Angela tries to shove her away. Useless. It would have been a feeble push against a normal person, and Tess might as well be made of concrete. Angela starts beating her hand against the side of Tess's face.

After Angela makes a last weak slap, Tess finally pulls her fangs out of Angela's flesh and steps back. Her eyes are wide. A tracery of blood rims her lips.

'Angel? What . . . Are you OK?'

'No.' It's all she's able to get out before her sight goes completely dark. She sways on her feet, and then her knees buckle.

'Oh, fuck,' is the last thing she hears before her head hits the floor.

There's only darkness until her eyes flutter open again. No dreams. And when she wakes up, she's thirsty. Terribly, terribly thirsty.

She tries to move her head. It feels like a stone, grinding against her neck. Her gaze falls on a pair of shoes, then travels up. Tess is standing there, staring at her intently.

'What . . .' Angela is barely able to croak out the word. Her voice is a strangled rope. She tries again. 'What did you do to me?'

'Well,' Tess says, 'I guess this means you won't be leaving me after all.' She brings her wrist to her mouth and tears at it with her teeth. 'Here.' She offers her arm to Angela. 'Drink it before I heal up.'

Barely aware of what she's doing, Angela clamps her mouth on the bleeding wound. The blood is tepid, and tastes stale. Unpleasant. She thinks it would be better warm. She gulps it down anyway.

Tess pulls her wrist back before Angela has done anything but take the edge off her thirst. She clutches after it, but Tess holds it away.

'That'll keep you for a little while, but it's no good long term. We need to get something else figured out fast. Because obviously what we've been doing isn't going to fucking work anymore.'

'Oh.' Angela notices that Tess is wearing a different dress. And her own clothes are stiff with long-dried sweat. She wonders how long it's been since she passed out.

Tess sits down next to Angela and strokes her hair. The self-inflicted bite on her arm is already healing, visibly scabbing over as Angela watches.

'This hasn't happened to me before,' Tess says, almost gently. 'I haven't ever been with anyone long enough. It takes years. But you got through it, and here we are. We'll have to work it out together, OK?'

Tess isn't looking at her. She's gazing off into the middle distance.

Angela doesn't answer. She closes her eyes again. It doesn't do any good. All of this is still happening, even if she can't see it.

She doesn't feel too hot anymore. She doesn't feel cold, either. She doesn't feel much of anything.

CHAPTER FORTY

Somerville
16 December 1999

Chloë is shocked out of a sound sleep when Entropy decides to use her solar plexus as a launchpad. A moment later, someone lifts the manuscript off her face. She blinks at Esther, who's little more than a blurry shape in the haziness that follows waking.

'You startled the cat,' Chloë says. She wipes clumsily at a trace of drool on the side of her mouth. She's fully dressed, and feels sweaty and stiff, the way she always does when she sleeps in her jeans.

'I'm sorry,' Esther tells her. 'I didn't mean to wake you. The door was open, and you looked so uncomfortable.'

Chloë becomes aware that she's been sleeping in an awkward position, lying on her back with her right arm and leg hanging off the edge of the bed. Her body must have contorted itself around the cat as she slept. It's happened before. She tries to sit up and finds that one leg is cramped and the other is asleep. Not to mention that Entropy's departure has left her feeling like someone punched her in the stomach. She gives up and flops back down.

She wonders if she should mind Esther wandering into her bedroom. But she can't really bring herself to care. It's not as if she was doing anything that couldn't be interrupted. Like working on her writing. Or in flagrante with her girlfriend. Ex-girlfriend. Small chance of either of those things happening. And if Chloë's underwear is all over the bedroom floor, Esther has seen plenty of it before in the course of cleaning the rest of the house.

Chloë's eyes fall on the red bra, draped over the headboard. Matching panties on the floor. They stand out like a beacon. All the rest are black or white or tan. Utilitarian.

She should put the red ones away. She doesn't want to look at them right now.

Light is streaming in through the window. She squints as her eyes adjust. Wasn't it dark when she started reading? 'What time is it?'

'About two in the afternoon.' Esther thumbs through the manuscript. Somewhere upstairs, the neighbours begin one of their bouts of noisemaking. Whatever they're doing is making the ceiling squeak, loud high-pitched squealing sounds. Chloë can't begin to imagine what it might be. Unless maybe they're having sex, although she's unable to picture the kind of sex that would produce metallic screeches. No matter what it is, there's little chance she's going to be able to fall asleep again.

'Could I have that back?' She makes a half-hearted gesture towards the manuscript in Esther's hands. 'I should finish reading it.'

'Let's see . . . a book of fables. It was so good it put you right to sleep, eh?'

'They're horrifying. And not even intentionally horrifying.' With some effort, Chloë manages to pull herself upright. 'In one of them, the five senses were arguing with each other, but made peace so they could all beat up the big toe. Because it was more different from them than they were from each other. It was literally a fascist children's story. You know, so kids can learn values.'

'That does sound dreadful,' Esther says, tossing the book onto the rumpled blankets. 'So. How did your date go?'

Chloë makes a short, bitter noise in her throat. 'Date? You mean our extended discussion of how horrible it would be if we stayed together?'

'Oh dear. And she seemed so nice when I met her.'

'Well, I don't think you were wrong. Mostly. I mean, there are issues, it's not an ideal situation. But it's complicated.'

Esther frowns. 'Complicated? If the two of you weren't to be, I'd expect it to be for a fairly simple reason.'

'No. She doesn't . . . I mean, she's done some fucked-up shit, if that's what you're talking about.'

Esther sits down on the bed next to Chloë, ageing mattress springs protesting noisily under her as she settles herself. 'So is that why you broke up, then? The "fucked-up shit"?'

'I guess so? Maybe? That's part of it, but I don't want to . . .' Chloë shakes her head. 'I don't know. I think it was the right thing to do, in the long run.'

'I see.' The frown on Esther's face deepens.

Chloë starts stretching her limbs until a sharp pain in her leg convinces her to abandon the idea. 'I'm going to experiment with being single for a while.'

'You were single for two years,' Esther points out.

'And there's nothing wrong with that! I should be able to take care of myself.'

After an uncomfortably long interval filled only with the sound of a squeaking ceiling, Esther says, 'Well . . . that's true.' Her voice is heavy with doubt.

'Hey! It *is* true!'

'Didn't I just agree with you?'

'No, you didn't,' Chloë replies crossly. 'Don't be disingenuous. That was a tentative, oh-my-god-you're-on-crack kind of, "Well, that's true." I wanted a positive, affirming, "Yes! That's true!" I've made a decision, and I feel good about it, OK?'

'Are you sure?'

'Yes, damn it!' Chloë shouts. 'I'm happy!'

'All right,' Esther says, if anything sounding more dubious than before. 'If you say so.'

Chloë rolls her eyes. 'Seriously, stop doing that.'

'Doing what?'

'Stop pretending to agree with me when you clearly think I'm being an idiot,' Chloë tells her. 'It's infuriating.'

Before Esther has a chance to reply, Ari knocks on the doorframe. 'Mind if I come in?'

'Sure, why not?' Chloë says. 'House party in my bedroom. You want to join in telling me how I'm screwing up my life?'

'Um, no thanks,' Ari says, looking perplexed. 'I thought I should let you know that I'm heading out of town. I wanted to say goodbye before I left.'

'Oh.' Turning to look at him, Chloë notices that he's bundled up for going outside. An overstuffed suitcase is sitting in the living room behind him. 'How long are you going to be gone?'

'Forever. I mean, I probably won't be out of town forever, most likely I'll be back through at some point, but I'm moving out.'

'What a pity,' Esther says. 'I'll miss our card games.'

'Wait, you are?' Chloë feels like the conversation has left her behind. On the other hand, she's not going to complain about cutting the previous one short. 'All right, I guess, but . . . you're paid up through the end of the month.'

'Keep it. I'm supposed to give two weeks' notice or something, anyway, right?'

'I think that's for quitting a job.' Chloë tries to remember the legal niceties, but she never looked them up. There's no reason to belabour the point, though. The situation wasn't altogether above board to begin with. 'Never mind, it's fine. Thanks for being laid-back about the cash – I could use it.'

'No problem,' Ari says. 'I need to head out today, so I thought it was only fair.'

'I'm sorry you're leaving. You've been a good housemate.' She's surprised to realise that what she's saying is the truth. 'Why do you have to go?'

'Because it's after the ides of December,' he answers, taking a sidelong glance at Esther for some reason. 'I've clearly done what work I can in this city. I can feel myself being drawn elsewhere. There are others in the world who need my help, and I must hurry to them, however far off they may be.'

'I see.' *Good housemate*, Chloë thinks, *but still a raving nut*.

'To be honest, I think I might have missed my chance here, whatever it was,' he adds confidingly. 'I guess it could have been that wrong number.'

On that incomprehensible note, Ari turns and heads out of the room, only to be immediately interrupted when Entropy drops onto his head.

The cat gnaws happily on his hair for a moment while Ari staggers under the sudden, unexpected weight. Just as he starts to regain his footing, Entropy springs off and scampers away, sending Ari crashing into the doorframe.

Chloë flinches in sympathy where she sits. 'Sorry about that.'

'Aw, I think he wanted to say goodbye.' Ari pats his disarrayed hair back into place as the cat disappears into the kitchen. 'I'm going to miss him.'

'I'm sure he'll miss you, too,' Esther says.

Ari finishes getting himself recombobulated and resumes his walk towards the front door, Esther following in his wake.

Chloë gets up and limps after them on her cramped leg. It's

quieter now; at some point, the mysterious noises upstairs ended with a final grating screech. When they reach the doorway, Esther hugs Ari affectionately.

'Farewell, dear,' she says. 'Take care of yourself.'

'And have a nice trip,' Chloë adds as they break apart.

'Thank you!' Ari says. 'And listen, I hope things go well with your thing with the other girl. It sounds like you've got a really amazing thing going on there with her!'

Chloë winces, but manages to keep smiling. 'Thanks.'

She sticks out a hand for a handshake as he spreads his arms for a hug. Chloë feels bad about that, so she tries to hug him as he promptly switches to a handshake. Eventually, they get it sorted out and hug awkwardly.

With a final wave, he walks out.

'Another goodbye,' Chloë says before the echo of the closing door has had time to fade. 'I seem to be doing a lot of that lately. It's going to be hard to find someone else who'll put up with this place.'

'At least you won't have a divine messenger wandering around the house anymore,' Esther says. 'I don't know about you, but it made me feel a bit self-conscious.'

Chloë starts dragging herself back to her bedroom. 'I actually stopped minding the freaky religion. It's more the terminal case of foot-in-mouth disease that I never got used to. I always love to hear about how wonderful my relationships are right after my girlfriend bites me and we break up, you know?'

'Well,' Esther says, 'I'm not certain he was entirely wrong.'

Chloë pauses in the doorway. She takes deep, slow breaths, and keeps her tone calm. 'I thought we were done with that argument.'

'No. We were interrupted.'

'Well, leave it,' Chloë warns her. 'I don't want to talk about this, OK? I don't even want to deliberately not talk about it. I want to forget the whole thing.'

'That sounds healthy.'

'I don't care how it sounds.'

'I can't help but be reminded,' Esther says, 'of the story of Ragnelle—'

Chloë spins around. 'Do you ever stop?' She can't prevent her agitation from leaking into her voice. 'What are you talking about? Ragnelle?' It takes her a moment to place the name. 'The King Arthur character? Why, are you going to tell me you had sex with her, too, back in the Middle Ages?'

'No, of course not. She's mythical.' Esther pauses judiciously, then adds, 'I did first hear the story three hundred years ago, but that was well after the Middle Ages.'

Chloë holds a hand up to stop her. It's shaking slightly. 'Oh, my God. No. Not now. I cannot deal with your strange, random bullshit right now. Look, I don't know what you're trying to do, or why you're so intent on dissecting my breakup with Angela—'

'I'm doing it,' Esther says, 'because I can see how unhappy you are.'

'Well, you know what?' Chloë yells at her. 'It doesn't matter! It's over! Stories aren't going to help!' Tears start leaking out of her eyes. 'Nothing's going to help.'

Esther takes a step back. 'I didn't—'

'We talked, we decided it wouldn't work, we said goodbye. There is no reason to have hope here. So I don't want to think about her anymore, OK? I want to forget it ever happened. One more miserable failure in my life. Fantastic.'

'I'm sorry,' Esther says softly. 'I wasn't trying to upset you.'

'I know,' Chloë says. 'But could you leave me alone for a while? Please. I need some time alone.'

Esther nods. 'All right.'

She doesn't say anything more. There's only the sound of the two of them breathing. Chloë finds herself missing the noise from before, the fuss of Ari leaving, the upstairs neighbours, even, perversely, the argument she's been having with Esther. Anything to fill the silence. Her thoughts are too loud. She wishes she could just feel blank.

She steps into the bedroom, and shuts the door.

CHAPTER FORTY-ONE

The Wedding Of Sir Gawain And Dame Ragnelle

The piquet deck holds many secrets. I learned most of them three centuries ago, from my dear sweet Julie, La Maupin.

She taught me about the cards when we were on the road after she rescued me from a nunnery. Nunneries were considered excellent places to stash inconvenient women in those days, and after a series of misfortunes I found myself imprisoned in a very dreary one. Fortunately, La Maupin discovered that she missed me lying by her side, so she spirited me out. Then, to cover our escape, she stole the body of a dead nun, put it in my bed, and lit the room on fire. The woman did not do things by halves.

However, the authorities looked askance at her actions, and she was tried in absentia and condemned to death for body snatching, arson, and kidnapping. I've always thought the last charge was unfair, since I'd run away with her quite willingly. We kept ourselves out of sight for all of three months before she got bored with hiding and headed off to Paris to become an opera singer. Until she did, though, we had very little to do during the day but play cards.

The king commuted her sentence eventually. She was an extremely good opera singer.

While we played, she told me that the figures on the cards were named for the great men and women of history and legend. Le Roi de Coeur, the King of Hearts, was Charlemagne, founder of the Holy Roman Empire. Hogier the Dane, slayer of the giant Brehus, was immortalised in the deck as Le Valet de Pique, the Jack of Spades. There were cards for Hector and Caesar, Judith and Athena. And for one woman I had never heard of – Ragnelle, the loathly lady, who was given La Dame de Carreau as her card – the Queen of Diamonds. I asked La Maupin for her story, and here, word for word, is how she told it to me:

One day, King Arthur was hunting in the Inglewood forest, a wild wood on the border of the Summer Kingdoms where the fey folk rule. In his eagerness to pursue a hart, the king had left the rest of his party behind. Which meant he was alone and nearly unarmed when he was surprised by Sir Gromer Somer Joure, a knight whom he had wronged.

'You have given my lands to Sir Gawain,' the knight snarled at Arthur. 'Why should I not kill you where you stand?'

'All would shun you if you slay me in an unfair fight,' the king replied to Sir Gromer. 'But perhaps we may find another way. Is there some task I might perform which would appease you?'

At this, Sir Gromer smiled, a certain malevolent gleam appearing in his eye. 'Indeed there is. Return to this place in a year with the answer to a question I shall give you, or else forfeit the life I could have taken today.'

Sir Gromer, as you may have gathered, was a bit of an ass. It's probably why King Arthur gave away his lands in the first place, but that's neither here nor there.

In any event, King Arthur swore that he would do it, and asked, 'What question would you have me answer?'

To which Sir Gromer said, 'What is it that women most desire?'

Sir Gromer departed into the wood, and Arthur returned to his hunting party, and thence to Camelot.

After some days, Sir Gawain noticed his uncle was distracted, and asked the king what was amiss. Sir Gawain, as it happened, was something of an expert on this kind of thing, having dealt in the past with a similar challenge from an invincible Green Knight. Essentially, he was the go-to person at court for all matters pertaining to hostile weirdos. So, when Arthur told him the nature of the dilemma, he immediately had a suggestion.

'Let us put this year to good use,' Sir Gawain said. 'We shall ride across the land asking one and all what the answer might be. Surely there is someone among your subjects who will know.'

And so they set out, questing for a solution to the conundrum. But of the hundreds of people they asked, all claimed to know the answer, yet no two answers were the same. One told them women most desire to be well dressed; another that they most desire to be well wooed; still another that they most desire to be well pleased in bed. Never did they receive an answer they could be sure was correct. All too swiftly, the year was nearly up and Arthur's life seemed all but lost. With heavy hearts, they approached the Inglewood forest.

Before they reached the spot on which King Arthur made his oath, though, a hideous monster appeared before them. She was a loathly lady with sharp blackened teeth, a foot-long nose, the ears of a donkey, and bleeding sores about her neck. Her staring red eyes had caused many a knight to flee in terror, her sickly green skin gave small children nightmares, and her feet smelled very, very bad.

'I am Dame Ragnelle,' she screeched at them. 'And your life is in my hands, King Arthur. For I know your task and know the answer you seek.'

At this, Arthur stayed his hand, which had been reaching for his sword. 'And what price do you ask for this knowledge?'

'Give unto me yon handsome knight to be my husband,' said

Ragnelle, pointing a clawlike finger at Sir Gawain, 'and you shall have the wisdom for which you quest.'

'I would order no man to do this,' King Arthur said. 'Not even to save my life.'

'But I may choose to do so if I wish,' Sir Gawain declared. 'And the year draws swiftly to a close. I agree to your terms, Dame Ragnelle.'

'So be it!' she said, and leaned forward to whisper words in Arthur's ear.

Armed with her answer, King Arthur sped off into the woods to meet Sir Gromer, arriving with only moments to spare.

'I had begun to suspect you would not return here,' Sir Gromer said, 'and that I would have to chase you down to slay you.'

'I am here, as I swore,' King Arthur said.

'But your life yet hangs in the balance. Have you an answer for me?'

'Indeed I do,' said the king, and repeated what Dame Ragnelle had told him. 'What women most desire is the freedom to make their own choices.'

Sir Gromer stamped his feet, and tore his hair, and gnashed his teeth, and rent his garments, and in general acted like the little prat he was. 'My sister Ragnelle must have told you this!' he shouted. 'That foul hag has betrayed me!'

But angry as he was, Sir Gromer acknowledged the king's answer was true, and told him he was free to go.

The marriage between Gawain and Ragnelle proceeded with all befitting ceremony. But on their wedding night, Gawain was astonished to find that Ragnelle had become a maiden as fair as sunlight on clear water.

'Now that we are wed,' she said to the knight, 'my curse is half-broken, and I shall be a monster only half the time. What do you wish – shall I be monstrous by day, when others will see us together, or at night, when we will be alone in each other's arms?'

Sir Gawain considered his reply. After he had given the matter some minutes of thought, he said unto her, 'The decision, Ragnelle, should be yours, not mine. It is not my right to command such a thing of you.'

At that, she smiled, and said, 'The curse is broken.' From that moment on, she became at all times the beautiful maiden she truly was. And Gawain and Ragnelle lived together in happiness for many years, until at last death parted them.

It's a lovely story, isn't it? I can recall, even now, the rise and fall of Julie's voice as she told it to me, and the sound of the rain pattering down outside the threshing barn where we were hiding.

I'll grant that it's not a perfect tale from the modern point of view. But when it comes to something that dates from the fifteenth century, I suppose you take what you can get. I agree with the moral, anyway.

Which is probably, come to think of it, why I was absolutely terrible at being a nun.

CHAPTER FORTY-TWO

Brookline
21 December 1999

Angela holds the knife against the soft flesh of her upper arm. She tells herself she's only testing to see how it feels. She doesn't have to go through with this. She can stop any time she wants.

The knife is a vegetable chopper from the kitchen. It's very sharp. Mike insists that all of the knives in the house be kept as sharp as possible. He's fond of saying that you're more likely to hurt yourself with a dull knife than with a sharp one. Probably true. Unless you're using one this way.

It's almost surprising that she hasn't thought of this before. But it never occurred to her until last week. She didn't consider it when she was with Tess, not even when things were at their worst. Then again, of course she didn't. You can take the Catholicism out of the girl, but there's a part that always says it's another mortal sin. Kills your soul.

These days she's far from sure that souls exist. And if they do exist, she's even less certain she has one to kill. Maybe there's nothing in the mirror because there's nothing really there. Just an empty shell, borrowing life from other people to move around.

Borrowing? Like she's ever going to give it back.

It's stealing.

Angela increases the pressure, aiming to make a small cut, a nick really. She braces herself in anticipation of pain.

It doesn't come.

She waits, sure that she'll start to feel it any moment now. But the seconds tick by, and there's nothing. Puzzled, she moves the knife away and looks at her arm.

There's no blood, no cut in the skin, no sign that she's done anything at all.

What the hell?

Impulsively, she chops at her arm with the knife, hard and fast. It bounces off. There should be a deep gash, but there isn't so much as a mark. She frowns, and places it further down her arm. She saws rapidly back and forth across her wrist. Pressing down, harder and harder.

Nothing. Nothing, nothing, nothing.

'You're fucking kidding me!' Angela says to her empty bedroom. She throws the knife to the ground. It lands with a clatter and skids a few feet across the basement floor tiles.

Stupid. She should have known this wouldn't work, right from the start. Tess showed her, if she'd been paying attention. Demonstrated it right in front of her, more than a year ago. It takes a vampire's fangs to break a vampire's skin.

Like the Nemean Lion, it occurs to her. Another monster that needed to be put down. She's not going to get a constellation out of it, though. They're all used up. Not to mention she's not important enough. No one bothers to remember the little monsters.

Could she do it that way? Use her own teeth, gnaw at her wrists until she bled to death? Probably not. Now that she's bothering to think about it, she remembers Tess's wounds closed a few seconds after a bite. She isn't sure she can bleed to death, anyway; it's not her blood in there, so losing it might only make her hungrier. Blood can't work the same way for her now – it's obviously not pumping oxygen around, not when her heart is a voluntary muscle, motionless and inert whenever she's not paying attention to it. Not when breathing is a choice.

She could always open up the drapes and take down the tinfoil. Then she'd have to spend the next ten hours or so sitting in her empty room, staring at the window. How are you supposed to pass the time on a night like that? Read a book? There must be a method that isn't so agonisingly prolonged. Beheading is supposed to do the trick, isn't it?

Angela can't come up with any practical way to bite her own head off.

'Damn it!' She takes a final kick at the knife, which skitters under her desk before stopping against the wall with a soft thump.

OK, then, she thinks as she leaves her room, heading upstairs.

There has to be something in the house she can make into a wooden stake.

CHAPTER FORTY-THREE

Quincy
22 December 1999

Chloë looks at the clock and is surprised to see that it's almost half past four. The sky outside the office's one small window is already darkening. It's the shortest day of the year, only nine hours of daylight total. Fifteen solid hours of darkness have just arrived.

She idly wonders if rich vampires ever arrange to spend winters in Alaska and summers in . . . Where would be appropriate? Tierra del Fuego? Get a little sleep during the paltry daylight hours, and then up again for a long night on the town. Or would that be uncomfortable, like slamming caffeine all day, every day?

How did sunset happen without her noticing? Where did all the hours go? She must have lost track of time. Her mind has been wandering in the oppressive silence of the empty room. She's been alone there the whole day. Mike told her Shelly isn't feeling well.

It could be another couple of weeks before she sees Shelly again; it's Chloë's last day at work before the holiday season starts. Unless she goes to their Christmas party, but Angela is certain to be there, so that would be awkward.

There'll be lots of parties coming up soon, one after another. First Christmas, then New Year's Eve. End of 1999, end of the world. That's on the news every day now, inescapable. Pundits fretting over what's going to happen to the computers, crazies predicting earthquakes, tornadoes, rains of frogs. It makes Chloë think of lying in bed with Angela, looking at the glowing stars on her ceiling. Talking about Orion and Prince songs and cities on fire.

Coming to work marks the first time she's left the apartment in days. She feels lonelier out in the world than she did sealed up in her room. She'd have thought being by herself would make the tiny office seem more spacious, but instead it feels claustrophobic. As if having another person in there helped to keep the walls apart. There are plenty of other people around at Compass Rose, but Chloë doesn't have any reason to go talk to them. Mike is almost certainly busy, and she's not about to bother some innocent accountant or sales manager because she's feeling down. She hardly knows most of her colleagues, anyway; she doesn't come in enough.

After her brief chat with Mike in the morning, she's only had one other conversation today, a phone call from an irate author. He'd harangued Chloë about the obvious lack of taste, insight, and talent of whoever it was that rejected his brilliant work. Since Chloë was the whoever-it-was who rejected it, the phone call hasn't helped her mood.

No one's going to notice if she leaves early today. She seals a final rejection letter into an envelope and tosses it onto the outgoing mail pile. She's just started to reach for her coat when the office phone rings again.

After a few rings' worth of internal debate, she scoots her office chair back to her desk. It's still business hours, and since Shelly isn't here to field the call, Chloë can't justify letting it go to voicemail. She grits her teeth as she picks it up, and tries to answer in as surly a tone as she can manage, just because.

'Compass Rose Books, can I help you?'

'What the hell,' Shelly says on the other end of the line, 'did you do to Angela?' Chloë is too surprised to answer. Shelly doesn't really wait for a reply, anyway. 'Seriously, what did you say to her?'

'I – Nothing! I didn't say anything. I haven't spoken to her for days.'

'I meant when you dumped her,' Shelly tells her impatiently. 'What the hell happened?'

'I didn't dump her! I mean, we dumped each other. It was a mutual–'

'Does she know that? Because she's not acting like it was a mutual anything.'

Chloë does her best to gather her thoughts. 'Shel, will you please tell me what's going on? Because I don't have any idea what you're pissed off about.'

There's a long pause before Shelly responds. When she does, she's clearly making an effort to soften her tone. 'I'm sorry. I'm kind of on edge, and I shouldn't take it out on you. Listen, Angela came home from that thing last week, from whatever talk you two had, and she looked like someone had killed her puppy. She's been acting weird ever since–'

'I don't think either of us was really thrilled about it.'

'Let me finish. I don't mean bad-breakup weird, I mean scary weird.'

'Scary?' Chloë asks sharply. 'What do you mean, scary?'

'I mean I'm scared for her. What did you think I meant?'

'So, she hasn't done anything to make you afraid of her?'

'What? No, of course not,' Shelly says. 'Why would you even ask that?'

'I don't know,' Chloë mumbles. 'No reason.'

'People don't ask that kind of question for no reason.'

'Look, I'm sorry I brought it up.'

'Chloë, I'm really worried about Angela, so if there's something I should know about–'

'She bit me!' Chloë blurts out.

'She . . . did what?'

'She bit me. On the neck. With her teeth.' Chloë fidgets with the phone cord, tangling and untangling it as she tries to think of an explanation that won't make her sound insane. There isn't one. 'Angela's a vampire.'

'Oh,' Shelly says. 'Huh. I thought it was something like that, yeah.'

Chloë is so taken aback she nearly drops the phone, barely fumbling it back into her hand and up to her ear before it clatters to the floor.

'You, uh, you don't sound very shocked.'

'Well, she's been living in my house for months,' Shelly says, a little too quickly. 'I'm not an idiot. You start to notice the oddities after a while. No food in the refrigerator, never up before sundown–'

'What aren't you telling me?' Chloë knows exactly what it sounds like when Shelly is trying not to give something away. 'What did you see her do?'

'Nothing! It was Mike. He's the one who figured it out.' Shelly sounds distinctly uncomfortable. 'He's been dropping some pretty broad hints for a while now, so it didn't really come as a surprise.'

'How did Mike know?' Chloë asks. *Am I the only one*, she wonders, *who didn't have a clue? I slept with her for a month and I never saw it coming. How dumb does that make me?* 'You know, I really wish one of you had said something.'

'What, you wanted me to tell you every strange thing I knew about the woman you were dating? My housemate? Come on, who does that?'

Chloë narrows her eyes, even though Shelly can't see it. 'You told her I was having problems with depression.'

'Oh. I wasn't trying to – I mean, I didn't make it sound like, I didn't say . . .' Shelly coughs. 'I kind of feel like I've lost the moral high ground here.'

'Yes.'

'Buy you a drink the next time I see you?'

'Please.'

'Are we OK?'

'I'll get over it.' Or at least, she decides, after everything that's been going on recently it doesn't seem worth arguing about. Someone drinking her blood may not have many upsides, but maybe one of them is a sense of perspective.

'Are you all right, after what happened?' Shelly asks. 'I mean the biting and everything?'

'I'm fine,' Chloë says. 'It wasn't . . . I'm fine.'

'Is that why you broke up?'

'Sort of. Maybe.' But that isn't completely true, Chloë thinks. It certainly isn't a fair answer. Not when she'd nearly volunteered to let Angela do it again, before that idea got unequivocally quashed. 'No. Not really. Look, forget anything I said about her being dangerous to you. That was a crappy thing to say. I don't think you need to worry about it.'

'If it matters,' Shelly says, 'I think she feels really, really bad about biting you. Putting together some of the things she said to me.'

'Yeah. I know.'

'Well. Listen, if you run into her, could you let me know?'

That's an odd question. Chloë sits up straighter in her chair. 'What do you mean? You're the one who lives with her.'

'Right, that's what I was calling about. I mean, originally.' A hint of anxiety has entered Shelly's voice again. 'She's been really upset, and she came up from her room last night acting, I don't know, agitated. I spent the whole night talking her down, I didn't get to sleep until, like, seven in the morning. And I woke up just now and went to check on her, and she's gone. Not in her room, not in the house, not anywhere. No message, no note, not answering her phone.'

Chloë feels a faint prickle of worry in her stomach. 'I'll keep an eye out. But I think I'm someone she doesn't want to run into right now. I doubt she's going to come to my place or anything.'

'If you do see her, though . . .'

'Sure. If I do.'

Chloë closes her eyes for a few seconds after she ends the call. She gathers up her handbag and coat. The sense of apprehension is still roiling in her gut, but there's not a lot she can do about it.

When she turns to the doorway, someone is standing in it. She jumps back and knocks her head against a shelf.

'Ow!'

'Hey, are you OK? It's me, didn't mean to startle you.' It's just Mike. Walking into the office, hand reaching out to her, a concerned look on his face.

'I'm fine.' Chloë waves his hand away and rubs the back of her head. 'What were you doing there?'

'I was going to ask if you wanted a ride home. I was waiting until you were off the phone.' His expression is carefully neutral, but he shifts his weight uneasily from one foot to another.

'How much of that phone call did you overhear?' Chloë asks.

'Not much that I didn't already know.'

'Right,' Chloë says bitterly. 'Because everyone knew about Angela but me, and no one bothered to tell me.'

Mike winces, just a little. 'I'm sorry about that.'

'You're sorry. OK. Fine.'

'I would have said something, but I really didn't think you were in any danger.'

'All right.' Her voice is getting louder. She tries to bring it back down. 'Forget it. You're not the one to blame.'

'She's been living with Shelly and me for most of the year without—'

'Sure.' Chloë already regrets bringing it up.

'There haven't been any problems,' he persists, not picking up on the hint.

'I get it,' she says tightly. 'Really.'

'I certainly never thought you were at risk of being—'

'Well, you were wrong!' Chloë snaps. 'I guess going without blood for a month makes her a little twitchy!' She's shouting now. She isn't even sure who she wants to shout at. Mike, Shelly, Angela. Herself. 'But don't be sorry, because it's not your fault I'm an idiot!'

'You're not—'

'Oh, yes, I am!' It's all too much. Everything that's happened in the past week. The bite, the breakup, Angela disappearing, Shelly yelling at her over the phone. Whatever dam was holding her mess of emotions back during work hours has cracked, and she can't stop the words from flooding out. 'I'm an idiot, I'm the one, single moron who can't see the obvious! Were you all laughing at me?'

'What? No! Why would you think that?'

'And now she's missing! Why is Shelly asking the idiot to find her? The idiot who's responsible for it, why would anyone . . . God, I'm worthless, I'm—'

Mike is holding her, and she's sniffling against his chest, trying as hard as she can not to cry. Again. How many tears is it going to take before she runs out?

'You're not an idiot, Chloë,' he says gently. 'None of this is your fault. I don't think that. I don't think Angela does, either, whatever's going on with her right now.'

'I should have done better,' she manages to choke out. 'I should have known. You figured it out.'

Mike studies the ceiling as if there's something intensely

interesting up there. 'About that. I had a big advantage there. She doesn't smell right.'

Chloë sniffles a final time, then tilts her head up. 'I never noticed that she smelled weird.'

'You wouldn't. I would. I'm a werewolf.'

Chloë blinks, and pulls away. She almost backs into the shelf again before her aching head reminds her that it's directly behind her.

'I figured that all things considered, you had a right to know,' Mike adds.

'You're kidding, right?'

'Why would I be?' He leans against the doorframe. 'Look, if you have vampires, why not werewolves? And vice versa, for that matter. I think that's why I clued in to what Angela is pretty quickly. I thought that if I existed, it wasn't such a big leap to make.'

'But you can't . . . you're going bald!' Chloë says, staring at the thinning hair at the top of his head. 'Wolves don't go bald!'

Mike exhales through his nose, almost a sigh, the corners of his lips turning down. 'I have canine atrophic follicular dysplasia,' he tells her. 'Dog pattern baldness. Runs in my family. When I go wolf, I look like I have mange.'

'You have got to be fucking with me.'

'If you want to find out, would you mind driving me home?' He glances out the window. 'It's a full moon night, and I've been hanging around here longer than I meant to. I'm cutting it pretty close to moonrise. I could manage it, but trying to get through rush hour Boston traffic makes me want to wolf out like you wouldn't believe.'

'Your game nights,' Chloë says faintly. 'When you leave early. This is why?'

'Yeah. Little joke. I hunt small game, sometimes, up in the Fells.' He dangles a pair of car keys. 'I really need to get going. You up for it?'

She hesitates, her hand almost going up to touch the place on her neck where she's been bitten. But, she thinks, this is Mike. Someone she'd have described as 'sane' and 'reliable' if anyone ever asked her. Someone who only moments ago was holding her and letting her get snot all over his shirt.

She can't spend her life not trusting anybody.

'Sure, why not?' she says. 'Let's go.'

He tosses her the keys and turns to stride down the hallway while they're still in the air. She hurries to catch up, stepping next to him as he pushes the button for the elevator. 'Shelly knows about you, right?'

'Of course she knows.'

'I'm sure everybody knows,' Chloë mutters to herself. 'Today is doing wonders for my self-esteem.' But the bitterness is mostly gone. At least it's clear why Shelly was so accepting of the notion of vampires. After a werewolf boyfriend it can't have been, as Mike put it, a very big leap.

'She didn't figure it out on her own,' he says. 'I had to tell her. You'd be surprised what people don't notice.'

'Not anymore, I wouldn't. Listen, I don't mean to be rude or any-thing, but just to check,' Chloë says, 'you're not going to bite me, right?'

'Don't try to balance a snack on my nose,' Mike answers as the elevator dings, 'and we should be fine.'

CHAPTER FORTY-FOUR

I-90 Turnpike, Massachusetts
22 December 1999

Angela is driving much too fast.

She watches with detached interest as the speedometer crawls up to 90 miles per hour, then edges past it. When she hit 70 a while back, the car started juddering and shaking like it was going to fly apart, but it's stopped doing that now. It's rolling smoothly down the freeway. She's staying in the left lane, occasionally overtaking another car. Only once in a while, though; the traffic is light, and mostly headed in the other direction. Towards the city rather than away.

She should have tried this before. She should have tried a lot of things. She has preternatural reflexes and an indestructible body – why hasn't she ever used them? So many possibilities, so many lost opportunities. Jumping off a rooftop. Walking on the ocean floor. Breaking into a zoo and petting the tigers. Although she's probably allergic to tigers. But still. Why hasn't she ever done anything?

Of course, it helps that she doesn't much care about consequences tonight. What does it matter if she gets a speeding ticket?

The scenery whips past, monotonous and dull in the glare of her headlights. Snow. Trees. Road. White and grey and black. The yellow line at the leftmost edge of the lane is the only visible trace of colour. White markers flash by every tenth of a mile, shining like flares with reflected light, hypnotic in their repetition. Her eyes follow them as they pass.

She has a lot of regrets. Leaving her thesis half-finished, for one. She'd really wanted to get that done. Find a job in the field. Add something, in her own small and insignificant way, to the sum of human knowledge. That was a pipe dream, anyway. It's been impossible long term ever since she turned. Grad school was one thing, but there aren't any postdocs and professorships waiting around for people who can't show up during the day. How would she go in to work? Teach class? Attend meetings? She's put off thinking about it, held onto the hope that a solution would eventually present itself. But the fact of the matter is, her career is going to end the moment she graduates.

There's a pickup truck ahead. A grey one, or one that looks that way in the faded hues of night. She passes it, flying past like it's standing still. Its headlights hover in her rear-view mirror, gradually growing smaller until they disappear.

She regrets not leaving Tess sooner.

She regrets not telling Chloë how she feels about her. Or at least not enough, and not in the way she really meant. She should have said so much more, told Chloë how much she loved reading her stories, how much she loved hearing her talk about her job and her cat. Angela should have said how astonished she was to find herself looking forward to getting out of bed every evening. How astonished she was to be happy.

Well, that's over with. She made sure of that herself. Chloë thinks the absolute worst of her, and Angela doesn't disagree. It's better if Chloë stays far away. It's better that she's safe.

She regrets hurting Chloë. Hurting anyone. She regrets that most of all. She should never have bitten a single person, not once, not even the first time. She should have let herself starve. She should have done back then what she's going to do tonight.

The speedometer is approaching 95 when the car starts to skid.

Angela slams on the brakes and twists the steering wheel. It's a mistake; the rear end of the car fishtails, drifting sideways across the wet asphalt. All she feels, she notices in a detached way, is an icy calm. No fear at all.

She wrenches the wheel in the other direction as the car slides off the road entirely, jolting up onto the median strip, spraying out a broad spatter of snow. The Corolla bucks and shudders as it hurtles forward over the uneven surface.

She keeps her feet off the pedals, countering every jounce with small movements of the wheel, getting the hang of it. She can do this. Her thoughts stay ahead of her hands, and her hands are fast, so fast, reacting the instant anything happens. She manages to keep it all just under control.

When the car slows down enough, she puts her foot back on the brake. She gradually glides to a halt, stopping a few feet away from the opposite lanes. The engine is still running. There isn't so much as a crack in the windshield, and she doesn't even have a bruise.

Vampire reflexes. Indestructible.

Her hands rest easily on the steering wheel, steady as the earth below, not shaking at all. How strange. Is it because she doesn't need to gasp for breath? Because a heart that doesn't have to beat will never beat too fast? But no, she's felt things since she turned – excitement, horror, anger, love. Maybe it's simply that she knows, bone deep, exactly how fast she can move.

She gets out to check the tyres and looks back at the long, diagonal furrow her car has ploughed through the snow. She's glad she didn't hit anyone. That's one thing she doesn't have to add to her conscience, at least.

The tyres look fine. An SUV whizzes past her, headed towards Boston. Then another. Neither slows down.

Angela gets back in the Corolla and shuts the door. Buckles her seatbelt with a firm click.

She's worried that she might be stuck in the snow, but when she shifts the transmission to low gear and gives the car some gas, it trundles forward without any trouble. Good. Being forced to stop here wouldn't change her plans, but she'd like to get where she's heading. Even if it doesn't matter, even if it doesn't make any difference at all.

She eases her car across the snow-covered grass, back onto the road, and drives more carefully towards her final destination.

CHAPTER FORTY-FIVE

Green Line to Park Street Station
22 December 1999

After dropping Mike off, Chloë takes the T downtown and tries to make sense of her life.

All right, so werewolves exist, she acknowledges, brushing a bit of dog hair off her coat. And they can go bald. And they really, really don't like rush hour traffic on Morton Street. None of this should have come as a surprise, all things considered. She starts to speculate about the dog crate in Shelly and Mike's house, then puts it firmly out of her mind. Their private life is none of her business.

How, she wonders, *have I already begun to get used to the presence of the supernatural in my life?* Well, she always wanted magic to be real when she was a child. She should have been more careful what she wished for, she supposes.

When she gets off at Park Street to transfer, her sneaker hits the wet floor with an audible squelch. The brick paving is sodden with the melted slush from thousands of boots. It soaks through her shoes and wets her socks as she heads downstairs to wait for the Red Line. She shivers in the cold, damp air, chilly as soon as she stops moving.

When the train comes, she doesn't get on.

Chloë can think of one place Angela might have gone. If Angela were feeling reckless, or curious. If the lure laid out for her succeeded at drawing her in. Chloë has certainly been curious herself, ever since she saw the flyer. Curious about Angela's past, about what Tess did to her.

She watches the crowd press into the subway cars, then turns around, heading back up the stairs. Up once again to the Green Line tracks, looking for a trolley that will take her a few stops back the way she came.

I should be trying to let things go, she thinks as one rumbles to a halt in front of her, the wheels squealing on the track. *Why am I doing this?*

Because if Angela went there, she might be in some kind of trouble. And even if she isn't, even if she's not there at all, maybe Chloë isn't ready to let things go quite yet. Not ready to forget about the girl with blonde hair and grey eyes.

One of Chloë's occasional impulses is hammering at the back of her mind, warning her not to go. Telling her to catch the next Red Line train and head home. Everyone knows what curiosity does, her instincts whisper.

She ignores it. When the trolley doors fold open, she steps in.

On Newbury Street, a frigid wind throws sharp crystals of ice into Chloë's face. The sidewalks are nearly empty. Earlier there might have been late Christmas shoppers in spite of the horrible weather, but now all the stores are on the verge of closing.

There are two types of art galleries scattered across Newbury Street. On the western end, they're a little more bohemian and a little less expensive, aiming for the students who hang out at Tower Records. On the east side, the galleries are posh and upscale, surrounded by pricy restaurants and boutiques. It's a ritzy part of town, considering that the whole neighbourhood is built on a garbage landfill and slowly sinking.

She's unsurprised to find that the gallery she's looking for is firmly on the eastern side of the street. The door opens with a faint jingle of bells, and Chloë steps into the warm indoor air.

She feels like a barbarian invader in her jeans and cheap coat, dripping meltwater onto the patterned carpet. There are only a few people inside; the gallery is closing in fifteen minutes, according to the sign on the door. A stocky man wearing spectacles is behind the counter, studiously ignoring Chloë as he leafs through a booklet. Two other people are wandering past the exhibited art, both of them with dyed hair, deep red and bright purple floating across the pictures like exotic birds. There's no sign of Angela anywhere.

Expecting to find her here was probably idiotic, in all honesty. Why would Angela revisit a part of her life that she ran as far away from as she could? What did Chloë imagine had happened – Angela fell for some kind of cunning trap and her evil ex jumped her and kidnapped her? In a public place? And what, exactly, was Chloë planning to do about it if she had? The whole idea was stupid.

She drifts over to look at Tess's work. It's not hard to find. Her photos are prominently displayed, lining a full wall beneath artfully arranged track lighting. Dozens of grainy black-and-white portraits and cityscapes. As Chloë examines them, she grudgingly admits they're striking.

There's a whole series devoted to Angela. Angela sitting on a bench under a streetlight, her hair illuminated by the soft glow. Angela dancing at a club, smiling and sweaty, her skirt flaring out as the camera catches her mid-twirl. Angela with a black eye.

And the picture from the flyer, uncropped and blown up to enormous size. Angela, naked. Bonelessly relaxed and vulnerable. Her nipples pale on her small breasts. Her labia slightly swollen in the aftermath of sex. A dark trace of blood smeared from her neck down to her collarbone.

'You have good taste,' a voice says next to her. Chloë turns, startled. She hadn't heard the woman with the red dye-job come up next to her. 'That's the best of the Fallen Angels. I'll let you have it for two thousand. Special deal.'

'I don't actually have two thousand dollars to spare.'

'Yeah, I didn't really think you did.' The woman's eyes flick to Chloë's coat, then her shoes, then back to her face. A small, odd smile is perched on her lips, only the left side of her mouth curving up, dimpling her cheek. 'You do have a bite mark on the side of your neck, though. Maybe a week old. Kind of hard to miss it, since whoever made it didn't bother to lick it clean. Wanna guess how I know that?'

Chloë wants to look around wildly for exits, run to the closest one she can find. She keeps her gaze fixed on the woman's incomplete smile instead. She has the uneasy feeling that running would be the most dangerous thing she could do.

'You must be Tess.'

'In the flesh.'

Everything about Tess is small except her clear brown eyes, which seem almost too big for her face. Her nose is small, her chin sharp. The top of her head barely comes up to Chloë's collarbone. Chloë has to tilt her head down to look directly at her. She feels ungainly just standing there.

It hadn't occurred to Chloë that she was showing the signs of a vampire bite. That if Tess was at the gallery, she might take notice.

'I thought Angela might have fucked off to Boston. It's not like she had friends anywhere else.' Tess's smile quirks up a little more, finally reaching the other side of her mouth. 'And you're her blood bank these days, huh? So much for all her bullshit about that. Where is she? Outside or something?'

'No.'

'She's not?' The grin slips away from Tess's face. 'She didn't even have the guts to come here herself?'

'Does that mean she hasn't—You haven't seen her?'

'Me? I haven't caught sight of her the whole time I've been in town. Not here, not at the clubs, not anywhere.' Tess gives Chloë a sour look. 'I suppose she was spending all her time snuggled up at home with you. How cosy.'

'You went around the clubs? Have you been looking for her?'

'No,' Tess snaps. 'Hey, what the fuck is going on? Why did you come here? Did she send you to spy on me? Bring back a report?'

'It isn't like that,' Chloë protests. 'She doesn't know I'm here. We're not, the two of us aren't . . . We're not together anymore.'

'Oh.' The anger fades from Tess's eyes. 'Can't have been that long ago, if you've still got bite marks. Did she break your heart, too?'

Chloë doesn't reply.

'Question still stands, though,' Tess says. 'What brings you to the gallery, blood bank? If you're not a spy and you can't afford a memento.'

It seems like a bad idea to admit she was hoping to find Angela. Not when she's trying to convince Tess she isn't there on some kind of espionage mission. Not when her instincts are screaming that the wrong word right now could be very, very dangerous. 'I guess I was curious,' she says. That's also the truth, as far as it goes.

'Curious. Are you sure that's it?' Tess steps in closer, tilting her head to keep her eyes locked on Chloë's. Close enough that Chloë should be able to feel her body heat. But she doesn't.

'What other reason would I have?' Chloë's throat feels dry.

Tess lays a hand lightly on Chloë's arm. 'Some people like getting bit. Can't get enough of it. Maybe they want to be vampires.' Her fingers gently encircle Chloë's wrist. 'Or maybe they get off on it. What do you think? Either of those sound like you?'

'No,' Chloë manages to get out. 'Not really.'

'You sure?' Tess asks, her voice low and intimate. 'Because if you miss it, I could help you out.'

'I'm sure,' Chloë says.

'That's kind of a shame. Because that means I should probably kill you.'

'What?'

Tess's hand tightens, clamping down, holding Chloë's arm in place. Chloë abruptly remembers Angela's startling strength. She's pretty sure she couldn't break the smaller woman's grip no matter how hard she tried.

'I'm definitely considering it,' Tess says. 'Got any reason why I shouldn't?'

Chloë turns her head, slowly, making no sudden movements, until her gaze takes in the other people in the gallery. The guy with the purple hair – almost a boy, really, barely out of his teens – is staring at them, a frown on his face. He takes a hesitant step in their direction. The gallery clerk remains planted behind the counter, idly flipping through his brochure. Chloë looks back at Tess, her eyebrows raised.

Tess purses her lips. 'You know, you've got a point. Russell knows enough not to say anything, but what's-his-name, pudgy over at the desk there, he could be a pain in the ass.' She tilts her head, considering. 'All right, come with me. If you scream, I'm going to have to kill the fat guy, too.'

Tess strides towards the back of the gallery, yanking Chloë along with her. Chloë bites back a yelp and looks over at the two men. The purple-haired boy – Russell? – is still watching them. The clerk doesn't even look up.

Chloë stumbles after Tess. Her arm is being wrenched so violently she thinks it might get pulled out of its socket if she tries to stop. 'Listen,' she whispers as they race past someone else's photographs, blurred images of fields and forests rushing by at the edge of her vision. 'If you, if you do this . . . There isn't any way, you can't . . .' She gropes after any argument against her own murder.

Her brain is numb, barely responsive. 'There'll be a body. You'll have a body in the middle of a gallery where you've got pictures showing, and someone's going to know—'

'Shut up,' Tess says, stopping short.

Chloë almost trips, but manages to catch herself before she falls. She recovers her balance as quickly as she can and makes an effort to get her bearings. They're at the far end of the room, past all the photos. They've come to a lurching halt at a door in the back wall.

Tess pushes it open, drags Chloë through, and kicks it shut behind them.

PART EIGHT
The Gruesome Killing Spree

CHAPTER FORTY-SIX

Deviance, Phoenix, Arizona
29 August 1998

'Why are we here?' Angela snaps.

Tess's expression doesn't change – remote, disdainful, her chin up, her mouth a thin, straight line. It's the same expression worn by practically everyone else in the club. Only her eyes are different, darting around like small fish as she steals a quick glance at each person they pass.

'Just follow my lead,' Tess says. 'I've been doing this a long time.'

Angela can barely hear her over a distorted, wailing guitar break. The music here is all blasted at top volume. Even 'Lullaby' got the ear-splitting treatment, and that song is half-whispered. She doesn't think much of the DJ.

'Doing what? What have you been doing a long time?'

'You'll see.' Tess watches as a woman in a top hat and velvet waistcoat passes by. It looks like she's aiming for dapper, but she isn't quite pulling it off. Her makeup is too thick, her hair too lank and dry. Angela sees Tess's fingers reach up to touch the camera hanging from a strap around her neck.

But right when she starts to lift it, the woman raises a hand to greet some friends. Tess dismisses her, her gaze flicking back to Angela. Her camera thumps back against her chest as she lets it go.

Tess's hand twitches towards the little handbag where she keeps her cigarettes, but she doesn't open it. She hasn't lit up since they got here. Angela wonders why; half the people around them are smoking, the ceiling nearly hidden behind a blue haze she would have found choking not so very long ago. Is Tess trying to keep her hands free for the camera? Why is it so important?

'Come with me.' Tess grabs Angela's arm and drags her deeper into the crowd.

This isn't one of their usual haunts – it's not Tess's favourite, which means Angela never comes here, either. Goth nights are scattered piecemeal across Phoenix, and this one is in the middle somewhere, not far from where the 51 crosses over the Grand Canal. A warren of dark rooms connected by narrow hallways, decorated with skull masks and chains and blacklights on the last Saturday of every month. Everything looks flimsy and temporary, quick to put up and quick to tear down.

If it's happening tonight, that means it has to be a Saturday. Tess bit her on a Wednesday. So she lost three whole days on the darkroom floor, lying there passed out. Or maybe lying there dead. She's beginning to think that's the more accurate way to think about it, since that's what happens when you stop breathing and your heart stops beating. She died. She just started moving around again afterwards.

Tess insisted they come here as soon as Angela was able to stand. She was still disoriented when Tess dressed her in the most revealing outfit she could find, then sat her in a chair and painted her face with lipstick, eyeshadow, blush. Tess had badgered her with instructions while poking at her with eyeliner. How to avoid breaking someone's fingers with a handshake. How to keep her fangs concealed. When

Angela asked if she could finish her makeup herself, Tess laughed and told her to go look in the bathroom mirror.

Even knowing what would happen, it was a shock to see nothing there.

Angela stops walking and pulls back on Tess's arm. Tess jerks to a halt, turning to face her with a frown.

'I'm not taking another step until you let me know what's going on,' Angela tells her. 'I'm tired, and thirsty, and really not in the mood. Why are we out dancing?'

Tess mutters something Angela can't hear over the music. 'Speak up,' Angela says, exasperated. 'You know, it would have been a lot easier if you told me before we got here.'

Tess takes hold of Angela's shoulders and stretches up on her toes so she can get closer. 'We're not dancing,' she hisses in Angela's ear. 'We're hunting. You're tired and thirsty? That's why we're here. So you'd better get in the mood, all right?'

'Oh,' Angela says. 'What . . . what are we hunting?'

'Who, not what,' Tess corrects her. 'Listen, here's who we're looking for. Someone out on their own, no friends. Lonely, maybe bored. Somebody who's going to be flattered if we give them any fucking attention at all. Young is good. Even younger than you. And drinking but not totally smashed would be great.'

Angela looks around at the sea of people. A writhing knot of shapes, dancing, talking, laughing, drinking. They blur into an undifferentiated mass, a single organism wearing a lot of black clothing. How is she supposed to tell what anyone's feeling? How do you spot the difference between someone who's here alone and someone whose friends have gone to the bathroom?

'I don't know how to start.'

'Leave it to me. Like I said, I've been doing this a long time.' Tess grins and, surprisingly, gives Angela a quick kiss on the cheek. 'Look, we might not find someone right away. Even if we do, it might not work out. Sometimes it doesn't. But it hasn't taken me more than a few weeks for a long time. I'll get us fed, don't worry about it. We're in this for the long haul now, you and me.'

Tess drops back down and begins working her way into the crowd again, weaving expertly through the spaces between bodies. The hem of her long dress swishes away from the clumsy stomping boots around it like it's a living thing. Angela follows behind, puzzling over what Tess said. They're in it for the long haul *now*? What were the past two years, the short haul? Why would finding someone take weeks? What is Tess looking for?

And when they do find someone, what are they going to do?

'There,' Tess says. 'Standing in the corner. No, don't look directly at him, keep looking at me. Watch him out of the corner of your eye.'

Angela keeps her face towards Tess and tries to use her peripheral vision. She registers a shock of bright-purple hair, a glum face staring out at the dancers.

'Don't get close until I step in next to him,' Tess tells her. 'Then you take his left, I'll take his right. Look sexy, and try not to say much.'

Tess eases her way towards him on a circuitous route, her attention wandering everywhere other than her destination. She cuts across the dance floor, an obstacle course of twitching bodies. Right through the area where her target is looking. She shoots a quick, impatient glance back at Angela, who hasn't moved. Angela walks towards her, making an effort to look sexy as she does it.

She suddenly feels very conscious of what she's wearing. Her top isn't anything but a glorified bra, and her skirt barely covers her ass. She's wearing thigh-high stockings, but they mostly draw attention to the exposed white flesh above them. She's worn all this before, of course, or something like it. But never for this reason. Never to serve as bait.

Tess has nearly completed her circuit, with Angela lagging a few steps behind. She's close enough now for a better look at Tess's selection. His features are a little too big for his face – a wide mouth, a prominent nose. Neither handsome nor ugly, maybe striking if you were looking for a compliment. He's wearing the requisite heavy boots and black trousers, and he's topped them with a jacket covered with buckles and straps. The jacket isn't the best look for him. It gives the vague impression that he's a member of a depressed drum-and-bugle corps. Sergeant Pepper's Lonely Goth Club Band.

His hair is beautiful, though. The exact shade of a lilac flower, vibrant and bright, looking like it grew there naturally. Angela wonders if he dyed it fresh tonight before he went out.

She steps in closer and sees a spray of acne along the line of his jaw. He looks young. Very young. Surely he had to be at least twenty-one to get in?

'Hey!' Tess shouts above the music, lifting her camera to her face. 'Don't move!'

The young man swivels around to look at her, blinking in surprise.

'Seriously!' Tess goes on. 'Can you freeze for, like, half a second? I want to get a good shot of you!'

He obligingly holds still while Tess takes the picture. He even poses a little, lifting his chin, although he doesn't smile.

Angela feels like she's been punched in the gut.

A small woman in a ruffled black dress, her face hidden behind a camera. 'This is going to need a long exposure time,' she told Angela. 'If you move, it'll blur out.'

She'd been a target. Two years ago, in the park. Someone lonely, bored, and flattered by any attention at all. That's all she was. She wonders if she was ever anything else.

'Perfect, thanks.' Tess puts the camera down and moves in next to him on his right. Her brow wrinkles slightly as Angela remains still, and she gestures with her head towards his other side. Angela steps forward slowly, and takes her place there. Boxing him in.

'I'm Tess.' She doesn't need to shout so loudly now that she's right next to him. *She looks completely harmless*, Angela thinks. Such a tiny thing, dressed up like an Edwardian doll. 'That's Angela. It's a pleasure to meet you.'

His eyes shift to Angela's chest when Tess introduces her, then quickly away again, his gaze settling between the two of them, carefully fixed on nothing in particular. 'My name's Russell,' he says. 'So was this, like, for a promotion or something?'

Tess shakes her head. 'Nah, I'm a photographer. I like to take a shot whenever I see anything striking. Like your hair.'

Angela is tempted to point out that his hair isn't going to show up very well on black-and-white film.

'Mine always fades to pink way too fast,' Tess says. 'What are you using? Manic Panic? Special Effects? It's gorgeous.'

Russell blushes. 'I get it done in a salon.'

'Cool. Can you tell me which one?'

Russell's blush is stirring uncomfortable feelings in Angela's throat and stomach. Hunger. She can feel something shifting around in her mouth. She fights hard to remember what Tess said about keeping her fangs in, tries to stay focused. Concentrate. She doesn't have to let it control her.

'Tell you what,' Tess says, linking her arm through his. 'Why don't we buy you a drink, as a thank you for the photo? And you can tell us who does your hair.'

'You don't have to –'

'We want to,' Tess cuts him off. 'Angela, let's bring this gentleman to the bar.' She waits expectantly, a quick motion of her hand coaxing Angela to take his other arm.

'Excuse me,' Angela says. She turns and stalks off across the club. Tess shouts something after her, but she doesn't pay attention.

She doesn't bother to duck around the people in her way, shouldering straight through the crowd instead. Someone stumbles and falls. She hears more shouts, different voices, but she keeps going until she reaches the door.

Past the bouncer, out the exit, into clearer air. There's a cluster of people gathered on the sidewalk, probably trying to get away from the noise. Most of them are red-faced from the heat, dripping sweat now that they're out of the club's heavy air conditioning. They're dressed ridiculously for the desert. One is wearing a leather jacket. Even what Angela has on makes more sense. Or at least at night it does; in the daytime, someone with her complexion baring this much flesh would develop skin cancer in a month.

Well, that won't be a problem. Not anymore. She's never going to see the sun again.

It's quieter out here, once the door swings closed. The sidewalk chatter is muted, and only the thumping bass makes it through the walls. She can hear her own thoughts again – until the door opens to let someone else out, which eradicates whatever she was thinking in a burst of sound.

She moves further away, heading into an alley between buildings. There are puddles left from a hard rain earlier in the day, the water steaming up from the hot ground. The brick walls look greasy, and the air is filled with a rank smell wafting out of an overfull dumpster. She finds a relatively dry spot next to it and sits down.

She tries to catch her breath, and discovers what it feels like not to have any breath to catch. Strange. Very strange.

Angela half expects to see the angel reflected in a puddle. But when she glances into one, its surface is nothing but a blank screen, speckled with dirt and bits of plastic. He's not in there, and neither is she. There's no one looking back at her at all. She isn't sure why she thought he might make an appearance tonight; it's been close to two years since the last time, when she finally decided she was done with that part of her past.

'What the hell, Angela?' Tess, at the mouth of the alley, coming closer.

'Leave me alone.'

'How about, no? How about you explain what your little freak-out in there was supposed to be instead?'

'What do you think it was supposed to be?'

'I don't know. You like to ruin everything?' Tess is standing next to her now. One hand is keeping the edges of her dress away from the puddles, the other is holding a lit cigarette. No reason not to smoke now, apparently. 'That guy was a good prospect. Why did you go and mess it up?'

'A good prospect for what?' Angela asks, her eyes on the grit swirling in the dark pools of water. 'Dinner? Or fucking?'

Angela can still hear the bass pulsing ever so faintly through the alley wall. She counts thirty beats before Tess says anything.

'You need to let me show you the ropes. It's important.'

'Did you know that whenever you avoid a question like that, you're pretty much telling me the answer?' Angela asks. 'I don't know where I should start. For one thing, and this is not even the most messed-up part of tonight, have you noticed I'm a lesbian?'

'Yeah, I'm not an idiot. I thought you might be squeamish about it. I was going to do that part by myself if you didn't want to.'

'That's supposed to make it better?'

'Look, we've only got two options here!' Tess snaps. 'We can fuck them, or kill them.'

Angela jerks up her head, shocked, to meet Tess's eyes. As far as Angela can tell, she's serious.

'What are you talking about? That's insane.'

Tess makes a frustrated, strangled noise in the back of her throat. 'Put it together, for once in your life. You can't drink from someone once and then let them wander off. They'll talk. That's a death sentence. So you build a relationship with them. Get them used to the idea. Gain their trust.'

'Get them under control.'

'If you want to think about it that way.'

Angela breaks her gaze away, puts her head between her knees. Muffling her laughter.

'What?' Tess asks her.

'Two weeks,' Angela manages to choke out. 'You had me totally under your thumb two weeks after I met you. I'm such an idiot.'

'Oh, angel, no.' Tess crouches down next to her, careful of her dress. She drops her cigarette into the water, where it goes out with a faint hiss, and reaches for Angela's chin. With a gentle tug, she tilts Angela's head back up. 'You're different. You were always different. You wouldn't have turned, I know you wouldn't have turned if it wasn't real. If you weren't special. No one else ever has, you're the only one. That's got to mean something, right?'

'So what happened to everyone else?'

Tess looks puzzled. 'What do you mean?'

'How do breakups work in this thing you've got going? How do you make sure they won't talk? Do they live through it?'

'Don't be crazy.'

Tess doesn't flinch, doesn't even blink. No matter how closely Angela tries to read her face, she can't see a reaction.

Although Angela can't help but notice that she didn't really answer, either.

'Look, this is the way things are,' Tess says. 'If you don't want it to be a guy, we can look for a girl. It'll be harder, guys are always going to be easier for the two of us to pick up, but we can do it.'

'That isn't the point.'

'You're right, it's not. The point is, it's food. Something we need to do to survive. It doesn't have to affect things between the two of us.'

'You think it doesn't matter?'

'No. It really doesn't.' Tess's eyes are wide with sincerity. Her hands land softly on Angela's shoulders. 'Not if we love each other.'

'Then I guess I don't love you enough,' Angela says. 'Fuck you.'

Tess slaps her.

Angela hardly feels it, but she reacts anyway. She launches herself at Tess, snarling, knocking her over backwards. Tess lands in a puddle with a splash. Angela scrabbles at her face with her fingers, not having any real idea what she's doing. Tess punches her in the stomach, hard. It knocks her back a little, but doesn't do much else. No breath to catch also means no wind to lose.

Angela's fangs have come out, and she's making a strange noise deep in her throat. She thinks she might be growling. Tess is halfway to her feet when Angela is on her again. Her teeth close on Tess's shoulder. The taste of Tess's lukewarm blood floods into her mouth. Tess snaps with her own fangs, missing Angela's face by a fraction of an inch.

They're both on the ground, flailing at each other with their fists, elbows, feet. Tess reaches for Angela's face, scratching at her eyes. Angela grabs at Tess's arm and bites again, her fangs sinking in deep. Tess struggles to pull away, then gets a knee in Angela's chest and pushes, shoving her back. Flesh tears and shreds as Angela's teeth are ripped away from Tess's wrist.

Both of them stand up warily, keeping an eye on each other. Tess's dress is wet, filthy, and torn in half a dozen places. Dark blood oozes out of her shoulder and arm. One of the straps on Angela's top has broken and dangles freely, leaving her almost exposed. She doesn't look down, but she knows her stockings must be a ripped and sodden mess. Nothing hurts, though. She doesn't even feel any scrapes from rolling around on the concrete.

'Got that out of your system?' Tess asks.

'We're done.'

'We better be.'

'Not with this,' Angela says. 'I meant, you and me. We're done. I'm done.'

'No. Let's go home and get cleaned up.' Tess holds out her hand. The one that isn't dripping blood. Angela doesn't take it.

'You can't say "no" here, Tess. You don't get to say "no". I'm not going back to your house.'

Tess looks impatient. Her hand is still out. Her wounds are already shrinking, the flow of blood slowing to a thin dribble. 'You're being totally irrational. You've got no place else to go before dawn, and you have no fucking idea what you're doing.'

'I'll come get my stuff in a few days. Don't bother smashing my computer, I've got everything backed up.' Angela walks past Tess, heading towards the mouth of the alley. She gets most of the way there before Tess says another word.

'You're not going to last more than a few days, not out on your own,' Tess declares. 'You're not going to last the night.'

Angela keeps walking.

'Did you get what you wanted from me?' Tess yells after her. 'Is that what's going on? You were waiting for this to happen, and now you're gone?'

'It's not a gift, Tess,' Angela says, not turning around. 'You screwed me over the way someone screwed you over. That's all.'

Angela wishes that were the last word, but of course it isn't. Tess follows her out of the alley, her face contorted with rage, screaming at her, calling her an ungrateful bitch. The goths hanging around outside the club door stare at them as they go by. Tess trails after her for blocks, past shuttered businesses and then darkened houses, yelling that she has to come back, that she's got no choice, that she'll regret this, that they're in love. The sidewalks are almost empty once they're away from the club, and the few people they pass look away quickly, cross to the other side of the street.

When Angela reaches the turbid, murky water of the Grand Canal, flowing sluggishly beneath the underpass, swollen with the recent rain, she jumps in.

The running water feels strange, like it's trying to push her away, but Angela ignores it and stays under. She starts swimming. Tess, at last, doesn't follow.

She doesn't come out until she hits Indian School Road. Maybe about a mile? She isn't sure. She crawls out onto the walking path that runs alongside the water. Drenched, filthy, and half-naked in the middle of the night.

She wanders down the road looking for a pay phone. First step, get a cab. Second step, find a place to stay. She wonders if she should head down to Tempe. She's technically got an office at the university, although she hardly ever uses it these days. But it's shared with two other grad students. Too dangerous, too much chance of someone coming in, even on a weekend.

She'll have to go to a motel. That should work. Put up the Do Not Disturb sign, spend the day in the bathroom, away from any windows. Later, she can think about finding someplace to stay for the long term. Someplace far, far away.

Before that, though, she has to figure out a way to survive. Without killing anybody. And without becoming anything like Tess.

CHAPTER FORTY-SEVEN

**The Parable Of The Beautiful Girl And The Gruesome
  Killing Spree
Appalachian Foothills, Western Massachusetts
22 December 1999**

Hey, man, thanks for the ride. I mean it. You would not believe how hard it is to hitchhike these days. Everyone is, like, convinced that I'm a serial killer who's going to brutally murder them. Leave the body in a ditch, that kind of thing. Boo! Ha ha, yeah, there's no trust anymore, you know?

Where am I heading? Well, I'm not entirely certain. I'm following a premonition and guided by a prophecy, but that's kind of a long story. All I know is that I'm heading west. And hey, I'll get to see more of this great country while I'm at it, right? I started hitching about a week ago in Boston. Got as far as Worcester on the first day. Stayed there the second day, too. Pretty much been in Worcester the whole week, honestly. Like I said, it hasn't been easy to get a lift. Nice city, though. Birthplace of the mass-produced Valentine's Day card, did you know that? Yeah, I think before Worcester, they were all handmade, one at a time. So, uh, that's something, I guess.

I spent most of my time there preaching. Yep, that's what I do, I'm a street preacher. You're absolutely right, it's a rough time of year for an outside job. I don't mind being out in the snow and the cold so much, but hardly anyone stops to listen when the weather gets bad. You'd think people would be more open to it this close to Christmas, but everyone hurries on by.

Hey, as long as we're stuck together in the car, you want to hear a parable? Pass the time? All right, then how about just a short parable? It won't be boring that way, me yakking away at you for the whole trip.

Great, great. I've been working on a new one. It's called, 'The Beautiful Girl and the Gruesome Killing Spree'.

Once upon a time, there was a beautiful girl.

The beautiful girl had been told all her life that the best thing she could ever do was be nice to everybody. Everybody in the whole wide world. Her parents told her this at home. Her teachers told her at school. Be nice. Be polite. Be quiet. Don't speak out of turn. Don't make waves. Make everybody else feel happy, and then you'll be a good person.

One day, the beautiful girl met a monster. I actually already went through this bit in a previous parable, and it's going to make the story a lot longer if I add it back in. Can I give you the quick version? OK, let's see – dancing, screwing, relationship, argument, bite. I think that about covers it.

So, anyway, there was this monster the girl was dating, and one day the monster started biting her, over and over. And the beautiful girl just took it. Because that was the *nice* thing to do. I mean, God forbid anyone feel bad about biting her! So she took it and took it and took it and took it until one day, she finally decided to stop being so goddamn nice about it. And that was the end of that.

But the problem was, all the rage from her entire life had come boiling up to the surface. Everything she'd buried under all that niceness. And it was making the girl hate herself because she wasn't nice anymore. Now, maybe all she needed was a good night's sleep and a whole lot of therapy. But she never got it. You want to know why? She was too pissed off.

No, no, bear with me here, I'm almost done. About a year later, the beautiful girl met another girl. That other girl was funny and smart and pretty and cool, and they got along great. Until one day the second girl pushed the wrong button and chomp! So much for that relationship, too.

And the first beautiful girl thought, if everything is going to go to hell, anyway, no matter what she tries, maybe she should just run with that. Maybe she should really go crazy and kill her goddamn monster ex. Maybe she should kill anybody who gets in her goddamn way.

Or maybe it would be better if she slit her wrists or crashed her car or took a gun and shot herself in the fucking head, or whatever the hell it would take to save everyone the fucking trouble! How about that?

Yeah, she thought to herself. How about that.

What's that? Listen, there's not too much more, and . . . Oh, you want me to get out here? Even though I'm not done with the parable yet? No, totally, it's your car, you call the shots.

The only thing is, this is kind of the middle of nowhere, isn't it? If you could maybe take me to the next town – no? OK, that's cool. Thanks for giving me a ride to, um, to wherever this is. Have a great day.

Bye!

CHAPTER FORTY-EIGHT

Newbury Street, Back Bay, Boston
22 December 1999

'Now,' Tess says as the door swings closed with a sharp click. 'You were saying?'

Chloë takes a rapid glance around the room Tess has brought her to, looking for any way out. Not that she could get to one with Tess tightly gripping her wrist. The door they came through is behind Tess, and firmly shut. There's another door across the room, an oversized one that looks like it might lead outside.

They're in a small area behind the exhibition space. Chloë glimpses framed pictures stacked against the wall to one side, a desk and photocopier occupying a nook on the other. She doesn't take the time to examine any of it more closely.

'They saw you go back here with me . . .' she begins, then quickly abandons that line of reasoning when she realises it might get the clerk killed. 'There's going to be a body.' *My body*, she thinks. *My corpse.* Chloë tries to calm her voice. If there was ever a time she needed to keep it together, it's now. 'There'll be questions, won't there?'

'Nah, it's not like I'm going to leave you in the room. I'll say I took you here to show you around, you left by the back door.' Tess gestures towards the exit with the hand she isn't using to keep Chloë pinned. 'It'll be true, sort of.'

This would be a particularly easy way to die, Chloë thinks. Not even her fault. Just something that happened. She doesn't want to, though. Not here, not now.

Good to realise that, if maybe it comes a little too late.

'People know I was coming here tonight. My aunt, my co-workers. I told them.'

'Now see, if you'd led with that, I might have believed you,' Tess says.

'I'm telling the truth.' Chloë doesn't think she could sound more like a liar if she tried. Why doesn't she say her story is entirely plausible? That'd be about as believable.

Tess frowns at her. It makes her look like an angry pixie. 'You know, it's a little weird that instead of begging and pleading, you're trying to convince me it would be inconvenient. Is that why she likes you? You're brave and stoic and shit like that?'

Chloë is fairly sure that it's raw shock driving her responses rather than courage. 'Would begging and pleading work?'

'No, not really. And you're right, by the way, this is very fucking inconvenient. You're making things a hell of a lot harder on me when I was looking for a quiet night. So, thanks for that.'

'Why kill me?' It's the only thing she has left to say. 'Why bother?'

'Why do you think? Cleaning up Angela's mess. She might even thank me for it someday.'

'I . . . I don't think she would.' Chloë can't keep the tremor out of her voice. So much for bravery and stoicism.

'So.' Tess pauses, and looks Chloë up and down as if she's trying to judge a dubious piece of meat. 'How is she these days, anyway?'

Tess sounds almost casual. Bizarrely so, given the circumstances.

'What?'

'It's a simple question,' Tess says impatiently.

'She's, um . . .' Chloë has no idea how to reply. How is Angela? Getting everyone worried about her? Not enjoying life as a vampire? That seems like it might be insulting.

'Come on, you might as well say something. What the hell does it matter?'

'She told me once she doesn't hate you for what you did to her,' Chloë says in a rush.

Tess goes very still. 'Oh, that's nice. She doesn't hate me for it. How nice.' Her tone is acid. 'And how about you? Does she love you?'

'What?'

'Is "what" the only thing you know how to say? Come on, tell me. Does she love you?'

Chloë doesn't know what the right answer is. Or if there is a right answer at all; for all she knows, Tess is simply curious.

She can feel her heart pounding in her chest. She counts the heartbeats. One. Two. Three. Four. She wonders if Tess can feel the pulse in her wrist. Or hear the thumps as they happen. They certainly seem loud enough.

'Maybe,' Chloë says. 'I mean, I think so. I think . . . yes.'

Tess squints at Chloë, leaning forward slightly, examining her face. 'You think so.'

Chloë nods.

Tess takes one last close look. Chloë isn't sure what she's looking for.

'Well.' She straightens back up again. 'It probably wouldn't have made a difference, anyway.'

'If you're doing this to take me away from her, you don't have to,' Chloë stutters out. 'We already broke up. It's done.'

Tess looks utterly stunned for a moment. When she recovers, her face becomes an angry mask.

'This isn't . . . Holy shit, I'm not doing this because I'm *petty*.' She practically spits the word. 'This isn't about that at all! We're talking about the fucking safety of my species here. It has nothing to do with her. You got that?'

Chloë nods mutely.

But if that's true, then why, she wonders, *did you ask me if she loves me?*

The reason won't matter in a few moments. Chloë can see Tess's fangs when she talks, gleaming with saliva. They come out either for hunger, she remembers, or excitement.

There's a look in Tess's eyes, cold and hard as glass, that Chloë recognises from somewhere. Alec's face, she realises. His eyes used to turn that way, too, sometimes. Always right before they had a fight. It's not pleasure, exactly, but anticipation. Preparation. Bad things are about to happen. It's a look, it occurs to her, that she's never once seen on Angela's face.

'Let me go.' Chloë isn't sure why she's bothering. Mostly from a sense that she shouldn't let this happen to her while she does nothing. She has too many years of that behind her. That's another epiphany arriving right when it doesn't matter anymore.

The bones in her wrist creak in protest as Tess's unyielding fingers clench harder, and she can see the muscles in Tess's body tense, like a cat preparing to spring on a toy. Tess opens her mouth wide, baring her teeth.

'*Let go,*' Chloë says again, desperation adding fierceness to the words.

Tess does, her hand leaping away as if Chloë's arm had suddenly caught fire. Both of them stand blinking at each other.

Tess's mouth snaps shut and contorts into a snarl. 'Huh. Nice trick,' she growls. 'Does it work if you can't say it out loud?'

Chloë doesn't know what she's talking about, and there isn't time to care. A clenched fist is already lashing towards her jaw in a blur. Chloë flinches away, trying to bring up her arms to protect herself, too slowly, too uselessly. '*Stay away,*' she yells.

Tess takes a step back just as the door behind her opens and purple-dye-job boy steps through it. They collide, the boy letting out a surprised grunt. Tess's fist swings wildly as she stumbles; it passes so close to Chloë's face she can feel the air stir.

Russell falls on his backside with a painful-sounding thud. Tess turns to glare at him, her expression changing swiftly from anger to exasperation.

The moment Tess isn't looking at her, Chloë runs.

She isn't sure what just happened, but staying to find out seems like the worst idea imaginable. She dashes across the room to the back door and twists the handle, silently cursing the time it takes to yank it open. At least it isn't deadbolted. She barrels through to the outside.

Her foot slips in the snow as she emerges onto a dark back street, lightless windows puncturing dull brick walls, metal grills covering loading docks. She manages to stay upright, picks a random direction and runs. As fast as she can, as hard as she can. She turns at the first corner she comes to, then the next.

Still running, gasping for breath, something painful happening in her side, she makes it onto an avenue with cars and people. Boylston Street, busy at almost any time of day. She changes direction, keeps running, dodging past a woman pushing a stroller, a man with a scarf wrapped around his face, bundled up against the cold. Everyone is walking slowly, too slowly. She needs to get past them; she needs to get away.

She doesn't look back. If someone is following her, she doesn't want to know.

CHAPTER FORTY-NINE

Appalachian Foothills, Western Massachusetts
22 December 1999

A few hours ago, Angela made a snow angel. She'd been lying on her back, gazing at the stars, when the urge to make one struck her unexpectedly. Since then, though, she's barely moved. She lies motionless in the impression her body has shaped in the snow. The moon is high in the sky, round as a sugar cookie. It looks small and remote, a far-off buoy floating above the bare branches of the oak trees.

She doesn't stir when she hears the sound of an engine from the distant road. As isolated as this place might be, a car still passes within earshot every hour or so, even in the middle of the night. Complete isolation is hard to find.

When she hears footsteps crunching in the snow behind her, she lifts her head and turns to see who's coming down the path.

It's a tall man with shoulder-length hair and soft, genial eyes, dressed in boots and jeans and a battered jacket. He drops a heavy suitcase in the snow a few feet away from her, and sits on it.

She recognises him, of course. He might not have wings and a halo like the figures in the stained glass windows, but she's seen him in too many bathroom mirrors to mistake him for anyone else. She isn't surprised he's shown up here, even though it's been so long since she last saw him face to face. He always did have a habit of appearing at the most awkward possible moment.

'Hi!' the angel says brightly.

Angela sits up fully. 'Hey.'

'How're you doing?'

She shows him a grim little scowl. 'Not so good, really. You?'

'Not bad, not bad.'

When the conversation seems to die there, he looks around at the scenery.

'Well,' he says, turning his attention back to Angela, 'it's a nice surprise to run into you.'

'A surprise,' Angela says drily. 'So you're saying that you just happened to come up here by accident? Total coincidence, nothing to do with me?'

'Pretty much.' He sounds somewhat sheepish. 'I got kicked out of a car a little way down the road.'

She looks him up and down. 'That's your excuse for dropping by? Why, because there aren't any mirrors around?' When he doesn't answer, she turns her eyes back to the stars. 'Fine, have it your way.'

'So, what are you doing all the way out here?' the angel asks.

She waves a hand upwards. 'Watching the sky.'

'Oh, yeah?'

'I'm trying to get a sense of place. Where I fit in to all of this. If I fit in to it at all.' She scans the constellations until she finds Canis Major, low in the eastern sky. 'That really bright star is Sirius,' she says, pointing at it as she names it. 'It's only eight and a half light years away, which is, like, next door, when you're talking about the whole galaxy. There's the Big Dipper, the Little Dipper, and Draco the dragon in between. And those stars way over there on the edge, right above the horizon, are in Leo, the lion. You can just see it, now. Any of those stars could have planets around them. And any of those planets could harbour intelligent life.'

'So, the whole universe could be filled with people?' he says. 'Civilisations around every single star?'

'Well,' Angela admits, 'probably not Sirius. That's a type A star. It can't be more than about three hundred million years old. Any planet would still be a molten lump at that point. But a lot of them could.'

The two of them regard the heavens together for a long minute.

'I don't believe in you anymore,' she says.

'That's OK,' the angel replies equably.

'I haven't believed in you for a long time, or any of the rest of it, no matter what they made me say at Confirmation. And I don't go to church at all now, not ever, and I'm inflamed with lust for other women, and . . . and I use birth control!'

The angel looks puzzled. 'Why?'

'Why what?'

'If you're into other women, then why do you use birth control?'

'Oh!' Angela turns slightly pink. 'It's a health thing. I get really bad cramps if I don't take them. And let me tell you, the fact that I still have a period has to be the least fair thing in the world. I mean, maybe I need to get rid of excess blood, somehow, but–'

He shifts uncomfortably. 'Is it important to you that we discuss this?'

'Forget it,' she says. 'The point is, you're a myth. You and the tooth fairy and Santa Claus – all of you are the exact same kind of thing. Not real.'

'You can think that, if you want. It's fine with me. Religion is supposed to be for people, not the other way around. If believing in me wasn't helping you, I hope you've found something that does.'

She narrows her eyes at him. 'That is not at all what I was taught as a child. It's certainly not the kind of thing you used to say.'

'Are you sure that was me you were listening to? I can be hard to hear past all the other voices, especially when I'm far away. It's the whole reason I came down here. That, and preaching my radical gospel.' He considers his words. 'Look, beliefs are stories we tell ourselves to make the world make sense. Those stories only matter if they mean something to you. I make up my own stories, why shouldn't you?'

Angela takes a few moments to puzzle that out. 'You make up your own beliefs? Are you saying you're a rebel angel?'

'No. At least, I choose not to believe so.' He flashes a grin at her, then grows more serious when she doesn't smile back. 'What I'm saying is that religions change. Interpretations change. And the crucial thing about them is what they accomplish, not what they are. So believe whatever you need to, whatever gets you somewhere better. Although if it matters,' he adds, 'I actually am sitting right here beside you, and maybe there's a reason for that, you know?'

She shakes her head, and turns away. 'You were going someplace interesting for a while there, but you had to end with that, didn't you?'

Angela starts to gather snow together into a ball, carefully packing it until it's round and perfect. It's good snowball snow, solid enough to hold a shape without being too heavy and damp. She tosses it from hand to hand and considers throwing it at the angel, but is irritated to find she can't bring herself to do it. It feels too sacrilegious, even if the religion he signifies isn't hers anymore. Even if he's not really there.

'Why are you out here, anyway? Was it just to look at the sky?' he asks. 'It's a bit cold for that, isn't it?'

'I don't ever get too cold,' she says, flopping back down in the snow. 'It seemed like a good place to come. I'm tired.'

'I can think of a lot of better places to catch a nap.'

'Not that kind of tired. More like, tired of everything. I'm tired of not being able to move on. I'm tired of everything always getting ruined by things that happened years ago. And I'm very, very tired of worrying that someday I'm going to go on a date and end up ripping out my girlfriend's jugular vein with my teeth and sucking the blood out of her still-warm corpse.'

The angel's eyes widen. 'Is that ... something you do a lot, or ... ?'

'No,' Angela says quickly. 'I've never actually done that. But what if someday I just snap?'

'Do a lot of people have that worry? Because I'm guessing it's not a common one.'

'Look,' she replies grumpily, 'I think I'm more likely to do that than most people, OK? I came way too close to it once. It would only be one step worse than what I've already done. Just a line I haven't crossed yet.' She traces patterns in the snow with a fingertip. Diamonds, circles, stars. 'I'm a mass of instincts. For a while I deluded myself into believing I could keep them under control. I was hoping that I might be able to act like a normal person again, but clearly I can't.'

'I don't know if anybody's really normal. I'm not normal. I'm a religious zealot, and I get kicked out of cars for telling weird stories. We've all got our issues.'

Angela rises fully to her feet, brushing the accumulated snow off her backside. Her clothes are soaked, and the dress is almost certainly going to spot; it's velvet. She supposes it doesn't much matter.

She looks out over the cliff. The sky looks no different than it did a few minutes ago, the stars moving too slowly for any change to be seen. A few wisps of cloud float across the moon.

'I was thinking maybe it would be better for everybody if I wasn't around,' Angela says. 'And I guess that's what I'm doing out here. Waiting for the sunrise.'

'What happens at sunrise?'

'You know,' she answers in a jocular tone, 'I'm not completely sure. The guy in *Nosferatu* sort of vanished, but on *Buffy the Vampire Slayer* you burst into flames, then crumble into ashes.'

The angel looks troubled by this. 'Here's an idea – let's not find out the answer.'

'I'm pretty much out of other options. Do you have any idea how hard it is to stake yourself?'

'That isn't what I meant.'

'I know.'

'You should get away from here. Go someplace safe.'

Angela looks down, not facing him, trying to make out the details of the landscape below. 'No.'

'You should.'

'Why?'

The trees down in the valley gleam faintly white in the moonlight, laden with snow. The distant stream is a silvery snake. She tosses her snowball and watches it drop down and down until she can't see it anymore.

She briefly wonders what would happen if she decided to jump instead. Probably nothing, if the knife attempt and the near accident in the car are anything to go by. She'd end up doing the same thing she's doing now, only in a different place, below at the bottom of the cliff. Tess didn't break any bones when she hammered her fist into cement, so a fall isn't likely to hurt much.

'I don't think the things you're afraid of are going to happen,' the angel says. 'I don't think you'll let them happen. Now that you've come close once, I don't think you'll let yourself get that far again.'

Angela frowns at that, her eyebrows furrowing as she stares into the gorge. 'You haven't got the faintest idea what I'm dealing with.'

'You think I don't know anything about people who drink blood?' he asks evenly. 'If you study Christian theology at all, the subject comes up. Kind of a lot.'

'That's not – that's completely unrelated.'

'Is it? Because it sure looks like you're making yourself into a sacrifice for other people's sins. Which is a lousy job, and it doesn't end well.'

'You don't know anything about my life, and you don't know what you're talking about.'

'You should get away from here.'

She grinds her teeth in frustration. Why did he have to come here? 'No. You're not the boss of me anymore. Don't order me around, and stop telling me what to do.'

'I'm not trying to order you around.'

'Then leave me the fuck alone!'

Acting on a sudden impulse, she throws herself over the edge of the cliff.

She drops straight down, time stretching until every instant has its own breadth, separated from the next. At first it's like flying, like how she imagined it might feel if she had any luck turning into a bat. Free in the air, high above the ground. The wind presses against her face, roaring in her ears; her dress flaps around her like a flag in a gale.

But the initial thrill wears off quickly, and something tight and cold replaces it.

It's too far, too much. The earth below is charging up to meet her. Seeing the ground rushing towards her, so fast, so very fast, she knows she's made a mistake. This isn't like a skidding car. This is different. Reflexes can't save her here. Nothing can. Impenetrable skin or not, she doesn't believe anyone, anything, could survive this.

She only wanted to leave, be somewhere else. But when she hits she's going to shatter like a china vase. Or maybe she's wrong about dying, maybe she'll live through it because of what she is and lie there broken and bleeding until the sun comes up, with no chance of getting away anymore, no chance at all.

Oh, crap.

Oh, crap, I'm never going to see her again, I'm—

She lands on her side in a snowdrift, the force of it slamming her all the way through to the ground beneath without slowing. She can feel the jarring punch of the collision in her whole body. The impact makes a sound like a muffled drumbeat.

It takes her a few stunned seconds to realise that nothing hurts.

She wiggles her fingers and toes. Nothing seems to be broken, either.

She wants to break into hysterical giggles with the giddy relief of it. Indestructible after all.

'You should be careful,' the angel tells her. 'You wouldn't want to dash your foot against a stone or anything.'

That puts a damper on her brief giddy mood. When it's gone, nothing is left but a remnant of the horror she felt during the fall, fluttering inside her rib cage like a flock of panicked starlings.

She sits up in the vaguely Angela-shaped crater she's made and spits out a mouthful of snow.

'That's . . .' she starts, trying to regain her composure. 'That's Satan's line. About the foot and the stone. In the Gospels.'

She can't make out much of her surroundings. It's darker here in the shadow of the cliff, the side of the mountain cutting off the moonlight. There's a stand of trees somewhere to her left, visible only because of the snow. Dim, pale clumps hovering in the air, outlining unseen branches. The angel is a blurry shape standing a short distance away.

She can barely make out his shrug in the darkness. 'If the Devil can quote scripture, it seems only fair that I can appropriate a few words back.'

Angela is beginning to get over her shock, rational thought slowly returning. *So it's back to this again*, she thinks. She should have known there was no real way to get away from him. What she's hearing isn't coming from outside of her, after all.

'You can't have made it down here so fast. It's not possible.'

'You're one to talk. Speaking of which, it's going to take you, like, an hour to make it back to your car. It's all the way up at the top.'

'What I'm trying to say is that now I can't even pretend to believe you're actually here.'

'Sure, you can,' he says. 'Inexplicable miracles and wonders? Totally my thing. Look, sunrise isn't going to leave a lot of time for second thoughts when it comes. You should leave. Find the real cause of your problems. Self-actualise.'

'The only cause of my problems is me.'

'You turned yourself into a vampire?'

Shaking off the last lingering shreds of terror, Angela pulls herself up to her feet. Once her legs are steady, she stalks towards him, heels crunching through the snow.

'I don't have to listen to you,' she says as she approaches him, 'because you don't exist.'

He exhales impatiently. 'All right. Let's say that's true. So what?'

'So you're fake. A memory. Entirely in my head. You are a figment of my imagination.'

Angela tilts her head up to stare a challenge into his eyes. She can see him better now that she's right next to him. They're standing close enough together that the fog of his breath touches her hair.

'If I'm all in your head, then who,' asks the angel, 'is telling you to leave?'

She doesn't have a good answer to that.

He seems very large, looming over her, and she feels small, a child talking to her imaginary friend. She'd trusted him then, before dogma and bigotry turned it all so sour. Before she grew up. Angel of God, my guardian dear.

Even if he was never real, there'd been a time when it was nice to believe somebody was listening.

'I don't have any other choices left,' she says, almost under her breath. 'None that I can stand to make, anyway.'

'Are you certain? Because I don't think I'd be here if that were true.'

'So what are they?' Angela wants to grab him and shake the answer out of him. There'd be no point, though. 'How am I supposed to live? What am I supposed to do?'

'If you stay here,' he tells her, 'you're never going to find out.'

She stares at him for a silent minute, turning that over in her mind, before she walks away.

After half a mile of trudging through the snow, she finds a road and starts the long journey back up to her car.

CHAPTER FIFTY

Public Garden
22 December 1999

Chloë doesn't stop running for blocks, not until she reaches the Public Garden, where she collapses on a snow-covered bench, gulping down cold air with deep gasps.

She takes a few moments to recover. Then she takes a few more to convince herself that no one is about to jump out from behind a tree and murder her. It's a useless worry, anyway. She's seen how fast Angela can move when she wants to; if Tess had chased after her, she'd already be dead.

Chloë wonders if she should be frightened for the two men she left behind in the gallery. She hopes not. Tess talked about Russell like he was her . . . accomplice? Henchman? And the guy at the front desk didn't see anything happen, in the end. No reason for Tess to disrupt her quiet evening a second time. If that's truly something that matters to her.

She certainly isn't going back there to find out. She shouldn't have gone in the first place. Going to see naked pictures of Angela. What a creepy thing to do. What had she been thinking?

The Garden is deserted. Nothing is in bloom at this time of year, and the weeping willows dip bare branches into the pond. The statue of the Good Samaritan is capped by a helmet of snow.

The rush of adrenaline that came when she was running is gone. She wearily gets up off the bench and trudges to the closest T stop. Heading far away from Newbury Street. Heading back home.

When she gets to her apartment, it's dark and quiet. Esther must be out doing whatever it is that Esther does. After she kicks off her sneakers, she finds Entropy napping on the bed, and she snuggles in next to him, still wearing her clothes. The cat stirs sleepily as she pets him. He nestles against her, purring and kneading his paws into her chest.

'I really want my girlfriend to hold me right now,' she whispers to Entropy. 'I want her to tell me happy endings are possible, and everything's going to be all right.' But Angela isn't her girlfriend anymore, and Chloë doesn't know where she is.

Even though she's exhausted, Chloë's eyes remain stubbornly open. She stares at the ceiling, her feelings too tangled to let her fall asleep.

PART NINE

Damn The Torpedoes And Eat Your Grapenuts

CHAPTER FIFTY-ONE

Club Congress, Tucson, Arizona
18 September 1998

She can do this, or she can be like Tess, or she can starve.

Those are her options, and she only has until the bartender gets around to mixing the drink to make the decision. Although she's already got a good head start going on that third possibility. If she doesn't get some blood down her throat soon, she's going to go crazy.

The girl sitting next to her is chattering away, telling a story, laughing. Layla. She's here at the club on her own tonight, and already far from sober. An undergraduate who wants to be a fashion designer. She'd said she liked Angela's trousers. They're leather with diamond cutouts all up the sides, the white flesh of her legs gleaming through the holes. Bait, although couture wasn't exactly the lure she thought she'd use to catch something. Someone.

'So I brought in a picture of the haircut I wanted, I mean an actual picture, two pictures even, front and back,' Layla says. 'And I said, "I want a reverse bob, just like these pictures, can you do that?" and she said, "Sure", and I should have known something was off, because her own haircut was, like, square, literally square, you know?'

'Not a good sign,' Angela acknowledges.

'I came out looking like a puffball, I can't even describe it.' Layla reaches up to run a hand through her hair, which at the moment is so short it's almost a crewcut. 'It was unbelievable, I was crying, actually crying, and I went somewhere else an hour later and got it all cut off, because I was afraid to go outside.'

This isn't really Angela's scene. It's an old hotel that's been turned into a music venue, better lit and more nicely furnished than any place she's used to going. The walls in the lobby are a pale yellow, with a pretty mural running across them near the ceiling. The room has broad windows, a red-orange floor, wooden pillars painted in bright patterns. She's never heard of the bands playing here tonight. Last of the Juanitas just finished a set. The Pork Torta is still setting up. She met Layla in the break between.

Angela feels conspicuous. Even in minimalist makeup, which is all she feels confident enough to put on right now, her clothes are setting her apart. Most of the crowd is wearing vivid colours. She's a black-and-white break in the design; she looks like a skunk set loose in the peacock enclosure. Layla's in a dress with shoulder ruffles that's the same lemon cream as the lobby walls. It almost glows against her deep tan. It leaves her neck completely exposed. There's warm rich blood just beneath the skin. Angela can practically smell it.

'And on top of the traffic,' Layla is saying, 'last time there was a football game someone stole a bench right out of our back yard. Right out of the yard! It's like every time they play at home, the whole city becomes an asshole.'

Angela tears her thoughts away from blood and biting. Stay calm, she reminds herself. You have to stay calm.

The two of them are standing at the bar, pressed close against it by other bodies, waiting on the Long Island Iced Tea that Angela ordered on Layla's behalf. They've been waiting for a while; a lot of orders went in before theirs.

Angela wonders if she can pull this off with so many people around, if she decides to go through with it at all. But she's fast, faster than a normal person could ever hope to be. And after years of watching someone like her pass for human, she knows that most people don't pay attention.

She isn't thrilled by how much she stands out here, though. By how memorable she is. But coming somewhere like this – not to mention driving a hundred miles out of her way to get to Tucson – means there's very little chance that anyone who frequents the goth clubs in Phoenix is going to show up and recognise her. And almost no chance that she'll run into Tess.

'Back off!' Layla says to a beefy guy trying to elbow his way past her to get to the bar. 'Wait your turn. I swear to God, some people. Have you seen The Pork Torta before?'

It takes Angela a moment to realise that Layla is talking to her again. 'No.'

'I think you'll like them. They're weird. Not gothic weird, it's a different kind of weird, but weird. They're kind of like a trash rock band meets high art.'

Angela is wedged uncomfortably against the bar herself, its rim jutting into her side. She wants to push back against the mob of people to give herself some room, but she doesn't dare to. She might end up knocking half of them over by accident. Strength isn't always an advantage when you're trying to be subtle. She can't ruin this. Too much depends on what happens tonight.

If she decides to go through with things, if she makes that choice, she'll only have to avoid Tess for a few more months. When Shelly and Mike's current tenant moves out, she'll tell her advisor there's a family emergency forcing her to leave town, some terrible protracted illness. It's close enough to the truth. She's a member of her own family, after all, and there's something terribly, terribly wrong with her.

She's got the whole trip planned out already. She'll drive when it's dark, stay in motels during the day. Motels have been a godsend. The receptionists have been remarkably easy-going about doing makeup checks for her. Hopefully it won't be too long before she's mastered putting it on sight unseen. And bathrooms and Do Not Disturb signs have been keeping her alive. A good motel, all by itself, is enough to take care of most of her needs.

Not all of her needs, though. She's so, so thirsty. She didn't know her mouth could get so dry, her lips, her throat. Her tongue feels like a pumice stone rasping against her gums. It's agony.

Moving to Boston is just one of the possibilities in front of her, though. It's her best one, no doubt about that; it isn't as if she has anyone else she can turn to for help. Her family already thinks being a lesbian makes her an unholy abomination. They've hardly talked to her since she came out to them. She isn't eager to find out how they'd react to her becoming a vampire.

But she'll only make it to Boston if she takes the final step here, tonight. And she hasn't done that. Not yet. She still has the choice.

The bartender is taking forever.

Layla just asked her something that she didn't quite catch. Angela responds mechanically to the half-heard question, stammering out an ambiguous answer that she hopes isn't inappropriate. Layla nods, and resumes talking as if nothing's amiss.

'I didn't honestly want to see the movie, but my friend dragged me there because she's obsessed with Wesley Snipes, I mean totally obsessed. And I had no idea what was going on the whole time, but he had this boomerang with knives on it that would cut people up and then fly back to him, so that was cool.'

Angela tries to pay better attention. It doesn't work very well. She's only able to dip in and out of Layla's flow of words, like a stone skipping across a stream.

She needs to stop distracting herself. She needs to make a decision. She can do this, or she can be like Tess, or she can starve.

She won't be like Tess. There, that's one option off the table. She will never be like Tess. She will never take a girl home, and hold her and bite her and fuck her and beat her when she tries to speak up. Not ever. Better to take one bite, lone and quick and brutal, than force anyone into that shuttered half-life. Or bring about the end of that life, years down the line.

She still doesn't know whether or not that final bite was an accident. And she has no idea whether Tess knew for sure that she'd come back from it if it happened.

Has Tess killed people? Even if she never admitted to it outright, she never denied it, either. Not really.

Angela won't do that. She will never do that. She won't kill anyone, no matter what. She may not have entirely decided where she's drawing the line yet, but wherever the line is, that has to be far, far past it. No coming back.

Her life does depend on secrets now, though. Tess was right about that much. Anyone could kill her by dragging her into the sunlight. Anyone who decides that she's a monster. They probably wouldn't even be wrong.

If she's going to bite anyone, she needs to make sure they don't remember it.

Out of the corner of her eye, Angela sees the overworked bartender putting together the ingredients of a Long Island Iced Tea. Easy, practised movements. Ice in the cocktail shaker, then vodka, then gin, then rum.

At first, she'd thought about finding someone so strung out on drugs they couldn't remember anything. But she doesn't have the faintest notion where to start looking for someone like that. Besides, that wouldn't be any better. Just easier. It'd still be assault. It's more honest if she does the drugging herself.

Assault. Violence. She has to look this in the face, if she's going to do it. She will attack people, and bite them, and drink their blood. Drink Layla's blood. Friendly, chatty Layla. Angela gave her blood willingly when she did it, and it won't be the same. That's not at all the same as having it taken.

'And the buses don't run past nine at night,' Layla says. 'So it's kind of like, you can go to see a movie, but you can't go home. You can't even walk home! There aren't any sidewalks!'

'Really?' Angela asks.

'I swear, you go outside of downtown, and it's like something's eaten every single sidewalk in Tucson.'

Tequila goes into the cocktail shaker. Triple sec. Lime juice. Sugar syrup.

She could let herself starve. Her other remaining option. Would that mean death? Possibly. But she wonders if she wouldn't die from it at all, if she'd simply keep existing as she is. If she'd get thirstier and thirstier, forever.

She's already pushed it almost as far as she can stand. Wasted so much time trying everything else she could think of. None of it worked. Hunger is constantly howling in her stomach. Metastasising through her mind, driving her insane. The yearning to feed is slowly taking over, beginning to blot out all other thoughts. It can't be that much longer before there's nothing else left, nothing but a frenzied monster, a raving maniac craving blood. She can feel it coming, like she used to be able to feel her mind start to fray from going day after day without sleep. That sense of something horrible lurking around the corner.

She shudders. Death would be better. Death would take away everything, too, but it would be over then. Unless her family was right all along and hell is waiting for her anyway.

'What's wrong?' Layla asks, frowning. She touches her fingertips to Angela's wrist, concern written across her face.

'Nothing,' Angela says. 'A touch of indigestion.'

'Did you have Mexican? I love Mexican, but it can get to you. I don't like Tex-Mex, though. The best I ever had was in New Mexico, have you ever been there? They put green chillies in everything, it's amazing.'

The drink has already been poured from the cocktail shaker into a highball glass. The bartender adds a splash of Coke, garnishes the rim with a lemon wedge. She finally sets it in front of Angela, briskly placing it down before turning to get to work on whatever she's making next.

Angela needs to choose. Right now.

She can do this, or she can be like Tess, or she can starve.

Don't forgive me, Angela thinks. *Don't forgive me, for I am about to sin.* A confession made to no one.

'Want to get away from the pile-on here?' Angela asks.

'Oh my God, yes,' Layla answers. 'Let's go, I can barely breathe.' She reaches for her drink with a tipsy, unsteady hand.

'Let me get that for you.'

Angela keeps her gaze locked on Layla's face, and drops the crushed tablets into the glass as she picks it up.

CHAPTER FIFTY-TWO

Somerville
23 December 1999

It's well past midnight, already a new day. Chloë's been restlessly pacing in the living room for half an hour. The shocked, blank numbness she sank into earlier has been displaced by jittery agitation. She tromps back and forth, back and forth, kicking aside any junk on the floor that gets in her way. A pair of underpants goes flying, landing half-on and half-off a bookshelf. When they were cleaning the room, they must not have found all the pairs Entropy hid. Or else he's started distributing them around the apartment again. She really should put her clothes away.

Chloë barely registers the sound of the key turning in the lock. It isn't until the temperature drops, the warmth leaking into the night through the open door, that she looks over to see Esther letting herself in.

'You're out late,' Chloë says.

'I was looking at the Christmas lights,' Esther replies as she bustles around the room, shedding her handbag and overcoat. 'Lovely new tradition. Before the eighteenth century, all we did was light a log on fire. Then the Germans starting sticking candles all over a tree, which was quite deranged – a terrible fire risk. But I'm glad it caught on. You didn't have to wait up for me, you know.'

Chloë doesn't even bother to roll her eyes at her aunt's absurdities. 'I didn't. I can't sleep. I've had a horrible day.' Chloë drops onto the ragged armchair with an audible thump, her legs folding up like paper fans. Now that she's stopped moving, it's as if they won't support her anymore. 'Angela's ex-girlfriend is a psychopath who tried to kill me. Angela is miserable and has run off somewhere – not because of the attempted murder, she doesn't know about that – and Shelly thinks it's all my fault. Oh, and a friend of mine from work is a werewolf. Everything's insane, basically.'

'Excuse me,' Esther says. 'Did you say someone tried to murder you?' It's the first time Chloë has ever seen her look taken aback.

'Yeah, a vampire attacked me. *Another* vampire!' Chloë's voice rises, her words speeding up. 'And this one wasn't just starving! She did it on purpose!'

'Oh, my goodness!' Esther crosses the room and perches on the arm of the chair. 'Are you hurt?'

'No, I mean, I – Not physically. Which doesn't make sense!' She's finding it harder to breathe, the terror she felt in the gallery making an unwelcome reappearance. 'I should be dead!'

'My poor girl!'

Esther wraps her arms around Chloë's shoulders and hugs her tightly. Chloë leans into the hug, grateful for the comfort. 'I have no idea how I got away. I said, "Let me go!", and she did.'

Esther goes very still. 'Ah.' She releases Chloë and takes a step back, looking her niece over thoughtfully. 'Good.'

'What?' Chloë is thrown by her aunt's abrupt change in attitude. 'What do you mean, "good"?'

'I always thought you had it in you.'

'Had what in me?' She peers at her aunt through narrowed eyes, her panic momentarily forgotten. 'Why are you being so blasé about this? What do you know?'

'I assure you, I'm quite dismayed. By the vampire attack, and by Angela going missing. Not the werewolf so much.'

'Of course not,' Chloë says sarcastically. 'Why would you be surprised by an ordinary werewolf?'

'We have more important things to worry about. Shouldn't you go looking for Angela?'

'What?' Chloë says again. She's becoming increasingly disoriented by the hairpin turns in the conversation. 'No! She probably hates me now. Can we go back to the vampire attack?'

'Are you still in danger?'

'I . . . don't think so, no.' Chloë never told Tess her name, much less where she lives.

'Then we should move on.'

'No, we shouldn't!' Chloë says. She wishes Esther would come hug her again. 'I can't – I wouldn't know where to start looking for Angela, OK? Even if I do find her, I'll only make things worse.'

'Hmpf,' Esther says. 'Because she was so glad to be rid of you, she wandered off into the night?'

'I can't believe you want to have this conversation again *now*!'

'We never had the conversation the first time,' Esther says.

'You know what? I'm done!' Chloë leaps to her feet. Out of the corner of her eye, she sees her underwear slide off the shelf and flop to the ground. She can't help but feel that the drama of the moment has been undercut. 'Thanks for the three seconds of sympathy for my near-death experience.' Chloë stomps towards her bedroom. 'I'm going to get some sleep. It's late.'

'You've been miserable since you broke up with her, Chloë,' Esther calls after her. 'From the sound of it, she has been, too.'

'We're wrong for each other, OK? I mope. She bites.'

'So, she bites. And you've been bitten before?' the old woman asks, arching an eyebrow.

Chloë stops short. 'Oh, that's very nice,' she snaps. Turning back around, hands on her hips. 'Very layered with double meaning. Well done.'

'Well, is that the reason you're being so pig-headed? You think that some night she's going to wake up next to you, see your neck lying there all exposed and delicious, and—'

'No! She isn't like that. I know that she . . . that she's done things, but she's doing the best she can in a rough situation.'

Esther taps her foot on the carpet. 'So what is the problem, then?'

'The problem is me, all right?' Chloë shouts. 'Is that what you wanted to hear? Crazy, crazy me. She's had enough trouble in her life, she needs someone who isn't . . .'

She trails off, unable to finish.

'Chloë . . .' Esther sighs and steps in closer. 'I don't believe that you're unlovable. All I see is someone wrecking things before they have a chance to start, just to spare herself the trauma of destroying it later.'

'That isn't what I . . . I mean, it's not what I want to . . .' Chloë pauses. 'Wait. I've heard that somewhere before, haven't I?' She wrinkles her brow, trying to remember. Suddenly, she does. 'Oh, my God. I can't believe you're giving me relationship advice from *Love Slave of the Night Creature*. And I can't believe you actually read *Love Slave of the Night Creature*.'

'It was on the floor, and looked interesting. But that isn't the point. You should go talk to her if that's the only thing stopping you.'

'It's not just— She had her own reasons for breaking up with me, too, you know.' Chloë glances at the window, but all she sees are blooming patterns of frost and her own tiresome reflection. The glass might as well be opaque.

The truth is, everything that Esther's saying has been hitting home. Chloë hasn't stopped thinking about Angela since the moment they broke up. Not even immediately after being attacked by Tess. And Chloë has felt none of the sense of relief she got when she ended things with Alec. Only a gnawing ache.

'Listen, suppose I thought talking to her was a good idea,' Chloë says. 'It doesn't matter, does it? She's missing, and Shelly says she's not answering her phone, and I've got no idea where she is. Remember?'

'Of course I remember,' Esther replies. 'You're more capable than you think. You handled a vampire attack, after all.'

'What has that got to do with . . .?' Chloë shakes her head, perplexed. 'And anyway, I don't know how I did that.'

'You did it, though. Didn't you?'

She pauses before answering. 'I . . . suppose I did.'

There's no denying that whatever she did at the gallery worked. She somehow made it happen. Although she can't quite see the connection to finding Angela.

'You should ask the cards,' Esther says.

Chloë swings around, looking quizzically at her aunt. 'Are you serious?'

'You don't know where she is. You don't know if she wants to see you. Do a reading.' Esther shrugs. 'Maybe you'll get some answers.'

There are dozens of reasons to reject the suggestion. But they all depend on the universe making sense, something Chloë is no longer certain is true.

'You know what? Why not?' She plunks herself down in the chair again, and pulls the coffee table closer. 'Lay them out.'

Esther sits across from her and takes the yellowing pack of cards from her handbag. She sweeps the table clear. Small knickknacks cascade off the edge, landing on the carpet with muted thuds.

Then, to Chloë's surprise, she hands the cards over.

'You do it.'

'Me? I thought the whole point was . . . I mean, I've got no idea what I'm doing.'

'You'll figure it out,' Esther says calmly.

'What pattern should I use?'

'Whatever you like.'

Chloë hesitates a moment longer, but then lays out the cards in the simplest order she can think of, the one she remembers from her childhood. Three crossed pairs.

'Would have been nice to have a better ambiance,' Chloë says, thinking about the last time her cards were read, in her parents' house with her parents gone. The lights low, the candles lit. In her memory, there are damask hangings on the wall, although she doesn't think that would have been very likely.

'We'll make do.'

'Right. Can't have everything, can we?'

Chloë flips over the first pair.

CHAPTER FIFTY-THREE

Newbury Street
23 December 1999

Tess isn't difficult to find. Angela thought she'd have to search longer, maybe come back another night. But as soon as she steps around the corner, she spots Tess from a block away, smoking a cigarette under a streetlight in front of the shuttered gallery. No one else is out on the snow-covered sidewalk, and there are hardly any cars driving past. This late on a Wednesday night, Newbury Street is a wasteland.

Angela came here straight from the mountaintop, rocketing past the exit that would have taken her home to Brookline, twisting around Copley Place and the library until she found a place to park. Find the real cause of your problems, the angel had said. Well, there she is, waiting all alone like she's got nothing better to do.

Angela watches her for a while, then approaches. Tess glances up when she gets close, and blows out a plume of smoke.

'Thought you might show up tonight,' Tess says. 'Did a little birdie come running to complain about me?'

Angela frowns, puzzled. 'What are you talking about?'

'Nothing.' Tess flicks her cigarette into a snowbank, where it lands on a soggy pile of butts. 'So why are you here, then?'

'Me? What about you? What are you doing in Boston?'

Tess hikes a thumb back towards the gallery. 'I have a showing. Not everything is about you, Angela.'

'Yeah, about that. I don't remember signing a release form.'

'So sue me.'

'Maybe I will.'

'Good luck with that.' Tess's lips curve into a smirk. 'Maybe take a look at the law first, though. Start with what happens when the model consents to have her picture taken.'

'You told me they were private!'

'When they were photos of my girlfriend, they were.'

Angela clamps her mouth shut on her next words. It's pointless to argue. Tess will only lead her around and around, contradicting herself whenever she wants to, lying if she feels like it.

'So you're here by complete coincidence?' Angela asks. 'No idea that I might be in town. No thought that I might notice my naked body on the flyer. You never went looking for me at the Fetish Fleamarket.'

'You seriously need to get over yourself. I went there to buy shoes.' Tess scowls. 'You saw me there, and you didn't say hi? Rude.'

'Five thousand miles round-trip, avoiding the daylight, so you could make an appearance at an opening-night gala with wine you couldn't drink and cheese you couldn't eat. And then, what? You've been hanging around the gallery ever since?'

'It's a big deal!' Tess protests.

'You've been out on the street all night!' Angela shouts. 'Smoking by yourself, waiting for me to drop by! Why can't you admit you wanted to see me?'

'Fine!' Tess yells back. 'Fine, I was hoping you'd come, so what? It's not the only reason I'm in town. But yeah, I thought the flyer might get your attention. I went by all the clubs, too, but since you've obviously been avoiding me, that was a waste of time.'

'You're complaining because you had a hard time stalking me?'

'I wasn't stalking you. What was I supposed to do? It's not like I had a phone number.'

'Well, here I am,' Angela says. 'So what do you want? To hurt me some more? What?'

A lone car speeds past, headlights throwing sharp shadows onto Tess's face. Angela steps aside to avoid being sprayed with slush. Tess stays still. She drops her gaze and scuffs the snow with her shoe, mumbling something Angela can't hear over the fading roar of the engine.

'What did you say?'

'I said, come back to Phoenix with me.'

Angela stares. 'Are you serious?'

'Yeah.'

'Why would you . . . ?' Angela presses her fingertips against her forehead, then lets her hand drop. She doesn't bother to finish the thought. This is typical behaviour for Tess – leading with insults and denials, ending with an emotional plea. The only real surprise is that she dropped the hostility so quickly.

'I'm leaving tomorrow,' Tess says softly. 'Come back with me. You were the only . . . You woke up. We were supposed to be together. You weren't supposed to leave.'

'Tess. You treated me like shit.' It seems like an inadequate way to describe it, after two years of misery with her, and a year of misery afterwards dealing with the fallout – or mostly misery afterwards. Not entirely, not for the month she was with Chloë.

'It'll be different now,' Tess says.

'You acted like it was my fault whenever you were in a bad mood. Which was all the time.'

'You're exaggerating.'

'Exaggerating?' The word comes out tight with outrage. 'You yelled at me and hit me and fed on me until I *died*.'

Tess's gaze lands somewhere past Angela, off in the distance.

'What if I hadn't woken up?' Angela asks. 'What then?'

'But you did.'

It's as close to an admission she might not have woken up as Angela is ever likely to get. 'You treated me like shit,' she repeats. 'Why the hell would I believe you've changed?'

'I haven't changed. You have.' Tess looks up at Angela, finally meeting her eyes directly. 'I had to do all that, when you were human.'

'Had to?' Angela can feel hysterical laughter bubbling up in her throat. 'Nobody was forcing you to hit me.'

'Don't pretend you don't know what I'm talking about.'

'What, you needed to protect your fucking vampire secrets?' Her voice is rising in pitch. 'That's a pathetic excuse, Tess. It's garbage.'

'It's the truth. You'll have to do the same thing. And the sooner you realise it, the better. You should come do it with me.' Tess's tone is almost pleading, the neediness behind her entreaty rising close to the surface. 'We're going to be like this a long time, and it gets lonely.'

'I can't put people at risk the way you do.'

'We don't really have a choice, angel.'

'Oh my God.' Angela shakes her head in disbelief. 'Do you ever listen to yourself? It sounds like you're reading out loud from a text-book on abusers.'

Tess jerks her head back as if slapped. 'Don't call me that.'

'Oh, you don't like that? Because every word you've said tonight has been a big red flag. "I had to do it, there wasn't any choice, any-one would have done it, it'll be different now!" You know what comes next? That I was really the one abusing you. That's what people like you say next.'

'Fuck you,' Tess snarls, all trace of softness gone, 'and your holier-than-thou bullshit. Like you're some gentle fucking flower. The first thing you did after becoming a vampire was try to rip my throat out. And you know what? You want another go at it now. Your fangs are already out.'

Tess is right; when Angela runs her tongue over her teeth, she can feel the telltale pinpricks.

'What have you been doing all year?' Tess asks. 'Living on happy thoughts and moonlight? Are you telling me you never got yourself a girlfriend and bit the shit out of her? Because you're lying.'

Angela keeps herself from flinching. 'I didn't . . . I'm not going to do that anymore.'

'Sure you won't. Because you're the *nice* vampire. The nice vampire wouldn't hurt anybody, right?'

'Stop it. I never meant to–'

'Oh, you didn't mean to?' Tess cuts her off, unrelenting. 'Good for you. Does the nice vampire not drink blood? Is that the way it works?'

'Stop it.'

'The nice vampire can blame everything on me.'

'Shut up!' Angela yells.

'Make me.'

Angela's muscles are tensed to spring. Because Tess isn't wrong about at least one thing. It would feel good to sink her teeth into Tess's flesh. An outlet for years of anger, taken out on its cause. There'd be something deeply satisfying, she thinks, about grabbing Tess by the back of her head and slamming her face into the sidewalk. Over and over. Angela's picturing it in her mind, already hearing the crack of the pavement shattering when Tess's head rams into it.

Tess is waiting, her hand already clenched into a fist, readied for a swing.

She wants this, Angela understands in an instant. *She wants me to do it. If she can't kiss me, she'll take punching me in the mouth instead.*

Angela forces herself to relax. 'I'm not playing that game, Tess.'

'What game?' Tess still has her weight on the balls of her feet, leaning forward, ready to fight.

'This one,' Angela says. 'Your game.' She wills her fangs to retract, easing them back up into her mouth. 'You want to hit me? Go ahead. You can't hurt me that way now.'

Tess remains motionless for a moment, then growls inarticulately and slams her fist into the lamppost.

It rings like a gong and tilts over sideways, fissures opening in the concrete where the base tears itself out of the ground. The bulb on top flashes and goes out, plunging them into shadow.

Angela's gaze flicks to the dented metal, and then back to Tess. 'I can see that things are really going to be different now.'

'Whatever you think you just proved—'

'When you leave town,' Angela tells her, 'don't come back.'

Tess lifts her chin. 'You can't tell me what to—'

'Don't come back,' Angela repeats, her voice flat and hard. Tess blinks, for once looking unsure of herself.

Angela turns and walks away. This time, Tess doesn't follow her, doesn't shout or threaten or make demands. Angela glances back at the end of the block and sees her standing in the same spot, motionless. A small figure that vanishes from Angela's sight as she rounds the corner.

She's shaken by what almost happened. By what she came close to doing a second time. But she has to admit there's a spark of pride there, too. She didn't let Tess goad her into another fistfight, for whatever that's worth. The temptation was there, but she didn't give in.

And she called Tess what she is, right to her face.

It won't change a thing, not really; Tess is probably already spinning it all in her mind to make herself out to be the victim. Nonetheless, saying it still felt like taking a breath of air after almost drowning.

She'll probably never completely escape the effects that Tess has had on her life. Not as long as she needs to avoid the sunlight. Not as long as she needs blood to survive. But maybe she can move forward. Move on to whatever comes after. One chapter of her life ending so that another can begin.

It isn't long before she turns onto Boylston Street, brightly lit even at this hour. The city lights throw reflections onto the darkened shop windows as she walks past. Not hers, of course. But in one of them she sees the angel. He gives her an approving nod. She nods back.

It seems like a good time to make her peace with him, to the extent that she can. He did annoy her into making some important realisations, after all.

When she reaches her car, she sits behind the steering wheel for long minutes before she puts the key in the ignition, looking out into the night through the windshield, her eyes fixed on nothing. All she has to do now is figure out where she's going next.

CHAPTER FIFTY-FOUR

Excerpt From Angela's Experimental Log

TEST #49A
SUBJECT: How far can I fall without dying?
METHODOLOGY: Jumping off a cliff
RESULTS: A long damn way
COMMENTS: I don't have much to add about the cliff-jumping. It wasn't performed in ideal laboratory conditions, so the data is sparse.

But as long as I'm jotting things down, anyway, there is one final vampire myth I'd like to write about.

It's not the only one left by any means. There are dozens of them floating around out there. I've heard that vampires can hypnotise people with their eyes. That they can command animals. That they can turn into mist.

To be perfectly frank, I have no idea whether or not any of those are true. I don't think they are, but it must be obvious by now that I'm guessing about a lot of things. Just like everybody else. I'm learning as I'm going.

So I'll stick with one I do know something about. Only a little bit, but something.

Myth number three: vampires are eternal and unchanging

Do vampires get older? I don't know. They're certainly hard to kill, at least in some ways. But they aren't eternal and unchanging. They can't be, because nothing is.

The universe itself is in motion. Other galaxies are flying away from the Milky Way. They used to be closer; go far enough back, and they were all clumped together at some single point of origin. The universe was born, and it's growing. And someday, almost certainly, it will die.

There's some disagreement about precisely how it's going to die. I think the evidence points to the Big Freeze. After trillions of years, new stars will stop forming. The remaining ones will run out of fuel and burn out – all the lights in the sky turned off. The temperature will approach absolute zero. Even black holes will evaporate. If it turns out that protons decay, then at some point there won't be any atoms left intact. A thin soup of random particles will be all that remains, a bunch of photons and leptons flying around in a nearly empty universe.

I find that reassuring.

It's not because I take comfort from the notion that the universe is going to fizzle out. Not exactly, anyway. Although with trillions of years to go, it's not worth worrying about.

But here's why it'll happen: right now, and for a long time to come, everything is growing and changing. Galaxies are moving. Stars are born and expand and collapse and explode. Nothing stays the same, and nothing stays still.

So I won't stay the same. I can't. I might or might not grow older, but somehow I'll be different.

Somebody important to me once said, 'One way or another, all bleeding stops eventually.' And it's true. You can die, or you can heal.

CHAPTER FIFTY-FIVE

'The past,' Esther intones as Chloë turns over the first pair of cards.

The King of Clubs, crossed by the Nine of Spades. Both upright in only one direction, not mirrored like regular cards, just as Chloë remembers from almost twenty years ago.

Other than that, though, the Nine looks almost modern. She wonders if the cards are really three hundred years old. And the King, Le Roi de . . . something. A bearded figure cloaked in red, one hand clutching a sceptre, the other resting on some kind of animal by his feet. A lion, that's right. The King's face is dark and glowering, his eyes staring at her. There he is. Hello, Alec. Her history, always reaching forward to mess up her future.

She tries to remember the last time she saw him, the day they met to file the divorce papers. Lunch with him first, both of them trying to be civilised. Neither with a lot to say. They were asked why they were filing, and a laundry list of hatreds came pouring out. She won't listen to me. We never stop arguing. She can't get a real job. We don't have sex. The clerk drily told them that 'irreconcilable differences' was all they needed to write on the form. Fine, they told her, put that down.

359

Differences that couldn't be reconciled. That look he sometimes got in his eyes before a fight. That's the real reason, to be honest. The one thing she could never be reconciled to.

Anyway, he's in the past. The cards say so. He can't touch her from there.

'The present,' Esther says when Chloë moves on to the next set.

The Ten of Hearts, crossed by the Ace of Spades. The Ace has an elaborate design around the single giant spade in the centre, a rooster crowing at the top of an interwoven circle of leaves and flowers, coins and crowns. Faded words in French she doesn't understand pass over and under the images. The card means changes, pathways, a decision point. Coupled with the Ten, it's hearts hanging in the balance.

They don't, of course, tell her which decision is the correct one. Only that the decision is an important one. Useless cards. She could have told them that herself. Story of her life.

You'd think, once you've figured out what your problems are, you'd be able to fix them. Turns out it doesn't work that way. They sit there, large and looming, while you muddle your way through the rest of your life. Slow growth, mistakes and setbacks, all the while hoping to wake up one day and realise it's been a while since you last felt like throwing yourself off a bridge.

'The future,' Esther says.

The Queen of Diamonds, crossed by the Queen of Clubs. The blonde Queen, with a melancholy look to her, elaborately dressed in jewels and a gown and holding a white flower to her nose. The darker Queen is facing out and to the right, her eyes on a fan clutched in her outstretched hand. She looks as if she's dancing.

Chloë studies the cards for a minute.

'I know where Angela is,' she says. 'Or at least, where she's going to be.'

'Good. You should find her.'

'Should I, though?' Chloë slides to the edge of the armchair, her fingers lightly touching the two central cards. The present. 'Let's face it, both of us are . . . there are some real problems here.'

Esther reaches over and puts her hand on top of Chloë's. 'Let me tell you something. Back when I was in high school, in the seventh century BC on the isle of Lesbos, Sappho once took me aside and said to me, "Esther, love is not something that can be caged in rules, but it can be poisoned with self-doubt. So, for once in your life, go for the gusto, seize the morning, damn the torpedoes and eat your grapenuts, because by all the gods, having a few problems does not automatically turn you into some kind of monster!"'

The corners of Chloë's mouth curl up. 'Really. She said that verbatim, I'm guessing?'

'Oh, not at all. She said it in dactylic hexameters, but I'm not even going to try.'

'It's a nice story,' Chloë replies. 'It's also completely ridiculous.'

'Stories matter if they affect you. Even ridiculous ones. Do you miss her?'

Chloë sighs. 'Yes. I really do. I miss everything about her. I want . . . I want to hear her laugh. And lie in bed next to her while she tells me about the stars. Or just see her face. Yes, I miss her.'

'I'd be willing to bet she feels the same way about you.'

'How would you know?'

'I'm old,' Esther says sagely. 'I can tell these things.'

Chloë looks at the Queen of Diamonds again. The short, pale stranger. Ragnelle, she remembers, is the name of the card. She didn't know that story when she was eight; she's read it in the years since. A very old tale of knights and maidens and magic. The loathly lady with sharp, sharp teeth.

'The cards say that if we get back together,' she says, 'I'm going to get bitten. Sooner or later.'

'Will that be something that happens to you or something you choose?' Esther asks.

The Queen of Diamonds doesn't have the hard stare of the King of Clubs. The Queen of Diamonds knows what women most desire. And she may be cursed with the teeth of a monster, but she has a human soul inside.

Chloë nods and stands up. 'All right. I guess I'd better get going, if I'm going to go at all.' She smiles at Esther. 'See you later.'

'I'm thinking I'll head out early in the morning tomorrow,' Esther says. 'Get out of your hair. I wouldn't want to overstay my welcome.'

'You're leaving?' Chloë is having difficulty imagining life without Esther in the house. 'You don't have to. It's been nice, having you here.'

'Thank you, dear. I'll miss you, too. But I should be on my way. Keep the cards, I'll get a new set.'

Chloë looks down in surprise at the much-used cards, still spread out on the table. 'Do you really want me to take them? If they're as old as— I mean, they're probably worth something.'

'I'm quite certain you should have them. And incidentally, a romance with someone who's going to live a long, long time isn't a bad idea for you.'

'Wait.' Chloë jerks her head back up. 'What?'

'Just a thought.'

'Are you sure?'

Esther nods. 'It does run in the family.'

'. . . huh.' As soon as Chloë comes down from her brief moment of shock, she considers Esther's words carefully.

They make a surprising amount of sense. It would explain all sorts of things that have happened recently, from the incident at the art gallery to the card reading itself. It might account for earlier events as well, for that matter. Incidents that have nagged at the back of Chloë's mind her whole life.

The impulses she sometimes has. The way people react when she speaks in a certain tone of voice.

Tess, dropping her arm. Maybe even Alec, agreeing to move out.

She finds herself responding to Esther's comment with a strange sense of recognition. After all, if the world has vampires and werewolves in it, why would witches be out of the question?

Which does raise the possibility that every story Esther has ever told her was the literal truth, but that's a little too much to handle right now. Chloë's open to a lot of things after all she's seen and done, but the possibility that her aunt might have actually met Sappho is a thought she'll have to kick into a corner until later.

'Am I going to need anything, other than the cards?' she asks. 'Should I get myself a hat and a broomstick?'

Esther grins. 'Those are entirely optional, dear. Although you're welcome to pick them up if you want.'

'What about other stuff I should know about? I've barely got any idea how this works. How do I use it? Are there things I should be able to do?'

'I'm afraid I can't be of much help to you there,' Esther tells her. 'I had an inkling you might be a dab hand with the piquet deck, but beyond that I've got no idea. It's different for everyone. More an art than a science, really, so I've already told you as much as I can. You'll have to find out the rest on your own.'

'Oh.' Chloë glances back at the cards, half hoping that they'll divulge further secrets immediately. They don't. 'That's kind of frustrating.'

'You're a smart girl, you'll pick it up quickly. I only had to hang around here for a couple of months before you took your first step in the right direction. The ones after that will come, be patient. And right now, get yourself out of the house and on your way before the night gets any colder.'

Chloë reaches for her coat.

'You know,' she says as she gets herself ready, 'the cards weren't exactly explicit. About what's going to happen tonight.'

'They seldom are, I'm afraid.'

'But that means I might not be achieving anything by going out now.' Chloë finds her handbag and slings it over her shoulder. 'She might not be OK. She might turn me down. Or we could both be too screwed up for us to ever be together. It might even just plain old not work out.'

'Well,' Esther says, 'there's always that risk.'

CHAPTER FIFTY-SIX

ManRay
23 December 1999

Angela pushes her gin and tonic a few inches across the table. It hits a patch of blacklight and starts to glow. Four hundred and fifty nanometres. Indigo.

She isn't entirely sure why she ordered it; she obviously can't drink it. And she has no desire to repeat her early experiments, back when she was trying to see if she could choke down anything other than blood. If it was larger than a single pea, there was a lot of vomiting involved.

If she bought the drink to fit in with the people around her, it wasn't worth the bother. No one's paying attention. There aren't many people in the club; the crowd is even thinner than the last time she was here. She has the low table by the far wall all to herself.

Everyone's at home getting ready for the holidays. There are decorations on the bar walls, scenes from *The Nightmare Before Christmas*. Jack Skellington and Sally holding hands. She's not certain whether it's meant to be ironic or kitschy or a genuine attempt at gothic seasonal cheer.

Anyway, other than her, the few people who came out tonight aren't lingering in the bar. They're over on one of the dance floors, not wanting to miss out on the last few sets. The wee hours of the morning are drifting away one by one, and the club will be closing soon. Music leaks out from the other rooms, growing louder and softer as doors open and shut, blending together and pulsing in her ears. She tries to disentangle the melodies, figure out the songs. 'Bela Lugosi's Dead' coming from one direction. 'Another World' from the other. Everyone's favourites, saved for the end.

Angela came here after leaving Tess, not for any particular reason. She isn't there to hunt. Not tonight, and not ever again. She can't do it anymore. Although she has no idea what she's going to do instead.

Maybe she should finally go home. Spend what's left of the night working on her thesis. She might as well, even if there isn't much point. It's possible that some solution will present itself, something will come up that would let her have a career after grad school. She can always hope so, anyway.

Or maybe she should do one of the things she fantasised about when she was driving to the mountaintop. Walk underwater, break into a zoo and put her hand on a tiger's flank. Finally take advantage of what she's become.

It occurs to her that she's never going to get another piercing. And no tattoos. Which has to be the most inane insight about invulnerability ever.

'Hi,' someone behind her says.

Angela looks up to see Chloë pulling a seat back and sitting down next to her.

She feels an almost electric jolt at the sight of Chloë's tall, lean body, tousled curls, and green, green eyes. Not someone she expected to run into here. Not at all. Chloë isn't dressed to get in, not even wearing the minimal basic black, just blue jeans and a T-shirt under the coat she's taking off. They must be letting everyone through the door at this hour.

Angela wants to say something graceful and perfect. The best she can come up with is, 'Uh . . . hi?'

'You know,' Chloë says, 'there's a girl here who's only wearing, like, a thong and a couple of adhesive doilies. Have you seen her?'

Angela smiles, tentative. 'I have. I think it's the same one from last time.'

'She's really kind of a show-off.' Chloë edges forward on the red velvet seat cushion, getting a bit closer. Hands on her knees. Eyes on Angela's. 'How've you been?'

'To be honest? I've not been all that great, the past week or so. You?'

'Sounds about right for me, too. Shelly's worried about you, by the way. You should call her.'

'Oh. I didn't think . . . I don't know. I don't know what I've been thinking.'

'Are you all right?' Chloë's voice is warm but serious.

'Yes,' Angela says slowly. 'Or I'm better than I was, anyhow. I guess I had some things I needed to figure out.' She looks at the table, where her finger is tracing the ring of condensation left by her glass. 'Had to have a chat with the imaginary guardian angel I'm supposed to have outgrown. Apparently my subconscious still thinks I need to be rescued by a dude. How lame is that?'

'I think if you have things to figure out, you're the one rescuing yourself. Whether or not the assist is imaginary.'

'I suppose.'

'So did you?' Chloë asks. 'Figure them out?'

'I don't know yet.' Angela looks back up to meet Chloë's eyes. 'Partly?'

'Hey, partly's good. Partly's something. You know, I was worried about you, too.'

'You were?'

'Yeah.'

They hold each other's gaze for a little while. Angela's smile becomes less tentative.

'So, read anything particularly bad lately?' she asks.

'Oh, a few.' Chloë grins and leans back, draping one arm over the backrest of her chair.

'Like what?'

'I read someone's erotic novel a couple of days ago. *The Seven Bedly Sins*.'

'Oh, my. Dare I ask?'

'It was pretty disturbing. The author was intent on cramming in a weird sex scene every five pages. Every five pages exactly, I checked. And once, when there was a weird sex scene in the trunk of a car that he needed more than five pages to describe, he interrupted it in the middle with a flashback to a different weird sex scene in an aquarium tank.' She sketches the settings in the air with her hands. 'It had nested layers of smut.'

Angela laughs. 'That's actually sort of impressive.'

'It was a submission for the "inspirational literature" line, too.'

Angela laughs harder, unable to stop, nearly doubling over. For once, she's glad she doesn't have to breathe. Chloë scoots forward again and brings her head close to Angela's.

'Listen,' she says, 'I've been thinking maybe we ended our last conversation a little too soon. Back at the café.'

Angela stops laughing.

She can't afford the hope that flares up in her chest like a lit match. Ignoring everything she'd rather say right now, she tries to smother it out.

'It'd be nice to believe that, but nothing's really changed.' Angela shakes her head. 'My only choices are . . . I don't have any choices.'

'Because you want to stop hurting people.'

'Because I'm going to stop hurting people. That's not something I'm going to do anymore.'

Chloë frowns. 'How were you planning to . . . ?'

'I don't know.' Angela flicks her glass with her finger. It chimes slightly, and wobbles, spilling a little gin and tonic onto the table. 'I suppose I have to think of something.'

'Let me help,' Chloë says.

'No.'

'Angela—'

'No.' Angela pushes herself up to leave. Chloë puts a hand over hers, silently asking her to stay. Angela could break free of it easily. There's no way Chloë could keep her there, not even if she tried a full body tackle. Angela stops anyway, still standing, neither staying nor going. 'Chloë, I'm not going to drink your blood.'

'Hear me out. How long did it take? Before you changed?'

'There isn't any point to this.'

'Just answer me,' Chloë says firmly. 'How long?'

Angela compresses her lips into a thin line. 'Two years,' she says. 'More or less.'

'Then we'd have two years to figure something out before it happens to me.'

She shakes her head. 'We don't know that. It's supposed to take years before it happens, but what if sometimes that means a year and nine months? I've got no idea what actually triggers it. And I'm not 100 per cent certain everyone comes out the other side of the final bite. In fact, I'm pretty sure most don't.'

'Then we won't let it get to that point. Give it a year, to be on the safe side. Just until 2001.'

'That's not the only danger!' Angela protests, her voice rising. 'There's other problems, you wouldn't be safe, you'd—'

'You're not going to treat me the way Tess treated you,' Chloë says.

She sounds so certain that it derails Angela's growing panic. 'How do you know?'

'Believe me, I know how to recognise the signs for that. You're not mean. Even if you think you are, you're not.'

Angela stares at Chloë. 'How can you possibly believe that? I attacked you.'

'You screwed up, once. I'll forgive you. Once. OK?'

'That was one hell of a screw-up,' Angela says flatly.

'Yeah, it was,' Chloë agrees. 'But you don't want to hurt me. I know that. It means something.'

She comes close to believing it when Chloë says it. But it doesn't matter. It can't matter.

Angela has pulled back as far as her arm will let her without shifting her hand away. Chloë's fingers are still on top of hers, gently resting there, not moving.

'Look,' Angela says, 'even, even if . . .'

'I trust you.'

Three simple words that sound wholly sincere. And Angela can't accept them, however much she wants to.

'I don't. I don't trust me. Not enough.' She has to bring it up. She can't let it lie there unsaid. Even though it's going to wreck everything. 'What if there's another screw-up, and what if next time I lose control and, and kill you?'

There's a pause while Chloë thinks about that. Angela looks down at her shoes.

Black cut-out heels. What a stupid thing to wear. Her feet should be frozen after all the time she spent in the snow tonight. But they're only wet. She can't stop being what she is.

'I think you won't let yourself get into that kind of state again,' Chloë says, her words soft, only barely audible over the music from the other rooms.

'I can't risk it.' Angela has to force herself to say it. 'I'm sorry, but no. I won't risk you.'

There it is. Everything out on the table. The greatest danger, the one that's come to be her biggest fear. The one that makes even a short amount of time together impossible.

'You know . . .' Chloë takes a breath. Angela looks up to see Chloë's teeth worrying her lower lip as she considers something. 'I might . . .'

'What is it?'

'If it comes to that, I might be able to protect myself.'

'No, you can't.' Angela flinches as fleeting images of fists and teeth pass through her mind. Memories she doesn't want. 'Believe me, against a vampire, any ordinary human doesn't have a chance. I would know.'

'Yeah, well, about that.' Chloë coughs. 'Apparently I'm not an ordinary human. I'm a witch.'

Angela had already started to draw her hand away from Chloë's. She stops mid-motion. Only their fingertips are touching. 'You're a what?'

'Possibly an immortal witch.' Chloë's gaze is fixed on their hands, keeping watch on that tenuous connection. 'And one thing I seem to be really, really good at is stopping people from attacking me. Tess took a swing at me earlier tonight—'

'She *what*? When did you see Tess? Are you OK?'

'I'm fine! I went down to the gallery, which was stupid, I know, and she figured out we were . . .' Chloë shrugs. 'She wasn't happy to meet me.'

'"A little birdie."' Angela's mouth tightens. 'So that's how she knew . . . I was dumb enough to go see her, too. She didn't bother to mention that she'd assaulted you. I should have . . .' Angela shakes her head. At least Tess is leaving town tomorrow, and Angela doesn't think she'll be coming back. 'Are you absolutely certain you're all right? She didn't hurt you?' Angela looks Chloë over carefully, although if something were wrong, she'd already know. An injury from Tess wouldn't be subtle.

'I held her off. That's what I'm trying to tell you. She couldn't lay a hand on me.'

'How?' There's no blood, no sign of a broken bone. And no reason to believe Chloë is making this up. 'How did you keep her away?'

'I think I may have done the same thing when you bit me. You let go when I told you to.'

Angela frowns, uncertain. Remembering Chloë saying, '*Stop.*' Remembering going still, unlatching her jaws, leaping back . . .

'I've done it a few other times, too,' Chloë continues. 'I might be able to do a lot of things, it turns out. Tonight I did what I guess you'd call a divination, and it told me you'd be at the "queen of clubs". Here. That's actually how I tracked you down. I think the piquet deck has a weird sense of humour.' She brings her eyes back up to meet Angela's. 'I was thinking I might be able to use the witch stuff to inoculate myself against vampirism. But I know I can use it to protect myself if you . . . if I ever need to.'

'How sure are you of that?'

'Sure enough.' There isn't any room for doubt in Chloë's voice. She glances meaningfully at the seat next to her. 'Do you, uh, want to stay and talk about this some more?'

Angela thinks back again, her forehead furrowed, trying to capture the exact moment in her mind.

Chloë told her to stop. And she stopped.

'. . . all right.' A little stunned, Angela allows herself to be coaxed back down, slowly lowering herself into the chair.

A line of tension in Chloë's arm relaxes, the folds in her T-shirt settling into looser shapes as her shoulders no longer strain against it. She breathes out through her nose.

'Glad that's settled.'

'Not everything's settled,' Angela says. 'That's only one of our concerns. What if we don't find any way to make you immune? Even in a year?'

'At least we'll have some time. Lots of things can get better with time.'

'Maybe,' Angela allows. 'I mean . . . maybe. How does it work, anyway? The whole witching thing?'

'I don't really know much about it yet. There are a few things I guess I have a knack for, but Aunt Esther said I'm going to have to learn the rest by doing.' She taps her fingers on the table thoughtfully, out of rhythm with both of the songs currently mingling in the bar. 'Maybe I should read as many stories about witches as I can. Get some ideas.'

'We could figure out some inoculation experiments as soon as we have something to work with,' Angela suggests. 'Run tests.'

Chloë smiles. 'Good thing I have a scientist to help me out with it. Should come in handy.'

'Mm.' Angela's mind is already racing ahead. They'll need to set up a schedule, keep records. It's going to be a tricky problem – how do you determine that someone isn't going to be affected by vampire bites? If any particular bite doesn't cause a reaction, that doesn't prove that the same will be true for the next. And it's not like they can set up a control group . . .

'So,' Chloë says, interrupting her thoughts, 'does this mean we, you and me, are we back together?'

Angela stops moving. 'Yes.'

'You're sure?' Chloë asks.

'Yes.'

She lets the match flare up, bright as a fireball streaking across the sky. She couldn't put it out now if she wanted to.

And she doesn't want to.

'Good,' Chloë says. 'Because I, I . . .'

Before she can say any more, Angela is once again out of her seat, this time in Chloë's arms, kissing her, quickly, eagerly.

'We'll work it out,' Chloë says between kisses. 'Vampire stuff, witch stuff, whatever. Everything. We'll figure it all–'

Angela cuts her off completely with a lingering kiss. Neither of them says very much for some time after that.

After a while, when they both finally pull apart, just a little, Angela asks, 'Do you want to dance?'

'Yes,' Chloë answers.

Angela stands up and holds out her hand. Chloë takes it, and Angela pulls her into another embrace.

Then she leads her out of the bar, through a door, onto one of the dance floors. Nine Inch Nails is playing there. 'Closer'. *Not the most romantic song in the world*, Angela thinks. But it'll do.

A lot of their problems haven't truly been solved yet, she reminds herself. And they're not likely to get solved in the next day, or week, or month. But that's OK. A year might be a different story. Maybe Chloë's right. Maybe they can have this. A life, a real one. Together.

CHAPTER FIFTY-SEVEN

ManRay
23 December 1999

They hold each other closely, slow dancing around the room, keeping lips next to ears so they can talk over the music.

A few of the other clubgoers smile at them as they pass. Including the girl in the stick-on doilies.

'So,' Angela says after a few minutes, 'is being a witch hereditary? Does it skip generations?'

'You're already totally casual about it, aren't you?' Chloë grumbles. 'Why am I the only one who's ever surprised by this stuff?'

Angela grins, and gestures towards herself. 'Hey, mythological monster here. It's going to take a lot more than that if you want to astonish me. And by the way, when did all this happen, anyway?'

'I just found out. It's been kind of a weird day. There's actually a lot of things I need to tell you about. Which reminds me, you and me and Shelly and Mike had better sit down and have a talk sometime.'

'What about?'

'I'd better let Mike say. But not anything bad. Nothing that can't wait until tomorrow.'

'All right.' Angela looks perplexed, but lets it go.

They're not even moving their feet now, just swaying from side to side. Not so much dancing as embracing. Angela turns her head to rest her cheek against Chloë's collarbone. Even when Angela is in heels, Chloë is still the taller one.

'Hey,' Chloë says as a thought strikes her, 'does getting back together mean I'm back on the list for tickets to lesbian New Year's?'

'I knew you had to have an ulterior motive. Don't want to miss the big blowout? The raffle, the fireworks, the lights going out on civilisation. Should be quite a show.'

'You never mentioned the raffle! No way can we miss it now, one of us might win a prize before the world ends.'

'Already got one,' Angela says, holding Chloë tighter. 'Want to come back to my place tonight?'

'Absolutely.'

Angela fits in Chloë's arms like she was meant to be there. If she could spend the rest of the night holding Angela, she would. She probably can, now that she thinks about it. There's nothing stopping her.

Maybe they'll only have a year together, or maybe they'll have a long, long time. But that's true for everybody, isn't it? Not just vampires and witches.

If Chloë had to guess, though, she'd bet on it being a long, long time. They'll get it figured out. They'll get it all figured out.

Angela lifts her head again and looks at Chloë, her eyes soft. The smile is still on her lips. Chloë feels something warm kindle inside of her at the sight of that smile.

'Maybe we can alternate every night,' Angela says. 'My place, then your place.'

'What about my cat? That's going to be a problem every time you come over, isn't it?'

Angela shrugs. 'I can get shots or something.'

'You'd do that?'

'Oh, come on,' Angela says. 'It's the least I can do.' A thoughtful look crosses her face. 'Shots might not be practical for me, though. Pills, maybe? I can manage pills. Anyway, I'll read up about it. You're giving me your blood, I think I can handle allergy treatments.'

'I guess I can't argue with that.'

'It'll be nice. We'll spend nights together. I'll work on my thesis, you'll write. We'll break for make-outs.'

'I'd like that,' Chloë tells her. 'I'd like that a lot.'

The music stops and bright lights illuminate the room, turning on with an audible clank in the sudden silence. The club is closing, and the handful of stragglers left stand blinking in the glare. A few of them shuffle towards the exit.

'Come on,' says Angela, tugging on Chloë's hand. 'Let's get out of here.' Chloë follows her towards the door.

'Um, just to warn you, I tend to draw from life when I write. Would you mind showing up as a character? Is that all right?'

Angela, if anything, looks flattered. 'No, I wouldn't mind that at all. That would be kind of neat, actually. If you don't mind putting the whole lesbian vampire cliché thing into your work.'

'You think you're a cliché?' Chloë snorts. 'What if I want to put myself in there, too? Do you know how many writers write about writers?'

'You're right,' Angela says. 'You're a much bigger cliché than I am.'

'Will you still love me when I'm trite?'

Angela pulls her in close, gently bringing Chloë's head down until their foreheads touch.

'Nobody's perfect,' Angela whispers to her, then dives in for another kiss.

ACKNOWLEDGEMENTS

So many people helped to make this book possible that it would be impossible to thank them all. I am certain to have forgotten some-one, so please accept my apologies in advance. Here are some of the people who helped me, whether it was with their support, feed-back, knowledge, or talent, during the process of writing *Love Bites*:

In Massachusetts – Shannon Hartzler, Claire Fry, Ron Rittinger, Jenny Gutbezahl, Amy Herzog, Jonathan Herzog, Kisha Delain, Charles Schmidt, Danforth Nicholas, Ian Vincent, Michele Markarian, Jason Taylor, and everyone at Playwrights' Platform.

In Arizona – Adrienne Perry, Allison Rose, Marian Wald, Janet Cooley, Guy Castonguay, Jillian Courtney, Eugenia Woods, and the members of Old Pueblo Playwrights.

In Oregon – Gretchen Icenogle, Michelle Seaton, Elizabeth Young, Ithica Tell, Gilberto Martin del Camp, and April Magnusson.

Elsewhere in the US – Gavin Hall, Mana Taylor-Hall, Justin Robin-son, Daniel Herman, Mark Herman, and Ronnie Apter.

In the UK – Armarna Forbes, Amanda Rutter, Whitney Curry Wimbish, Jack Jackman, Edinburgh Creative Writers, and Rogue Writers Edinburgh. And of course my amazing editor Molly Powell, as well as Emma Thawley, Ian Critchley, Jo Fletcher, and everyone else at Jo Fletcher Books.

Everywhere – Beth Biller.

Thanks so much to all of you!